Praise for Rachel Vincent and *Menagerie*

"[*Menagerie*] is a dark tale of exploited and abused others, expertly told by Vincent."
—*Library Journal*, starred review

"As depicted by Vincent, Delilah is magnificent in her defiance of injustice, and the well-wrought background for her world sets the stage for her future adventures in this captivating new fantasy series."
—*Publishers Weekly*

"Vincent summons bold and vivid imagery with her writing, especially with the otherworld aspects of the carnival."
—*Kirkus Reviews*

"Well paced, readable and imaginative."
—*The New York Times*

"Vincent creates a fantastic world that is destined to pique your curiosity...
As Delilah Marlow slowly uncovers a side of herself that she never knew existed, you'll sympathize with her...desperate to see her succeed."
—*RT Book Reviews*, Top Pick!

NEW YORK TIMES BESTSELLING AUTHOR

RACHEL
VINCENT

MENAGERIE

MIRA®

MIRA

Recycling programs
for this product may
not exist in your area.

ISBN-13: 978-0-7783-1932-0

Menagerie

Copyright © 2015 by Rachel Vincent

For questions and comments about the quality of this book, please contact us at
CustomerService@Harlequin.com.

www.MIRABooks.com

Printed in U.S.A.

This one is for my husband and children, who suffered with me through three years, several rewrites, a shifted release date and the loss of my longtime editor while I wrote *Menagerie*. It's been a long road, but I think it's been worth it, and I can't thank you all enough.

MenAgerie

PART 1

EXPOSÉ

Twenty-five years ago…

The heat rippling over the surface of Charity Marlow's blacktop driveway was one hundred twelve degrees. It was nearly one hundred nine in the shade from the scrub brush that passed for trees in her front yard.

She sat on a white iron bench in her backyard, picking at the paint flaking off the arm scrolls. A glass of sweet tea stood on the empty plant stand to her right, thinner on top, where the ice cubes melted, thicker on bottom, where the sugar settled.

Inside, the baby was crying.

She'd been going for close to three hours this time, and Charity's arms ached from holding her. Her head throbbed and her feet were sore from standing. From pacing and rocking in place. Her throat was raw from crooning, her nerves shot from exhaustion, and her patience long worn thin.

She'd decided to go inside again when the last ice cube had melted into her tea, and not a minute later.

Not a minute earlier either, even though the top of her head felt close to combusting from the heat of the sun.

She stared at the cracked earth beneath her feet, at the hands in her lap, watching her own fingers shake from exhaustion. Then she stared at her tea as the ice cubes shrank before her eyes, and still the baby screamed.

Then, the last ice cube melted.

Despair swallowed Charity like the whale swallowed Jonah, but she held no hope of being spit back out. Her arms felt like they were made of iron as she lifted her tea.

She closed her eyes while the top of her skull burned in the blazing sunlight. "Lord," she whispered, condensation dripping over her fingers from the outside of her cold glass, "won't you take this angry child and give me a quieter, happier one in her place?"

As soon as she'd said the words, she regretted them. Words spoken in pain and exhaustion are rarely meant, and Charity Marlow's were no exception.

But there was no taking them back.

The moment the last word fell from her lips, the baby stopped crying.

Setting her glass down, she listened harder but heard only silence.

She stood and rounded the bench, headed for the kitchen door. By the time she got to the house, she was running. The screen door slammed behind her and her sandals slapped the floor, competing with the thunder of her own heartbeat in her ears as she raced down the hall.

She stopped in the nursery threshold, one hand clenched around the glossy white door frame, breathing too fast. Too hard. Her chest felt like it was constricting around her heart, as if her ribs were laced up too tight.

"I didn't mean it. *Please*, I didn't mean it."

The baby was dead. Charity was sure of it. She'd committed the worst sin a mother could commit, and now she was being punished.

But there was no answer from above, so she had to take that next step forward. And the one after that.

By her third step into the nursery, she could see a chubby little fist propped against the pastel crib bumper. Anguish swelled up from her heart and caught in her throat, a lump she couldn't breathe through, yet couldn't swallow.

One more step, and she could see the whole crib and the baby lying in it, eyes peacefully closed.

Charity sobbed and sagged against the crib rail, one hand on her daughter's round little stomach.

The child's eyes fluttered open, and Charity's shocked gasp was like a crack of thunder in the silent house. Her eyes filled with tears of joy and relief and she reached to pick up the child, already scolding herself for being such a superstitious fool.

Then the child smiled at her and Charity froze, her fingers inches from her daughter's pale pink jumper. Chills raced up her spine and goose bumps erupted all over her body.

The child laughed—surely no purer sound of joy was ever heard—and she stepped back from the crib, fear crawling beneath her skin.

The baby laughed again, and she took another step back, then another, and another, until her back hit the pale yellow wall. In that moment, as confusion, guilt and fear met within her, calling into question everything she'd thought she understood about the world and her place in it, Charity Marlow knew only one thing for sure.

That was *not* her baby.

Fourteen years ago...

The whistling tones of a calliope organ rang out from a speaker mounted over the carnival gate, the playful notes tripping up and down the musical register with a spirited energy. The kids from Franklin Elementary buzzed with anticipation, whispering excitedly to one another as they fidgeted in two semistraight lines. The music seemed to feed their enthusiasm and fray their patience.

As she approached the gate, ten-year-old Delilah Marlow clutched her brown-bag lunch and stared at the graceful form in front of her. The woman handing out tickets wore a red sequined leotard with a black feathered hat, black stockings, and shiny black slippers. Her lips were painted bright red. Her blue eyes practically glowed beneath dramatic sparkly lashes and thin dark eyebrows that ended in a jewel-studded curlicue at each of her temples.

She was the most glamorous thing Delilah had ever seen.

"Here you go, sweetheart." The costumed woman handed her a shiny slip of red paper. Delilah's gaze lingered on the sequins and feathers as the woman handed tickets to each of the other five fifth graders in the group, and to Mrs. Essig, their young homeroom teacher. "You all enjoy your visit, and remember to look but not touch. Especially you!" She patted the brown spikes sticking up all over Matt Fuqua's head. "With that hair, you might just be mistaken for a werewolf pup!"

The other three boys laughed and elbowed Matt, but fell into a sudden awed silence as another woman in red sequins passed by—walking on her black-gloved hands. Her tiny waist was bent backward at a severe angle, so that both of her bare feet dangled over her head, her toes nearly touching the top of her skull.

Delilah couldn't stop staring.

Shelley Wells linked her arm with Delilah's as they stepped through the gate and into the carnival. "How does she *do* that?"

"She's a circus freak." Matt marched past the girls as if he owned the whole midway. "My dad says some of them are just as weird as the monsters they got in cages."

Mrs. Essig hurried to catch up with him, shooting an apologetic glance at the red-sequined woman. "They're *human*," she whispered fiercely as she grabbed the back of Matt's shirt to keep him from wandering down an offshoot of the main path on his own. "That's all that matters."

Matt pulled free of his teacher's grip. "Are we *sure* they're human? My dad says sometimes you can't tell just from lookin'. Remember the reaping?"

Mrs. Essig nodded stiffly, but Delilah knew their teacher didn't *actually* remember the reaping, and neither did Matt Fuqua. Only old people *actually* remembered the reaping, and most of them didn't like to talk about it, because they'd all known someone who'd died. Or killed. Or been taken.

Remember the reaping? wasn't just a question. It was something parents said in hushed voices. Something priests advised while they made the sign of the cross. Something politicians shouted from behind podiums. *Remember the reaping* was a warning not to let history repeat itself. A reminder for humanity not to let its guard down.

Remember the reaping was an American way of life.

The teacher rubbed her forehead and pinched the bridge of her nose. Delilah recognized both gestures. Mrs. Essig was getting another headache.

Matt shrugged, oblivious to his teacher's discomfort. "My dad says you have to be careful who you trust, because the reaping could happen again."

According to Delilah's father, Matt Fuqua was just smart enough to be dangerous. Others who'd warranted the same description included congressmen from the wrong side of the aisle and that eight-year-old from Memphis who'd figured out how to put his mother's car into Neutral before he realized he couldn't reach the brake.

Just smart enough to be dangerous, it turned out, wasn't really very smart at all.

For the next hour, Delilah and her classmates wandered along the crowded sawdust-strewn midway, clutching their lunches and staring in awe at every vibrant spectacle they passed. They didn't have access to the entire menagerie. The owner had generously offered a complimentary midway "preview" for all of the local schools, with the hope that curious parents would later attend the whole carnival at full price. But what they did see was enough to impress even the most jaded fifth grader.

Along with the tantalizing scent of the food carts and the game booths boasting all the bells and whistles, costumed circus performers gave abbreviated demonstrations to cheering children and stunned teachers. A man in a red velvet jacket and dramatic black eyeliner swallowed a series of swords on a small dais, while Delilah rubbed her throat in empathy. Five acrobats in red-and-black sequined leotards formed an inverted pyramid, their bodies bent and twisted into complicated shapes. And set back from the midway, behind velvet ropes to hold the audience at a distance, a man and woman in matching top hats and shiny red-and-black costumes juggled lit torches and breathed fire into the air.

Everywhere the children turned, a new spectacle awaited, each more extravagant than the last. But the real draw was a series of stunning hand-carved and brightly painted circus wagons that had been hauled out to line the midway. Each wheeled cage displayed a different cryptid the children had only ever seen on television, the internet, or in books. Handlers in black slacks and bright red shirts stood by, ready to answer questions or prod creatures into displaying their bizarre and sometimes unsettling features.

The first wheeled cage held a brownie, a small gnomelike

creature with a long nose and pointed ears, which Matt labeled "boring" and Shelley pronounced "cute." Another held a cockatrice—a miniature dragon with dark, unsettling eyes that stared up at them from its rooster-like head. The creature had scales that glittered with each elegant movement of its long whip of a tail. Its sharp talons clicked against the metal floor of the cage, and Delilah stumbled backward when it opened its curved beak and let out a terrible crow.

The exhibit most popular with the boys, other than the woman who could twist her body until she was standing on her own skull, was a dog with three heads, each growling and snapping at the other two. As they watched, a woman in a sparkly red bustier and black skirt tossed a bloody hunk of meat into the cage with an artistic flourish. The boys in the audience cheered as each third of the dog fought viciously over the single dinner all three mouths had to share.

All Delilah could think was that the dog must have been awfully hungry to keep stealing food from itself.

While the rest of the group remained spellbound by the savage snapping dog, Delilah wandered toward the next wagon, where a cluster of kids from another school had gathered. She had to push her way to the front of the whispering, pointing crowd, and her first glimpse of the creature in the cage stole her breath. It was like nothing she had ever seen. Or rather, it was like *several* things Delilah had seen, but never in such a seemingly random compilation of mismatched parts.

The cryptid was the size and general shape of a lion, its body covered in smooth golden fur ending with a long, slim, tufted tail. Each of her four paws was wider than Delilah's whole hand, but even more incredible was the huge pair of eagle-like wings growing from the creature's back, its feathers fading from dark golden brown at the base to nearly white at the tips. Yet what really caused the commotion was the fact that the creature's front feline paws grew up into deeply tanned human arms and shoulders, which supported an equally human neck and a human head with long, dark hair.

From the biceps up, the creature in the cage looked like a normal woman.

Mesmerized, Delilah glanced at the plaque wired to the front of the wagon. Sphinx, it read. The cryptid was a forty-three-year-old sphinx named Hecuba, who'd been taken from her mother's nest on a Greek mountainside just weeks after she was born.

Delilah tried to imagine the creature in her natural habitat. Flying across the Greek countryside on huge powerful wings. Swooping to catch a goat or lamb in her razor-sharp claws, then taking the prize up to a massive nest on the side of a mountain. That would have been incredible to see.

Could Hecuba remember any of that life? Delilah couldn't remember anything from when she was only a few weeks old.

The sphinx turned in her tight quarters, ready to pace several steps to the other end of her cage, but when her gaze met Delilah's, Hecuba froze. Her eyes were gold and round like a cat's, and the left one peeked at the child through a curtain of dark hair. But no cat had ever looked at Delilah like Hecuba was looking at her. No bird had either.

The sphinx glared at her the way her mother did in church, when Delilah kept clicking the ballpoint pen but couldn't be scolded during the prayer.

The sphinx was looking at Delilah as if she wanted to say something.

Hecuba blinked, then continued pacing, but every time she turned toward the fascinated child, their gazes locked and Delilah's curiosity was piqued again.

"Can we ask her questions?" she asked the sphinx's handler, a large man in jeans whose thick arms were crossed over a simple red employee T-shirt. There were no top hats or sequins for handlers assigned to the most dangerous cryptids—nothing that could distract from the safety regulations.

"Questions?" The handler frowned down at her, as if he found her request very odd. "You can ask anything you want, but don't expect an answer. She don't talk. Even if she could, it'd probably be nonsense. Having a human head don't mean she has a human brain."

Delilah decided to give it a try anyway, because what other kind of brain could be inside a human head? She stepped closer to the cage, but stopped when the handler stuck one arm out to keep her at a safe distance. "Hecuba?" she said, and the sphinx stilled when she heard her name. "Do you remember Greece?"

The sphinx blinked, then narrowed her eyes at the child. A human tongue peeked from between her dry lips to wet them, and Delilah's pulse quickened. Hecuba was going to answer. She, Delilah Marlow, was going to be the first person in history to carry on a conversation with a sphinx!

"Ha!" Someone shoved Delilah's shoulder, and she stumbled to the left. When she turned, she found Matt Fuqua leering at her. "Did you really think it was going to answer you?" Matt and his friends laughed at Delilah while her cheeks burned.

Mrs. Essig quietly rounded up her group and announced that it was time to eat their bagged lunches.

As they headed down the midway toward the petting zoo, which boasted a picnic area and hand-washing station, the parade of performers and exhibits continued. Matt stepped into the path of an acrobat doing backflips down the sawdust-strewn path, and if Mrs. Essig hadn't pulled him out of the way, he would have wound up tangled in a knot of bendy limbs and sequins.

Shelley whispered into Delilah's ear that Mrs. Essig should

have let him go. Death by circus acrobat would have been the most interesting thing ever to happen to him.

The petting zoo was a fenced-off area at the end of the midway. Inside, a series of small open-air pens had been arranged across from a collection of long folding picnic tables. Mrs. Essig claimed the end of one table for her six field-trip charges and shooed them toward a hand-washing station at one end of the exhibit.

Delilah dropped her lunch bag on the chair she'd claimed, then followed Shelley toward the boxy plastic sink and soap dispensers. While the boys splashed each other and used more paper towels than they actually required, Delilah and Shelley wandered slowly past the enclosures, oohing and aahing over the young beasts on display.

Instead of the usual collection of lambs, piglets, and newborn bunnies, the menagerie's petting zoo held werewolf puppies, a centaur foal who pranced around her pen with hair the color of wheat flying out behind her, and the most adorable little bundle of white fur identified by the sign hanging from its pen as an infant yeti.

There was also a young giant—a three-foot-tall toddler wearing a folded tablecloth as a diaper. The giant's forehead protruded grotesquely and his legs were knobby and twisted. After a second of staring at him, Delilah decided that the huge toddler was much more scared of the taunting children than they were of him.

Shelley's favorites were the werewolf pups. The plaque hanging from their pen said that they were five years old and had been born right there in the menagerie. They had a baby sister, according to the petting zoo's "nanny"—a woman in black overalls and a stained red apron. But the infant was still too young to be separated from her mother, so Shelley and Delilah would have to come back with their parents to see the full display at night, if they wanted a glimpse at the only baby werewolf in the menagerie.

At the last pen before the hand-washing station, Matt and his friends had gathered, wet fingers still dripping, and were shouting to be heard over one another as they stared into the pen. "What's going on?" Shelley said, elbowing her way through the small throng of boys with Delilah at her side.

"There's no sign, so we're taking bets about what's in the pen," Matt explained. "I've got a homemade fudge brownie up for grabs, from my lunch, and Elías is throwing in a candy bar."

Delilah peered into the pen and discovered the source of the mystery. Three forms sat at the back in a semicircle, facing away from the crowd. The one on the left was the smallest and the one on the right was the largest, but all three wore what seemed to be threadbare nightgowns. Without their faces visible, their species was a total mystery.

"I say they're cyclopses," Matt declared.

Delilah shook her head. "Cyclopses are giants."

"Actually, there's a pygmy species native to a small island near Greece." Neal Grundidge pulled a used tissue from his pocket and swiped at his runny nose. "They're people-sized."

"They could be satyrs," Elías said. "We can't see their feet from here."

"Hey!" Matt shouted, gripping the pen with both hands. "Hey, turn around! We paid for freaks, so show us some freaks!"

"This field trip is free," Shelley reminded him, but Matt only wedged one sneakered foot into the pen and climbed up a foot.

"Get down!" Delilah whispered fiercely, as the nanny started toward them with clenched fists and narrowed eyes. "You're going to get us all in trouble."

"We're not leaving until you turn around, freaks!" Matt shouted, propelling himself another foot up the six-foot fence.

The creatures on the right and left of the semicircle hunched even closer to the center, but the one in the middle slowly began to turn.

Delilah held her breath, and Matt dropped onto the ground but clutched the fence with both hands. All six of the classmates watched, spellbound, as the form in the middle stood on human legs and feet and turned to face them. Long dark hair hung over her face, obscuring the source of her monstrosity, and silence fell over the fifth graders as they waited, frozen.

Finally the girl in the dress lifted one human-looking hand and pushed her hair back to reveal...

A perfectly normal-looking little girl.

"Awww!" Neal frowned. "She looks like my little sister."

"What is she?" Elías asked, as the nanny approached.

"She's not a she, she's an *it*," Matt insisted, backing solemnly away from the pen. "That's the most dangerous kind of freak. The kind that looks like us. She must be a surrogate."

"Are those her sisters?" Neal asked. "Surrogates don't have brothers and sisters."

"She's an oracle," the nanny said. "All three of them are. Right now they mostly find lost things and guess your middle name, but someday, they'll be able to see the future."

"You think they'll see another reaping?" Shelley whispered.

Delilah hardly heard her best friend's question. When her classmates had bored of the normal-looking freak and moved on to eat their lunch, Delilah stood alone in front of the pen, staring at the child oracle, who stared right back at her through haunting golden-brown eyes. The girl was a couple of years younger than Delilah, and a lot skinnier. Her nightgown was stained. Her hair was tangled and dirty, her bare feet caked in mud. There was no food in the oracles' pen, nor any furniture at all.

When Delilah finally turned away from the girl on the other side of the fence, bothered by something she couldn't quite put into words, she could feel the oracle watching as she walked all the way back to her table and sat with her friends. That unseen gaze followed her as she pulled a sandwich from her brown bag and stared at it, suffering a sudden loss of appetite.

Finally, as she opened her carton of milk, Delilah's grim tangle of thoughts cleared enough for one to shine through. If that girl was a monster, anyone could be a monster. That's why the world was so terrified of another reaping. Because just like last time, humanity would never see it coming.

But if monsters could look like humans, and humans could look like monsters, how could anyone ever *really* be sure that the right people stood on the outside of all those cages?

"Three hundred one thousand babies were born in hospitals across the United States in March of 1980. Not one of them made it home from the hospital."

—Opening lines of a 1996 documentary entitled
The Reaping—America's Greatest Tragedy

ROMMILY

A bead of sweat rolled down Rommily's brow and soaked into the thin blanket beneath her head. In midsummer, the inside of the cargo trailer was always sweltering, and being accustomed to the dark and the heat and the relentless jostling from the road wasn't the same as being comfortable. But then, comfort wasn't a concept she remembered very well anyway. She'd been sold to the menagerie as a skinny six-year-old with wide honey-brown eyes, clinging to her older sister's hand while she whispered reassurances into her younger sister's ear.

At twenty, Rommily was still thin and her eyes were still wide and honey brown, but the rest of her was all grown-up.

For the past decade of their fourteen years in captivity the oracles had shared a single cage on wheels, just wide enough to let them sleep side by side and just tall enough to stand up in. Rommily's entire world consisted of 192 cubic feet of space, which she shared with her sisters. What little time they didn't spend staring out at the world through steel mesh was spent performing, in chains.

Rommily could recall little of her life before the menagerie, and what memories she still possessed had taken on the hazy quality of a half-remembered dream.

The overloaded semi rolled to a stop with a familiar groan and the harsh squeal of brakes, and her body rocked with the motion. Near the front of the trailer, the pup whined in her cage, and at the rear one of the cats snorted, startled from sleep by the sudden loss of forward momentum.

The cats, she knew, always dreamed of trees, of wind and earth and prey. The pup dreamed about her mother. Rommily remembered their dreams clearly, though she hadn't been able to peek into them in months.

She sat up on the threadbare quilt that served as her pallet in the summer and her blanket in the cold. She glanced at the sister on her left, then at the sister on her right, both still asleep in spite of the narrow empty space she had left between them. She could hardly see them in the muddy darkness, but she knew their shapes by heart.

On the left was Lala, with her perpetual baby face and thin frame, dirty toes peeking from beneath her long layered skirt, even with her legs curled up to her chest. Lala was the youngest of the three, and the smartest, according to most.

On the right was Mirela, whose bountiful figure endured, though she was fed no more than the rest of the livestock. Mirela had a spine of steel, a fact evident in her proud posture. Mirie would not bend. Not for food, not for sleep, and not for comfort. Deep down, her sisters understood that if she were ever pushed too hard, she would snap, and the recoil might kill them all.

There wasn't enough room to move around in the steel crate, so Rommily sat with her knees tucked up to her chest and stared into the cage across the narrow aisle that ran down the center of the cargo trailer. A set of eyes flashed in the dark, reflecting what little light filtered through the vents in the top of the wide-load trailer.

The minotaur was awake. If he ever slept, Rommily couldn't

tell. Every time she woke up on the road, the bull was watching her. Not just looking at her. *Watching* her. She wasn't sure of much anymore, but she was sure of that.

The rumble of the engine died, and in its absence voices echoed from outside, shouting orders and barking replies. Rommily couldn't tell what time it was from the muddy light overhead, but the time of day never mattered anyway. Regardless of the hour or the weather, the roustabouts would start setting everything up the moment they arrived at the site, the latest in an endless blur of rural county fairgrounds. Lost time was lost money, and if there was anything old man Metzger wasn't willing to lose, it was money.

Something scraped the outside of the cargo trailer, and Lala rolled over in her sleep. Metal creaked from the left and right as the other livestock began to stir in their cages. The acrid scent of fresh urine wafted from the front of the trailer and Rommily's nose crinkled. Someone's bladder control had failed. Probably the pup's. But that was no surprise, considering how long they'd been locked in the dark.

A sudden violent squeal of metal ripped through the voices echoing from outside, and Rommily's eyelids snapped shut as mental images rolled over her. Visions still came like that sometimes, triggered from deep within her by a sight, scent, or sound.

"Take the key and lock her up," she mumbled.

The bull's eyes narrowed as his attention to Rommily intensified, but she didn't notice. She could no longer see anything but what played in her head, and even if she actually understood what she saw this time, no one else ever would. They hadn't been able to make much sense of anything she'd said since the rainy night they'd found her wandering between the cages on some Midwestern fairgrounds, drenched to the bone and dripping with enough blood to drive the cats into a frenzy.

Rommily knew that she understood more of the world than it understood of her since that night, but that frustrated her much less than the brutal realignment of her divination. Her third eye saw mostly the end of life now, and each vision chipped away a little more of her sanity. Mirela worried that she was too far gone already. Rommily worried that Mirela was right.

"Jack fell down and broke his crown," she whispered, and the words ran together like watercolors on canvas.

On her right, Mirela sat up, took one look at Rommily, then shoved her other sister's shoulder. Lala groaned and opened her eyes, ready to grump, but when her gaze fell on Rommily, the words died on her tongue.

Before either of them could try for the thousandth time to interpret their sister's words, the mighty groan of steel obliterated any attempt at communication. A second later, their cage began to tremble as the floor of the trailer shuddered beneath it.

The trailer wall behind the bull's cage separated from the ceiling with a great creak. Harsh daylight poured in through the ever-widening seams at the top of the wall and down both sides, blinding the occupants inside as the wall, hinged at the bottom, folded down like a ramp the full length of the trailer.

The effect was like opening one long side of a box to reveal its contents. Anyone unaccustomed to the sight would have been astonished by the number of wheeled cages lined up inside, neat as a child's blocks put away for storage.

But Rommily and her sisters, and the pup, and the cats, and all the others—they only stared out at the circus unfolding before them with tired, glazed eyes.

The bull didn't turn to look, not even when several big

roustabouts in dusty jeans and matching red shirts climbed the ramp at his back. Their heavy boots clomped against the metal floor, and they began opening locks and pulling heavy iron chains from the axles beneath the bull's cage.

The minotaur was bigger than all three of the oracles combined, and it took eight men—all of them big and strong, and accustomed to the work—to control the roll of his cage down the ramp. If left to gravity, his cart would crash heavily into whatever blocked its path, and if there was anything old man Metzger liked less than wasted time or lost money, it was broken equipment.

While several of the roustabouts stayed behind to sedate the bull, then let him out of his pen and fit him with a work harness, the others climbed the ramp again to fetch the horse cages. The centaurs couldn't bear a load like the minotaur, but all beasts of burden would be put to heavy labor of one sort or another.

To keep them healthy enough to work, they were given extra food.

To keep them relatively safe to work with, they were given regular sedatives, which kept their minds dull.

Rommily watched as the minotaur was harnessed, leather straps fitting over his largely bovine head and massive, heavy horns before lying across enormous cords of human neck muscle. He blinked at her through a medicated daze. His attention didn't falter even when the lot superintendent started shouting orders and waving his arms, directing carts of brightly colored costumes and decorative wagon casings—huge hand-carved frames, which would be mounted on the sides of the cages when they went on display.

Mirela and Lala sat on their knees on either side of their sister, and together they watched the pre-carnival dance, a laborious routine they knew well. Everyone had a job. Every job was important. The last time someone forgot to double-check a lock, three people had died. Four, if you count the creature that got loose.

But no one ever counted him.

The beasts of burden were put to work unloading the other cages. The oracles watched, mute, as pairs of large men hauled huge posts toward the fairgrounds. Women drove tractors pulling carts full of supplies, hay, and feed.

Rommily's fingers folded around the steel mesh in front of her when the roustabouts came for her cage. The animal exhibits had been unloaded and all that remained were the specialized-service acts. The succubi. The sirens. The oracles. Soon they would be cleaned up, decked out in bright colors, and acclaimed on the midway as dancers, singers, and fortune-tellers. But that was all for show. For profit. For later.

For now...

The rattle of chains and the metallic screech of wheeled cages. Sweat-stained clothes and growling bellies, and the aged stench of travel.

The oracle sisters rocked with the jostle of the cage as they were rolled off the trailer. They squinted against the harsh sunlight. Rommily breathed deeply in the open air, but even outside the stale livestock trailer, the menagerie still smelled like captivity. Like straw and animals and sweat and manure. Like rust, oil, and exhaust.

The bull passed the oracles' cage pulling two of the wolves' pens, linked end to end. His gaze caught on Rommily again, and he veered so sharply that the man pulling his harness turned and beat him over the head with a thick baton. Rommily could only watch, and when the small procession had gone, her focus fell on a sign revealed by its passing.

Welcome to the Franklin County Fairgrounds.

Rommily shook her head, and her grip on the steel mesh

tightened. When she opened her mouth, the commotion of the menagerie swallowed her voice before even her sisters could hear it. But the words echoed in her own head long after they fell from her tongue.

"...we all fall down..."

DELILAH

On the morning of my twenty-fifth birthday, I woke up to find that Brandon had left four glossy red tickets on my nightstand. They were made from nice card stock—definitely keepsake quality—covered in glittering, scrolling black script. My hand shook as I picked them up. I knew what they were before I even read the print.

> Admission For One
> To Metzger's Menagerie
> The Largest Traveling Zoo
> In The Northern Hemisphere

I left the tickets in the glove box during my shift at the bank, where I spent most of the day trying to tune out the excited chatter of my fellow tellers. About half of my coworkers also had tickets. The other half couldn't afford to go.

Nothing pays very well in small-town Oklahoma, and usually that's okay, because there isn't much to do in the land of red earth anyway, until you get up to the capital or out toward Tulsa. Hell, you can't even get full-strength beer with your dinner unless you pay for an import.

But the menagerie hadn't been within driving distance of Franklin County in nearly fifteen years, and it might never come back. Everyone who could borrow money or call in a debt would be there to see the spectacle.

Including me.

Brandon had spent a fortune on the tickets, and it didn't really matter that I would rather drive to the city and spend my birthday at the ballet, or a concert, or even a baseball game. As my mother had told me all my life, the true gift was in the intent, and my boyfriend had meant well.

He always meant well.

That evening, Brandon took my hand as we wandered down the fairground midway behind my best friend, Shelley Wells, and her boyfriend, Rick. Barkers cried out from both sides of the path, challenging us to pin the tail on the centaur, or knock down pop-up silhouettes of satyrs with a rubber-tipped archery set, or shoot the shell bras off mermaid figurines with water guns. Calliope music played at a volume only small children and the near-deaf could actually enjoy.

The noise scattered my thoughts and scraped my nerves raw. We hadn't even gotten to the menagerie section of the carnival yet and I was ready to go home.

"Hey, Lilah, did you see they have a minotaur?" Shelley pointed to a twenties-style poster tacked up next to a spinning ride advertised as "guaranteed to make you hurl."

"They didn't have him when we were kids."

I nodded, and she turned to walk backward, facing me while she shouted above the jostling, buzzing crowd. "You see a minotaur in school?"

"No. They're pretty rare." We'd seen very few live cryptids in class, and minotaurs were among the least likely to ever be studied by undergrads. They bred slowly in captivity and gave birth to only one offspring at a time. Most experts believed they'd be extinct within a century—a tragedy few in the U.S. would recognize.

"You shouldn't have quit." Shelley turned to face forward again, taking Rick's arm, then called to me over her shoulder. "You would've been a great crypto-vet."

"I didn't quit. I just didn't go to grad school." For a while, though, that had been the plan. I'd finished my crypto-biology degree and had already been accepted into two crypto-veterinary programs before I'd realized that the only jobs legally available in the U.S. for crypto-vets would have required me to lock up my patients. Even the ones with human faces.

Those jobs were at places like Metzger's Menagerie.

Or worse: research labs, in which scientists tested everything from cosmetics to biological weapons on creatures protected by neither human law nor ASPCA regulations.

Disillusioned by those prospects, I'd moved back home to Franklin, where the median income was less than two-thirds that of the national average and my best guess on the median vocabulary looked even less promising.

A jewel glittering among small-town clods of red clay, Brandon was a newly minted pharmacist with a future in the family business. He read books and spoke in complete sentences. We'd been together since the month I'd come home from college, and—poor gift-giving skills aside—he was a very nice guy. And he truly loved me.

The only part of me that had been relieved to find such a morally ambiguous birthday present on my nightstand was the part that had half expected an engagement ring.

I wanted to be more than a small-town bank teller married to a small-town pharmacist. But I had no idea what "more" might look like, and the certainty that I'd know it when I saw it had faded with each day spent in Franklin. All I ever saw was Brandon, and all he seemed to want to see was me.

And a traveling zoo full of bizarre beasts.

The actual menagerie was behind a second gate at the end of the sawdust-strewn midway, a design no doubt intended to pull people past countless opportunities to spend money on their way to the main attraction—the only part of the carnival not offered on a yearly basis by the county fair.

Brandon and I caught up with Shelley and Rick at the menagerie gate, where another line had formed. I recognized several of the people in the crowd as account holders from the bank, but without my name tag—Hello, My Name is Delilah. Can I Interest You in a No-Fee Savings Plan?—they didn't seem to recognize me. The family in front of us had three small children, each clamoring to touch the shifter kittens and phoenix chicks in the petting zoo. At the gate, the parents were reminded that certain areas of the exhibit, namely the succubus tent, would be off-limits to anyone under eighteen.

Rick snickered like an overgrown twelve-year-old and Shelley elbowed him. I thanked the universe for my mature, stable, predictable boyfriend, then realized that I'd just found three different ways to call Brandon boring.

When we got to the front of the line, an elderly man in a red sequined vest and a black top hat took one look at Shelley, then bowed low and pulled a bouquet of real daisies from his sleeve. He presented them to her with a flourish from one knee, heedless of his cracking joints.

Delighted, Shelley returned his bow with a curtsy, spreading the hem of an imaginary skirt, and even I couldn't resist a smile. Then she and Rick helped the poor old man to his feet.

The ticket taker resettled his hat on his head. "First time at the menagerie?"

"Kind of." Shelley stuck her nose into the daisies and sniffed. "Delilah and I saw some of it when we were kids. They didn't bring out any of the exotic stuff, though."

"Well, then, you're in for a treat!" He glanced at our plastic full-pass bracelets, then waved us inside with a grand, white-gloved gesture. "Trust me, ladies and gentlemen. You've never seen anything like *this* before."

However, that could only be partly true, no matter what they had on display behind velvet curtains and in gilded cages. Gone were the days when centaurs roamed the plains in herds, with flocks of thunderbirds beating powerful wings overhead, but we'd grown up seeing cryptids of all sizes, shapes, and colors on television and in movie theaters. They were the villains in our horror movies, most of which drew on the reaping for inspiration. They were the hidden terrorist threats in our thrillers, the bumbling bad guys in our comedies, and the subject of scientific study in nearly every documentary I'd ever seen.

That's where traveling creature features had the market cornered. Anyone could see a werewolf on television, but the average citizen could only see one live at the menagerie. If he or she could afford the cost of admission. And Metzger's had the most diverse collection of any cryptid zoo in the country.

Metzger's was stunning. I couldn't deny that, even as I stopped to scrape a thin coating of manure and sawdust from the sole of my left boot onto the grass.

Compared to the Tilt-A-Whirl and corn-dog portion of the carnival, the menagerie was practically circus finery. The lights were brighter and the colors more vibrant. Even the boisterous organ music felt more sophisticated and dimensional. Costumed performers wandered the midway with flaming batons, balloon bouquets, and souvenir top hats, giving the menagerie the same glamorous, exotic appeal I remembered from my visit as a child. The red sequined costumes had been updated, as, presumably, had the employees wearing them, and the scents of fried dough and roasted meat still made my mouth water.

But the guilt twisting my insides into knots couldn't be calmed by junk food, and the glass of wine I'd had in place of my pre-carnival dinner hadn't helped in the least. The small line of People First protesters shouting, "Remember the reaping!" outside the front gate had only made the whole thing worse.

The People First activists wanted the menagerie to leave Franklin County. We had that much in common. However, they didn't object to the inhumane treatment of cryptids in captivity—they were scared that the cryptids would escape and embark upon another devastating human slaughter.

What they didn't seem to realize was that if the menagerie's oddities escaped, *we would see them coming.*

We hadn't seen the reaping coming. The cryptid surrogates had pulled off the greatest con in all of history—so meticulously executed that we didn't realize the scale of the infiltration until it was far too late. Six years after the first wave, we'd *still* had no idea that our losses numbered more than three hundred thousand.

Fearing locked-up cryptids that didn't look human would do us no more good than suspecting our own neighbors and relatives of being monsters, as we'd done for decades after the reaping. But scared people can't be reasoned with. Scared politicians can't be talked down from their podiums. Scared nations pass reactionary laws without bothering to consider how much powder those legal snowballs will gather as they roll down Capitol Hill. Eventually, yesterday's outrage becomes today's normalcy.

Reactionary legislation had spawned outfits like Metzger's, where anything and everything not deemed to be human could be locked up and put on display with no limits, no boundaries, and no regulations except those meant to protect employees and spectators. Which made people like me—the admittedly quiet minority—profoundly uncomfortable.

My tension headache told me I shouldn't have accepted the tickets. My queasy stomach said I shouldn't be celebrating my birthday at the menagerie where, as a child, I'd been shocked to see three malnourished little girls locked in an animal pen wearing no more than a few filthy scraps of material. Because when *I* remembered the reaping—inarguably the most profound tragedy to ever strike the U.S.—I also remembered the millions of innocent cryptids who'd been rounded up and thrown in prisons or shot on sight for resisting arrest.

By the time I was born, several years after the reaping was discovered, the government had begun denying citizenship and legal rights to any living being only partially human, as well as to any hybrid of two or more different biological families.

What that meant was that ligers and mules were protected by the ASPCA because they were both hybrids of two animals that share the same biological genus and family. But because the griffin is a hybrid of two different classes—Mammalia and Aves—and three different orders—Carnivora, Artiodactyla, and Squamata—it isn't recognized as a natural animal but as a cryptid "beast." Anything considered "unnatural" under such legislation was denied protection under U.S. law.

That secondary national tragedy, a clean sweep of everyone not wholly human or "naturally" fauna, had been brushed under the rug, and even mentioning it made my friends and coworkers look at me as if I'd just set fire to the U.S. flag. So I'd stopped talking about it. But I hadn't stopped feeling it.

Yet deep down, I was dying to see the strange and amazing creatures I'd studied in school, for all the same reasons that had led me to major in crypto-biology in the first place. I wanted to see the beautiful selkie emerging from her sealskin. The troll, so tall and thick he couldn't stand up in most human-scale buildings. The man who could turn into a cheetah at will. The part of me that objected to the confinement and abuse of such beings was the very same part that *needed* to see them for myself.

To understand.

Metzger's had no right to exploit the creatures in its custody, but that wouldn't end whether I looked at them or not. And who better than I to truly appreciate, rather than taunt or mock?

At least, that's how I rationalized my warring desires to both condemn and experience the spectacle.

At the center of the menagerie, towering over everything else, was the big top, an enormous red-and-white-striped circus tent with three sharp peaks that cast an ominous shadow over the fairgrounds. The entrance flaps remained tightly closed until a paying guest was admitted, making it impossible to catch even a passing glimpse of the mysteries within. Around the perimeter of the menagerie stood a series of smaller tents and attractions, and branching from those were a series of themed subsections. Everything from the posters and cages to the costumes and music was designed with a vintage feel so that it seemed as though we'd stepped back in time.

Up first was the bestiary, where cryptid animals lounged or paced in sideshow cage wagons modeled after circus train cars from the early 1900s. They had bright, intricately carved frames and huge wooden wheels, and the beasts within were visible from both sides, through thick iron bars reinforced with sheets of modern steel mesh.

The mesh was a recent requirement, after a twelve-year-old had lost her right hand to an irritable troll in a carnival out West somewhere, a few years back.

Shelley oohed and aahed over the chimera, a beast with the

body and claws of a lion, two heads—one lion, one goat—and a snake for a tail. "Delilah, look how thick and smooth his fur is!" she cried, her nose inches from the side of the cage. I gently tugged her back by one arm. Anything with claws *and* venom should be appreciated from at least two feet away. "So glossy!"

But when the creature turned to pace four steps in the other direction—the full length of its cramped quarters—I noticed that the fur on the goat head's side was matted and dirty. Obviously that half didn't self-groom.

"Here, kitty, kitty!" Shelley called, and the snake growing in place of the beast's tail hissed at her.

"He's not a kitty, Shell," Brandon said. "He's a ferocious beast capable of tearing you apart with three different jaws at once."

"He's not a he." I pointed at a sign attached with twists of wire to the bars on one end of the cage car. "*Her* name is Cleo. She's eighty-six years old, as of last spring," I said, still reading from the plaque. "Born in the wild well before both the reaping and the repeal of the Sanctuary Act, and still in her prime today." I stepped back for a better look. "Poor thing. By the time she dies, she'll have spent three-quarters of her life in a cage."

Rick rolled his eyes. "They're animals, Delilah. They don't even know where they are."

"We're *all* animals. From the taxonomy kingdom Animalia. And you don't know what she knows or feels. Have some respect. She's your elder."

Rick laughed as if I'd made a joke. He tried to put one arm around me and when I pulled away from him, I tripped over a rock and had to grab one of the cage's bars to keep from falling. The heavy cage rocked just a little, and the chimera twisted toward me faster than I would have thought something with three heads could move. The snake hissed and the lion head roared.

I froze, intuitively trying not to trigger any further predatory instinct, but Shelley screeched and jumped back.

Rick laughed at her. Brandon pulled me away from the cage and didn't let go even after I'd regained my balance, my heart still racing.

"Don't touch the exhibits," a deep voice growled, and we turned to find a large man in a bright red baseball cap standing near the end of the chimera cage. His red polo shirt bore the Metzger's logo and the name embroidered over his heart read Gallagher. His hair was thick and curly beneath his cap and his eyes were dark gray. "Unless you want to lose a lot of blood."

"I tripped." In the glare from the setting sun, I noticed several old scars on his face and his forearms, and I wondered how many of those had come from beasts he was in charge of. And how many of them he deserved.

"Cleo's in an iron cage, surrounded by steel mesh," Rick said. "What's she going to do, roar until our ears bleed?"

The man tugged the bill of his red cap down, shading more of his strong features. "Only a fool believes his eyes over all other senses."

Shelley laughed out loud while Rick fumed, and when I turned back for another glimpse of the large man in the red hat, he was gone.

Shelley and I dragged the guys toward the next cage: *Panthera leo aeetus*. Commonly known as a griffin.

Rick and Brandon were fascinated by the griffins, both perched on dead tree branches bolted to the ends of their massive aviary on wheels. They had the hindquarters of a lion and the majestic head, wings, and front claws of an eagle.

An eagle on the physical scale of a lion.

I'd seen them on television and studied them in school, but I'd had no appreciation for their size until I stood in front of them. They must have weighed at least five hundred pounds each.

Brandon shouted at one, unrebuked by another large, gruff handler, and was rewarded when the griffin suddenly threw his enormous wings out and flapped, as if he'd dive at us. We all gasped and backpedaled. The griffin pulled his dive up short at the last second, and I noticed that a patch on his right wing, along the top ridge, was bare of feathers at exactly the spot his wing would have hit the bars, if he hadn't stopped.

The griffin made a horrible avian screech and I covered both my ears, but when he settled on a branch closer to us, still riled up from being teased, I realized that his sharp eagle's beak and incredible wingspan were far less intimidating than his feet, a lethal cross between a lion's claws and a bird's talons.

They were huge. And sharp. I noticed a dried chunk of raw meat wedged between his first and second digits.

My heart ached for him. The griffin was obviously meant to soar the skies and stalk the plains in wide-open freedom. None of which he would get in the menagerie. Yes, griffins could be dangerous, but so could bears and sharks and alligators, yet we didn't round them all up and throw them into cages.

After the griffins came the phoenix. Shelley was disappointed when it refused to burst into flames, then rise from its own ashes for her personal amusement, even though the signs wired to its cage said the poor thing wasn't due for a "rebirth" for nearly another month. I thought it was beautiful, even without the flames. The phoenix had a long graceful swan-like neck with plumage in vibrant graduating shades of red, yellow, and orange. Its broad sweeping tail would have made any peacock jealous.

After the bestiary, we skipped the "Natural Oddities" sec-

tion, which promised us trolls, ogres, goblins, and other assorted humanoid creatures of legend. Brandon led the way
toward the "Human Hybrids" section, where the sign at the
entrance promised us "bizarre and fascinating combinations
of man and beast."

"Come forward, come forward!" the uniformed man at the
tent entrance called, waving us closer with both white-gloved
hands. "Metzger's guarantees you've never seen a spectacle like
this, no matter what other shows you've attended. No one else
on earth has such an extensive collection of grotesque mergers
of human and animal flesh as you'll find in this very tent. Wolf
and man, horse and man, fish and man, bird and *woman...*" He
winked at Rick. "We've got it all! And don't forget to take a
peek at our world-famous minotaur! You won't find another
like him anywhere else in the continental U.S.!"

"It sounds really freaky," Shelley said.

"That it is, that it is." The talker bowed deeply, top hat in
hand. "But you've got these lucky gentlemen to keep you and
your friend safe." He gave the guys another faux-confidential
wink, and I almost laughed out loud. Brandon got nervous
when he heard coyotes howl at night.

The man in the top hat glanced at our bracelets, then held
back a canvas flap with a practiced flourish.

"Seriously, what's it like in there?" Shelley asked before
Rick could push his way inside.

The carny shrugged with an evasive smile. "Some people
love it. Gives others the willies. But what I *can* tell you is that
you can't truly know who you are in here—" he laid one
gloved hand over his red sequined vest "—until you've been
through *there*." He pushed the tent flap open wider.

Brandon, Shelley, and Rick stared into the darkness.

I stepped inside.

"Shock and grief echo across the United States this morning with the news that more than one million children died overnight, most reportedly killed in their sleep. Government officials and residents alike watch, stunned, as the reports continue to pour in, raising the death toll by several thousand per hour..."

—As reported by anchor Brian Richards on
U.S. Morning News, August 24, 1986

DELILAH

My ears roared with my own pulse as my friends followed me through the low entrance into the soaring tent, where a circle of faux-vintage wagon cages surrounded a bright red circus ring. The ring was empty except for a tall stool in the center, dramatically illuminated by a stark spotlight. Unoccupied bleachers lined the shadowy perimeter of the space, set up for a show to come later that night.

The farm scent was much less noticeable in the hybrid tent, where all the exhibits were at least part human, but there was yet more hay beneath our feet and the prevailing ambient noise was still the whisper of paws against hard surfaces and the occasional clomp of hooves.

Like the wagons in the bestiary, those in the hybrid tent had solid steel—or iron?—end panels, complete with massive, heavy-looking couplings with which they could be connected to the other cars. In theory. However, the rust on the hitches made me doubt that they were ever hooked to anything for very long.

Though we couldn't see inside the cars with their end panels facing us, we could see into the wagons across the ring, where vaguely humanoid beings paced, slouched, or sat in the corners of their cages, wearily trying to ignore their audience.

A woman in a red sequined leotard and red-trimmed black top hat stepped forward when we got to the entrance of the ring, defined by padded crimson ropes strung between two shiny metal posts. "Welcome to the human hybrids tent, where every genetic atrocity you can imagine is on display to satisfy your curiosity!" Her name tag read Wendy, and she was cradling something in the crook of her left arm.

"Oh!" Shelley rushed toward the woman and the small bundle she held. "He doesn't look so atrocious!"

Wendy gave her a slick, indulgent smile. "No, this little guy is damn near adorable." She leaned into the light and I saw that she held an infant satyr, whose furry brown goat legs ended in tiny hooves. His chubby little belly and everything north of it was human, except the tiny horns growing from the sides of his skull.

I'd never seen anything cuter in my life.

"His mother just fed him, and I was about to take him back to the petting zoo." Wendy twisted toward the circle of cages with hardly a glance at her young charge. "His mother's the one at the back of—"

"Oh, can I hold him first?" Shelley asked, already reaching for the infant.

"I...um..." Wendy sputtered, obviously unsure how to answer. "I guess. Just for a second." She laid the child in my best friend's arms, while Rick and Brandon watched, dumbfounded.

"His fur tickles." Shelley ran one finger down his fuzzy shin and over his hoof, but the child's eyes never fluttered. He didn't even seem to feel the touch.

"Why isn't he moving?" I asked Wendy.

She shrugged. "He has a full belly. He's passed out cold."

That much was true, but it had nothing to do with the state of his stomach. I gently pulled back the baby's left eyelid, then his right. "He's not full, he's sedated." I frowned up at Wendy. "Why would you sedate an infant?" I demanded. Brandon put one hand on my shoulder to calm me, embarrassed by what he no doubt saw as an irrational tantrum on my part, but I shrugged him off. "He's not a threat. He's a baby."

Wendy's patronizing smile faltered. "If the reaping taught us anything, it's that a threat can come in any size." She took the baby back, and with it, her bright, cheery expression, which now looked as false as her ridiculously long, ridiculously red fingernails. "Now, if you'd like to see the kind of monster this little guy will grow into—" she swept her empty arm toward the wagon car on our left "—start here and follow the circle counterclockwise."

My gaze followed the path formed between the outer loop of wagons and the inner, twelve-inch-high circus ring. Several other customers were clustered at various points on the path.

"When you get to the far side of the circle, go through the gate to the adjoining tent for a look at our special exhibits."

Rick's eyes brightened. "Is that where you keep the mermaids?"

She nodded and gave him an almost intimate smile, as if she were letting us in on a special secret. "Along with a couple of our other rare specimens. Including the Brazilian *encantados*—dolphin shape-shifters—and our world-famous minotaur."

Brandon shoved Rick's shoulder. "I *told* you there were mermaids!"

Wendy's smile grew, and she was now ignoring me completely. "Just make sure you stay on the path and out of the center ring."

"Why? What happens there?" Shelley asked.

"At the eight-o'clock show, one of the werewolves will do

a live shift. I've seen it a million times, and it's *still* incredible. You *can't* miss it!" She laughed at Shelley's worried expression. "They're chained the whole time, even inside the safety cages, and they're surrounded by armed handlers, too." She gave each of us a full-color glossy pamphlet. "And the ten-o'clock show is *stunning!*" She gestured toward the ring with a familiar, wide-armed wave. "The draco sets two rings on fire and the cat shifters jump through them." Her arm rose gracefully to take in the soaring ceiling of the tent. "They put a bird net around the whole thing, and the harpies make several breathtaking dives. I guarantee you've never seen anything like it. It's the highlight of the evening."

I stared at the pamphlet. I *wanted* to see the draco breathe fire and the harpies swoop and dive, but wanting something didn't give one the right to have it. While I could rationalize my willingness to walk through passive exhibits I found fascinating yet morally repulsive, I could *not* justify sitting through a show in which sentient creatures were forced to perform against their will.

Though the prices Metzger's was able to charge made it clear that I took the minority viewpoint on that.

"Do the shows cost extra?" Rick asked.

"Um…let me see your bracelet." Wendy glanced at the wrist he held out. "Nope, you guys have the deluxe admission. You can go anywhere and see anything, except for the staff-only and staging areas."

"Awesome," Shelley said.

Wendy smiled and wished us a great evening, though her smile staled when it landed on me, then gestured for us to enter the ring. As we approached the first huge circus wagon, I glanced back to find her talking to Gallagher, the handler in the red cap, who'd snapped at me for touching the chimera cage.

They were both watching me.

I made myself turn back to my friends just as Shelley gasped. "He's so big!"

For a second, I thought she was talking about the huge handler, and I almost nodded in agreement. Then I realized she was staring into the first cage, a silver-trimmed green masterpiece with fleurs-de-lis and stylized howling wolf heads carved into the corners. I hurried to catch up with my friends and as soon as I stepped in front of the first cage, labeled Claudio—Werewolf, I lost my breath.

Claudio was *beautiful*.

His eyes were golden, like multifaceted bits of amber, and while they were clearly wolf eyes, they contained an obvious understanding—a self-awareness that ordinary wolves' eyes didn't have. His fur was thick and silver and glossy, and when he paced into the half of his cage that was lit from the overhead lights, I saw that his silver coat was actually made up of many different shades of black, white, and gray. His fur shifted with each movement, the color rippling and buckling as each individual hair reflected the light at a slightly different angle.

I stared, transfixed.

Claudio growled at us softly, padding back and forth in a cage that was much too confined, because Shelley was right. He was huge.

"I didn't realize how big they'd be," Brandon said.

"Ordinary wolves don't get that large," I whispered, uncomfortably aware that the shifter could both hear and understand me, assuming he spoke English. "One hundred seventy-five pounds, max, for males. Most are closer to one-fifty." By contrast, Claudio was two hundred pounds, by my guess—a wolf the size of a grown man—and in spite of an obviously confined lifestyle, he looked lean and powerful.

"The reality isn't like the old monster movies," I said, still speaking softly because somehow that felt more respectful of Claudio. "They don't have superpowers. They're strong and fast because they're wolves, but they're not superstrong, or superfast."

"Yeah, but even a regular wolf can rip a man's throat out," Brandon said, and I couldn't argue.

I stepped closer to the cage, fascinated, and Claudio snarled at me, lips curled back to reveal a muzzle full of lethally sharp teeth. The lump in my throat threatened to cut off my airway. "I'm so sorry," I whispered, and the growling stopped. Claudio blinked and tilted his head in an oddly human display of surprise, and that stream of guilt trickling through me swelled into a veritable river, until my veins surged with it.

Claudio didn't belong in a cage, and just by coming to observe him in captivity, I'd become part of the problem.

Anger on his behalf uncoiled like a living thing deep inside me and I gasped at the hot, unsettling sensation in my belly.

"Lilah!" Shelley called as she moved on to the next cart, a green-trimmed silver inverse of the werewolf's, with full moons carved into the scrolling frame. "There's a girl wolf!"

Claudio's snarling resumed, more intensely than before, a reminder that he not only heard everything we said, but understood us, as well.

The plaque on the next circus wagon read Geneviève— Werewolf, but at first glance, the cage appeared empty.

"I don't..." Something flashed in one dark corner of the cage, two pinpoints of yellow light, there, then gone. Then there again.

Geneviève was blinking.

Curiosity got the better of me and I squinted, trying to get a better look at her, but I could barely make out a small, hunched form in the shadows.

"I can't see her," Rick complained. "What good are two-hundred-dollar menagerie tickets if the exhibits are just going to hide?"

"I think she's scared," I said. Brandon took my hand, and Shelley nodded mutely.

"*She's* scared? She's the monster. We're supposed to be scared of *her*." Rick scowled, already walking backward toward the next car, which, according to the sign, held one of only four adlets currently living in captivity.

Adlets were the wolf version of a satyr, stuck in an in-between state with both canine and human features. They were also cannibalistic, highly aggressive, and one of the most effective arguments in favor of keeping cryptids locked up.

"Hold on a minute, now, you don't want to miss this," a voice called from the darkness behind the werewolf cages. Hay crunched beneath heavy footsteps, and a moment later something clanked against the bars on the rear of Geneviève's cage.

The light reflecting from her yellow eyes blinked out.

Claudio's snarling deepened and from our right, the adlet responded with a fierce, eerie howl of its own. On the other side of the ring, hooves and paws scraped the floors of other cages as the captives paced nervously.

Unease gathered in the pit of my stomach and crawled along my arms. My hair stood on end. The hybrids' anxiety was both obvious and contagious.

"Just a sec." A handler stepped into the light falling over and through half of Geneviève's cage. He was a stout, balding man in a Metzger's T-shirt but no vest, hat, or sequins whatsoever. His shirt was stained with sweat, his boots caked with dirt, and a lit cigarette dangled from his mouth. This was a behind-the-scenes man if I'd ever seen one. He held what looked like a thick stick. "This ought to get her up for you."

Geneviève whined, and the sound reminded me of a puppy we'd had when I was in middle school, before she'd chewed up the legs of my dad's favorite chair and he'd made us give her away.

Claudio growled, accompanied by a snarl from the adlet, and when assorted hisses, growls, and the clang of metal rang out from across the ring of circus wagons, I realized that the entire hybrid section of the menagerie knew exactly what was about to happen.

"Last warning, Genni," the handler said, and though her whining intensified, her eyes did not open. Too late, I realized that the handler's stick was actually an electrified cattle prod.

"No!" I shouted, and dimly I was aware that I'd squeezed Brandon's hand hard enough to make him flinch. My other hand had crushed the glossy pamphlet.

"It's okay," the handler said. "She makes us do this all the time." He shoved the cattle prod through a small hole in the steel mesh at the back of her cage.

Geneviève yelped in pain, and Claudio's growling crescendoed until it was almost all I could hear. The handler jabbed the traumatized werewolf one more time, and she scuttled out of her corner and into the light.

Rage filled me like a bonfire lit deep inside my soul. Geneviève was a little girl, no more than thirteen years old. She trembled on the floor of her cage, knees drawn up to her chest, heels tucked close to her body in an attempt to cover herself. She wrapped her arms around her legs and buried her face in the hollow between her knees, letting her long, tangled blond hair fall down her nearly bare back.

"Oh…" Shelley breathed, clearly horrified, and this time Brandon's hand clenched mine. None of us seemed to know what to say. Even Rick looked uncomfortable.

"Stand up, honey, and let them get a look at you," the handler said, as Claudio continued to growl and pace in his cage. The male werewolf couldn't see Geneviève, but he obviously cared about her, and he clearly knew what was happening. "I'm not going to tell you again," the handler taunted, his cigarette bobbing with every word, and the girl-wolf began to tremble.

The cattle prod scraped the iron bars on its way into the cage, and Geneviève stood faster than I would have thought possible. She scrambled toward the front of her cage to escape the weapon, her eyes still squeezed closed, as if her refusal to see us somehow meant that we wouldn't see her.

In that moment, I wished more than anything in the world that I'd made my friends sit through a boring birthday dinner with me instead of using Brandon's tickets, so that at least we could have spared Geneviève this one moment of humiliation in the string of such instances that no doubt comprised her entire existence.

Genni's hair brushed the base of her spine and did much more to cover her than the white bikini bottom and tube-style swimsuit top she'd been made to wear. Her arms and legs were thin and her rib cage was plainly visible through her skin. The outsides of her thighs were peppered with pairs of red welts that could only be burns from the cattle prod.

Little Geneviève obviously resisted her handler quite often. I wasn't sure whether to be relieved by that fact or horrified by it, so I settled for a deep sense of awe that a child so young had survived—so far—an existence I couldn't even imagine.

On display. Nearly naked. Ordered to perform, and tortured for refusal.

I hated myself for being there to see it.

I started to head to the next cage and relieve Geneviève of the audience that gave her handler the chance to abuse her. But then she opened her eyes, and I was too mesmerized to move.

She had Claudio's eyes. Exactly. Beautiful golden wolf eyes in a little girl's face.

"Open your mouth, Genni, and let them have a look at your

teeth." The handler circled the end of her cage, still carrying the cattle prod, and Geneviève scuttled away from him. The name embroidered on his shirt was Jack. The tip of his cigarette glowed red in the shadows.

"Genni…" he warned, and when Claudio started howling, Jack banged on the end of the male wolf's cage with the fist holding the cigarette. "Pipe down, Papa!"

Understanding crashed over me with a devastating weight and stunning intensity. The father was caged feet from his half-naked daughter, unable to protect her, yet forced to hear every offense heaped on her.

"Genni!" Jack shouted, and she turned on him, hissing, hair flying, her lips curled back to reveal long, sharp canines among the teeth in her otherwise human mouth.

"Ain't that somthin'?" Jack took a long drag on his cigarette. "Have to file 'em down once a month, or she's likely to bite a finger off when we groom her."

"You *groom* her?" Brandon sounded sick. Shelley looked pale, and Rick was staring at his feet.

"Have to. That one won't do nothin' on her own. Has to be prodded into brushin' her own teeth in the mornin'." He brandished the forked end of the cattle prod at her and she hissed again, then retreated to the back of her cage. "No, no, don't sit down, Genni. Give the good people their money's worth." Jack turned back to us. "Wanna hear her howl? She's got a helluva voice, that one. Not much for speaking, but she howls like her mama did."

"Did?" I didn't want to ask, but I wanted to know. "She died?"

Jack shrugged, and the tip of his cigarette left squiggles of light dancing in front of my eyes. "Who knows? Sold her off last year." He turned back to Geneviève, who stood in the darkest corner of her cage. "Give us a howl, darlin'."

But Genni had had enough. She sank to the floor against the rear wall of her cage and vanished into the shadows again, closing her eyes so the twin points of yellow light disappeared.

Jack moved toward her with the prod again, and the fire burning in my belly burst into a full-body blaze.

"Leave her alone," I said, and when the entire hybrid tent went silent around me, I realized that my voice sounded...different. Not lower in pitch, but larger somehow. More robust.

Brandon, Rick, and Shelley turned to look at me, their eyes wide. Distantly I realized that my scalp had started to tingle and that the heat blazing deep inside me now threatened to burn me alive.

It was a boundless and terrible heat. And it was not entirely unfamiliar.

Creatures in cages all around the tent turned to stare. Sounds I hadn't even realized I was hearing suddenly ceased— the snort of something equine; steady small splashes from the special section across the ring; and the constant rustle of feet and hooves on hay.

Jack was too intent on causing pain to notice the sudden silence. "It's no trouble." With his back to us, he moved toward the center of the cage to lengthen his reach. "It's just—" he twisted something at the base of the prod "—a little jolt." He shoved the cattle prod between the bars and through the mesh, and Geneviève howled when the tip touched her right calf.

"Get the hell away from her!" I shouted, and my hair rose on my scalp, as if the power sparking through me had charged it at the roots. It floated around my head, not in thin tendrils, but in heavy ropes of hair, twisting around my face in my peripheral vision.

My pamphlet fell to the ground. Brandon dropped my hand. Shelley made a strange noise as she and Rick backed away from me.

Jack pulled the prod from Geneviève's cage and turned, his mouth already open to yell at me. The first syllable died on his tongue. The cattle prod thunked to the ground. My hands found the sides of his head, and dimly I was aware that my fingers looked too dark, the nails long and vaguely pointed.

I gripped his skull and felt several tiny pops as my nails pierced the skin at his temples. Jack's eyes rolled up into his head and his arms began to twitch. His teeth clattered together and sweat poured from his forehead. Blood dripped from his temples.

I saw it all, but none of it sank in. I registered nothing in that moment except the sparks still firing inside me, firing *through* me, out the tips of my fingers and into Jack's head, where every synapse fried within him eased a bit of the demand for justice seething inside me.

How do you *like it?* I demanded, but my mouth never opened. My tongue never moved.

Shelley screamed. The sound of her terror cut through my rage and I pulled my hands from Jack's head in one swift movement. I stumbled backward, horrified by what I'd done, sucking in great gasping breaths that did nothing to soothe the fire burning deep in my chest.

What had I done?

The handler wobbled on his feet. Blood leaked from four pinpoint holes on either side of his balding scalp. Eyes unfocused, he thumped to his knees on the ground, then felt around in the hay without ever looking down. His thick fist closed around the cattle prod he'd dropped and he twisted a knob on the end as far as it would go. Then he raised the prod as high as he could in both fists and rammed it down on his own thigh. The forked tip plunged through denim and into flesh.

The handler began to convulse. For a moment, no one else

moved. The entire hybrid trailer watched Jack electrocute himself. Then hooves and paws began to pound against their cage floors. Wolves howled, something avian screeched, and several human mouths cheered.

"What did you *do*?" Shelley wailed.

My heart pounding, I turned to see my friends staring at me in horror, backing slowly toward the adlet cage to get away from me.

Rick tripped over the low circus ring and went down on one hip.

"I…" I looked at my hands and blinked to clear my vision, but my vision wasn't the problem. The problem was my hands. They were too long and bony, my fingers ending in narrow black points. I had needle-claws, where I'd had normal fingernails before.

Blood dripped from the tip of one. I shook my head in denial of what I was seeing—of what I'd done—but instead of settling over my shoulders, my hair was twisting around my head, if the standing-on-end feeling in my scalp could be trusted.

I backed away from the handler still electrocuting himself and from Geneviève's cage, where she stared at me through yellow wolf-girl eyes. Panic dumped adrenaline into my bloodstream and I suddenly itched to run. To escape.

"What the *hell*?"

I turned to find Rick staring at me, one dusty brown cowboy boot on either side of the bright red circus ring.

Another handler stepped out of the shadows and kicked the livestock prod from Jack's hands. He stopped convulsing, but his eyes regained no focus. His mouth hung open.

"What *are* you?" Wendy, the woman in the sequined leotard, demanded, and I could only blink at her, because I had no answer. Yet even in my mounting terror, I knew that if I'd had an answer, I shouldn't give it to her.

You are normal. You are human. You are ours. The memory of my mother's bedtime mantra played through my head as it always had in moments of fear and doubt since I was a small child. It had never in my life felt more relevant. Or more like a total lie.

The handler in the red cap pushed Wendy aside and stomped toward me, reaching out for me. Then, suddenly, his gaze darted over my shoulder. "Wait!" he shouted, and I turned to run.

The last thing I saw before my skull exploded in pain and the world went dark was the face of the hybrid tent ticket taker in the top hat as he swung a felt-covered mallet at my head.

ATHERTON

The call came over the radio at 7:04 p.m., while Wayne Atherton was eating a cheeseburger in the driver's seat of his patrol car.

"All units, respond with your location. We got a problem up at the fairgrounds."

Wayne dropped his burger into the grease-stained bag and answered with food still in his mouth. "This is officer oh-four. I'm just off Highway 71, a mile past Exit 52." Known locally as the Sonic exit. Wayne finished his bite while four other deputies responded with their locations, then Dispatch came back over the radio with a squawk of static.

"No details yet, but there's an ambulance on the way to the menagerie and they're requesting all the backup we can send. Oh-four, you're closest, but I'm sending everyone else your way. Be careful. And don't forget your iron kit."

The iron kit. *Shit.*

Wayne slammed the gearshift into Drive and pulled onto the highway without checking for oncoming traffic. He only remembered to turn on his siren when the car he nearly ran off the road blasted its horn.

"Dispatch, how're those details coming?" he demanded as

he sped down the dusty two-lane highway toward the Franklin County fairgrounds. "I need to know what I'm walking into."

A month before, a cop down near Dallas had lost an arm to an ogre drunk on Kool-Aid and impatient for his dinner.

"Oh-four, you're headed for the hybrid tent, set up near where they put the Tilt-A-Whirl at the county fair. Not sure how it happened, but it sounds like one of the hybrids got loose and injured a menagerie employee."

"A hybrid?" Wayne stomped on the gas pedal and began scanning the side of the road for the familiar faded wooden sign marking the entrance to the fairgrounds. What he knew about cryptids would easily fit between the cardboard pages of a toddler's picture book, and the only hybrids he could even name were mermaids and werewolves. "No civilian casualties, Dispatch?"

"Well, I doubt the carny's a cop, Wayne," Grace said in that exasperated tone she usually saved for after hours.

"You know what I mean. No customers hurt? No locals?"

"Hang on, oh-four." Dispatch went silent for a minute, and just as Wayne was turning onto the wide gravel path leading to the fairgrounds, Grace came back on the line. "We're only hearing about the one injury so far, and Metzger's says no one else is in immediate danger. Secondary report says the perpetrator is restrained."

Perpetrator? "If this is a hybrid attack, there's no perp, Grace. You wouldn't characterize a tiger that escaped from the zoo as a perpetrator, would you?"

"I don't make the reports, I just dispatch them. But I'm coming up with all kinds of new ways to characterize *you*."

Wayne laughed, picturing Grace chewing on the cap of her pen. "What kind of injury are we talking about, Dispatch?"

"We're not clear on that yet, oh-four, but the folks at the carnival seem to want us to take the cryptid into custody."

"This is the Sheriff's Department, not the pound!" Franklin County wasn't equipped to hold most cryptids, much less keep them for any extended period of time. Hell, some of them wouldn't even fit in a standard jail cell!

"You're preaching to the choir, oh-four. Just haul ass and watch your back."

He hated it when Grace talked like she was his boss instead of his girlfriend. Especially over the radio, where anyone could hear. But as usual, she was right. "I'll check in as soon as I know what's going on."

Wayne turned off the siren but left his lights flashing as he rolled through the menagerie's open gate, where carnies in elaborate red-and-black costumes waved him on. He drove straight down the midway with his foot on the brake, honking to warn everyone who hadn't noticed his blue-and-red strobe. Where the midway forked, another pair of menagerie employees waved him to the right, through another gate, and a minute later, Wayne could see the commotion. A large group was being held back from the entrance to a big circus-style striped tent by a crimson velvet rope and a staff of large red-clad men.

He got out of his car, lights still flashing. The crowd made way for him, and when he got to the front, he headed straight for a woman in a leotard and top hat and a man in a black Metzger's cap. "Deputy Wayne Atherton, Franklin County Sheriff's Department. Who can fill me in?"

The employee in the black cap stuck his hand out for Wayne to shake. "I'm Chris Ruyle, the lot supervisor."

Wayne had no idea what a lot supervisor was, but he walked and talked like the boss. "What happened, Mr. Ruyle?"

"We were hoping you could tell us." Ruyle lifted the closed tent flap and gestured for Wayne to go in ahead of him. Inside, a woman lay on her side on the ground, a familiar head of dark wavy hair spread all around her. Her hands were bound at her back. With iron cuffs.

Wayne dropped to his knees at her side. "That's Delilah Marlow." She'd been a couple of years behind him in high school, and all he really knew about her was that she'd been ready to shake the red dirt from her shoes on her way out of town since before she could even walk. No one had expected that girl to come home after college, much less stay. "Dispatch said the victim was an employee. What the hell happened?" A large purple bump was already starting to rise on one side of her skull. "What did this?"

"I did."

Wayne looked up at the man who'd spoken. Then he looked up some more. The man held a black top hat and wore a red vest with *Lerner* embroidered on it in scrolling black print.

Wayne stood, anger bubbling up from his guts. *Damn out-of-towners beating up on local girls.* Franklin County wouldn't stand for such things. "I thought this was a cryptid attack."

"It was," Lerner said. "But the creature wasn't ours. She was yours."

"Mine?" Wayne followed Lerner's gaze to Delilah Marlow's unconscious form. There was hay caught in her hair and blood beneath her fingernails—defensive wounds if he'd ever seen them. "You got five seconds to start making sense before I arrest you for assault and battery."

Lerner stared at him unflinchingly, and Ruyle cleared his throat to catch Wayne's attention. "Officer Atherton, the victim is over there." Ruyle pointed toward a small crowd of flamboyantly dressed carnival employees gathered around a man seated on the ground with his mouth gaping open, staring at the hay beneath him. A trickle of blood seeped from each of his temples. A line of drool hung from his open lips. "This *girl* is the creature, and I can assure you she doesn't belong to Metzger's. So what I need to know from you is just what exactly this Delilah Marlow is, and what the hell she did to my handler."

Martin,

I'm sure you've seen the news by now, and I'm very sorry to have to tell you that your sister Patricia and her family are among the thousands of victims of this morning's national tragedy. I wanted to call, but your phone number wasn't in Patty's address book, and she was in no shape to find it for us. She and Robert are both in total shock. They lost four of their children overnight, and the police aren't sure exactly what happened. All we do know is that Emily, the six-year-old, was the only one who survived...

—From a hand-written letter by Hannah Goodwin to her brother-in-law and his family, August 24, 1986

DELILAH

A soft buzzing woke me up. Not like a bee or a fly, but like...electricity. I was lying on something hard, rough, and cold, but the cold was all wrong. I could feel it not just against my face and arms, but against parts of me that should have been insulated by my clothes.

My eyes flew open as I shoved myself up with both hands, but the glaring assault of fluorescent light—the source of the buzzing—was like a spike driven through my skull. My arms gave out and my eyes fell shut. My cheek slammed into the floor, and I sucked in a shocked breath.

The floor. I was lying on the cold, hard floor. Naked.

My pulse racing, I lifted my head carefully and had to breathe through a wave of vertigo. My head throbbed fiercely. Light painted the insides of my eyelids red. I sat up on my knees, shivering, and folded my arms over my chest to cover myself. Then I opened my eyes again.

The glare was no longer crippling, but my headache was. I blinked and my eyes started to adjust to the light, but the world was a blur. Another blink, and several dark stripes came into focus.

No, not stripes. Bars. Thick iron bars.

Panicked, I scrambled away from them on my hands and knees until I came to a gray brick wall. I leaned my bare back against it, my knees pulled up to my chest, and finally made myself look at my surroundings.

I was in a corner cell with two walls of iron bars and a rough concrete floor.

No.

My heart pounded hard enough to jar my whole body with each beat. The adjoining cell had a hazard-orange floor with No Occupancy painted on it in black block letters.

No, no, no, no…

Across a wide aisle from my cell were other, normal cells.

Jail.

I was in *jail*. Because I'd turned into some kind of monster and stuck my fingers through that carny's *skull*.

But that wasn't possible. I wasn't a monster, and I had never hurt anyone in my life.

Yet I could remember exactly how that man's flesh had felt beneath my fingers. I could still feel the resistance his skull had offered, then that satisfying *pop* when my fingers had breached it.

Nonononono. I buried my face in my arms and squeezed my eyes shut, but the images were still there.

A dangling cigarette.

A cattle prod lying in the hay.

Blood dripping down the sweaty man's face.

What the *hell* had I done? *How* had I done it?

Tears rolled down my cheeks and I swiped at them with both hands. This couldn't be happening. I wasn't a cryptid. My parents were human. I didn't have so much as a birthmark to be examined, much less feathers, or horns, or scales.

Yet in that tent, I'd had… What *had* I had, exactly? Weird

hair? Pointy fingers? That didn't fit the description of any cryptid I'd ever studied.

I examined my hands. They were trembling uncontrollably, but looked normal, other than the blood dried beneath my fingernails.

I pulled handfuls of long, dark hair over my shoulder. My hair looked normal. Whatever I'd become had left no trace of itself. How was that even possible? The vast majority of cryptid species can't blend in with the human population— not even shape-shifters. I'd officially learned that on day one as a crypto-biology major, but like everyone else, I'd actually known it my whole life.

So how could whatever kind of creature I was blend in well enough to hide itself not just from the rest of the world, but from me? How could I not know what I was?

What else did I not know about myself? If I couldn't put faith in my own humanity, how much of the rest of my life was a lie?

I didn't mean to do it.

Terrified, I mentally relived that surreal memory over and over, trying to understand what had happened. The only thing I was sure of every single time was that I hadn't *intended* to turn into a monster and shove my fingers through a man's skull. I'd seen it happen. I'd felt it happen. But I hadn't *made* it happen. Not on purpose anyway.

And that meant I could no longer trust my own body.

I didn't realize I was pounding my head into the brick wall at my back until the repetitive thuds finally broke through the vicious cycle of my memories.

The fierce throb in my head felt like my brain was trying to burst through my skull. My hands wouldn't stop shaking. The concrete floor had sanded raw spots into my knees and my palms, as well as on more tender patches of bare flesh.

This couldn't be happening.

On my right, a door squealed open on rusty hinges. Startled, I turned to find a sheriff's deputy heading down the center aisle toward me. He carried a tall stool under one arm and a bundle of familiar material beneath the other.

The sight of my clothes in his hand triggered fresh tears as I scooted along the wall at my back. When I hit the far corner, I stopped, cradled by solid brick on two sides. I tucked my legs up to my chest again and crossed my ankles to cover my most private parts. I was as shielded and defended as I could get, yet I'd never felt more exposed or vulnerable.

"Hi." The deputy set his stool down in the aisle, out of reach from my cell.

I rested my chin on my left knee and let my hair fall forward like a curtain, hoping all he could see were my shins, hair, and eyes.

"Do you remember me?"

He did look a little familiar, but no name came to mind.

"I'm Deputy Wayne Atherton. You were a couple of years behind me in school."

Wayne. Yes. We'd had a history class together my sophomore year.

"Where am I? Are you in charge?"

"This is the Franklin County Sheriff's Department. You've been taken into custody as a cryptid living under false pretenses. And as far as you're concerned, yes, I'm in charge."

"Did—" My voice cracked, so I cleared my throat and started over, my face flaming. "Did you take my clothes off?"

"No, that was a couple of guys from the SWAT team the sheriff called in to assist with your transport. Dr. Almaguer said he would only examine you while you were still unconscious. To check for species-identifying features."

Dr. Almaguer. My teeth began to chatter and I set my chin

on my knees to make it stop. They'd called in a small-animal veterinarian to examine me—the very man who'd once put my dad's farm dog to sleep.

The deputy propped one foot on the lowest stool rung and set my clothes on his lap. "He didn't find anything, Delilah."

Because there was nothing to find. How else could I not have known?

"Are you going to give my clothes back?"

"That's up to you," he said.

I closed my eyes. He was going to interrogate me in the nude. Because he could.

"What are you?"

"I don't know."

"Make this easy on yourself, Delilah. Just tell us what you are, and you can have your clothes back." The deputy shifted on his stool and my underwear slid from the pile of clothes and landed on the floor. He didn't notice, but my focus snagged on that bit of fabric. I would have told him anything I knew for a single scrap of my own clothing. But there was nothing to say.

"I told you, I don't know what I am. *Please* give me my clothes." My cheeks were burning, but my teeth still chattered. "I'm freezing."

"Yeah, the sheriff runs warm, so he keeps the air turned down low. Especially in the summer." Atherton shifted on the stool again, and his tone softened. "Delilah, I can't help you until you help me. I got orders. So why don't you tell me what you are, and I'll not only give you your clothes back, I'll get you some water. Or something to eat. Are you hungry? Your friends said you didn't eat much dinner."

"Are they here?" Shelley's scream still echoed in my aching head. Brandon's look of horror was imprinted on my retinas. "Can I see them?"

Deputy Atherton started to shake his head, and I buried

my face in the crook between my knees, sniffing back fresh tears. "Please," I said into my lap. "I didn't mean to hurt anyone and I have no idea what happened. *Please* just give me my clothes and let me see my friends."

Atherton sighed. "Ms. Wells had to be sedated. Her boyfriend took her home."

My throat felt thick, my tongue clumsy. "Is she okay?"

"She's terrified. She's not the only one. The news is out, and people don't feel safe, knowing you were born and raised here. Knowing you went to school with their children and spent the night at their houses—and they didn't have a clue. People are starting to remember the reaping, Delilah."

Oh, *fuck*.

Terror pooled in my stomach like acid, eating at me from the inside. "They don't think I'm a surrogate, do they?" I peered at him over my knees. My hands started shaking again. "Because I *swear* I'm not."

"How can you know that, if you don't know what you are? You look human, and you lived among us for years. Just like the surrogates. What are we supposed to think?"

Panic slowed my brain, yet sped up my words. "This is totally different. I wasn't hiding or lying in wait, planning something. I didn't know I wasn't human. I *still* can't believe what happened. You have to tell them that. Tell the sheriff I'm not one of them."

"How do I know that's true?"

Terror scattered my thoughts into a maelstrom of disjointed theories. *Think, Delilah!* "There were hundreds of thousands of surrogates, but there's only one of me."

The deputy shrugged. "So far. For all we know, you could be the first in a whole new wave."

"No, that's not what I am!" My arms tightened around my

shins, drawing my knees tighter against my chest. "I don't have any siblings."

"Having grown, healthy siblings would work in your favor. Being an only child does not."

"Okay... But I'm an adult!" Surely they'd figured *that* much out when they'd taken my clothes off. "The surrogates were six-year-olds."

"Yes, but even cryptids age. The surrogates are now thirty-five years old. Wherever they are."

But no one knew where they were, and that was the problem. As soon as they'd been discovered, Uncle Sam had rounded them up like rabid dogs, and no one knew whether they'd been shot, or studied, or cryogenically frozen for later. And that was fine, because the surrogates truly *were* dangerous. They were the fucking devil's spawn.

If the government thought I was one of them, I would disappear, too.

"I'm not a surrogate." I pushed hair from my face with one hand and sat up as straight as I dared without clothes on. "I didn't steal any babies. I've never hurt a soul in my life before tonight, and *I don't know how that happened.* Think about it. If I'd known what I was, why would I go to the menagerie? Please, Deputy. You have to believe me. I'm not conspiring against humanity."

Atherton exhaled slowly. Then he stood, still watching me, and shook out my blouse. "I believe you." He stuck my shirt between two of the bars and dropped it on the floor. "But I'm not the one you have to convince." Next came my jeans, bra, and underwear, each dropped just inside my cell. "Get dressed."

I glanced at my clothes, then back up at him. "Are you going to watch?"

He blinked, obviously startled by the thought. "Of course

not." When he walked down the aisle away from my cell, I realized that Atherton wasn't the enemy. He was just doing his job.

Unfortunately, his job was to extract information I didn't have, in order to help the sheriff—

Help the sheriff what?

End life as I knew it?

I lunged for my clothes, then dragged the whole pile back into my corner, where I shimmied into my underwear as fast as I could. I turned my back on the bars to put my bra on, in case he turned around, and had just stepped into my jeans when the brutal reality of my new situation hit me over the head like that carny's mallet, swinging straight for my soul.

I'll never go home again.

My legs buckled beneath me and my knees slammed into the concrete. My jaw snapped shut with the impact, but I hardly felt it. I was a cryptid living under false pretenses, and no one would care that I hadn't known. Most probably wouldn't even believe that.

I pushed my arms through the sleeves of my shirt, but had trouble buttoning it. My hands wouldn't stop trembling.

Gone. Everything I'd ever had was probably already gone. My job. My apartment. My car. My clothes. Cryptids weren't allowed to own property or enter into contracts. Including leases.

"Deputy Atherton, I think I need to talk to an attorney." My voice had almost no tone and very little volume. I seemed to be hearing myself from one end of a long tunnel.

He turned and headed down the aisle toward me again. "They're not gonna give you a lawyer, Delilah. Cryptids aren't citizens. You have no rights in the U.S. of A., in Franklin County, or in the incorporated township of Franklin. You are now the property of the state of Oklahoma."

Property. No rights.

"Unless they decide you *are* a surrogate," Atherton continued. "If that happens, the feds will come for you."

And I would never be seen again.

I clutched my half-buttoned shirt to my chest and scooted back into the corner, pressing my spine into the seam where both brick walls met. The world seemed to be shrinking around me, as if someone were sucking all the air out of a vacuum-sealed bag. I couldn't breathe. I couldn't think.

"Is your mother still over on Sycamore?" Deputy Atherton asked, and a fresh bolt of fear opened my lungs. "They're sending someone to pick her up."

"Leave her alone." My gaze snapped up to meet his, and his brows rose. "She has nothing to do with this. She's human."

"You thought you were human, too, and you were wrong about that. Is there anything we should know before they knock on her door?"

I held his gaze in silence.

"They're already on their way, Delilah. If you know something that will keep her from getting hurt, you need to tell me."

"She sleeps with my dad's shotgun under her bed." I crossed my arms over my knees and stared at the ground. "Better call first and let her know you're coming. That, or send an ambulance in advance."

Atherton's brows rose. He unclipped a radio from his belt and relayed my mother's itchy trigger finger to someone in Dispatch.

My bare toes curled on the concrete, and I wished for a pair of shoes. My racing thoughts had stilled into a single bold question mark, and the mental silence was almost as confining as the bars caging me.

"So, what happens now?"

He pulled a thick, rusty pair of medieval-looking iron cuffs from a pouch at his back. "Come on, Delilah. Get up. It's time to meet the sheriff."

DELILAH

"Turn around and stick both hands between the bars."
The theory seemed to be that my hands were my weapons, and that with them restrained in iron behind my back I would be much less of a threat.

I complied, and the cuffs closed over my wrists one at a time. They were heavy, and the weight felt both surreal and brutally degrading. But surely if I were going to have any adverse reaction to iron—which would narrow my species down to one out of *hundreds* of kinds of *fae*—the bars on my cell would have triggered it already.

Iron was the only way that we knew of to identify the *fae*. Most of them had one feature or another that clothes wouldn't cover—feathers, a hollow back, vines growing in place of hair—but glamour was a better disguise than any clothing, contact lenses, or wigs could ever hope to be.

Once I was cuffed, the deputy let me out of my cell and guided me down the aisle. He didn't touch me. In fact, he seemed to be walking a couple of feet behind me until he had to come forward and open the door at the end of the aisle.

The moment I stepped into the open front room of the sheriff's station, all phone calls and typing ceased. The ambient nervous chatter died, and everyone turned to watch me be escorted across the room. None of the stares were friendly. Even the people in handcuffs looked at me as if I were a slimy clump dug from their shower drains.

My face flamed. I wanted to hide, but the best I could do was let my hair swing forward to shield part of my face.

Several feet into my barefoot walk of shame, I saw Brandon sitting in a cracked plastic waiting room chair. I tripped over my own nerves and Deputy Atherton started to catch me, then changed his mind. I saw the moment it happened. He was reaching for me, probably out of instinct, then suddenly recoiled. He *flinched*—as if I were a snake about to strike, when really I was falling face-first toward the dingy yellow floor tile, unable to catch myself with my hands cuffed at my back.

Brandon stared at his shoes as I staggered, then awkwardly regained my balance on my own. I recognized tension in the cords standing out from his neck, as if he wanted to look, but was fighting the urge.

"Brandon," I called once I was steady, and my voice cracked on the first syllable. His jaw clenched, but he didn't look up. My flush deepened. "Brandon." Raw desperation echoed in my voice and a couple of strangers sneered at the tender bits of my heart and soul I'd exposed.

My boyfriend of four years was the only person in the room not watching me.

"Brandon, *please*." My cheeks were scalding and my throat ached. But I *couldn't* believe he would abandon me without a word. He knew better than anyone else in the world aside from my mother that I would never hurt someone on purpose.

Deputy Atherton took me by the arm, evidently having gathered the courage to touch me in the face of my humiliation. "Come on, Delilah."

"No." I jerked free of his grip, and people all over the room flinched. "Say it, Brandon," I demanded, and at first he didn't move. Then my roommate and lover—one of my very best friends—stood and marched toward the exit, as if he wanted to run, but pride wouldn't let him. "Brandon! Say it, you fucking coward!"

He froze halfway to the door, and my heart stilled along with him. Then slowly, Brandon turned. His eyes were red. His jaw was clenched. He looked at me as if he didn't even know who I was.

"How could you do this to me?"

"I didn't—"

"The whole thing was a *lie*," he shouted, and I flinched. "*You* were a lie! I trusted you. I told you everything. I ate with you and slept next to you, and the whole time you were some kind of monster, just using me as part of your human camouflage. There *is* no Delilah Marlow."

"No, that's not true. It was all real! I didn't know!" I took a step toward him, but Atherton grabbed my arm again, and several other deputies placed hands on the butts of their guns. "You have to believe I didn't know."

"I don't know what to believe." Tears shone in Brandon's eyes, but anger glowed in his cheeks. "I was in love with a woman who never even existed. I can't believe I ever let you—" His sentence ended in an inarticulate sound of disgust, and something deep inside me cracked apart. Some delicate part of me collapsed like a demolished building, leaving only broken shapes and sharp edges.

"Don't blame yourself, son," a middle-aged man called out from the waiting area. "We were all fooled in the eighties. I lost my aunt, uncle, and six cousins to those chameleon bastards, may they rot in hell."

Cheers erupted all around me, and suddenly my ribs felt too tight.

"But I—I'm not one of them! I'm not—"

"Baby killer!" a woman shouted from the waiting area.

"Remember the reaping!" a man in regular steel cuffs shouted, though the cop who shoved him back into his chair didn't seem to dispute the sentiment.

A cop in his thirties stood from behind his desk and strode toward me, and I thought he was going to take over for Deputy Atherton and get me out of there—until he spit in my face.

I blinked, stunned, as spittle dripped down my cheek.

"Damn it, Bruce!" Atherton hauled me toward another door.

Across the room, Brandon shoved the press-bar on the front exit and when he stepped into the parking lot, he took my last shred of hope with him. If my own boyfriend wouldn't stand by me, who would?

The front door closed behind Brandon, and I sniffed back tears that stung like utter rejection and humiliation. My hair fell into my face as Wayne led me into another hallway, several strands clinging to the spit on my cheek.

Finally, Atherton closed the door behind us, shielding me from the rest of the world. Or maybe shielding it from me.

In an interrogation room, I followed his instructions without truly hearing them. In my mind, the front door of the sheriff's station closed over and over, and all I could see was the back of Brandon's head.

"Delilah," Atherton said, and I realized he'd already said my name at least twice.

"What?" I blinked to clear my head and looked down to find myself sitting in a cold plastic chair with my arms looped around the back. A tug against my cuffs rattled chains I had no memory of, which evidently ran between my handcuffs and a metal loop set into the ground. I couldn't stand or even twist much in my chair without pulling my arms out of their sockets.

Before I could ask if all of the metal was really necessary, a second deputy knelt to slap a set of iron shackles around my ankles and connect them to that same hook in the ground, behind my chair. When he stood, I tried to lean forward, but the pain in my shoulders stopped me. I tried to cross my ankles, but the shackles were in the way. I couldn't move more than an inch in any direction, and that sudden severe confinement made my throat close. The room had plenty of open space but I couldn't use any of it. Plenty of air, but I couldn't seem to breathe any of it.

"Struggling will only make it worse," Atherton said, and while there was no malice in his voice, there was no willingness to help either. "Just try not to think about it."

But I couldn't seem to manage that until the door opened, and Sheriff Pennington stepped in from the hall. He commented on my restraints with an incomprehensible grunt, then sat in the chair across a small folding table from mine.

Pennington folded his fleshy arms on the table and studied my face. "Delilah Marlow?"

I nodded, desperately trying not to squirm. "Am I under arrest?"

He snorted, then swiped at his nose with the back of one hand. "No, and I wouldn't arrest a dog for bitin' either. I'd just put the bitch down in the interest of public safety. You won't be charged, and you won't be Mirandized, because you no longer have any rights, you devious piece of shit. As long as you're under my jurisdiction, I can do whatever I want with you, and I can't imagine your lot would improve if the feds take over."

His blatant threat bounced around the inside of my skull,

and anger overtook my fear for the first time since I'd woken up in a jail cell. "This isn't right, Sheriff."

"I deal in law, not morality." Pennington paused for a moment, evidently to let that little cow chip of irony sink in. "What are you exactly, Delilah Marlow?"

"I don't know," I repeated. He lifted one skeptical eyebrow, and I shrugged as best I could with my hands tightly bound behind me. "Look, if I knew, I'd tell you just to prove I'm not a surrogate."

"Unless you *are* a surrogate."

"If I were a surrogate, I'd lie. Either way, you'd have an answer. But I *don't know* what I am. I didn't know I wasn't human until tonight."

"We don't know what the surrogates were either, do we?" Pennington pulled a palm-sized notebook from his front pocket. "So that doesn't really rule anything out for you."

I tried to find a more comfortable position, but the chains kept relief just out of reach. "Well, we know what they weren't, and none of those little monsters looked anything like I did tonight."

"About that…" the sheriff continued, flipping open his notebook to reveal a single page of pencil scrawling. "Let's put our heads together and come up with some possibilities that might keep you out of federal custody, shall we?"

And finally something in his voice clued me in. Sheriff Pennington didn't want me to be a surrogate either, because that would put me beyond his authority. The Justice Department had claimed jurisdiction over all of those cases before I was even born.

"Here're the facts, as they were relayed to me. One, your voice changed in depth and—" Pennington glanced at the notebook on the table in front of him "—quality. Says here it was deeper than it shoulda been, and it felt—" another glance at his notes "—*large*. Whatever that means. Two, your eyes changed color. Not just the irises, but the entirety of your eyeballs." He made a vague gesture encompassing most of my face, and I shuddered at the thought. "They became white, shot through with dark veins. Does that sound about right?"

I could only give him a painfully wrenching shrug, trying to hide the tide of horror washing over me. "I couldn't see my own eyes." And I'd never heard of a cryptid species which fit that description.

"It also says here that the veins in your face became black, like dark spiderwebs beneath your skin. Do you know anything about that?"

"No." But I could imagine how terrifying it would have been to see. No wonder Shelley was scared. No wonder Brandon could hardly look at me. I'd spent four years studying cryptid species, yet couldn't even identify my own. If *I* couldn't understand what I'd become, how could they?

Pennington glanced at his notebook again.

"What about your hair? Witnesses say your hair took on a life of its own."

"Sheriff, I'm assuming that if you spoke to my friends, you know that I was a crypto-biology major, with an emphasis in human hybrid species. I should know what I am. But I truly have no clue. Before tonight, I didn't even know the question needed to be asked. All I know for sure at this point is that I'm no longer a bank teller." I was no longer a driver, or a tenant, or a girlfriend, or a best friend.

I was nothing other than the property of the state of Oklahoma.

My eyes fell shut and I sucked in a deep breath.

The reality—the true *enormity*—of my loss suddenly hit me in a way that the mere intellectual understanding of it hadn't been able to. When the interrogation was over, they weren't going to send me home. I *had* no home. I was never going to count another cash drawer or make another pot of coffee ever again, no matter what I did or said. Everything that I had ever been or done or loved was gone. Delilah Marlow no longer existed.

No, Brandon was right. Delilah Marlow had *never* existed. My entire life was a delusion. A fantasy. A lie I hadn't even known I was telling.

The reality was pure hell.

Pennington closed his notebook and crossed his arms on the table again, watching calmly as I fought total, devastating terror. "Before you start feeling too sorry for yourself, keep in mind that a man almost died because of you, and up at County General, they're not sure he'll ever regain normal brain function."

A bright spark of anger surged up through my fear, and I seized it. "He electrified a little girl!"

Pennington turned to Atherton, who was stationed next to the door. "She's talking about one of the beasts?"

The deputy nodded and pulled his own notebook from the pocket of his khaki uniform pants. "A pubescent *canis lupus lycanus*. Female." He looked up and pocketed the notebook. "A thirteen-year-old wolf bitch. The rep from Metzger's says they have trouble with her all the time, and the customary motivational method is a low-voltage poke with a standard cattle prod."

"She was covered with electrical burns!" For a second, I forgot I was chained to the floor, and when I tried to stand, I nearly dislocated my shoulder. Both Pennington and Atherton reached for their guns.

I froze. "Relax." My pulse raced so fast the room started to look warped. "I can't even open a jar of pickles, much less break through solid steel and iron."

Atherton glared at me. "Delilah, she's not a child, she's a wolf." The deputy slid his gun back into its holster, but the fact that he didn't snap it closed made me nervous. "An animal."

"Then why was she wearing underwear?" I demanded, and the sheriff and his deputy looked at me as if I'd lapsed into Latin. "Okay, just think about it. When we put wolves on display in a zoo—a *regular* zoo—we don't put underwear on them because they aren't self-aware enough to feel modesty or adapt to social conventions and restrictions. But Geneviève was wearing underwear, which means the menagerie understands that she's *thoroughly* self-aware. And if she's self-aware, why is it okay to put a *child* on display in skimpy undergarments, then shock her with a cattle prod when she doesn't want to be seen in nothing but her underwear? You can't have it both ways."

I sank back into my chair, only aware that I'd been straining against my restraints when my joints started screaming at me in protest.

Atherton and the sheriff stared at me for a moment, obviously unsure what to say. Then Pennington dragged his chair closer to the table and scowled at me with confidence born of ignorance. "According to the law, your werewolf bitch isn't a person. She's a monster, and monsters are offered no protection under the law because them and their kind slaughtered more than a million innocent children during the reaping alone. Who knows how many others they've killed one at a time? If werewolves are self-aware, why didn't the pack that tore that family apart up in the Ozarks last month use that self-awareness to decide not to kill innocent people?"

"First of all, that was a pair of adlets, not a pack of werewolves, and second, self-awareness isn't the same as a moral compass," I argued. "I don't believe every cryptid should be allowed to roam free, just like I don't believe every *human* should be allowed to roam free. We have psychos, too. People kill their coworkers. Kids kill their classmates. Parents kill their own children. Those people are every bit as monstrous as the worst cryptid predator you can point to, yet they're human, just like we are."

Atherton and Pennington stared at me, and unease churned in my stomach. "There is no *we*," the deputy said, and though I'd known that for several hours by then, hearing him verbally exclude me from the rest of humanity added another layer of pain to that brutal certainty. "Delilah, you're not human."

"Yeah, well, I guess you're going to have to take a blood sample to figure out what I am, because I don't know."

"Actually, we took one while you were knocked out." The deputy glanced at my arm, which was when I noticed the small bandage in the crook of my left elbow. "They had to send it up to Tulsa. Your sample's the lab's number one priority, but it'll still take several days."

I collapsed against the back of my chair, and my aching shoulders sagged with relief. "Then I guess we're in for a bit of a wait."

The interrogation room door creaked open and we all turned as another deputy stepped into the doorway. "Mrs. Marlow's here."

Sheriff Pennington stood and gave me a grim scowl. "I'm not very good at waiting, so you better hope your mama can shed some light on the subject. Otherwise, things are gonna get real bad for you, real damn fast."

State agencies report that more than 12,000 parents have been arrested in connection with the August 24 murders of more than 1.1 million children, and an unnamed source in the FBI tells the *Boston Gazette* that that figure is still rising...

—From the front page of the *Boston Gazette*, August 28, 1986

CHARITY

When Charity Marlow's phone rang at 12:04 a.m., she knew without even glancing at the caller ID that something was wrong. No one ever called in the middle of the night to say everything was fine.

Ten minutes after she hung up the phone, Charity had dressed, brushed her hair, and brewed a pot of coffee. The deputy who knocked on her door declined a travel cup, so she made him wait while she fixed one for herself because "questioning" sounded like the kind of ordeal that would require coherence on her part.

Coherence was the very least of what Charity Marlow owed her daughter, but it was all she had left to give.

On the way to the sheriff's station, she sat in the passenger's seat of the patrol car and sipped quietly from her cup, and not once during the drive across town did she ask why Delilah was in custody. Charity had been both waiting for and dreading that night's phone call for nearly twenty-five years.

At the station, in a small room equipped with bright lights and cheap chairs, she sat across a small scarred table from Matthew Pennington, who'd held the title of sheriff for the past twelve years in spite of her consistent vote for whoever ran against him. Two armed deputies were stationed at the door, one on each side, and Charity saw no reason to pretend she didn't understand their presence.

"I suppose you want a blood test," she said before the sheriff could even open his mouth.

He nodded, but she read irritation in the stiff line of his jaw. Pennington liked to run the show. "We've got a phlebotomist from County General waiting for that very thing. Of course, you'd be saving us all a lot of time if you could just tell us what you and your daughter are."

Charity set her travel cup on the table. "Sheriff, if I weren't human, I wouldn't exactly feel inspired to bare my soul to you and your gun-toting hee-haws." She tossed a glance at the deputies beside the door, both of whom scowled at her. "But I *am* human, and your lab should be able to confirm that with little more than a microscope. And since you clearly know otherwise about Delilah… Well, I'd be just as interested as you are in what the lab has to say about her blood sample."

Pennington leaned back and crossed thick arms over the brown button-up shirt stretched tight across his soft chest. "You're telling me you don't know what species your own daughter is?"

Charity nodded. "In fact, considering that you have her in custody, I'd guess you know more about her genetic origin than I do."

"Well, you'd be wrong there." Frustration deepened the sheriff's voice even beyond the chain-smoker range. "I have her medical records. The blood test they ran at birth says she's human."

Charity nodded again, but made no comment.

"According to her record, she hasn't had blood drawn since the day she was born."

"I believe that's accurate."

"She's never been sick?" Pennington leaned forward, arms folded over the table, and Charity winced at the acrid bite of cigarette smoke clinging to his uniform. "Not once in twenty-five years?"

"Every child gets sick at some point, Sheriff. But Delilah never had anything I couldn't treat myself."

"Because you're an RN."

Charity sat a little straighter in her hard plastic chair. "Actually, I'm a nurse practitioner."

"That's right," the sheriff said, but she saw right through his sudden recollection of her employment history. "You finished your MSN when Delilah was three. Was that so that you could legally treat her yourself?"

"In fact, it was. And as her primary medical caregiver, I found no reason to run further blood tests on a perfectly healthy child." Charity looked right into the sheriff's eyes. "But I would be willing to tell you what I *do* know, if you'll go first."

The sheriff's flustered flush was so bright that one of the deputies stepped forward to see if he was okay. Pennington waved the unspoken question off and glared at the woman seated across the table.

"What we know, Mrs. Marlow, is that your daughter got worked up during a tour of the menagerie this evening and turned into the kind of creature that should have been lookin' outta one of those cages, instead of looking into 'em. She grabbed a carny by the head and sank her fingers into his skull, and when she finally released him, he turned his livestock prod up as far as it would go and rammed it into his own leg."

Charity's bold spirit—a thing of wide repute in Franklin County—faded like a blossom gone dry in the sun. She closed her eyes to hide her thoughts from the sheriff, and the face that flashed behind her eyelids belonged to a woman she hadn't seen in twenty-five years, but would never in her life forget.

"Lilah actually hurt someone?" More than two decades of secrets, lies, and guilt swelled within her as she examined every fear and doubt she'd ever had about the daughter she loved more than anything else in the world. More, even, than the husband whose heart had given out at the age of fifty-seven, beneath the burden of their secret. "I didn't think she was even capable of violence."

"Why don't you tell us what you know?"

Charity crossed her arms over her favorite blue summer sweater and when she leaned back in her chair, a gray-streaked strand of straight brown hair fell over her ear.

"Keeping your secret can't help her anymore, Mrs. Marlow," Wayne Atherton said. "We can't help her either, if we don't know what she is."

Unlike Pennington, Atherton truly seemed to want to help, so Charity cleared her throat and took a long sip of her coffee. "Almost twenty-five years ago, my six-week-old daughter disappeared from her crib."

"You're telling us that Delilah was kidnapped?" Pennington prompted after a moment of silence, but Charity only shook her head.

"I'm telling you that my daughter *Elizabeth* was kidnapped. Her middle name was Delilah, so that's what I called the changeling left in her place."

For one long moment, neither the sheriff nor his deputy spoke. Charity couldn't even be sure they were breathing.

"Changeling." Pennington seemed to be tasting the word, as if he might want to spit it back out. "So, you're saying the *fae* took your baby and left a surrogate in its place? There hasn't been a confirmed surrogate exchange since the reaping." The sheriff laid both thick hands flat on the table between them.

"Mrs. Marlow, are you telling us that your daughter is part of a second wave of attack?"

Atherton slipped quietly out of the room.

"No." Charity set her coffee down and looked straight into the sheriff's eyes, so that he couldn't possibly mistake any part of her bearing or intent. "This is different. I don't know what those little monsters were, but Delilah isn't one of them."

The sheriff crossed his arms above his belly. "How can you be sure? Does she look like Elizabeth?"

"I haven't seen Elizabeth in twenty-five years, Sheriff, but as infants, they were identical."

Pennington's scraggly gray brows rose. "Sounds like a surrogate to me."

"You're wrong." Charity lifted her cup in one unsteady hand and took a sip of the cooling coffee. Then she set the cup down and took a long, deep breath. "Delilah *was* sent to deliver pain, but not by instilling terror on a national scale like the surrogates. She was left in Elizabeth's place to punish *me*. And I got exactly what I asked for."

"What—"

Charity held up one hand and spoke over the sheriff. "Elizabeth was a beautiful child, but she had an ugly temper. She cried for days and nights on end. I couldn't eat or sleep. I couldn't think straight. One day, when she was six weeks old, I prayed that the Lord would take my brand-new baby girl— the center of my existence—and send me a quieter, happier child in her place."

She pulled a tissue from the purse in her lap and dabbed at first one eye, then the other. "Now, it may be that a lot of women in my position do the same thing, and nothing comes of it. But I…" She leaned forward, and fresh tears fell from her eyes. "Well, Sheriff, I said my prayer out loud. And it wasn't the Lord who heard me."

"Who heard you?" the remaining deputy whispered.

Charity twisted in her chair to give him a censuring glance. "Believe it or not, Deputy, no one claimed credit for replacing my daughter with a more pleasant doppelgänger." She turned back to the sheriff. "So I did some research and learned that I could get in touch with whoever took my daughter if I were to nurse the child for a week, then smear a bit of her blood on a mirror and state my own child's name." More inclined toward logic than superstition, Charity had thought the whole thing sounded gruesome and crazy, but the truth was that since the reaping, anything seemed possible. The sheriff eyed her doubtfully, but she continued. "It worked! A woman appeared to me in my bathroom mirror, holding Elizabeth from some room I've never seen before."

"What did she say?" the deputy asked, and the sheriff scowled, but let the question stand.

"She said that in a year, if I had taken proper care of the changeling and still wanted my daughter back, Elizabeth would be returned to me."

"This woman in the mirror?" The sheriff's skepticism was fading beneath undeniable curiosity. "Did you get her name? Her species?"

"She wouldn't tell me any of that. But she looked and sounded as human as Delilah did."

"So what did you do?" Pennington said, and from across the table, Charity could see that though he held a pen, the notebook page in front of him was completely blank.

"We cared for Lilah as if she were our own. She was a delightful child. Happy and affectionate. We came to love her—I felt *guilty* for how much I loved her, when my own daughter was missing." Charity folded her hands on the table and took a deep breath. "Then the one-year mark came and went, and Elizabeth never reappeared."

"Did you try the blood-on-the-mirror trick again?" the sheriff asked.

Charity nodded. "Several times, but my summons went unanswered."

"And you never got her back?" the deputy guessed, clearly transfixed by the story.

Pennington waved one hand to silence the deputy, and when he turned back to Charity, she met his gaze with tear-filled eyes. "No, I never got Elizabeth back," she said. Then she took a deep breath and gave voice to a fear that had lived in her soul for twenty-five years, but had never before been spoken aloud.

"Sheriff, I think my Elizabeth was never returned because I loved Delilah more."

DELILAH

The weight of my mother's confession steadily pressed the air from my lungs until psychological suffocation felt like a very real threat. I tried to lean forward, staring intently through the one-way glass into the room where she sat, but again chains and cuffs held me painfully short of where I wanted to be.

However, the real trauma went much, much deeper. Brandon had been wrong—there really *was* a Delilah Marlow. But I wasn't her.

I closed my eyes and took a deep breath, trying to take it all in. Trying to understand.

I wasn't my mother's daughter.

That devastating revelation triggered a landslide of loss, leaving me crushed by the debris of my own life. I had no real name or family. No birthplace or birth date. No true identity. Added to the confiscation of everything I'd ever owned, that left me with nothing but a body I could no longer trust. Though according to Pennington, *that* was now owned by the state of Oklahoma.

This can't be real.

What was I, if I had no name, no friends, no family, no

job, no home, no belongings, and no authority over my own body? What *could* I be?

Maybe I was just the good little girl my mother'd begged for. Or maybe I was the monster Sheriff Pennington believed me to be. Maybe I was the first enemy soldier in a secret war against humanity. But could that even be true, if I didn't know about it?

A strange creak cut through my thoughts, and Deputy Atherton turned away from the window to look at me. "Delilah? Are you okay?"

When I opened my mouth to tell him just how far from okay I was, the creaking stopped. I'd been clenching my jaw so tightly we could both hear the stress.

"You really didn't know about any of that?" he said, pointing beyond the glass at my mother.

I shook my head. Even after hearing it, I wasn't sure I truly understood. All I knew for sure was that I was a changeling of unknown origin sent to torture my mother. And that somehow a punishment meant to last a year had lasted a lifetime. For what? For loving me too much?

That wasn't fair to her. She was a *good* mother. Yet if whoever'd taken Elizabeth Delilah Marlow—the *real* Lilah—had brought her back, where would that have left me? Would I have been raised by the woman in the mirror? Was she my mother?

No.

Charity Marlow had been living with her secret for twenty-five years, maintaining her silence to protect me, mourning her real daughter—a baby who'd looked just like me—in private, because the world could not know of her loss. That *made* her my mother, even if we shared no blood.

Had my dad known?

Yes.

Suddenly my father's periodic melancholy made sense. What had he seen when he'd looked at me? Could he see the difference between me and his Elizabeth? Had he loved me as much as my mother did?

Had he blamed her for the loss of their true child? Had he blamed *me*?

"If you tell the sheriff I let you watch, he'll have my badge." Deputy Atherton's statement sliced through my thoughts so suddenly that it took me a second to understand what he'd said.

I sniffed, unable to wipe either my eyes or my dripping nose. "I won't tell him." As the only person to show me even the slightest bit of compassion, Atherton was the closest thing I had to an ally. "Thank you for letting me see my mom. What's going to happen to her?" I whispered, still staring through the glass.

He shrugged. "If she's human, she should be fine."

"She harbored a cryptid for twenty-five years. That's a felony, Deputy."

"She was protecting her kid. The sheriff would never…" Atherton didn't bother to finish. We both knew the sheriff would.

"Mrs. Marlow," Pennington continued from the next room. "As an officer of the law, I have to ask, why didn't you turn the changeling over to the proper authorities when it became clear that your daughter was never going to be returned?"

The changeling. He wasn't even using my name anymore. I'd become a thing.

"She didn't know she wasn't human," my mother said. "*I* didn't know for sure. If I'd given her to the police, they would have put her in the state refuge, where she'd have been less than a snack for the first troll or ogre to find her. She was a baby, Sheriff."

"Yes, and I'm sure she was adorable." Pennington leaned

back in his chair again, and though I couldn't see his face, I could picture his patronizing expression perfectly. "A few years ago I saw a baby tiger in the zoo, over at Tulsa. It was behind a thick wall of glass playin' with its handler, chasin' a bit of string with a stuffed mouse tied at the end. That baby tiger was the cutest damn thing I ever saw in my life." He paused dramatically. "A year and a half later it ripped that same handler's arm off and bit through her jugular."

My mother didn't even flinch. "You're suggesting Lilah is like this tiger?"

"I'm tellin' you she's worse. The tiger acted on instinct. Your Lilah made a deliberate decision to—" Pennington crossed his arms over his chest. "Well, we're not sure what she did to that poor man. What we *are* sure of is that if you'd done your civic duty when she was a baby, we wouldn't be sittin' here now. I suspect the state's attorney will have a few things to say to you about that, but I could put in a word on your behalf, if you were to help us out. We really need to know what she is. You must have seen *something* when she was growing up that could help us. There musta been signs that she was different from the other girls."

"There weren't, Sheriff," my mother insisted. "That's why it was so easy for me to believe she was human, no matter where she came from. Lilah was normal. She was smart, and kind, and always the first to go to bat for the underdog. I was always *so* proud of her."

My mother's face blurred beneath tears I couldn't hold back.

"So, you never saw anything strange about her hair? Or her eyes? Or her hands?" Pennington asked, and my mother shook her head. "Not even when she got riled up about something?"

"No. There was never anything like that." My mom leaned forward, her arms folded on top of the table, and I recognized the fierce look in her eyes. "Look, Sheriff, I have no idea what Lilah did to that man, but I have no doubt that he damn well deserved it."

Deputy Atherton twisted a knob at the bottom of the glass, and my mother's voice went silent. He pressed a button on the same panel, and the glass frosted over until it became reflective again. My viewing was over.

"She loves you."

"Yeah, and I'm afraid that's going to get her in serious trouble." I rotated my shoulders in the futile search for a more comfortable position as he slid into the chair across the table from me. "What's next for her?"

The deputy exhaled and pushed a strand of brown hair from his forehead. "Pennington's approved a rush order on her blood test, so we should hear back within twenty-four hours, assuming she's human."

Because identifying one of thousands of cryptid species by blood was complicated, but confirming humanity was pretty quick.

"She'll have to stay here until we're sure, though."

"Can't you just let her go home? She's no threat, Deputy."

Atherton shook his head. "Standard procedure, for public safety. Anyone suspected of having cryptid blood has to stay in custody until the results are in. I'll take her some coffee and a stale cinnamon roll, but that's the best I can do."

"What about me?" I shifted in my seat, trying to ease the pressure on my shoulders. "Am I going to sit in a cell until they figure out what I am?"

"Looks like it, and you should probably consider that a stroke of luck. Pennington's had a couple of the guys out front looking at options for where to send you since before you woke up, and the very best of them is going to make this place look like a luxury hotel."

A fresh jolt of fear tightened my chest. "Please tell me Pennington's not the final authority."

Atherton shrugged. "The law's a little fuzzy on that. If that carny was in the morgue instead of the psych ward, Pennington would have to call in the state police. That's standard for all capital offenses. But since he doesn't have to make that call, he's probably not gonna. If you turn out to be a surrogate, you fall under federal jurisdiction, but that's another call he's not going to make unless he has to."

"So my fate is in the hands of the sheriff of a county with fewer than fifteen thousand people in it." My mouth was dry, and my hands had gone numb, but because I wasn't human, they could keep me as long as they wanted without so much as a sip of water or a trip to the bathroom.

"Yes, but I think you're better off here than you would be in state custody." The deputy folded his hands on the table while I watched him through a strand of hair that had fallen over my eye. "The state reservation is over capacity. They're sendin' the overflow straight to an R & D holding facility, and that place..."

Atherton stared down at his hands, and the fact that he was clearly stalling made my heart beat too hard.

Cryptid research and development was big business, with both the government and the private sector, but regulation was virtually nonexistent. Animal activists raised hell if a pharmaceutical company wanted to test new shampoo on a sewer rat, but R & D could inject environmental toxins beneath a selkie's removable seal skin all day long and no one blinked an eye.

"They don't tag 'em or count 'em, Delilah. I made a couple of calls, and a guy in records told me that since the lab opened fourteen years ago, they've sent in more than five times the max capacity—all kinds of cryptids—and there's no record of any of them ever officially leaving the facility. But they fire up the industrial incinerator about once a week."

My pulse jumped, and I struggled to keep breathing slowly. Evenly. "What's the alternative? Hotel California?"

The deputy nodded. "Otherwise known as the Oklahoma Cryptid Confinement Center."

"Same thing." Because there, every sentence that wasn't a life sentence was a death sentence.

"The only other option I can think of would be a private collection. I know this guy out in—"

"No." Chills shot up my spine. Werewolves on leashes, declawed and walking around like pets. Selkies and naiads swimming in giant koi ponds. Fauns serving drinks at private events in nothing but gold chains and collars. I shook my head vehemently. "I'm nobody's pet."

"That's not up to you." Atherton leaned back in his chair, his forehead crinkled in irritation. "I'm going out of my way to help you, and your appreciation looks a lot like ingratitude."

Indignation sharpened my vision until I finally saw the deputy clearly. "You want me to be *thankful* that you're willing to sell me as a living party favor instead of sentencing me to a cryptid prison?"

The deputy's eyes narrowed. "You need to take a good, objective look at what you're facing here, Delilah. OCCC is an open-population cryptid prison. There are no guards. No cells. No rules. Helicopters make periodic supply drops on the grounds. You'd fight for every scrap of food and clothing until the day some troll or adlet eats you for breakfast. Is your pride really worth dying for?"

Fuck! I closed my eyes and clenched my fists over and over, wishing that the rest of me would go as numb as my fingers.

"And at least in a collection you'd be alive and in good

health. No collector is **going to let** any serious damage come to property he spent good money on."

Property. Damage Money. I would be an exotic pet. An insured asset in some rich prick's ledger. Because even animal lovers keep dogs on leashes.

The deputy shrugged. "I could say something to the sheriff about a private collector," he offered. "He'd have to think it was his own idea, but that shouldn't be hard. He still thinks it was his idea to install a vent fan in the men's room, and—"

"That *was* my idea." Pennington pushed the door open and marched into the interrogation room. Atherton's jaw tightened and his gaze dropped to the table between us for a second before he stood to relinquish the chair. "But I like where your head's at, Deputy." Pennington settled across the table from me, and the chair groaned beneath his weight. "I've found a fella out near the panhandle who's lookin' to replenish his collection. He doesn't care what flavor of freak you are, so long as we pass along the results of your blood test as soon as we have 'em."

My chest felt so tight I could hardly breathe. "What kind of collection?"

"Well, I guess calling it a collection is kinda puttin' on airs. Fella actually calls it a reserve."

Wayne frowned. "Sheriff, are you talking about Russell Clegg's operation? He's running a game park over there, bringing hunters from all over to—"

Pennington twisted to look up at his deputy, and the chair creaked again. "Atherton, shut your mouth. You know no such thing."

I swallowed convulsively, struggling to hold down what little dinner I'd had as horror washed over me in waves. "You can't just let them chase me through the woods and shoot me down like a deer!" I wouldn't stand a chance, with hunters wearing infrared goggles and hound dogs following my scent.

"Handin' you over to Clegg will save the great state of Oklahoma thousands of dollars a year in upkeep, and in the process, I'll be making the streets of Franklin County a safer place to live. Folks want you gone, Delilah. Voting folks."

"I thought you couldn't send me anywhere until my blood test comes back."

The sheriff shrugged. "After talking to your mother, I agree that whatever you are, you're probably not a surrogate. If the test says otherwise, the feds can seize you from Clegg just as easily as they could seize you from me, and as long as my check has cleared, I could not give a—"

The door to the interrogation room flew open, startling us all.

"What?" Pennington roared at the deputy who stood in the threshold.

"There's a man out 'ere wants to talk to ya, Sheriff. It's about Lilah Marlow."

"What about her?"

The deputy shrugged. "He said he'd only talk to you. We put him in the next room, now that they got Mrs. Marlow moved to a cell."

The sheriff nodded. "I'll be there when I'm done in here." His deputy disappeared into the hall, and I glanced at Atherton with my brows raised, silently asking what he knew.

He only shrugged.

As the sheriff turned back to me with more questions, I stared at my own reflection in the one-way mirror, wondering who was looking back at me from the other side, and why.

I'd already been threatened with prison, a collection, and a hunting reserve. How much worse could this stranger's plan for me possibly be?

"Ladies and gentlemen, our lead story continues to grow stranger and more disturbing. So far, in every single one of the reported cases of this mass prolicide—the killing of one's own children—it appears that one child in each family has survived, completely unharmed. Even more bizarre—all of the surviving children are six years old, each born in the same month—March of 1980."

—Continuing coverage on the *Nightly News*, August 30, 1986

RUDOLPH

"Just twist that button next to the window, and you'll be able to hear what they're saying." The sheriff's deputy still had one hand on the doorknob, clearly eager to leave the observation room. Rudolph Metzger was neither surprised nor offended. Often locals were almost as unnerved by menagerie workers and their close proximity to the beasts as they were by the beasts themselves. "They can't see or hear you. The sheriff will be with you shortly," the deputy added on his way out.

Rudolph exhaled slowly when the door closed behind the officer, leaving him alone in the dim interrogation/observation room with Gallagher.

One hundred and twelve years.

That's how long the menagerie had been in Rudolph's family. The Metzgers had been bringing quality live entertainment to small towns all over the U.S. since before cell phones and personal computers. Since before the internet brought footage of dangerous and exotic creatures into private homes with one simple click of a mouse.

Since long before the reaping and the repeal of the Sanctuary Act.

Back then, business was simple and the creature carnival was smaller. Beasts only. The chimera. The phoenix. The basilisk. Nothing with human parts could be caged or put on display, but business was good because outside of zoos and traveling menageries, private citizens couldn't get an up close look at a griffin without getting their eyes pecked out or their limbs ripped off.

But the technological boom had not been good to traveling circuses.

Rudolph shrugged off bittersweet nostalgia and waved a hand at the button on the wall, his gaze focused on the occupants of the room beyond the one-way glass. Gallagher stepped forward to twist the knob, and voices filled the room.

For a while, Rudolph only watched, uncomfortably aware of the fact that if the woman hadn't been chained to both her chair and the floor, he would've had no idea she wasn't, in fact, a woman at all. She was a monster. A female monster, certainly, but *not* a woman.

Only humans can be men and women.

But she *looked* like a woman, and that was a problem.

Most monsters could not hide for long among humanity—monstrosity shone through, even among the most normal-looking of creatures. Werewolves, for instance, had wolf eyes and canines even in human form. *Ifrits* gave off an unnatural body heat and had hair the color of flames. Sirens' eyes often came in colors foreign to humanity. Each species had its tell.

But this one…

After five minutes of studying her, scrutinizing every visible part, Rudolph could see no sign of aberration. Of course, the same was true of oracles, until their eyes clouded over in the grip of second sight.

"You're sure?" he said, still staring at the female chained to the chair. Strands of her ordinary dark hair hung over her ordinary blue eyes. She was ordinary, in the human sense, but somewhat attractive.

Yet another problem.

Gallagher nodded without pulling his gaze from the subject behind the window. He was a man of few words, but he was also a man of strong instinct and no bullshit, both qualities the old man considered himself to have in spades. If Gallagher said this beast was more than she seemed, then she was more than she seemed.

She was also the kind of exhibit that could make or break a menagerie. Rudolph could not afford the risk she represented, nor could he afford to pass up the crowds she could draw. The profit she could bring.

When the Sanctuary Act was overturned, mere months after the reaping, traveling menageries began to evolve into modern creature features, complete with humanoid and hybrid exhibits as well as specialty shows. Demand was high and regulations were few. Insurance was optional and inspections were rare in most venues. Costs were low and profit margins were wide.

At first, Metzger's had flourished.

Yet by the time Rudolph's father passed the reins on to his middle-aged sons in the late 1990s, everything had begun to change. Rubes had become skeptics accustomed to movie magic and special effects. Audiences were harder to impress and less willing to pay for the privilege. Safety regulations, inspections, and insurance for traveling menageries had become astronomic expenses in an age when customers could sue a restaurant over too-hot coffee.

Rudolph's three brothers—and their prissy, gold-digging wives—wanted no part of the circus lifestyle, and after he bought them out to keep them from running Metzger's into the ground with their own disinterest, the menagerie's liquid assets were nearly drained.

Fortunately, Rudolph had a head for figures and an eye for beasts. He could tell at a glance which werewolf pup was the hardiest of the litter and which centaurs could subsist on oats and water without compromising their stamina. Rudolph knew just how to coax the livestock into breeding, and exactly when to sell which offspring to supplement income during the rough winter months when traveling was restricted by the weather.

Thanks to Rudolph's talent and attention, Metzger's had survived when many other menageries folded. But survival wasn't enough. He wanted Metzger's to flourish!

Gallagher's discovery could help make that happen.

"We can't show her like that." Rudolph waved one hand at the glass, and Gallagher nodded. "If people think she's a surrogate, no one will come see her. And if it looks like we've put a human woman in a cage, the rubes will feel sorry for her and we'll be the bad guys. You'll have to bring out her beast. Show them she's a monster—but not a surrogate."

Gallagher scowled. "*I* will have to...?"

Rudolph sank onto the edge of the table to relieve the pressure on his bad hip. "She was your idea. She's your responsibility. I want to see the eyes, and the veins, and the claws. The audience *needs* to see those things. You will train her."

"We don't know what she is." Gallagher's focus returned to the room behind the glass. "Hell, it sounds like *she* doesn't know what she is."

"If we've never seen anything like her, the audience won't have either. Play up the mystery until you figure it out." Rudolph glanced up at the large handler's harsh profile. "She's dangerous, Gallagher. Don't underestimate her."

"She stuck her fingers through Jack's skull. There's no underestimating that."

"No." Rudolph's tone demanded his employee's full attention, and Gallagher turned again. "No matter what she can do when her beast shows itself, she's more of a threat in her human guise. Look." He pointed through the glass, where the female's jaw was clenched in anger while tears still stood in her eyes. "She's not just scared, she's *indignant*. She thinks she deserves better than she's getting."

For several minutes, they watched through the glass while the female made demands and begged for exceptions.

"She wasn't in hiding here in bumfuck, Oklahoma," Rudolph said. "She wasn't trying to pass for human. She thought she *was* human. The world thought she was human. When audiences look at her, they will see themselves, locked up and helpless. When the other exhibits look at her, they will see possibility. Opportunity. She grew up with freedom and human privilege. She's smart, she's loud, and she has a severely inflated sense of self-worth. Her delusions make her dangerous."

Gallagher nodded slowly, and they both stared through the window again while the female shouted at the sheriff, as if fear fueled her spirit, rather than cowing it.

Rudolph shook his head to disguise the chill traveling up his spine. This female could incite riots. She could save the carnival—or be the end of everything he'd been working toward his entire life.

"You must break her, Gallagher. She is the spark, and if that spark kindles, it will burn my menagerie to the ground."

DELILAH

With no clock or watch, I couldn't be sure how long I sat alone in the interrogation room chained to the floor, but it felt like forever. At some point during my isolation and immobilization, the threats I was facing—prison, private collectors, exotic game parks—began to coalesce into a steady baseline of anxiety. My new normality, it seemed, would be fear, and once that became clear, my other, lesser complaints began to stand out.

My shoulders were a constant source of pain—dull when I sat still, sharp and paralyzing when I tried to move. My hands had gone numb again, and no amount of finger wiggling would bring back pins and needles.

My bladder, though, was the real problem, and the inability to take myself to the restroom was one fresh hell of an indignity.

When the door finally opened again, I started to insist on a bathroom break, but one look at the sheer joy on Sheriff Pennington's face stole the words right off my tongue. The hair on the back of my neck stood up; his pleasure couldn't mean anything good for me.

Pennington strode into the center of the room and waved one pudgy arm at me. "There she is. Make it quick."

Two men eyed me from the hallway. An adrenaline-charged bolt of fear shot through me with one glance at them, and I forgot about my pain and discomfort. I recognized the large man in the red baseball cap even before I saw that *Gallagher* was embroidered on his Metzger's Menagerie polo.

The smaller, older man wore a slick-looking button-down shirt in that same shade of red, tucked into a pair of pleated black pants. He pushed past the deputy into the interrogation room, where he stared down at me from across the table.

My skin crawled under his methodical assessment. His gaze was cold and quick, efficiently inventorying my features without pausing to notice intelligence in my eyes, or tension in my frame, or fear in the rapid rising and falling of my chest with each breath.

My focus snagged on the crow's feet branching from the corners of his eyes and the wrinkles framing his mouth like nested parentheses. The script on the left side of his shirt read Rudolph Metzger.

"Any health issues?" Metzger glanced over his shoulder at Pennington, then turned again to study the chains binding me to my chair. "Allergies? Seizures? Anything communicable?"

"What the hell?" I demanded as Deputy Atherton stepped into the room, but he could only shrug. Pennington may have thought of me as a thing, but at least he'd talked to me like a person. Rudolph Metzger might as well have been examining the teeth of a racehorse.

Gallagher only watched from the doorway, his expression as featureless as the wall behind him.

"Regular bowels and menstrual cycles?" the old man continued, addressing me for the first time.

My cheeks burned. "Are you fucking serious?"

When I refused to answer, he turned back to the bewildered sheriff. "Normally we'd wait for the lab results on a cryptid of unknown origin, but since half a dozen of my own people witnessed the incident, we'll take her. You get half up front, and the other half when we have her blood work in hand. We can't register an exhibit without it."

"No." My pulse raced so fast the room started to look unsteady. "Hell, no. I am not joining the circus."

"It's not a circus, it's a carnival," Pennington said, while I tried to breathe through my fear and fury.

"Actually, it's both," Metzger corrected, without acknowledging that I'd spoken. "The menagerie itself is technically a circus—a single traveling unit, whose employees live, eat, and work together. But we engage carnival-style independent contractors who bring their own food carts, game booths, and rides at each stop." His contemptuous gaze settled on me. "This transaction doesn't require your approval. You're not joining my menagerie. You're being sold into it."

"Well, I can guaran-damn-tee you that requires *my* approval," Sheriff Pennington growled.

"Of course." Metzger glanced at his employee. "Gallagher, write the man a check."

Gallagher pulled a long checkbook from behind his back.

"Hang on now. We're gonna need more than half up front," Pennington insisted. "If you don't even know what she is, she must be rare, and rare is expensive."

Metzger gestured for the sheriff to precede him into the hall, and he took the checkbook from Gallagher on the way. "Let's talk money. But keep in mind that I'm the one assuming all the expense and risk…" Their voices faded when the door closed, and through the window set into it, I saw both men gesturing as they negotiated.

Gallagher watched me from his station near the door. His

focus only strayed from my face when he studied the chair and the chains holding me in place, and after a second, I realized he was checking for weaknesses in my bindings.

"Deputy." My heartbeat hammered in my ears. "Please don't let him do this."

Atherton sank onto the chair across from me and leaned over the table. "There's nothing I can do, Delilah."

"Talk the sheriff out of it. Tell him you heard Russell Clegg pays big."

"You'd rather be hunted than sit in a cage?"

I'd rather do neither, but the drive to the panhandle would give me several hours to think. Maybe I could break free at a rest stop. The chances of that were slim, but with Metzger, my chances of escape dropped to zero; the county fairground was only a few miles away.

"Delilah." Atherton cleared his throat and glanced at the table between us. "I think you should keep your head down and roll with the punches on this. These guys look like they're prepared to do this the hard way."

"You should listen to him." Gallagher's voice was like the rumble of distant thunder.

Before I could respond, the door opened again and Metzger walked into the interrogation room as if he now owned not just me, but the entire Franklin County Sheriff's Department.

Pennington followed him, holding two checks. He handed one to a deputy whose name I couldn't remember. "Write up an invoice and send that in with it to the state treasurer, up at the capital." The deputy left, and Pennington folded the other check and stuffed it into his own back pocket. "Deputy, give 'em the keys."

"No. Please!" I thrashed against my bindings, though I knew that would do no good. I couldn't help it.

Atherton stood and gave me an apologetic look as he fumbled with his keys.

Pennington rolled his eyes, then snatched the key ring and tossed it to Gallagher, who caught it one-handed. "It's the big one with the black rubber grip."

"No." Despite the pain, I struggled frantically while Gallagher thumbed through the keys. "You can't just *sell* me!" I shouted, and a deputy with baby cheeks and big brown eyes jumped, startled by my outburst. "You can't sell *people*! How could you all just go along with this?"

"You wanna sedate her?" Pennington asked, as Gallagher found the right key and pried it from the ring.

Metzger gave him a contemptuous huff. "It's never safe to introduce chemicals into the system of a cryptid before you know its species. Reactions vary widely. This one was raised human?"

Pennington nodded.

The menagerie owner sat on the edge of the table in front of me. "Do you have family?" he demanded, and I realized he had yet to address me by name.

When I only glared up at him, the grinding of my teeth drowned out by the panicked rush of my own pulse, Pennington answered for me. "We got her mother in a cell. Not her real mother. Charity's human, best we can tell."

"I don't know how you *can* tell, considering how normal this specimen looks. I'd keep an eye on the mother," Metzger said, and when Pennington nodded, the menagerie owner turned back to me, his voice carrying a soft, measured menace. "You're going to come peacefully, because if you don't, I'll see that your mother is charged with harboring a cryptid and public endangerment."

I studied his dark brown eyes, looking for the bluff, but I found none. He would have my mom arrested with no more regret than when he shook the dust of Franklin County off his boots and led his rolling prison into the next town.

"Fine." I couldn't drag my mother down with me, so I made myself sit still, battling competing urges to both fight and flee.

When the tension in my frame eased, Metzger stood and turned to the sheriff. "That would never have worked on a surrogate. The feds have no claim on her." He nodded to Gallagher, whom I could feel looming over me from behind, then the old man and the sheriff wandered into the hallway, talking about the proper restraint technique of a "human-lookin'" cryptid.

I jumped when Gallagher's hand settled onto my shoulder. "Relax." His voice was low and carefully controlled, but the word was spoken so close to my ear that I could feel the breath it rode on. His hand slid down my arm, like a handler strokes a horse's flank, to soothe her.

"Don't touch me!" I snapped through clenched teeth, and the light pressure of his fingers disappeared.

"I'm going to unthread the chains, then I'm going to help you up and lead you to the truck." He spoke softly as he worked, filling me in on each step before he carried it out, and when I looked up, I found Wayne watching, his expression trapped somewhere between anger and fascination. "I'll have to hold your arm as we walk," Gallagher continued. His hand brushed my bare foot, and the shackles fell away. "That's standard safety procedure."

"Do I look that dangerous?" I asked as he knelt behind me.

"Appearance isn't relevant to threat potential."

Metal clanged on the concrete, and suddenly my arms felt weightless, free of the burden of several pounds of iron chain.

The old man turned at the sound, and Gallagher tugged me up by one arm while he pulled my chair back with his free hand. My legs ached, and I wanted to stretch them. My fingers started tingling, as feeling returned, and I rolled my sore shoulders to help the process along.

When I turned to look up at Gallagher, I had to look way up. He was six foot six, if he was an inch. Maybe even taller. He returned my gaze with no visible thought or emotion, the face of a soldier. Or a stone statue. I got the feeling just from looking at him that unlike Deputy Atherton, Gallagher was burdened with neither empathy nor compassion.

Atherton, however, was suddenly nowhere to be found.

"Is she a biter?" Metzger asked the sheriff. "We brought a muzzle."

Pennington shrugged. "I'd keep it handy. That one's got a mouth like a snake."

Metzger's eyebrows shot up. "She has venomous fangs?" He pulled a small notebook from his jacket pocket. "That should narrow things down."

Pennington shook his head, looking confused. "No, she's a smart-ass."

The old man stuffed the notebook back into his pocket and stalked past him, gesturing for Gallagher and me to follow. "You should use more care when describing cryptids, Sheriff," he shot back over his shoulder, as Gallagher tugged me along. "In my line of work, similes are often indistinguishable from description."

Pennington mumbled something rude, then pushed past us into the front of the sheriff's station.

When Gallagher pulled me into the room, I had to fight for a deep breath. My gaze lost focus as it skipped from face to face in an open reception area that should have been nearly empty at 2:00 a.m. Some of the staff had stayed to help identify my species or find some place to send me. Others had stayed because there'd never been a cryptid outed in Franklin County, and I was big news.

Still others, based on the staggering hatred shining in their eyes, had evidently come just to spit on me.

"Lilah!" My mother's voice cracked beneath the weight of my name. I turned toward the sound and saw her standing, unrestrained, next to Deputy Wayne Atherton.

"Mom!" I shouted.

But Gallagher kept pulling me forward, still barefoot, after Metzger, denying me the goodbye Atherton had obviously risked his job to give me.

"Where are you taking her?" my mom demanded from across the room. I wanted to turn again, but if they thought I was resisting, Metzger might demand my mother's arrest on the spot and Gallagher might produce his muzzle.

Other questions followed my mother's, and when a woman's commanding tone and professional cadence rose above the others, I looked up to see that Channel 5 had sent a small crew from Oklahoma City.

A new foreboding settled through me like sand sinking through water, and suddenly my legs felt too heavy to move. Someone had alerted the media. More reporters would follow.

"Folks," Pennington began, and I groaned when I saw him standing with his hands on his hips, feet spread wide, ready to address the public as their leader in arms. Naturally, I'd been apprehended in the middle of an election year.

As soon as the crowd turned toward the sheriff, Rudolph Metzger stopped in the middle of the station and Gallagher pulled me to a halt several feet behind him. "Ladies and gentlemen, I understand your curiosity, but I don't yet have the answers to most of your questions." The menagerie owner's voice carried with even more presence and authority than the Channel 5 reporter's, and the crowd abandoned Pennington in favor of the man who'd probably been talking for the menagerie since before he could grow a decent beard.

"What I *can* confirm for you is that Delilah Marlow has been exposed as a cryptid hidden among the good people of Franklin County, and I have agreed, on behalf of Metzger's Menagerie, to take possession of her in the interest of public safety, effective immediately."

"What is she?" The reporter thrust a microphone at him, and I realized that her cameraman had framed the shot so that Gallagher and I were both visible over Metzger's shoulder.

"How was she exposed?"

"Was anyone killed?"

"What will you do with her?"

"Is she the only one?"

Metzger smiled for the crowd—I saw it in profile—and graciously waved off the questions. "That's all I'm prepared to say tonight, but I'm excited to announce that thanks to our new acquisition—" he aimed an elegant gesture my way, and I dropped my head when I saw countless phone cameras aimed at me "—Metzger's has agreed to extend our engagement in Franklin County to indulge the hometown crowd. Come see us tomorrow night, when we will unveil our latest exhibition. We'll answer what questions we can for you then."

Horror pitched me into a stunned fog. I didn't hear the questions lobbed at us as we continued through the lobby toward the door. All I could think about were words like *acquisition*, and *exhibit*, and *hometown crowd*, and what they meant strung together in the same sentence with my name.

"Lilah!" My mom lurched forward and reached for my arm, with Deputy Atherton just a step behind her.

Gallagher slid between us without missing a step as he hauled me across the floor.

"Lilah!" She followed as closely as he'd let her. "I'll fight this. I'll get a lawyer. I'll get you out of there, honey."

But since the reaping, no court had ever deigned to hear a

case brought forth by a cryptid. Some courts were even refusing to hear witness testimony from cryptids. And if she
dragged him into her fight, Pennington would arrest her just
to keep her out of his hair.

"Mom, don't," I said as she jogged to keep up. "I'm fine.
Really. So just...don't. Okay? Promise me."

"Lilah—"

"Promise me!" I begged, as Gallagher tugged me through
the front door and toward the dark parking lot, where a win-
dowless Metzger's van was double-parked on the first row, beneath a light pole. I dragged my feet until a rock cut into my
bare sole. "You have to trust me, Mom. It's better this way."
For you. But if I said that aloud, she wouldn't stop fighting
until we were both behind bars.

Gallagher pulled me to a stop behind the van, where another handler in a red Metzger's shirt opened the rear doors,
then helped lift me into the cargo area. I twisted in his grip
to see Deputy Atherton dragging my mother back into the
sheriff's station. Her tear-streaked face was the last thing I
saw before the van door slammed shut on life as I'd known it.

PART 2

CONFINÉ

ROMMILY

The oracle sat up in the dark, suddenly wide-awake. She wasn't sure whether the images still burned into her brain were from a dream or a vision, but there was little difference between the two anymore.

Rommily clutched the side of her cage to pull herself onto her knees in the narrow space between her sleeping sisters. Her gaze skimmed dead grass and muddy hoofprints dimly lit by lamp poles on the edge of the parking lot, but she saw none of that. The oracle's eyes were filled with another place and another time. Though she could no longer trace the threads connecting the present and the future, she understood that they were drawing closer together with every beat of her heart.

Something thunked in the dark, and Rommily's focus— a fragile thing, at best—was yanked back into the present. A door squealed open, tracing a skewed rectangle of light on the ground in front of the nearest staff trailer, and a dark silhouette emerged. The backlit outline joined another shadowy shape, then voices spoke, accompanied by the heavy footsteps of two men with rough hands and cold hearts.

"Thumb on the scale," the oracle mumbled as the handlers stomped past her cage. One was still pulling his shirt on while the other scrubbed sleep from his face with both thick hands, cursing the phone call that had awakened him.

"Balance restored." Rommily's voice carried more volume than before, and Mirela stirred on her left, one foot peeking from beneath her brightly colored skirt.

In the distance, two points of light snaked toward the menagerie on a narrow gravel road. Rommily's grip tightened around the steel grid caging her as the hum of the engine grew louder. A current of anticipation fired through her, crackling in her ears like static. Humming in her throat like a melody.

"The blind lady."

A van pulled into the parking lot and reversed into position with the crunch of gravel. The old man got out of the passenger's seat, and Rommily retreated from the edge of her cage as he rounded the vehicle, limping on his bad hip. The old man missed nothing.

The driver stepped out and slammed his door, and the oracle scooted farther into the shadows. She watched, unseen, as the drowsy handlers opened the rear doors of the vehicle. The large man with gray eyes and a red hat jumped out of the back of the van and lifted a young woman in chains from the darkness that hid her.

The oracle's gaze narrowed on the dimly lit figure. The woman's dark hair hung limp and her eyes were dull with exhaustion, but Rommily had seen her true face. She knew the terror it could inspire.

"She won't serve her dish cold," the oracle mumbled, almost giddy with joy as chill bumps rose all over her skin. "And two graves won't be near enough…"

DELILAH

The van rolled to a halt, then shifted into Reverse, sliding me across the bench seat. Gallagher grabbed my arm to stop me from falling. He hadn't moved an inch or said a word since we'd left the sheriff's station, and his stony silence left me with nothing to think about but the inevitable indignity of being displayed in a decorative cage for an audience of my own friends and neighbors.

The van stopped again. Footsteps stomped through gravel, then the doors flew open, and a jolt of adrenaline set my chest on fire. "Please, no," I mumbled, staring out into the yellow glare of several light poles. I wasn't ready. This *couldn't* be real. How could my fate possibly be up to two men and a checkbook, with no attorney, no trial, and no defense?

How could I have fewer rights under the law than a stray dog had?

Stray dogs were never responsible for the mass slaughter of American children. Everyone knew that.

I hadn't killed any kids either. I hadn't brainwashed any parents or stolen any babies. But that hadn't stopped Sheriff Pennington from selling me to the first man to walk in with a checkbook. Cryptids would forever pay the price for the horror of the reaping.

Metzger stared into the cargo area with his arms crossed over his red satin shirt. His showman's bearing and voice had been abandoned, along with his jacket and his red suspenders. All that remained of Rudolph Metzger, the menagerie front man, were the polished black boots he still wore and the top hat, now held in his left hand. Behind him stood two more large handlers, who looked gruff and irritated to be on the job in the middle of the night. Like Gallagher, they wore nothing sequined or shiny. These men were the power and sweat behind the glitz and the glamour.

I was officially behind the scenes of the menagerie.

Gallagher jumped down from the van, then lifted me out by both arms and set me down on gravel. Rocks cut into my bare feet. My shoulders ached and my wrists were raw from the heavy cuffs fastened at my back, but no one offered to take them off. No one gave me any shoes, asked my name, or addressed me directly at all.

"What is she?" the handler on the left asked. According to his shirt, his name was Wallace.

"She is a mystery." Metzger thumped his top hat to knock dust from it. "She's new and exotic. Very rare. That's the angle anyway, until her blood test comes back. Play it up."

The owner pulled Gallagher aside, leaving the other handlers to glare at me, bulging arms crossed over broad chests. They were a human wall, and I would not be able to breach it.

"My daughter's getting remarried on Friday, and my wife and I are watching her kids during the honeymoon." Metzger had to look way up to talk to Gallagher. "I'll catch up with the menagerie two weeks from today. You have that long to break her in and train her."

Break me in? Train me?

I sucked in breath after rapid breath, but couldn't seem to get enough air. The night was uncomfortably dry and warm, but my veins had become arctic channels, pumping tiny icebergs through me to pierce and sink all hope.

"That won't be long enough, sir." Gallagher's voice was so low and deep that I could hardly hear him. "She's spent a lifetime—"

"Make it happen," Metzger demanded.

I hunched around the cold knot in my belly, struggling to absorb everything I was hearing through filters of shock and exhaustion. Nothing felt real. Nothing but the iron cuffs.

"Delegate some of your other responsibilities and make this your primary concern," the old man said. "I want her turning a profit when I get back, or I'm selling her to Vandckamp to recoup part of my loss, and you'll make up the rest from your own paycheck. For the next six months. Understood?"

Gallagher nodded, and panic tightened my chest until I could hardly breathe. Who the hell was Vandekamp?

"Get her processed, then put her on the row. Tomorrow, start breaking her." Metzger marched off toward a long line of campers and 18-wheelers, many painted with menagerie images in the same retro style as the posters hanging all over town.

His instructions echoed in my head.

Break me? Like a stick for kindling or like a pony for riding? Break me like a date, or like a heart, or like a promise?

In the end, it wouldn't matter. I had no intention of being broken.

Metzger's footsteps faded, and I turned back to Gallagher, fighting to convert my fear into fuel for the sparks of rage flickering deep in my soul.

My entire existence was in his hands, which meant he was the biggest obstacle to my escape.

I studied him as he gave Wallace and the other handler a series of instructions involving words like *crate*, and *blanket*, and *padlock*. Gallagher was big. He was tall, and broad, and solid enough to make the others—large men in their own right—look almost delicate. I would not escape by overpowering my handler physically.

But there were other ways to overpower. My mother had shown me that in every battle from the PTA presidency to the great flower-bed debate of 2008, in which she and her army of petunias had sent my father's ground cover packing. Pride. Love. Jealousy. Hatred. Insecurity. Any weakness can be exploited, and everyone has a weakness.

When we were in the eighth grade, I'd used a bully's insecurity to humiliate her, after she'd accused Shelley of cheating off her on a test, when the opposite was actually true. In college, I'd helped a friend get revenge on a cheating boyfriend by exploiting his rampant lust. And once at the bank, I'd used my boss's trust in me to get him fired after he cheated on his wife in the vault.

Gallagher might be bigger than the other predators I'd encountered, but as my father always said, the bigger they are, the harder they fall. Finding Gallagher's weakness would be the key to setting myself free.

Gallagher pounded on the trailer door with his thick right fist, his left still wrapped around my arm in a grip that didn't actually hurt, but probably couldn't be broken. My legs ached and my ankles were chafed from walking in iron shackles, and what I'd learned from slowly, awkwardly climbing the steep porch steps in them was that even if I could have pulled free from my captor, I wouldn't get very far if I tried to run.

The porch light came on over our heads, illuminating the aluminum steps beneath us, the dented metal door, and the mud-splattered white vertical siding of the menagerie's mobile office—a modular trailer, which could be lifted onto a flatbed truck and hauled from city to city, intact.

Gallagher had called it "the silver wagon," but neither descriptor fit.

The door was opened by a tall thin man wearing a red satin Metzger's jacket in spite of the stifling heat of the midsummer night. The name embroidered over his heart was Ruyle, and beneath that his title read Lot Supervisor.

I hated him with every cell in my body, even before Ruyle took one look at me, then snorted. "I can't believe the old man bought another free-range freak."

Free-range? Because I hadn't grown up in captivity?

The supervisor stepped back, and Gallagher tugged me into the cramped one-room office. Inside there was barely enough room to breathe, thanks to two cluttered desks, four lockable filing cabinets, a mini-fridge, and a whiteboard schedule covered with employee names, time slots, and various menagerie act assignments.

The board slid out of focus as I stared at it. I would be listed there soon—not by my name but by my species, or by some number assigned to me on a list of inventory.

"You'd think the old man would have learned a lesson after that free-range dark elf we picked up near Atlanta last year," Ruyle continued. "That was a real clusterfuck."

Gallagher only grunted.

Ruyle kicked the door closed and turned to study me. My skin crawled beneath his appraisal.

"What is she?"

Gallagher shrugged. "She doesn't eat live flesh, read minds, tell the future, shift into an animal, or have an allergy to iron."

Ruyle made a spinning motion with his index finger, and Gallagher turned me by both shoulders, so the supervisor could finish his assessment. "No horns, hooves, claws, or fangs. Do a thorough check for feathers, scales, and fur when we're done here."

"I don't have any of that." I tried to turn and appeal to Ruyle directly, but Gallagher stopped me with one heavy hand on my shoulder. "I was examined at the sheriff's station, and they didn't find anything."

"Oh, I think we're going to want to see for ourselves." Ruyle's hand settled on my lower back, then slid low over the curve of my hip. I tried to step away from his touch, but Gallagher's grip on my shoulder tightened, holding me in place.

Rage blazed beneath my skin like a fever. "Don't touch me."

Ruyle stepped into sight again, his disappointed gaze lingering on my mouth. "Not a succubus, then. Damn shame. They would have lined up for miles to be sucked dry by her."

The mental image made me gag. The supervisor laughed while I swallowed convulsively to keep from vomiting. I *loathed* him. "What, does that offend your delicate sensibilities?"

I stared straight into his eyes, standing as tall as I could. "If I'd eaten anything tonight, you'd be wearing it. Consider that my official opinion of your business model."

Gallagher's grunt actually sounded amused.

Ruyle seized my chin in a brutal grip and I gasped, shocked by the casual cruelty. I tried to pull free, and his hold tightened until my teeth cut into my cheek and I tasted blood.

"Free advice, freak. Just because you *can* talk doesn't mean you *should*." The supervisor looked up at Gallagher without letting go of me. "If the sign out front read Ruyle's Menagerie, cutting their tongues out would be an official part of the welcome package."

Gallagher said nothing, so Ruyle turned back to me. "If

I have to go find a muzzle for you, you'll wear it for a week straight, even if we have to feed you through a straw."

When he let go of my chin, I glared up at him, blinking back angry tears. "Aren't you afraid I'll scramble your brain and leave you drooling in a puddle of your own urine?"

"With your hands cuffed behind your back?" Ruyle's mouth laughed, but his eyes didn't.

"I won't always be cuffed, though, will I?" None of the "exhibits" I'd seen had been restrained within their cages.

The supervisor's eyes narrowed into angry slits beneath his deeply furrowed brow. "Three." His gaze slid up to Gallagher again. "My money's on three days before the old man sells her to R & D. Or I feed her to the adlet. We've got a pool going." Ruyle pointed to his desk, where an old pickle jar held a handful of wrinkled five-dollar bills. "You want in? The dark elf made it a week and a half." His contemptuous gaze narrowed on me. "But I'm betting she won't make it half that."

"Get on with it," Gallagher growled, while I stared at the jar of cash bet against my survival.

Ruyle rounded his desk and dropped into the chair behind it, looking up at me with both arms folded on the cluttered plywood desk. "You're what? Twenty? Twenty-two?"

"Twenty-five, today." Gallagher sank onto the edge of a two-drawer filing cabinet, without letting go of my arm. He'd either seen my driver's license, spoken to my friends, or read a report at the sheriff's station.

Ruyle's brows rose. "Hell of a birthday, huh?" He leaned over his desk and his gaze narrowed on me. "Look, twenty-five years is a long time to spend living a lie, and I'm sure you got real comfortable with a bunch of liberties and amenities you never really had any right to. Most in your situation don't make it in the menagerie because they can't let go of the past. But if you want to prove me wrong and cost me a small fortune in fives—" he gestured to the jar of cash "—that's exactly what you'll need to do. Forget about your friends, and your family, and your car, and your job, and any other defunct delusions. They were never really yours in the first place. If you can accept your place, you could be pretty comfortable here." His hard-eyed gaze took on a lascivious gleam. "I'll see to that myself. But if you make my job hard, I will make your life a living hell."

"She's *my* charge." Gallagher's hand tightened around my arm, tugging me closer. I fought the urge to pull away from him.

Ruyle nodded. "True, you're Gallagher's problem until you're broken in and turning a profit. But I'm his boss, which means that ultimately, just like all the other beasts, you're my problem. Understood?"

"Yeah." I shrugged, trying not to let the pain in my shoulders show. "You're the boss, so you have a lot of problems."

Ruyle's jaw clenched. He glared at Gallagher. "Three days. And that's a generous estimation." Then he picked up a form from a pile of papers scattered across his desk and turned back to me. "As the lot supervisor, I'm in charge when old man Metzger's gone, which is most of the time. Even when he's here, he leaves the real work to me and our boss of livestock." He threw a careless gesture at Gallagher, without looking away from me. "Obviously, you're the livestock. I'm sure a lot of this comes as a shock, after the way you were raised, so if you have any questions…" He shrugged. "You'll figure it out."

Ruyle scribbled something on the form in front of him. "Put her in crate forty-two. With any luck, it still smells like cat piss from that leopard shifter we leased from All American." He spun the form around and slid it across the desk toward my new handler. "Give this to Nellis and tell him we'll use one of the spare wagon casings for now. I'm not going to have Alyrose fix up something special until we know your new pet's a keeper."

"Crate?" I turned to Gallagher, wincing when the cuffs cut into my ankles. "You're going to put me in a box?" Would they at least punch holes in the top, so I could breathe?

"It's just a cage on wheels," Gallagher said. "A circus wagon with the decorative casings removed for transport."

Ruyle leaned back in his chair and laced his fingers behind his head. "I think you're onto something, though. I'm sure we could find a shipping crate to stuff you in. Yesterday's high was one hundred twelve degrees." The manager shrugged. "It'd be a real shame for you to broil in your own sweat because you couldn't keep your mouth shut."

Survival instinct stilled my tongue, but terror ate away at me from the inside. He was right. I couldn't survive the menagerie. I couldn't live in a cage. I couldn't be someone else's property.

Panic crept in from the edges of my mind, where lurked all the horrifying possibilities I hadn't yet let myself consider. They could do whatever they wanted with me. *To* me. I closed my eyes and breathed deeply, trying to tune Ruyle out, but the best I could do was mentally distance myself from the miserable existence his forms and decrees were outlining for me.

In addition to a crate number, he assigned me to uniform group C and hygiene plan A, with the caveat that if I became a security risk in the bathroom, I would lose the privilege.

Having never considered hygiene a privilege, I wasn't entirely sure what a downgrade from plan A would mean.

The supervisor also assigned me to the omnivore meal plan and gave me a wagon number, which would indicate my position in the "take down" and determine which of the menagerie's custom-built, wide-load 18-wheelers I would be "shelved" in for transport.

I couldn't fully process all the new information, and I didn't even try. But by the time Gallagher escorted me from the silver wagon, accompanied by the clank of my heavy iron bindings, the takeaway was clear.

Everything I'd ever owned had been taken. Everyone I'd ever known was gone.

I'd become the property of Metzger's Traveling Menagerie.

"According to the most current numbers, more than three hundred thousand human families lost a total of almost one million children in last week's massacre, and all of them appear to have been killed by their own parents. But what's really strange, Bill, is that the authorities are saying not *one* of those parents remembers a thing that happened in the early hours of August 24. Could *all* of those parents have been acting in some kind of subconscious state?"

—From an NPR interview with William Green, the world's foremost authority on hypnotism, September 3, 1986

DELILAH

The county fairgrounds ladies' room. Six stalls—four toilets and two showers—and a sink-lined walkway. Grimy concrete floor. White cinderblock walls, dripping with slimy condensation.

As an eight-year-old, I'd vomited in the third stall from the left after a bad chili dog at the fair. At thirteen, I'd borrowed Shelley's makeup and applied it in front of the very last sink, a willful violation of my dad's "not until high school" rule. And a week after my eighteenth birthday, I'd stood outside the fourth stall while Shelley took the pregnancy test she hadn't had the nerve to take at home alone.

But I'd never been marched down the abandoned midway in the middle of the night by a man the size of a small building, passing darkened game booths and locked-tight food stalls on our way into that bathroom. I'd never looked into the mirror and seen finger-shaped bruises rounding my chin or dark circles forming beneath each of my eyes.

I'd never been ordered to strip in front of the curtain-less shower while three men watched, their expressions ranging from Gallagher's objective professionalism to Mustache Man's leering grin of anticipation.

"I'm going to uncuff you, and you're going to take off your clothes and turn a slow circle so we can visually check you for species-identifying marks or features," Gallagher said. "Then you'll step into the shower and thoroughly wash your hair and your body."

"No," I said, and irritation narrowed his gray eyes. "Please don't make me do this. I don't have any marks, I swear."

He scowled and turned me by my shoulders for access to the cuffs at my back, but I spun around again before he could dig his keys from his pocket.

"I get it, okay? I don't have any rights. I'm just a piece of meat you're going to lock up in a metal box." Each word killed a little more of my soul, but desperation kept me talking. "I can't stop you from doing whatever you want with me."

"Damn right," the man with the mustache said, but I only exhaled and kept my gaze on the boss of livestock.

"You can make me strip. But I'm asking you not to. As a kindness. I have nothing left but my dignity. Please let me keep it."

Gallagher blinked, and for just an instant, he looked...surprised. Then the professional blinders slid back into place, locking me out of his thoughts. "There are rules. If you refuse to follow them, we'll have to cut your clothes off and bathe you ourselves, and there is *much* less dignity in that."

I nodded, my jaw clenched to keep my chin from trembling, and as I turned to give him access to the handcuffs, he exhaled.

"I think we can forgo the flea and lice treatment."

"Ruyle says no exceptions on that." Mustache Man picked up a commercial-sized bottle from the box at his feet. "We can't afford an infestation." The name on his shirt identified him as Clyde.

"This morning she was a bank teller with manicured nails."

Gallagher slid his key into the cuffs with the scrape of metal. "She's probably cleaner than you are."

Clyde scowled, but didn't push the issue.

Gallagher released my left hand, then my right, then turned me by my shoulders to face him again. He knelt to unlock my ankles, and Clyde leered at me over the top of his boss's red cap.

I crossed my arms over my chest, shielding myself from the pending visual violation. "Okay, how 'bout a compromise?" I said to the top of Gallagher's head as he freed my left ankle. "I'll strip and shower without a fuss, saving everyone a lot of time and effort—but not in front of them."

Gallagher shook his head without looking up at me as he unlocked my ankle. "Until we know what you're capable of, federal regulations dictate a three-to-one ratio of handlers to unrestrained cryptids."

I shrugged. "So make them turn around. How many of you really need to see that my back isn't hollow and my ass isn't covered in scales?"

Gallagher stood, towering over me with my shackles in hand, and I watched anxiously while he weighed the risks and benefits of my proposal. "If you try *anything*, I will never be able to trust you again. Do you understand what I'm telling you?"

A stubborn thread of anger steeled my spine as I stared up at him. "Let you see me naked, or you'll make my life hell?"

"This isn't about seeing you naked."

"Right." I rubbed my sore wrist, left raw from the sheriff's department's restraints.

Gallagher turned me by both shoulders, and I held his hard, gray gaze. "At the back of the menagerie, in a tent trimmed with a red ribbon, sit four of the most beautiful women ever seen on this earth. Succubi crave physical contact and take off any clothing we don't practically glue to their skin. So understand, Princess Vanity, that yours is not the most coveted flesh in this carnival."

I blinked, surprised by the longest speech I'd heard from him.

"It's almost dawn," Gallagher growled. "Get moving." He glanced at each of the other handlers. "You two turn around."

Only slightly mollified, I reached into the shower stall and twisted the knob. Water exploded from the showerhead and I held one hand beneath the flow, waiting—hoping—for it to warm while Gallagher fielded protests from Clyde and the other handler, whose name was Freddie. When the water was as warm as it was going to get, I turned to find the boss of livestock watching me expectantly while the other men stood between us, facing him, but turned away from me.

Their stiff bearing and crossed arms spoke volumes, but so did their obedience. They weren't willing to cross Gallagher.

I turned away from him, and my hands shook as I pulled my sheer blouse and cami over my head together in one quick movement. Despite the warm night, I had to clench my jaw to keep my teeth from chattering. I could practically feel his gaze on my back.

My fingers fumbled with my bra hook, and by the time I pushed my underwear to the floor and stepped out of it, I was trembling all over. Reducing the spectators from three to one hadn't helped as much as I'd hoped. I was still naked and vulnerable in front of a stranger.

"Extend your arms," Gallagher said, and I jumped, so on edge that any stimulus from the world around me—the splatter of lukewarm water from the shower, the tick of Clyde's old-fashioned wristwatch, the scent of bleach emanating from the toilet stalls—was a shock to my system.

I held my arms out, silently commanding them not to shake.

For a moment, there was only silence behind me. Then, "Turn around."

Exhaling slowly, I turned and looked Gallagher in the eye, silently challenging him to look away first.

His gaze held mine for several seconds. Then he made a visual inventory of the rest of me, evidently ticking off the parts I did and didn't have on some mental list.

When he was done, Gallagher gave me a quick nod. "Shower," he said, then he glanced at each of his subordinates and gave a brief report. "Nothing of interest."

I stepped into the shower, my face flaming as the other men snickered. Something landed on the shower floor at my feet and I looked down to find a clear plastic shower kit containing a tiny bottle of shampoo and a small bar of soap.

The razor was notably missing, and I had no intention of lingering long enough to use the little tube of depilatory cream.

I washed as quickly as I could, and when I turned off the water, Gallagher nodded to Clyde, who tossed a threadbare white towel over his shoulder. I had to scurry across the concrete, nude and dripping wet, to catch it before it hit the filthy floor.

The radio clipped to Gallagher's waistband buzzed as I wrapped the towel around myself. When I reached for my clothes, he paused with the radio in hand and shook his head. "No personal clothing." He nodded to Clyde again, who knelt to pull a wad of gray fabric from the same box that had produced the ratty towel. Clyde tossed the garment over his shoulder, and I caught it with one hand, holding my towel closed with the other.

"What?" Gallagher said into his radio as I shook the material out and held it up.

"The crate's ready," a voice said through the static.

"Be right there." He clipped the radio to his belt again and eyed me expectantly. "Let's go."

I held the dress up for him to see. "This is it?" Uniform C had turned out to be a very thin, very short gray peasant dress, sleeveless and gathered at the waist. It was better than the werewolf girl's tube top and bikini bottom, but not by much.

He frowned at Clyde. "Give her the rest of it."

Clyde dipped back into his box for a much smaller wad of material, and a second later I caught a pair of white cotton underwear, tangled around a cotton bra with no wires. They were clean, and approximately the right size, but worn thin.

"These are used."

"Uniforms are community property," Clyde said without turning. "You get whatever's clean, and if you're lucky, it'll fit."

Clenching my jaw so hard my whole face ached, I stepped into the underwear without taking off the towel, then turned away from them to put the bra on and pull the thin dress over my head. When I was clothed, Gallagher nodded to his men.

They turned as I was wringing water from my hair with the towel.

"Much better." Clyde eyed the dress and my dripping hair, but I didn't understand what he meant until I glanced in the mirror behind him.

I looked like a peasant from the Renaissance Fair. Or a servant from a fairy tale—a child's story, not an actual tale of the *fae*. I certainly didn't look like I hailed from a world of cell phones, high-speed internet, and mass-produced blue jeans. And that, of course, was the point.

The uniforms, like the cages, were a visual demarcation between humanity and everything else. A symbol of the gulf imposed between us, which they probably considered espe-

cially important in my case, because I had no features to identify me as other than human.

Less than human, according to the satisfied glint in Clyde's
eyes.

"Use the toilet. You won't get another chance for a while."
Gallagher's focus shifted to Clyde as he backed toward the
door. "Watch her while I check her wagon."

When he was gone, I stepped into one of the stalls, but
Clyde's hand stopped the door when I tried to close it. He and
Freddie watched, tranquilizer rifles held ready, as I urinated.

Maybe I should have been relieved that they didn't make
me squat in a box of litter.

NALAH

The centaurs were snoring again. Every few minutes, one of them snorted like a horse in a stable, and the sound was like a knife ripping through the fragile fabric of the young *ifrit*'s slumber.

Nalah pushed a heavy braid over her shoulder. Light from the waxing moon shone on crimson strands threaded with so many shades of gold and orange that her hair seemed to shift and jump like live flames. No human ever had hair of such colors, nor copper eyes ringed in bronze that flashed like sparks from a bonfire.

By most accounts Nalah was one of the most beautiful *ifrits* ever born into the *djinn* peasant class, and she could never, even for a second, be mistaken for human.

On her left, Adira groaned and rolled over on her own blanket. "I can't sleep," she moaned, blinking wide blue eyes at Nalah in the dark. "The beasts reek, and it's too hot to move."

"Apologies, Princess," Nalah murmured in the soothing tone she'd mastered as a child. There was nothing she could do about the beasts, and even less she could do about the heat, but she *was* sorry for it. She understood that being caged with her was both a blessing and a curse for Adira.

Nalah was a loyal companion and an even better attendant—she was well-trained in both arts—but the heat an *ifrit* radiated by nature contributed nothing to the princess's physical comfort in the summer. Not that there was much comfort to be found in the menagerie, where royalty and mongrels were treated with equal contempt. "Let me fix your bed, then I will brush your hair. That always helps you sleep."

Adira crawled off her blanket and tucked her knees to her chest in the farthest corner of their small cage. There wasn't much room in which to move, but Nalah made do, as she had for the entire year they'd been captives of Rudolph Metzger and his prison on wheels. In seconds, she'd refolded Adira's blanket into as thick a pad as she could manage. When the princess curled up on the makeshift pallet, moonlight shining on her pale skin and gossamer hair, Nalah folded her own blanket into a pillow and slid it beneath the princess's head.

Nalah scooted to the far side of their cage, so that any breeze that rolled through would hit Adira first, unimpeded. Then she began to run her fingers through the princess's long silvery hair, gently untangling it by hand, since they had no comb or brush, nor any other luxury, save each other's company. As she worked, Nalah hummed a traditional lullaby, one of a dozen she'd mastered by age eight, though the language and the legend it told were not her own.

"I miss the water. Do you remember the pools and fountains at home?" Adira whispered, and the wistful crack in her voice broke her companion's heart.

"I remember them fondly," Nalah said, though Adira's home was not her home. Adira's fountains were not her fountains. Adira's people were not her people.

"The water was so clean. So clear. So cold." She shifted on the makeshift pillow and moonlight glittered in her hair like sunshine on a shallow stream. "I'd give my kingdom for a fucking *glass* of water, much less a fountain."

Her kingdom.

Adira actually had a kingdom. She would have had two, if not for the menagerie. If not for imprisonment, and poverty, and long absence from the world of shimmering lakes and fountains she was born into.

Nalah let memories take her as her fingers combed through the princess's hair out of ingrained habit, yet what she remembered was not the glittering fountains and cool pools of Adira's childhood, but the roaring flames and cozy hearth fires of her own. Roasted meat, straight off the spit. Grilled fruit and charred marshmallows on sticks. Hot, thick vegetable stews and warm teas sweetened with honey. The remembered taste of sizzling hog fat and seared tomatoes took her back to the feasts of her youth, and memories might have become sweet, warm dreams if not for the unexpected light bobbing in the night a hundred feet away.

The *ifrit*'s fingers paused. Her copper eyes narrowed, trying to focus on a face in the dark, but it was the outline of his form and a familiar gait that finally brought recognition. Those, and the silhouette of the cap on his head.

"Gallagher!" Nalah gasped. Her hand flew immediately to her mouth, as if she could stuff the word back inside, but it was far too late for that.

"Ow!" Adira clutched her head, and Nalah was humiliated to realize her clumsy fingers had pulled out several strands of her companion's hair.

"Apologies, Princess," she breathed, but Gallagher had heard, and he was headed their way.

"You two should be asleep," the handler growled, tugging the bill of his cap lower on his forehead. Something clicked near his hand, and the flashlight was extinguished, momentarily blinding the girls with the sudden darkness.

Adira rose, propped on one thin arm. "You try sleeping in a cage surrounded by livestock."

"I've slept under much worse conditions," he said, and Nalah flushed at the scorn in his tone. She dreaded his disapproval, even when it was not aimed at her.

"How close are we?" Adira demanded when his censure floated right over her head.

"Close." He spoke so softly Nalah had to strain to hear him. "We've hit a delay, but we're still close."

The princess huffed impatiently. "What kind of delay?"

"The kind that's none of your business."

"You're being paid. Everything you do is my business."

The handler stepped closer to the cage and his voice became a fierce rumble. "I haven't been paid yet, *Princess.*"

Adira made an angry sound deep in her throat. When she began to braid her own hair, pointedly ignoring him, Gallagher's gaze fell on Nalah. "Try to get some sleep," he said softly.

The *ifrit*'s heart pounded so hard her dress trembled over her chest with each beat. "My needs are few and insignificant," she assured him, and the dismayed look he gave her burned all the way to her soul.

When the thud of his footsteps faded into the night, Adira laughed. "Your needs are not so insignificant after all," she teased. "Nor are they difficult to fulfill. If you offer yourself, he will have you."

"I couldn't." Nalah's cheeks flushed and the heat emanating from her swelled with humiliation.

"*I* could. Shall I offer you to him?"

"Only if that brings you comfort, Princess."

At her companion's expected reply, Adira gave a satisfied cluck of her tongue, and Nalah's flaming face began to cool.

Her fingers found the princess's hair again, and she repaired the braid Adira had botched.

Moments later, the princess sat bolt upright, sniffing the air like a hound on the scent of prey. "Water." Her voice shook with anticipation. "Clean water. I need it, Nalah."

"Of course. Where…?"

"There." Adira pointed into the dark, and a second later the shadows shifted with movement. When the form came closer, Nalah recognized both the handler—the others called him Wallace—and what he held: a bottle of water. Fresh and unopened.

She rose to her knees and cleared her throat to catch his attention. When he looked her way, Nalah released the shoulder strap holding her thin dress on and let the material fall over her calves on the floor of her cage, highlighted by a pool of moonlight.

The handler came closer, licking his lips as his gaze wandered over her firm bronze flesh. "What does Her Highness require tonight?" His words were sharp with sarcasm, but his willingness to oblige was as obvious as the bulge beneath his zipper.

"Water," the princess said, seated at the back of the cage with her legs neatly folded beneath her. "You may take her, in exchange for the bottle in your hand. Full and unopened," the princess added at the last second. They'd been burned by vague phrasing before.

"Done." The handler fumbled to open the door, then pulled Nalah from the cage as he tossed the water bottle inside. He locked the cage with one hand, the other bruising her arm.

Adira had drained the bottle of water with a satisfied belch before the first ugly grunt echoed from the shadows behind her cage.

DELILAH

Gallagher cuffed my hands in front of me with regular steel cuffs and led me out of the bathroom onto the deserted midway, where he took the tranquilizer rifle from Clyde. "You two turn in her clothes, then hit the sack. I got it from here."

"You sure?" Freddie eyed me while I curled my bare toes on the rough sidewalk.

Gallagher gave him a terse nod.

Freddie took off after Clyde, with the box containing my stuff tucked under his arm.

Gallagher took my arm and marched me toward the rear exit of the fairgrounds.

I looked up at him, but the bill of his hat shielded most of his face from the couple of lampposts we passed beneath. "Aren't you afraid I'll try to liquefy your gray matter?"

"You don't know how. That's as much a problem for me as it is for you."

"Are you sure?" The paved path ended at the open gate. The grass was scratchy but surprisingly cool against the soles of my feet. "I could just be biding my time, waiting for you to get careless."

The huge ring of keys attached to his belt jangled and

clanked with every step. "I'm never careless. And if you knew
how to turn back into…whatever you are, you would have
tried to kill us and escape while you were uncuffed."

"I'm not a killer." No sense denying that I was a flight risk,
especially when I spotted a double line of circus cage wagons up ahead. They were great hulking shadows cast into the
larger darkness by a line of tall lampposts.

Gallagher made a skeptical sound deep in his throat. "Of
course you're a killer. You just lack experience in the field."

"You don't know anything about me."

One dark brow rose in the shadows beneath the bill of his
cap. "You're an only child. Labeled 'gifted' in elementary
school. High school salutatorian. Undergraduate degree in
crypto-biology from Colorado State—on scholarship—then
you came back home to handle deposits and withdrawals at
the local credit union."

I stopped walking to stare up at him. "How do you know
all that? *Why* do you know all that?"

"My job is to break you. The more I know about you, the
easier that will be."

My gaze fell and I stared at my bare feet, mentally wading
through shock to process not just what he'd said, but the utter
lack of emotion with which he'd said it. His job was to break
me, and he would do that with no more regret than when he
got dressed and brushed his teeth in the morning. Breaking
me was just something else on his to-do list.

Yet he was the only one at Metzger's who'd spoken to me
like a person.

"Why did you make those other handlers turn around?" I
would already be one step closer to broken if he had let Freddie and Clyde watch me shower. Was that kindness just a setup
for my inevitable psychological fracture? Show me mercy now,
so that later his cruelty would seem all the more cruel?

Gallagher shrugged his massive shoulders. "I don't have to start breaking you until tomorrow."

"And that won't bother you because you think I'm a killer?"

For a second, I thought he'd actually answer. Then Gallagher tugged me forward again.

"I— Ow!" A jagged rock bit into my heel and sent sharp pain up my leg. I hopped on my left foot, reaching to clutch the bruised sole of my right before I remembered my hands were cuffed again.

Gallagher hauled me upright before I could fall over.

"Can I at least get a pair of shoes?"

"I can't issue anything that would help you escape." He took my arm again. I couldn't pull free, so I dragged my feet in silent protest, as well as out of caution. The dark grass suddenly felt like a minefield waiting to cripple me with every step.

For several minutes, I followed him in silence, watching the ground for rocks I probably wouldn't be able to see in the dark anyway. Then an odd equine snort startled me and I looked up to find the double line of circus wagons just a few yards away.

"Home sweet home," Gallagher said, and that fact—the visceral reality of it—hit me like sledgehammer straight to my soul.

My feet stopped moving and my mouth fell open. I inhaled as deeply as I could, but the air tasted foul. Like tyranny and manure.

"This can't be happening." The world teetered around me, and the very ground seemed determined to toss me like an angry bull. I dropped into a squat, knees and back bent, gasping, but no matter how much air I sucked in and spat out, I couldn't get a satisfying breath.

"Delilah. Stand up."

"This isn't real," I gasped, my elbows propped on my knees, hands hanging limp, cuffs and all. "This *can't* be real."

"It is, and making me drag you to your crate won't change that. Stand up."

But I could hardly hear him over the roar of oblivion devouring everything I'd ever had or been, leaving only an empty shell of me tethered to my brutal new reality by cuffs and chains.

"I'm having a nightmare," I murmured. But that wasn't quite right.

I was *living* a nightmare.

Gallagher squatted next to me and tilted my face up until I saw his gray eyes, finally illuminated in the beam from a light pole. "A cage locks other people out as much as it locks you in, and sometimes that's for the best."

"You're locking me up to protect me? You really expect me to believe that?"

"I'm locking you up to protect everyone. Where you live is not up to you anymore, but *how* you live is still your choice. I can make things a little easier for you, if you'll make my job easier for me."

Fresh anger flared in the pit of my stomach. I tried to shove him back, but that was like trying to push over a tree with my bare hands. "You're no better than your boss, offering to make me comfortable—for a price."

Gallagher's gaze hardened until his eyes looked like onyx pebbles. "I'm far worse than Ruyle." He grabbed my arm and pulled me upright. His hand tightened around my arm, and when I flinched, he let me go. "But I wasn't propositioning you. Do *not* insult me with that assumption again."

"So then, what were you offering?"

"You help me get you ready for exhibition, and I'll do what I can to make your adjustment less traumatic."

Indignation burned in my veins. I didn't *want* to be exhibition-ready, and there was no way to make any of this less traumatic. They could lock me up, but they couldn't force me to cooperate. Let them sell me—hell, let them kill me. If I'd realized anything since being sold into the menagerie, it was that I had nothing left to lose.

I turned my back on Gallagher without a word and marched toward the circus carts on my own. He caught up in three huge strides, and a few yards later, he pulled me to a stop in front of an empty steel cage on wheels. It was the last cart on the first of two parallel rows of circus wagons and the only one without a stunning, brightly colored decorative frame— a naked version of all the other cages.

One steel mesh panel had been slid open along its track. The base of the wagon was a custom steel trailer two feet off the ground, and before I could even process the fact that there were no steps, Gallagher lifted me by the waist and set me inside the cage on my knees. The door slid shut behind me with a horrifying clang and I spun around to find him threading a padlock through two metal loops to hold the sliding panel closed.

"Wait!" Panic echoed in my voice. "Please don't do this." My eyes watered, and my throat felt so tight I had to force the words out, because this was my very last chance. "I'm not dangerous."

Why the *fuck* had I let Brandon drag me to the carnival? It was just as depraved a spectacle as I'd imagined, but I'd never expected to become trapped inside it. If I'd insisted on a birthday dinner instead, I'd be curled up next to him in bed, blissfully ignorant of the horror I'd narrowly escaped.

"I don't belong here!"

Gallagher clicked the padlock closed. "You're no different from the rest."

I couldn't argue with that. No one belonged in the menagerie.

"What about these?" I held my hands up and rattled the cuffs.

He flipped a steel peg free from its loop on the outside of my cage, and a small panel in the mesh folded down, low enough that I had to sit to slide my hands through. He pulled a key from his pocket and removed the cuffs. Once I'd retracted my hands, he closed and locked the panel.

And just like that, my world was reduced to a four-by-six cage hardly tall enough for me to stand up in.

I sat with my legs folded beneath me, and the clang of my cage being closed echoing in my head. Gallagher watched me through the steel mesh. I couldn't read his expression—it was shrouded in shadows—but I heard the jangle of metal as he clipped his key ring to a loop at his waist. "Try to get some sleep. Tomorrow won't be easy."

As if my evening had been a stroll through a moonlit park.

It took every bit of restraint I had to keep from pleading with him again to let me go. That wouldn't work anyway, and I was done with begging.

"Fuck off," I said through clenched teeth.

Gallagher tugged his cap lower on his forehead, then retreated into the dark.

I stared in the direction of his fading steps until I could no longer hear them, then I crawled into one corner of my cage and leaned against the solid aluminum end wall, my knees tucked up to my chest. The diamond-patterned aluminum floor was hard beneath me, and the fresh, shallow claw marks were the only sign of recent occupation by the leopard shifter Ruyle had mentioned.

When my eyes had adjusted to the dim light and shadows, I realized there was a blanket at the opposite end of my cage, half-unfolded from being tossed inside. There was no pillow and no sleeping mat, and I'd been offered neither food nor water. Inmates on death row were treated better.

Of course, inmates on death row had constitutionally guaranteed rights.

I considered the blanket for a few seconds, then I closed my eyes and rested my chin on my knees. It was too hot out to sleep anyway.

"What are you?" The strange voice rumbled softly from the darkness to my left, and my eyes flew open. Two points of light shone from the shadowy depths of the green-and-silver wagon across the aisle from mine.

I stared back at the bright eyes without lifting my chin from my knees.

Metal creaked and the green cage rocked as the weight within it shifted. A man wearing only a thin pair of gray shorts crawled out of the shadowy side of his cage into the area lit by a nearby light pole. Long lines of tight, lean muscle stood out beneath his skin, and each movement he made was smooth and graceful.

"What are you?" he repeated, the words low-pitched and gravelly.

"I'm a person."

"But not a human, or you wouldn't be here. So what are you, really?" A strand of silver hair fell over his gaunt face, hiding one shining eye.

"I don't know. My name is Delilah."

"*Pas plus,*" he said. "Not anymore. They call me Claudio."

"They call you…?" I frowned, considering his odd phrasing. "Is that not what your mother named you?"

"My mother gave me life, and milk, and silver fur and golden eyes, but no true name, other than Little Gray Pup." Those bright eyes blinked again, studying me even as I studied them. "Claudio is the name on my pedigree. It's all I've ever been called."

Little Gray Pup. Claudio.

All at once, I recognized the wolf heads and fleurs-de-lis carved into his wagon frame. "You're the werewolf," I whispered, curling my fingers through the wire mesh. "The girl is your daughter?"

He nodded. "Geneviève."

On the tail of the name, a soft whine came from the dark cage to his right, and I found two more eyes shining at me. No cage stood across from the pup's. Mine was the last in my row.

"Go back to sleep, Genni," her father whispered, but affection softened his voice. The lights winked out when his daughter closed her eyes and I realized that because of the solid end panels, I could see into her cage from across the aisle, though he could not. But I couldn't tell from those two lights in the dark whether she was in human or canine form.

"Merci." Claudio's words were so soft I almost mistook them for the rustle of cloth from the cage to my right. "For what you did for her. Thank you," he repeated. "I am so very sorry for what it cost you."

. . . I didn't know what to say. His daughter was the reason my life had been ripped from me, but I didn't feel worthy of his gratitude. I'd made no conscious decision to act on Geneviève's behalf. I'd had no idea what I could do, or what I would be sacrificing. I hadn't acted, I'd merely reacted.

I was no martyr.

For a long time, I stared at the end panel of my own cage, too overwhelmed to truly focus on anything. I was listening to the snorts and shuffles of the unseen assortment of my fellow exhibits, assuming Claudio had fallen asleep, when his gravelly voice floated toward me again from across the aisle.

"The mystery of your species is a blessing, Delilah." My

name sounded foreign and beautiful, graced with his French accent and the lupine depth of his voice. "Do not rush to solve it."

"Why not?" I whispered, as his eyes flashed at me in the dark.

"It costs them less to breed new exhibits than to buy them, but they will not try to breed what they cannot identify."

Horror rolled over me in overlapping waves, and my crate seemed to rock like a boat at sea. Psychosomatic vertigo.

"Is that how you...how you got Geneviève?"

"And the four before her, each sold when they got too big for the petting zoo. She's the only one they've let me keep."

But he'd lost her mother. Grief was thick in his voice, and his pain made me ache deep, deep inside, both for his bleak past and for my own grim future.

Claudio retreated farther into his cage, and the rustle of rough fabric and the creak of metal told me he was curling up on his blanket to reclaim slumber.

DELILAH

I was still wide-awake, the werewolf's horrific warning echoing in my mind, when the sun rose to shine on my new hell. The only improvement morning brought was daylight, and after twenty minutes of starkly illuminated clarity, I decided I preferred the dark.

Daylight made it impossible to miss the filth caked into the seam where the floor of my cage joined the end panels, or the ribs showing through Geneviève's skin, even in wolf form. Or how the cheetah—werecheetah?—in the cage on Claudio's other side was missing several patches of fur, which was how I discovered that in cat form, her skin was patterned just like her fur.

The sun still hung low and heavy on the eastern horizon when the rest of the carnival came to life. The tantalizing scents of bacon and coffee reminded me that I hadn't eaten since dinner the night before.

"Flags up!" a woman's voice shouted.

When I pressed my face against the wire mesh side of my cage, daylight showed me what the night had hidden. A young woman in an apron stood in front of an arrangement of plastic tables and folding metal chairs, setting out salt and pepper shakers.

Behind her, a large man in an apron manned an open-sided food truck, scrambling eggs and flipping bacon.

At the woman's cry, a steady procession of Metzger's employees began meandering past the rows of caged chattel toward the scent of breakfast. They formed a line—half of them large men in red polo shirts—and filled trays with heaping portions of steaming food. Coffee was poured, knives and forks clanked, and boisterous conversation rose above it all.

"Don't start drooling yet," a raspy female voice said, and I turned to find one of the cheetah shifters—now in human form—watching me from the black-and-silver cage wagon to the right of Claudio's. She was small and delicately built with smooth dark skin and a tiny waist, and she had the most beautiful orange-gold eyes I'd ever seen. According to the plaque wired to her crate, her name was Zyanya. "We don't get bacon and eggs from the pie car. Not for free anyway."

Pie car?

I decided not to ask what "not for free" meant.

"I wasn't expecting them to share." I turned back to watch the buffet line. "But I *had* kind of assumed the staff would live on corn dogs and fried Twinkies. That's what I'd eat if *I* lived in the carnival. Under other circumstances," I added with a glance at the cage floor beneath me.

"What's a Twinkie?"

That time when I turned back to the row of carts across from mine, I found Geneviève watching me with her knees tucked up to her chest, tangled golden hair hiding most of her small body like a curtain.

"Um. It's a little yellow cake filled with cream. When they're deep-fried, the outside gets crunchy, and the middle is all gooey and sweet. I'd pick a fried Twinkie over scrambled eggs any day." But I realized from the puzzled look in her golden wolf eyes that a child raised in a cage had probably never tasted either.

"Junk food comes from the grease carts, which are part of the carnival, not part of the menagerie," another woman's voice called, but her wagon was too far down the line for me to see. "They don't open until the gates open."

"Who's speaking?" I asked, my face pressed to the wire mesh.

"That's Lenore," Zyanya said, running one hand through her short-cropped dark curls. "One of the sirens. Before she was exposed, she used to sing at some county fair in Alabama."

"Mississippi," Lenore corrected. "Then one day I got sloppy, and they pulled me offstage and locked me up."

"You grew up human?" I *really* wished I could see her.

"I grew up *passing* for human," she said. "All it took was a good pair of contact lenses and a little self-control. But nothing good lasts forever, right?" The bitterness in her voice was an eerie echo of my own.

She'd grown up hiding in plain sight, and I'd never known I needed to. Lenore and I were two sides of the same doomed coin.

The staff members ate quickly, and as each stood to return his empty tray, another stepped forward to claim the open seat. Neither Chris Ruyle nor Rudolph Metzger appeared. Neither did Gallagher. Obviously the management took its meals apart from the common rabble.

As crew members passed the line of cage carts on their way back from breakfast, most stopped to stare at me. I could only stare back at them, bitterly aware that twenty-four hours earlier, my life might have made most carnies jealous, but now they looked at me like people look at dogs in the pound. As if I *might* bite, but I'd *definitely* give them fleas.

From bits of overheard conversation, I discovered they were placing bets not just on how long I would last in the carnival after my "free-range raising," but on what my species would turn out to be.

After breakfast, I watched the aproned man and woman clean up the pie car, while a steady procession of performers wandered past my cage on their way onto the fairgrounds to rehearse. Without their costumes, makeup, and equipment, I couldn't match most of them with their acts, but I passed at least half an hour trying to.

Around midmorning, I recognized the heavy clank of horse trailers being opened from farther down the rows of carts, followed by the clomp of hooves first on metal ramps, then on earth. Those were sounds I knew well, having grown up on a farm, and I could tell from the absence of equine snorts and whinnies that the handlers weren't unloading actual horses.

Minutes later, several handlers led a line of six centaurs by my crate, and I couldn't help but stare.

They were beautiful.

Regal and proud, despite the chains and the drugged glaze of their eyes, the centaurs marched on four strong horse legs with their human shoulders squared and heads held high. The first two were Belgians, thick and powerful, their builds capable of heavy labor—a fact the staff would no doubt exploit. They shared the same dark brown coat, smooth, tan human skin, and stark blond hair, and after a closer glance at their nearly identical square chins and straight noses, I concluded that the first two centaurs were brothers. Or maybe cousins.

After the Belgians came a beautiful white Arabian, who looked almost delicate following the draft horses. She had dark eyes, fine, sculpted features, and long white hair that fell down her back to the juncture of her human and equine halves. Unlike the bare-chested men of her species, she wore an elastic sports bra of the same drab gray as my dress.

I couldn't identify the breeds of the fourth and fifth centaurs, one male, the other female, but the sixth was unlike anything I'd ever seen. He was a hybrid of man and what appeared to be white-tailed deer, based on the distinctive reddish-brown summer coat and white underside of his tail. His human half—well, one-third—was elegantly muscled with a dramatically thick neck, obviously necessary to support the massive six-pointed antlers growing from his otherwise human head.

I couldn't imagine where they kept him. His rack wouldn't fit into a standard horse trailer.

Each pair of centaurs was led by a single handler, and though the men holding the ropes were roughly half the size of the captives they escorted, the centaurs showed no inclination to resist. That was surely due, at least in part, to whatever drug had slowed their steps and glazed their eyes.

I watched the deer-man until he passed out of sight. I'd never studied anything like him in school.

"What is that last one called?" I asked, turning to Claudio, and I was almost ashamed of the interest ringing in my own voice. It was that very curiosity that supported the market for exploitative shows like the menagerie in the first place.

Claudio started to answer, but Zyanya beat him to the punch, blinking orangish cat eyes at me from her cage. "He's a cervuscentaur. The ringmaster says it every night in his spiel. The proper name for the others is actually hippocentaur."

I'd known that much. *Hippo* was the Greek word for *horse*.

On the heels of the centaurs came a line of four satyrs, which—unlike centaurs—walked upright on only one set of furry, hoofed legs. Led by a single handler, they were linked by a chain running through cuffs around their goat legs. My heart ached for them, bound together like slaves, clad only in flimsy loincloths, and my sympathy was compounded when I noticed that their ankles had been rubbed free of fur by the padded leg irons.

The satyrs were much smaller than the centaurs and couldn't carry a pack-load, but I had no doubt they would be used as beasts of burden.

As the satyrs passed, I heard the squeal of unoiled wheels, followed by the light clang of metal, which I recognized from the fold-down panel Gallagher had opened in order to remove my cuffs the night before.

When Claudio perked up in his cage, staring eagerly down the aisle, I realized that our breakfast was being served—absent the scents of coffee and bacon.

While I sat cross-legged in my wheeled pen, a new sound arose so subtly it took me a moment to realize I'd been hearing it for at least thirty seconds.

There was a thudding. A repetitive, earthy thunk, like a hammer striking the ground over and over. The sound came closer and closer, and when Gallagher stepped into sight holding a thick rope, I blinked, surprised.

He adjusted his red cap without even a glance in my direction.

A second later, the minotaur appeared, led by Gallagher's rope, tied around a copper ring piercing his bovine nose. I fell back onto my heels in astonishment. He was huge.

Eryx. I remembered his name from the posters nailed up all over town, and the minotaur was easily reminiscent of the mountain he was named for.

He was at least seven feet tall, and easily half again as wide as Gallagher, from shoulder to shoulder. Eryx stood on two powerful legs, neither fully bovine nor human, but some combination that merged huge hooves and shaggy brown hair with a mostly upright skeletal structure and the heavy musculature necessary to support such a massive creature.

His chest and arms were human, enormously muscled, and deeply tanned from years spent laboring under the sun, clothed in nothing but a much larger version of the satyrs' loincloth. The shaggy brown hair began again on his colossal human shoulders and thickened all the way over a massively muscled neck before growing thinner and shorter over his bovine head. Above and behind a drooping set of cow ears grew a pair of curved, whitish horns so thick at their base that I could hardly have wrapped both hands around them.

I stared with my mouth hanging open, only dimly aware that the thudding was the sound of the minotaur's hooves hitting the ground. I must have made some noise, because Eryx stopped, his long tail stirring dust on the ground. His heavily lashed, brown-eyed gaze met mine, and I recognized surprise in the widening of his oddly expressive eyes.

His eyes were human.

When the slack in the lead rope tugged on his nose ring, the minotaur snorted and tossed his head.

Gallagher stopped and looked back. "Eryx," he called to the minotaur. But he was looking at me.

The bull-man snorted, then he turned to follow his handler, leaving me to stare after them both.

"He's something, isn't he?"

I jumped, startled by the disembodied voice. Chris Ruyle, the lot supervisor, stepped into sight from the end of my cage. He leaned with one shoulder against the steel frame and I scooted back to put as much space between us as possible.

"One of only three mature male minotaurs in the country. The old man paid a quarter mil for him three years ago, and he costs a fucking fortune to feed. Draws a real crowd, though." Ruyle pulled a stick of gum from his pocket and unwrapped it, then dropped the sliver of paper on the ground. "He's not as tall as a giant, but he weighs more than one. Something about bone density and muscle mass. Guess how much he eats. Go on, guess," he insisted, but I only stared back at him. "That big bastard eats fifteen pounds of high-protein feed a day, just to maintain his size. Fortunately, he pulls his own weight, and then some. No machine built can raise a tent better or faster than a minotaur. Pound for pound, they're stronger than an elephant and easier to control than a giant."

"Fascinating," I said, and though I was actually fascinated, I let nothing but boredom leak into my voice.

"If you think about it, he's the perfect menagerie freak. He works hard, brings in customers, and never talks back. Or at all, for that matter."

"He can't speak?" The question flew out before I could swallow it, in spite of my determination to show no interest.

"Nothing but snorts and *mooooos*. Which is just as well, considering there's nothing really going on up here." He tapped his own skull, and I refrained from pointing out the irony in the gesture. "His brain is more cow than man. Eryx may be as big as a giant, but he's as simpleminded as a child."

"Children are universally young, not universally stupid," I mumbled.

"Enough about the bull." The supervisor's grin chilled me from the inside out. "Today's your big day."

"Emancipation?" I swiped one arm across my brow. "Whew! That was fast."

"Exhibition. Tonight you get to show the hometown crowd the real you."

My arms tightened around my knees. "I won't perform."

Ruyle stepped so close to the cage that the wire mesh brushed the tip of his nose. His gaze hardened. "You *will* perform, because if you're no use to the menagerie, the old man won't care much if the quality of your care…declines." His gaze held mine long enough to punctuate the less-than-subtle threat, then he glanced over my shoulder when something rattled on the other side of my cage. "Breakfast!" He made a face at whatever was being served behind me. "I'm more of a waffles-and-sausage man, myself, but you know what they say about beggars, right?"

Ruyle wandered away, whistling, and I turned to see Clyde, the mustached handler I'd met the night before, pushing a large stainless steel cart in the aisle between the two rows of cage wagons. He stopped in front of Zyanya and scooped a bloody serving of raw meat onto a plastic tray, then slid it through the fold-down panel in the side of the cheetah-shifter's cage.

Zyanya snatched the tray and set it on the floor of her pen. She growled softly as she ripped into a sloppy cut of raw meat with human hands and teeth that must have been at least part-feline. While I watched her in equal parts disgust and fascination, Clyde served two more carts in line with my own, then gave small, bloody portions of meat to both Geneviève and her father.

Finally, the handler parked his cart in front of my cage and pulled a clipboard from a slot next to the trays. He ran one finger down a list I couldn't see, then nodded to himself, replaced the clipboard, and pulled one of the last three trays from the stack. "They don't know what you are yet, so you get a little bit of everything."

Clyde pulled a slice of white bread from an open bag and dropped it onto the largest compartment. He dipped a small plastic bowl into a stainless steel tub of water on top of his cart, then set it in the tray compartment designed for a cup. Then he scooped two small chunks of cooked meat from the center tub onto my tray and opened the panel in the side of my cage.

Clyde shoved the tray at me. Water sloshed over the edge of the bowl and soaked into my bread.

I grabbed the tray before it could fall, and my stomach growled in spite of the unappetizing nature of the meal. "What is this?" I poked at a dark blob of meat with one finger, because I hadn't been given any utensils.

Clyde glanced at my tray. "Looks like…turkey kidney. And maybe a chunk of liver."

I gagged and set the tray on the floor of my pen. I'd never been able to stomach organ meat.

"Oh, you're too good for innards?" Clyde slammed the lid on the center serving compartment. "That shit's full of vitamins and packed with calories. You really gonna waste perfectly good meat little Genni over there would be grateful for?"

I glanced past Clyde to see that the werewolf pup—still in human form—had finished her meal and was licking her semi-clawed fingers clean.

"Give it to her." I turned back to the handler. "No reason for it to go to waste."

Clyde looked at me as if I'd lapsed into Greek. "You want to give away your breakfast?"

"Just the meat. She needs it worse than I do anyway." I pushed my meal toward the closed panel, and he shrugged, then opened it. When I slid the tray halfway out, he scooped up the liver and kidney with one hand, then shoved the tray back at me and slammed the panel shut.

The handler crossed the aisle to the pup's crate, and my heart ached when the wolf-girl sat up, her golden-eyed gaze eagerly glued to the meat in his hand.

"Your new neighbor has a gift for you, Genni." Clyde held up the turkey organs, and Geneviève's mouth fell open, her attention still tracking the meat.

The handler's fist closed and he squeezed until dark red bits of turkey oozed between his fingers. When his hand opened, the meat fell to the ground in front of Genni's cage. "Don't forget to thank her," he stage-whispered to the young were-wolf. Then he wiped his messy fist on a towel hanging from the cart and pushed the whole thing back down the aisle without even a glance back at me.

Genni's howl followed him.

Her hunger echoed deep within my soul.

Eryx

The minotaur stood in the shade of the brightly striped big top tent, chewing tasteless feed pellets and watching flies crawl on a pile of dung dropped by one of the centaurs when his handler refused to give him a bathroom break. The carnival staff tended to forget that hybrids were as much human as they were beast, but that wasn't the biggest blind spot in humanity's collective psyche.

Eryx had long ago realized that the only true difference between the hybrids and most of their handlers was that the handlers hid their beasts on the inside. A wolf will growl to warn that it's angry and a bull will paw the ground before charging. Rattlesnakes rattle, cats moan and hiss, and hyenas grunt and cackle. But a man will smile right in your face as he drives a knife into your heart.

Such was the nature of humanity, as Eryx understood it.

When the minotaur reached for his feed pail, his chain clanked and he glanced in annoyance at the big iron leash fastened to the cuff above his right hoof.

As he chewed, the groan of metal and the clomp of hooves drew his gaze to the somber procession passing the big top. It took all four satyrs to pull Finola and Lenore in their wheeled cage, though both sirens were more bone than flesh, lately. But the sirens didn't interest him. Neither did the succubi who followed, Zarah and Trista—twisted sisters, from twin birthing cries to shared cages, customers, and comforts. Nor did the two succubi in the cage behind them, whose names he'd never cared to remember. A pair of centaurs hauled each of their cages, but it was the fourth cart in line—the one pulled by the buck and the Arabian—that captured Eryx's attention.

Rommily.

Her name echoed in his heart and his chest ached when he saw her.

She sat between her sisters, Mirela and Lala, all three on their knees, one colorful skirt flowing into the next on the floor of their cage. Rommily's hair was long and dark, loose curls pulled into looser waves by their own weight, and he knew exactly what those waves would smell like, if he'd been close enough to catch the hot breeze blowing through her crate.

The interactive exhibits were bathed nearly every day. They were groomed, and perfumed, and styled, because they would have personal contact with the customers, the very thought of which made Eryx's fist clench around a handful of feed pellets, grinding them into powder.

He let the pulverized protein slide through his grip into the massive feed pail, then he set the bucket on the ground and bent to drink from the trough filled just for his use, because a minotaur could not easily utilize a cup, bowl, or fountain.

Eryx had never minded the trough, but the other limitations of his bovine features bothered him more with every passing day. Sometimes the inability to speak seemed much crueler a constraint than the chains, harness, and cage that restricted his every movement.

Though the bull's muzzle was not suited to human speech, his eyes and ears functioned perfectly.

When he stood, wiping water from his snout with the back of one thick hand, Rommily and her sisters were gone, headed to the tent where Mirela and Lala would read palms and tell fortunes once the carnival opened. Rommily was no use inside the tent since the night they'd found her wandering in the rain, so she stood outside with the talker, one ankle chained to a tent stake, a living advertisement for what customers would find inside.

Even separated from them by a wall of canvas, she was never far from her sisters, a blessing Eryx knew she cherished, even if she could no longer clearly express such thoughts. He could see it in the way she clung to Mirela's hand when they chained her. In the way she whispered frantic, likely impenetrable secrets to Lala as their handler unlocked the cage. Rommily no longer had lucidity, but she still had her sisters.

Eryx had never met another minotaur. He'd never even seen another of his species in person, except for his mother. Though sometimes he could remember her smell and her warmth and the feel of her coarse hair when he awoke from dreams of her, he had no clear mental image of what she looked like. He didn't even know her name.

The minotaur's earliest true memory was of a box, big and rough, with splinters that dug into his fingers and the sharp points of errant nails that slashed at his face when the floor pitched and tossed him into the sides of his confinement.

He'd spent three days in that crate with only a blanket, a few bottles of water he didn't know how to drink from, and a contraption that dispensed feed pellets when he pressed on a big blue button. Sometimes he heard human voices, but more often he heard bleats, and neighs, and whinnies, and even the occasional hiss. Eryx lost control of his bladder on the second day and he was mortified by the accident, but there was no one around to see him hang his head and ram his infant horns against the sides of the box when he could find no other way to express his distress.

When the floor had finally stopped tilting, he'd heard voices and felt the rumble of a truck beneath his box. Then the world had stilled around him, and there'd been a great squeal of nails being pried loose as one side of the crate was forced open. Daylight had blinded him as a chorus of aahs rang out from around the box. An instant later, small, eager arms had enfolded him. Eryx blinked as the child who'd embraced him dragged him onto a sunlit lawn bedecked with streamers and balloons, scattered with people in lavish clothes eating cake from little glass plates.

Rodney had turned six the day he received Eryx as a birthday present, but already the three-year-old minotaur outweighed him by fifty pounds.

Twenty-five years, eight hundred pounds, and three owners later, Eryx had yet to meet another of his own species or spend more than five minutes at a time unrestrained, but on his good days, he could almost remember little Rodney's last name. On the great days, he remembered the stories Rodney had read to him, and the colorful pictures in his big storybook, and the feel of delicate paper and brittle crayons between fingers that had been as thick and strong as a man's before the bull was five years old.

When the great days came more and more often and the good days began to run one into the next, Eryx had realized that something was changing. He was stronger now. He could feel that with every beat of his massive heart. With every step he took and every breath he drew and every movement of every muscle in his body.

The injections were not working. Not as they had before

anyway. The carefully formulated mix of drugs designed to keep the minotaur, centaurs, and satyrs docile enough to be controlled yet strong enough for heavy labor had ceased to be effective on Eryx. Maybe he had grown, and his handlers had failed to compensate with a higher dosage. Or maybe his body had become so accustomed to the chemical cocktail that it no longer affected him as it once had.

The only thing Eryx was sure of was that no one had noticed the clarity of his focus or the increase in his strength, and he had no intention of letting them. As long as his steps were slow and deliberate and his attention seemed labored, no one would look beyond what they expected to see from the carnival's prized beast of burden.

They wouldn't see what was right beneath their noses until it was far, far too late...

DELILAH

The ground beneath my wagon was strewn with fresh hay, and for the first time since I'd been hauled from the back of the Metzger's van in chains, I couldn't smell manure.

"Where are we?" The tent my cage sat in was about fifteen feet across and square. It was dimly lit by several floor lamps with filmy red shades. A folding screen stood near the back wall of the tent beside two round collapsible tables, each holding a neatly folded red-and-purple bundle of cloth. Tablecloths, I assumed. But I couldn't help thinking they'd make great pillows.

If my exhausted estimation could be trusted, I hadn't slept in twenty-eight hours. I'd had nothing to eat but soggy bread in at least fifteen.

"Please tell me this isn't where the succubi…do their thing," I said with a glance at the red lamps.

Gallagher dragged the third and final table toward the two against the rear wall. "This is the fortune-tellers' tent. The oracles work here—two of them anyway—but they won't need to set up for several hours, so we have a little time." Yet the tense line of his jaw told me that wouldn't be long enough for whatever he had planned.

"I have nothing but time. Literally. I have nothing else."
I sat on my knees on the aluminum floor of my cart to keep
my thin dress from riding up, and the diamond plate pattern
bit into my skin.

Gallagher set the table down with a thump, and when he
turned, his expression was as featureless as a stone wall and
about as yielding. He pulled a cord attached to one canvas
panel and the first of the two open flaps fell closed, cutting
off most of the sunlight within the tent. When he reached for
the second cord, my pulse tripped.

"Don't close that!"

He pulled the cord, and as the last flap fell, the outside world
disappeared, leaving me alone with a man more than twice
my size, whose job description included the phrase "break
Delilah."

He seemed to be looking at me, but I could hardly see him
in the dim lamplight. "We have work to do."

"I won't perform."

"All you have to do is sit there and look...beastly."

I scooted forward until nothing but wire mesh and my
own resolve stood between us. "Even if I knew how to look
beastly—and I don't—I wouldn't play along, and no punishment you can dish out would be worse than putting me on
display like an animal." I sucked in a deep breath and pressed
my palms against the floor of my cage to keep them from
trembling. "Nothing."

Gallagher crossed huge arms over his broad chest, and even
though I was seated in my cage, I still had to look up at him.
"You're wrong about that."

The truly horrible thing was that I believed him. I'd never
been hit or gone hungry. I'd never been electrocuted, robbed,
or even really threatened. The worst things that had ever
happened to me in my life had happened in the past eighteen

hours, and I wasn't naive enough to believe I'd seen the worst the menagerie had to offer reluctant captives.

"But I am a caretaker," Gallagher continued, and I wondered how many of my thoughts he'd been able to read on my face. "My job does not typically include causing pain."

"So, what is your job, exactly?"

"In the menagerie we all have many duties. But in general, I oversee the handlers and make sure the livestock is clean and healthy enough for work—both manual labor and exhibition. *You* are a special assignment. We need to uncover your species and draw it out for the public to see."

"That doesn't sound very pleasant."

Gallagher shrugged. "I don't think I'll have to hurt you."

His pragmatic address of my biggest fear surprised me. He wasn't making a threat; he was making a prediction. But I couldn't take it seriously. Everything that had happened to me since I'd first entered the hybrid tent had hurt in one way or another.

"And why is that?"

"Because I believe you truly don't know how to become the beast we all saw yesterday, and hurting you won't change that." His delivery was so sensible. He'd ruled out abuse because the time and energy spent causing me pain wouldn't be worth expending if it wasn't justified by the desired result.

I couldn't decide whether that made him more or less preferable to Ruyle, who was clearly willing to hurt me just for sport. Or pleasure.

"So, if torture's off the table, what's the plan?"

Gallagher scruffed his red baseball cap back and forth over his dark close-cropped hair. "If we can figure out what you are, we'll know how to trigger your transformation." He glanced at the watch on his wrist. "We really need to get started."

"Repeating the word *we* isn't going to make me feel like

I'm part of some team effort, and neither will playing good cop to Ruyle's bad cop. I'm not going to develop Stockholm syndrome or fall for reverse psychology." I scooted to the back of my cage and sat with my knees tucked up to my chest, my dress pulled down as much as possible to keep me covered. "I'm not going to help you turn me into an exhibit."

Gallagher pulled a chair from beneath one of the tables at the back of the tent and sank into it in front of my cage. The metal groaned beneath his bulk. "If you don't cooperate for me, the old man will assign you to someone else—probably Ruyle or Clyde—and your new handler will likely take his title a lot more literally than I do."

I shrugged, as if that prospect didn't completely terrify me. All I had left was free will. If I let them take that, I would truly have nothing.

"And if that doesn't work, the old man *will* sell you."

"To Vandekamp. I heard." I spread my arms, taking in the entire carnival full of atrocities. "How much worse could his menagerie possibly be?"

Some new bit of understanding settled behind his gray eyes. "Vandekamp doesn't run a menagerie. He keeps a private collection, and everything in it is for rent." Gallagher leaned closer to the cage, and something in his voice—something bleak and raw—kept me from looking away. "The man deals in exotic fetishes, Delilah. Vandekamp will break you, or he will let someone else pay for the privilege," he said, and every piercing word deepened the gash in my soul. "If you don't know how to access your inner monster, you'll have no hope of defending yourself."

I took deep, slow breaths to calm my roiling stomach. "Are you trying to scare me?"

Gallagher stood and threaded his fingers through the wire mesh between us. His grim stare captured mine. "I'm trying to convince you to unlock your arsenal. Why would you damn yourself to the role of victim when you could be scary enough that even if you *do* spend the rest of your life in a cage, no one would *ever* fuck with you?" His grip rattled the steel mesh and his gaze intensified. "I can see the destructive potential in you, Delilah. You're dangerous, and you could unleash that to your own benefit. Let me help you learn how."

You're dangerous. His words echoed in my head, and they made sense. They felt good.

Too good.

I hadn't yet found his weakness, but he'd found mine.

"Smart," I whispered, without breaking his gaze. "Trying to manipulate me into cooperating so I can protect myself." As if that were working for any of the other "dangerous" exhibits.

Gallagher let go of the cage. "You're going to believe whatever you want."

"Yeah. I am." Finally, he seemed to understand the inalienable certainty that had kept me running on no sleep, under threat of starvation, abuse, and exploitation. "That's one liberty you and this circus of inequity can't take from me." The anger slowly smoldering in my chest flared into true flames. "I can believe whatever I want, and unless you muzzle me, I can say whatever I want, and even if you cut out my tongue, I'll write whatever I want on the floor of my cage, in my own blood." I rose onto my knees and gripped the side of my cage. I was high on the truth, and on my own embattled nerve.

"If you cut off my hands, I'll write with my feet, and if you cut off my feet, I'll write with my nose, and if you cut that off, you may as well cut my whole head off, because no matter how you slice and dice me, you can't control what I think, or what I feel. You can keep me locked up for the rest of my life, however brief that may be, but you can never, ever own me. So why don't you march out there and tell Ruyle, and tell

Metzger, and tell the guy who tacks up the posters, and the woman who sews the costumes, and the men who drive the big trucks that the only thing I have to say to any of you tyrannical bastards is *fuck you* and the circus train you rode in on. Now get the hell out of my face. I'm not going to help you."

I sat with my back against the end of my cage, spine straight, and tucked my feet beneath me. My heart hammered so hard it was all I could hear. I'd practically dared him to throw his worst at me, and I was sure I would regret that as soon as the real pain started. But pain and regret couldn't negate the truth, and I'd needed him to hear it as badly as I'd needed to say it.

Gallagher stared at me for a second, and I couldn't read his expression. He took a single step back and his eyes narrowed. "You're your own worst enemy, Delilah. When you decide to put all that passion into self-preservation, you let me know. But you better decide soon, or you'll lose the chance."

Then he turned and pushed his way through the tent flap, leaving me all alone with my thundering rage.

"Maggie, I need you to pull the medical records of every child born in the month of March 1980 and start making copies. The FBI is sending someone over for them this afternoon. If they're requesting records from every hospital in the country, there's bound to be a run on ink drums. Better stock up now."

—Memo from the Health President and CEO of Mercy General, Oklahoma City, dated September 4, 1986

DELILAH

"What is that?" I asked, eyeing several wet smudges of color smeared on a thin plastic board.

"Special effects makeup." A short woman in jeans and a red Metzger's shirt angled her palette so I could see the paint she was blending with a short pointed palette knife. She had spiky purple-and-blond hair, and nails with tiny saber-toothed cat skulls painted on them.

Surely she was as much a work of art as whatever she'd been painting.

One of the rougher handlers, Clyde, shoved me into a dentist-style reclining chair upholstered with as much duct tape as vinyl. My teeth clacked together when I landed and the upholstery creaked beneath me.

"Alyrose used to work in Hollywood." He pinned me down with one thick hand on my sternum while a skinny teenager with a healed-crooked nose cuffed my wrists to the arms of the chair.

Clyde's thumb strayed south of professional contact, and when I tried to object, he pressed harder, leaning with his weight on my chest until I couldn't breathe. I thrashed, rattling the cuffs. My flailing foot hit the kid trying to cuff my ankles to the chair.

Clyde chuckled. "An hour in here, and no one will know what an uncooperative little freak you are." The last cuff clicked closed around my ankle and he stepped back.

I pulled in a desperate breath. When the world rushed back into focus, I found him watching as I recovered from suffering he'd dealt out as casually as he might slap at a buzzing fly.

He was waiting for my reaction.

I shouldn't have taken the bait, but after no sleep and virtually no food, my restraint—fragile from the start—had been compromised. "Can she disguise what a sadistic asshole you are?"

He pulled his fist back, but he didn't look angry; he looked gleeful.

I squeezed my eyes shut, straining against my restraints. Bracing for the blow.

"Clyde!" Alyrose screeched, and I opened my eyes to find her holding him back with both hands, black paint smeared across his forearm. "I don't have the time or the skill to disguise a broken cheekbone. Get out of here. And take Abraxas with you."

Abraxas—the boy with the crooked nose—shuffled backward to stand near the door.

"She's a troublemaker, Aly," Clyde insisted through clenched teeth, glaring at me.

"So am I." She pointed her palette knife at the exit. "Get out."

Clyde pushed the door open. "I'll be right outside." He shoved Abraxas down the narrow porch steps, then followed him and slammed the door at his back.

"Why am I here?" I tried not to struggle against the cuffs, but just knowing I couldn't get up made me desperate to try.

"You're here so I can bring out your inner monster with the aid of a little cosmetic magic." Alyrose squirted dark paste from a thin tube onto her palette. "It's not a long-term solution, but since only a few people have actually seen your transformation, makeup should work for tonight."

"And if I refuse?"

Her smile looked genuine. "Gallagher says you're too smart for that."

Interesting.

While Alyrose blended colors and mixed translucent pastes and gels, I craned my neck to see as much as I could of her narrow, cluttered camper. Garment racks lined two walls, stuffed with clothes in every imaginable color and texture. High on one wall, a shelf was lined with foam mannequin heads, each wearing a different wig in a rainbow of colors, lengths, and styles.

The mallet lump on the side of my skull throbbed when I rolled my head to the side, noticing a small cluttered folding table. Amid piles of ribbons, buttons, straight pins, hot glue sticks, cloth flowers, and lace sat an open laptop, where Alyrose had obviously been designing a new poster for the carnival.

A surgical stand stood next to my chair, its shallow stainless-steel tray full of makeup sponges and brushes laid out as precisely as any surgeon's tools.

"You really worked in Hollywood?"

She closed a bottle of what looked like black paint. "For a little while. I only worked on one movie, though. *Nightmares from Hell.* Did you see it?"

I shook my head, and my hair snagged on a duct tape patch on the side of the headrest.

Alyrose shrugged and set her palette on a small table near my feet. "It went straight to DVD."

"And now you do makeup for the menagerie?"

"Oh, hon, I do *many* things for Metzger's. Money is tight and time is short, so we're all multitaskers. I design and maintain costumes, create posters, help groom the female exhibits where needed, and maintain a running inventory of all the supplies necessary for all of that."

"Do many of the others fake their transformations?"

She laughed. "No, I mostly cover bruises, brighten pale skin, and lighten dark circles. Sometimes I exaggerate trademark features, to make the exhibits look more exotic, but you're the first chance I've had to work real magic in years. Which was Gallagher's idea, of course."

Eagerness emanated from her voice, and as relieved as I was to have temporarily escaped the demand to "transform," I wasn't thrilled to have become Alyrose's new pet project.

She sat on a chair in front of her laptop. A few mouse strokes later, the poster she'd been working on disappeared, and a startling image replaced it. The face on-screen looked familiar, but bizarre.

My breath froze in my throat when I finally recognized the monster as myself.

My irises were *gone*. My eyes were a milky white, shot through with gray veins branching like tree limbs. More veins branched over the skin around my eyes, so dark they were almost black against cheeks so pale my skin might never have seen the light of day. My hair seemed to float around my head in fine tendrils, but I knew that if she'd had video instead of a still shot, those tendrils would be writhing. I'd heard about it. I'd felt it. But until that moment, I hadn't seen it.

It didn't seem possible. Even staring right at the evidence, I couldn't make myself believe what I was seeing.

"Where did you get that?" My voice was a ghost, so thin it seemed to have no substance.

"YouTube. Hasn't gotten many hits yet, so we should be

able to fudge the details a little. I have solid white contacts, but I can't draw veins on them." She spun on her stool to face me, her gaze distant as she thought. "I'd love a few more reference images. Have they figured out what you are yet?"

"No." And I changed my mind nearly every minute about whether or not I wanted to know.

I couldn't turn away from the screen. I looked horrific. Monstrous. "Someone posted this online?" The magnitude of my living nightmare had just exploded.

"Yes, luckily for us." Alyrose rolled her chair toward me, opening an opaque plastic bottle. "We have a strict 'no photography' policy, but it only applies to the exhibits, and you weren't ours yet, so…" She shrugged and squirted pale liquid onto a makeup sponge. "We'll start with your skin tone. Gallagher promised they'll have you dimly lit, and no one will be closer than three feet from you, so I think I can pull this off, if you cooperate. What do you say?"

I nodded, not because I had no choice, though that was basically true, but because she'd *asked*. Maybe treating me like a person was just her brand of manipulation, but as long as she was playing nice, I would do the same.

The alternative, I knew, would involve Clyde.

For the next hour, while she painted me to look like the monster I could hardly believe I was, I lay in Alyrose's repurposed dental chair under bright lights, trying not to feel grateful for the air-conditioning, and the quiet, and the relative solitude, because those were not things they had any right to deny me in the first place.

When the costume mistress was done with my face, she cleaned her equipment in a bathroom I couldn't see from the chair. I stared through an open doorway at an unmade bed and a portable television sitting on a chair. Alyrose's camper was both home and studio. And transportation. Everything she owned fit into those three rooms.

Twenty-four hours earlier, I might have pitied her, but now her meager assets represented wealth and luxury I could never again attain.

As low as personal possessions ranked on the list of things I'd lost, I couldn't help missing my clothes, and my shoes, and my bed.

I no longer owned anything but thoughts and memories, and with each minute that passed, I volleyed between outrage and grief over my loss.

Alyrose came back, wiping her wet hands on a clean white cloth, and made several more swipes on her computer track pad. The image of my face on her screen was replaced with an image of me from the waist up, facing away from the camera, my hands raised, as if I were reaching for something. Jack, the handler with the cattle prod, stood between me and Genni's cage, mostly blocked from view by my body and hands.

She pressed a button on her keyboard, and the picture got bigger. Two clicks later, the screen showed only my pixelated right arm and the left side of Jack's face, blessedly blurred beyond recognition. "I can't get much detail from this, but it's the best shot I could find of your hands and arms. On the bright side, no one else will have a more accurate image to compare to the final product."

Alyrose turned from her computer and picked up a narrow, shallow box from the table, then rolled closer to me in her chair. She opened the hinged top of the box and tilted it so I could see several long, thin, sharply pointed pieces of black plastic, textured like finely grained wood. "These are your new fingernails."

"What are they?"

She set the box down and lifted one of the pieces into the

light. "They're resin special-effects claws from a haunted house I worked on several years ago. They may be a little big, but we can trim them to fit, and in dim lighting, they should do the trick. But once we get them on, you're not going to be able to use your hands."

I shrugged, which was awkward with my wrists secured to the arms of the chair. "It's not like they let us play cards."

Holding one of the claws and a tube of theatrical glue, Alyrose frowned down at my fingers. "If I uncuff you one wrist at a time, are you going to be a problem?"

I shook my head. I *would* get a chance to escape—the universe owed me that—but one uncuffed hand wasn't going to do it.

Alyrose asked Clyde for the key to my cuffs, but he refused to hand them over on the grounds that I was dangerous and deceitful. She shut him up with the assertion that if I knew how to become a monster, her services wouldn't be required in the first place.

Clyde uncuffed my left hand, but refused to leave the trailer while only three of my four limbs were restrained.

She scowled up at him from her stool. "Why don't you see if Ruyle has approved her wardrobe? I can't get her dressed without her costume."

"I'm not leaving you alone with her."

Alyrose's thin paintbrush clattered onto the surgical tray. "I dress the oracles and sirens all the time with no one but Abraxas here to help, and nothing's ever gone wrong."

"They're trained, and sedated, and predictable, because they know their place. This bitch is dangerous and delusional, and the old man won't let us drug her until we know what she is. You should have seen her last night, trying to bargain with Gallagher, like this is some damn hotel and we're the staff sent to wait on her! She wasted half her breakfast this morning because she thinks she's too good for organ meat, and—"

"I didn't waste it, I tried to donate it. *You* threw it on the ground!"

Clyde flushed. "One more word and I will muzzle you!"

"A muzzle would ruin the makeup," I pointed out, thrilled by the opportunity to strip away his choices.

Suddenly Clyde's broad form loomed over me, backlit by the lights shining down at my chair. His face came closer, stale coffee breath wafting over me, and I was suddenly, absurdly aware that I hadn't brushed my own teeth in almost twenty-four hours. "What part of 'sold to the menagerie' do you not understand?"

His rage fed my reckless euphoria. He couldn't stand having his authority challenged, and that made him easy to manipulate.

I was in chains, but *he* was losing control.

"The legality. The iniquity. The reality." I shrugged again. "I don't understand any of it, really."

"Well, let me help you out with that. You don't decide how food gets distributed." His fists slammed into the arms of the chair, and I flinched as the entire structure shuddered beneath me. "You eat what you're given or you go hungry. You do what you're told, or you go hungry." He grabbed my arms and lifted me until the cuffs cut into my wrists, and that's when I realized I'd poked the bear a little too hard.

I had the power to piss him off, but not the power to calm him down.

Terror squeezed my eyes shut.

"If that isn't enough to keep you in line, you better get used to this chair, because Alyrose will be covering up your bruises *every damn day*."

"Clyde," Alyrose scolded, while I stared at the back of

my own eyelids, trying to stop shaking. I was certain with every passing second that he was about to punch a hole right through my face.

Instead, he drove his fist into my stomach so hard that for a moment, I was aware of nothing but pain.

My body tried to curl around the agony spreading through my midsection, but the cuffs prevented that. Tears filled my eyes, then ran over, and I was left gasping for air I couldn't use.

"Now look at her eye makeup!" Alyrose cried, but I hardly heard her.

I couldn't make sense of this violent new existence, where terms like *justice* had no meaning, *bondage* was a state of existence, and *hell* was the forecast for the rest of my life. One word began to play over and over in my head. It was the most powerful word I'd ever known, yet the most worthless syllable ever to be uttered by someone wearing more chains than actual clothing.

No. No. No. No. No…

I sucked in a breath, then lost it on the tail of a sob that racked my entire body. The physical reality of defiance had come as a shock. It turns out that expecting pain can't really prepare you for it.

"Clyde. That's enough." Alyrose's voice was soft, but firm. "Get the hell out of my camper and go track down her costume."

I couldn't see him with my eyes squeezed shut, but I could measure his fury by the strength of each puff of breath that hit my face. For several tense seconds, he loomed over me, and I was afraid he'd take another shot.

But finally he stood. My chair rocked with the release of the armrests, but I kept my eyes closed as the camper door squealed open. His footsteps became heavier and more solid against the wooden steps outside.

"Get in there and keep an eye on that cryptid," Clyde said, and when the door slammed shut behind him, I opened my eyes to find Abraxas staring at me, wide-eyed, as if he were afraid to look away even long enough to blink.

I exhaled, and my heart finally stopped trying to beat a hole through my sternum. My entire midsection felt hot and swollen.

"Well, you certainly haven't made a friend out of Clyde." Alyrose picked up her paintbrush and returned to the dark veins she'd been tracing on the back of my left hand.

"Does he have *any* friends?" My voice sounded weak. It still hurt to breathe.

She shrugged. "He's kind of an ass, but he's good at what he does."

What he does?

"Is he the source of the bruises you cover up?"

Alyrose's tiny paintbrush stilled midstroke. "Some, yes." She sat up and rolled her chair toward my head until she could look straight down into my eyes. "Delilah, it's okay to pick your battles. Clyde doesn't forgive or forget easily, and provoking him will only get you hurt."

"So you think I should shut up and do as I'm told?" No surprise there.

"I think that the sooner you accept reality, the easier your life will become."

And that was the problem. As nice as Alyrose was, she was still human, and she still worked for Metzger's, and the bottom line for her and for everyone else employed by the menagerie was that I wasn't just inhuman, I was *less* than human, therefore unfit for concepts like liberty and justice. The reaping wasn't going to be forgotten anytime soon, and people weren't just angry about it, they were still afraid.

Fear is a powerful, often irrational emotion, and mass fear

on the scale of what followed the reaping has the power to shake any society to its core. As long as the world remembered, they would live in fear of all cryptids—regardless of whether or not any individual among us was truly dangerous.

Of course, not everyone supported stripping cryptids of all rights. But the dissenters were few among a dangerous and violent many, and most found it easy enough to simply ignore the problem—the way someone opposed to animal cruelty could still eat meat, I'd been guilty of that very thing myself. I'd abandoned the idea of becoming a crypto-vet because I didn't want to participate in the cruelty. But then I'd just come home and ignored the problem.

Looking at Alyrose and Abraxas, I realized that even some of the menagerie staff seemed to be doing the same thing. They weren't all hurting the captives, but neither were they trying to change anything.

Submission was the only solution they could conceive of to fix my problem. But with the imprint of Clyde's fist still throbbing in my stomach, I was much less interested in fixing a problem than in becoming one.

ROMMILY

The oracle curled her toes, and dirt squished between them. She liked standing up. She liked walking and staring up at the sun, turning her face into the breeze, even if the breeze was hot and dry.

Rommily lifted her arms, letting the wind blow through her hair and caress her fingers and make a whooshing noise in her ears. The crowd around her stilled as patrons watched the girl in the bright skirt, a matching handkerchief tied over the top of her head, her golden-brown gaze fixed on the sky. Adults stared and children pointed at her chains, their only clue—absent the white eyes that accompanied a prophesy—that the oracle dressed as a fortune-teller was a captive of the menagerie rather than a flamboyantly dressed patron.

Rommily could hardly feel the chains. She could hardly see the crowd or smell the popcorn. She didn't hear her handler when he told her to step back, but Kevin was used to her unfocused eyes and wandering steps, so he took her by the shoulders and guided her back into her usual spot against the front of the tent.

Even lost in the labyrinth of her own mind, as she'd been since that night in the rain, she understood that Kevin wasn't truly focused on her. She'd had a bad morning. Rommily had vague memories of screaming, and hands, and a sharp prick in her arm. But she was generally very little trouble for Kevin, and when neither Ruyle nor Gallagher was watching, his attention tended to wander toward the siren tent across the midway.

The canvas at Rommily's back rustled in the wind, but the stakes had been driven deep and the material was too heavy to truly ripple or flap.

Several feet away, the talker was well into his ballyhoo, the rise and fall of his words designed to pull people into the tent, where they would sit across a small round table from a pretty oracle whose chains were hidden by long skirts and colorful tablecloths. Mirela and Lala would look into the customers' eyes and hold their hands, then deliver some small glimpse into the future.

Your next child will be a girl.

Your boss will recommend you for a promotion.

Your wife will find her lost wedding ring.

The oracles saw much more than they were allowed to say, because revealing that the new baby will have spina bifida, the boss's recommendation will be overruled, and the ring will be found in the neighbor's bed would have a discouraging effect on the cash flow.

Rommily used to sit in one of those chairs and sell incomplete information to people she would never meet again. But the things she saw now could not be sold, even if there'd been no fracture between her visions and her ability to express them.

A small boy stopped in front of her and reached for the chain stretched between her feet. His father pulled him away, then met Rommily's suddenly white-eyed gaze.

Her eyes narrowed. "Blood poisoning," she whispered. "Bacteremia."

The man picked up his child and hurried away from the fortune-tellers' tent.

"Hush, Rommily," her handler said into her ear, tugging on the cuff of one black leather glove. "You'll drive away the customers." He knew better than to look into her eyes or touch her bare skin.

Rommily heard Kevin, but the sounds falling from his lips meant no more to her than the shuffle of shoes on sawdust, the crackle of a paper hot-dog wrapper, or the excited screams from the Zipper.

She took a step forward, and the chain connecting her ankles left a trail in the dirt. A woman with orange-streaked hair glanced up from her fried pie and met Rommily's eerily blank gaze.

"Pneumonia," the oracle whispered, and Kevin took her by the arm.

A boy with a pimple on his chin tried to snatch a bite of his girlfriend's ice cream cone, and when she pulled it out of reach, the back of her right hand bumped Rommily's bare arm.

"Cancer," the oracle said.

The girl frowned at her. "What?"

"Brain. Left hemisphere. Inoperable. There's nothing we can do. I'm so sorry."

Startled, the girl dropped her ice cream and ran into the crowd, leaving her boyfriend to chase her, but by then, more people were looking at Rommily.

"Fire," she said to a woman wearing jeans a size too small, then Rommily's focus skipped from face to face in the gathering crowd. "Collision. Heart failure. Suicide." She didn't know what all the words meant, but she heard them clearly, as they would one day—decades later, in many cases—be spoken

202

to grieving friends and family members. "Aneurism. Natural causes. Overdose. Cirrhosis. Cardio—"

"That's enough!" Kevin pulled Rommily back against the tent and stepped in front of her to draw her attention from the crowd. For one fleeting instant, he accidentally looked into her strange, blank eyes.

"Multiple gunshot wounds to the torso," she whispered, and her eyes filled with tears.

"I know." His gaze fell to her chin and he dropped her arm. "You've told me."

"Running, and screaming, and blood."

"Rommily…"

"This is the man all tattered and torn, that kissed the maiden all forlorn." She put one finger beneath his chin and pushed up, trying to make him look at her, but Kevin swatted her hand away.

"Ruyle won't be happy if I have to put you back in your cage, and I don't think you will be either."

The oracle's mouth snapped closed, and a tear rolled down her cheek. The talker lured a few bystanders into the fortune-tellers' tent, promising 100 percent accuracy, and the crowd began to flow again.

Rommily was quiet for a while, and Kevin's attention began to roam. People wandered in and out of the tent, buzzing excitedly over Mirela's and Lala's predictions, and the sun continued to sink slowly toward the horizon.

When the wind died down and the sun slid behind the siren's tent, casting Rommily in shadow, she began to fidget with the folds on her skirt and shuffle her bare feet. Something was coming. She could feel it before she saw it, and when the bull rounded a curve in the midway, pulling a cart draped with stained canvas, led by the handler in a red baseball cap, Rommily began to wring her hands.

As the cart passed, its rear wheel bumped over a rut in the path and a seam in the canvas fell open. Half of a pale, black-veined face appeared in the gap, and a single cloudy white eye met the oracle's similar gaze.

A sudden onslaught of images sucked the air from Rommily's lungs and the warmth from her limbs, sending her stumbling into the front of the tent.

"Secret Mary," the oracle said, but the words were too weak to be heard. "Secret Mary!" she shouted, and people turned to stare. Kevin reached for Rommily with one gloved hand, but she pulled away from him, still focused on the canvas-covered cart. "Princess Sara. Jane, and Pip, and Oliver."

The bull stopped pulling, and the cart sat still on the midway while Kevin tried to rein in his charge, and still that white eye stared through the gap in the canvas.

As her handler tugged her into the tent, Rommily's shrill cry echoed into the crowd, and beyond.

"Fate's bastards, every one, and you least among them!"

DELILAH

"The makeup and claws are bad enough." Gluing the claws on had ruined my recent manicure, erasing the only remaining evidence that I'd ever been anything other than an animal in a cage. Only the threat of being placed under Clyde's supervision kept me from ripping the prosthetics from the ends of my fingers and scrubbing my face clean on the hem of my dress.

I'd told myself that cooperation wasn't submission; it was survival. But there was a limit to what I would endure in silence. "I won't wear that, and you can't make me."

"Wrong on both counts." Gallagher closed the tent flap, and that time I was actually relieved to be free of the curious, invasive gazes from carnival staff passing behind the tent in the makeshift alley that served as a supply path during business hours. He hung the black dress on the outside of my cage. But "dress" was a label the costume didn't deserve. It was more like scraps of black satin held together with sequins and a prayer.

"Really?" I propped my hands on my hips, careful of the fake claws, and challenged him with one arched brow. "I guess you could knock me out or sedate me and change my clothes for me, but don't you think the customers would be disappointed to find your shiny new exhibit lying unconscious on the floor of her cage?"

Gallagher's grim scowl was inspiration enough for me to continue.

"Or you could try to wrestle me into that thing the hard way, but Alyrose won't have time to repair any damage done to her masterpiece." I held my painted arms out for emphasis, and the glare from the light mounted on the center pole flashed on the tips of my fake claws. "You really should have made me change before she spent all that time and effort on makeup."

"I would have, if Ruyle had signed off on the costume in time." Gallagher stepped closer to the cage, but the bill of his cap left his face deeply shadowed. "You have to put the costume on, Delilah."

But we both knew the only card he had left to play was the violence card, and for no reason I could understand, he still hadn't laid it on the table.

Maybe his humanity ran more than skin-deep.

"Why are you here, Gallagher?"

"Because this is my job, and I *can't* let you get me fired."

But there was something he wasn't saying. His frame was too tense, his jaw too tight.

Gallagher squared his broad shoulders and cleared his throat. "You are out of options. You have to wear the costume. We all have to do things we hate. That's the nature of life."

"This isn't life, it's captivity. What do you hate doing?"

"I hate seeing you caged."

"Right." I sat on my heels. "You're the one keeping me caged."

"That doesn't mean I like it." He tipped his cap back and I could see his eyes, but I couldn't make sense of the visceral conflict I saw in them.

Conflict of what? Ideologies? Or something more personal? Loyalties?

"I hope you *do* find freedom someday, and I hope you tear some heads off in the process," he continued, holding my gaze so that I could see the raw candor in his, along with the risk he took with every word he spoke. "But I won't be the one who lets that happen. I *can't* be the one."

His voice had gone tight and deep, as if the words bruised his throat, and there was something new in his eyes when he said them.

"Because you can't lose this job."

"That's right." His hand settled onto the black satin still hanging from the side of my cage. "Which is why you have to put on this costume."

"I'm not even sure *how* to do that." I studied the scraps of black cloth hanging against the side of my cage, searching for some structure I understood. A skirt. A bodice. A waistline. I saw none of that. "If the audience isn't supposed to see bruises, this thing's going to be a problem."

"Bruises?" Gallagher's brows furrowed, and I realized I should have opened my argument with that.

"Just one, really." I closed my eyes so I wouldn't have to see him look as I lifted the hem of my dress to reveal the dark purple blotch on my stomach.

"Son of a bitch," he growled.

I dropped my hem and opened my eyes to find him scruffing his cap over his hair.

"Clyde?"

I nodded. "Does this mean my exhibit is canceled?" Had I gained a reprieve *and* gotten Clyde in trouble?

But Gallagher shook his head. "We can't cancel your debut. I'll have to find you something more modest to wear."

Modest sounded promising.

He scowled at the skimpy black costume. "I could borrow something, but the oracles wear too much, the sirens too little. Alyrose will know what to do." His scowl deepened as he glanced at his watch. "Sit tight."

"As opposed to prancing down the midway?" I said as he pulled the tent flap back, but he let the canvas fall closed without so much as a smile.

He'd only been gone a few minutes when the tent flap rose again.

"That was fa—" My words tumbled into a tense silence when my gaze fell not on Gallagher, but on Clyde, who was carrying what appeared to be a yard sign, turned away from me.

He laid the sign on a table already piled with boxes and supplies as the canvas fell closed behind him. "Why aren't you dressed?"

"Because my costume won't cover the bruise you left on my stomach." I expected knowledge that his boss was angry to take some of the wind from his sails, but when he only stalked closer to my cage, my confidence wavered. I backed toward the far side of the cart. "Gallagher went to Alyrose for an alternative, but he'll be back any minute. Any second," I amended with a closer look at his face.

Spite rode his features like violence rides a bullet.

"Well, no matter what you'll be wearing, you'll have to come out of that thing first." Clyde eyed the gray dress I still wore. "Why don't we surprise him and take care of that?" He shrugged, faking amiability while my pulse rushed so fast I felt dizzy. "One less thing on his to-do list."

"No," I said, but Clyde was already headed for the table by the closed tent entrance.

He reached for something behind a box on the table and lifted a long black stick with a forked tip and a red handle.

An electric stock prod. Perhaps the very instrument of torture that had landed me in captivity in the first place.

A jolt of fear lit my lungs on fire until I realized the real problem was that I'd stopped breathing.

Clyde carried the prod toward me like a sword. "I'm going to open your cage, and you're going to get out slowly and handcuff yourself to the side. Then I'm going to cuff your other hand, and if you so much as twitch, I will shove this stock prod somewhere where the welt won't show." He flicked the costume with one finger. "No matter what Gallagher brings back, it won't cover much, so my choices are pretty limited."

Air slid in and out of my lungs so fast it couldn't have been much use to the respiratory process.

"Calm down. You'll be fine if you cooperate. Ready?" Clyde pulled a key chain from a clip on his belt. He opened the lock on my cage, then slid the panel back with a metallic clatter. Cattle prod held ready, he tossed a set of handcuffs through the opening at me. "Put that around your right wrist."

"It'll mess up the makeup," I said with as much confidence as I could manage.

"Not if you're careful."

I studied him for a second, looking for any sign that he might hesitate to electrocute me, and when I found none, I clenched my jaw and clicked the metal loop around my right wrist, careful not to damage the prosthetic claws. Clyde was right. The theatrical makeup wouldn't rub off without some serious pressure, and if either of us had to put pressure on my bound arms, I'd have bigger problems than damaged makeup.

"Now crawl out of there and fasten the other cuff through the wire mesh."

Hay crunched beneath my feet, poking at my bare soles. My left hand shook as I secured my right to the front of the cage, but it shook even harder when Clyde slapped half of a second set of cuffs around my left wrist. I resisted instinctively when he tried to pull my arm back, but when he threatened my thigh with the cattle prod, I gave in, biting my lip to hold back the protest poised behind it.

This was payback. The bastard wanted to see my fear, and I would have swallowed my own tongue to hide it from him.

Still wielding the prod, he cuffed my ankles to opposite wheels of the cart, which was only possible because the leg irons were separated by a fifteen-inch length of chain, designed to let prisoners walk.

And just like that, I was bound, spread eagle, to the front of my cage.

Clyde laid the cattle prod on the ground and went back to the table, where he picked up a large pair of scissors.

"Wait. You don't have to do that. Just uncuff me and I'll put the costume on. I swear." I was well beyond caring if it messed up the fake claws or showed off a bruise. Gallagher's threat had been accurate—life with Clyde as my handler would *truly* be hell.

"Shut up and hold still." He knelt in front of me and began slicing up the left side of my thin linen dress.

Fear thickened my tongue. "Won't Alyrose be mad about the damage?"

"Nah." The blade was cold against my hip as it sliced through first the dress, then the side of my underwear. "We got a couple hundred of these, and shit happens, ya know?"

I felt sick thinking of how often "shit" probably happened in the menagerie.

"I bet you had a real nice childhood, didn't you? Good schools? Birthday parties. Vacations. Right?"

My nausea swelled with the realization that Clyde's barbaric lesson actually had a point. And that it was starting to sink in.

I wasn't immune to the realities of life in captivity. The fact that I could read and add and navigate a map didn't make me the exception; it made me an object lesson. A target for all the handlers who'd grown up with fewer advantages than I'd had and who now had the opportunity and determination to prove themselves my betters.

Material fell away from my skin and I closed my eyes. Clyde's scissors cut through the side of my bra. He stood and looked down into my eyes.

"Did you go swimming and skating with your human friends? Let human boys touch you? You let all those boys think they had something good and clean, didn't you? Something sweet and soft?" He severed both the shoulder of my dress and the strap of my bra in the same cut.

The soft snip made me flinch, but I clenched my jaw, determined not to give him the reaction he was after.

"I bet you never told them you were a dirty animal. A monster wearing a girl's face. What would they have said if they'd known? How do you think they feel now that everyone knows what you are?"

My resolve faltered when he stepped back to look at me, half-covered in flayed linen. In that moment, I understood that the menagerie was filled with two sorts of people. Those who felt that the inhumane treatment of cryptids was unfair, but needed the work. And those who were attracted to jobs like Clyde's because the position of authority came with a socially acceptable outlet for the true evil that burned within them.

I blinked away tears. Wars were not won from crying.

"Well, we all know where you belong now, no matter what you look like. As soon as you figure that out, your life's gonna get a whole lot easier."

Clyde's barbarically illustrated point came through loud and clear. The only way to avoid being forcibly put in my place was to step into it voluntarily. To give up any claim to humanity and admit that I belonged to Rudolph Metzger, because he'd bought me, and he could do whatever he wanted with me, and no one would stop him because the law wasn't concerned with the well-being of subhuman species. Not even those who'd acquired the prefix less than twenty-four hours before.

The choice wasn't really a choice at all. Fighting them every step of the way could get me killed. But if I submitted, I would die a little every day until they were able to drive my walking corpse like they drove the centaurs and the satyrs. Maybe they'd drug me, once they figured out what I was, but maybe they wouldn't have to.

How much trouble could I possibly be once I'd given up the possibility of ever being free?

Two more snips severed the material over my opposite shoulder, then the other side of my underwear, and scraps of ruined fabric pooled on the straw beneath me.

That linen dress had felt insubstantial when I'd worn it, but hindsight assigned it the strength of armor. I would have done anything to have it back.

Clyde stared. He looked simultaneously ravenous and satisfied. I wanted to cover myself, but the cuffs held me in place, exposed and vulnerable, wearing nothing but the shredded remains of my dignity.

I closed my eyes. The world seemed to be spinning too quickly, and I prayed that it would sling me loose. Dislodge me from this living hell.

Clyde stepped so close I could feel his breath on my face. He brushed hair from my shoulder, and my eyes flew open. "Don't touch me."

He only laughed and my skin crawled while his gaze wandered. "Do you want to know what you're worth?" He slid his fingers into the hair at the base of my skull and pulled my head back, so that I had to look up at him. "Can you guess what the old man paid for you?" The coarse cotton of his uniform shirt grazed my skin.

I held as still as I could. It took most of my concentration to keep my eyes dry, my mouth closed, and my psyche intact.

"Fifteen thousand dollars. Ten for the state of Oklahoma, five made out to the honorable sheriff himself—though that part's off the books. I bet that's less than your car cost, isn't it? Less than a year at your fancy college. If you turn out to be too much trouble, he'll sell you for half that and take the rest out of Gallagher's salary, but none of that reflects what you're really worth. Do you know what you're worth, beast?"

When I didn't answer, Clyde pulled back on my hair until I couldn't close my mouth. Until my throat was stretched so tight I could hardly breathe. "You are worth *nothing*. No matter what the old man paid for you. No matter how much money you bring in for the menagerie. You will never be worth what it costs to feed and clothe you, no matter how little you eat and wear. Do you under—"

Suddenly he flew backward and his hand was ripped from my hair. I sucked in a startled breath, then lost it entirely when Gallagher spun Clyde around and slammed him into the side of the cage, inches from my left hand.

The boss of livestock pressed his forearm into the smaller man's windpipe, pinning him to the bars. "If you ever hurt her again, I will rip your limbs off and feed each distinct part of your corpse to a different exhibit."

I gaped at him, my heart pounding.

"Back off." Clyde's voice was weak and scratchy from the pressure on his throat. "I was just having a little fun with the uppity bitch."

"She is mine."

"I'm not," I insisted, though every self-preservation instinct

I had was telling me to shut up and let them fight it out. "I'm not anyone's."

"Mine," Gallagher repeated, pressing even harder with his forearm. "The old man assigned her to me. I'm the boss of livestock. It's my paycheck on the line, and you will *not* fuck with my paycheck. Got it?"

"Fine," Clyde croaked. "I was just trying to help, but whatever."

Gallagher let him go but refused to back away, so the smaller handler had to sidestep him, rubbing his throat.

"Go see that the centaurs are fed and watered, and make sure Abraxas picks out their hooves before the show."

Clyde stomped toward the closed tent flap, his gait stiff, his fists clenched. "Ruyle sent over the temporary sign. He'll need a name for her by next week."

"Noted." Gallagher picked up the stock prod, and I couldn't tell whether he intended to confiscate it or find a very special place to store it, so Clyde couldn't forget it next time. "Go."

Clyde left—quickly—and as soon as he was gone, Gallagher turned to me, still holding the stock prod. Anger had dilated his pupils and clenched his jaw, and with one look at him, a fresh bolt of fear shot up the length of my spine.

He dropped the prod on the table and pulled a ring of keys from a clip on his belt, the anger melting from his bearing. "I'm not going to hurt you, Delilah."

Relief washed over me, and it was harder than ever to resist feeling grateful for common decency disguised as gallantry. Gallagher wasn't going above and beyond. He wasn't risking his job for me. He was hardly even doing the decent thing— that would have required setting me free.

But that was very difficult to keep in mind, after what he'd just stopped. Which was why I had to reinforce the idea.

"I'm not yours," I said, still miserably aware that I was completely naked.

He thumbed through the keys. "You're my responsibility."

"That's not the same thing, Gallagher. There's a principle at stake."

His brows rose as he crossed the hay-strewn ground toward me, and his attention never wandered south of my eyes. "I thought your *survival* was at stake. You want me to call Clyde back so I can clarify?"

"Don't be an asshole."

Gallagher stopped several feet away, scowling. "You've grown bold, for a woman chained naked to a cage."

I tried to shrug. "You said you wouldn't hurt me."

"And my word is my honor."

The words echoed in my head. Something about the way he said it—the formal cadence—surprised me.

He unlocked my left wrist, and I dragged my focus back on task. *Escape.* Nothing else was more important. "So, all the keys work on any set of cuffs?"

"I'm going to pretend you didn't ask that." Gallagher stared at my right hand while he unlocked it, and in spite of his proximity and of the fact that he'd seen me naked the night before, he took no liberties.

He plucked my butchered dress from the ground and handed it to me.

I covered myself as best I could, trying to ignore the bits of straw caught in the linen, poking me in sensitive places.

"Are you hurt?" Gallagher knelt at my feet, and I stared down at the top of his red cap.

"Just my pride."

"A flesh wound, then." Metal clicked, and the cuff fell away from my left ankle. "No mortal blow was ever struck through someone's pride."

"Says the man standing fully clothed and untethered."

"Valid point." Gallagher left my right ankle chained to the cart while he retrieved a wad of black cloth from the table. "Put this on."

"I can't, not with the claws." I wiggled the fingers of my left hand while my right carefully clutched ruined linen to my chest. "What is it?"

"It's the best I could do." He slid a sheer, snug black tank top over my head, then over one arm at a time with more professional detachment than I'd seen from the doctor during my last physical.

Gallagher dropped into a squat in front of me and held the matching underwear near my left ankle. "Step through here." I slid my foot through the leg hole of the black bikini bottoms, then had to wait while he unlocked my other foot.

For about fifteen seconds, I was completely unrestrained, and the urge to somehow recognize the occasion was overwhelming. But I wasn't stupid enough to make a bid for freedom in broad daylight, only half-dressed, with a very large handler only inches away. Instead, I stepped through the second opening, and as he perfunctorily slid the material into place, looking to the side to give me as much privacy as possible, I swore to myself that I'd find another, better opportunity to run.

Soon.

"Thanks," I whispered, and saying that one word cost me a good deal of pride. I didn't want to be grateful for a kindness I shouldn't have been dependent upon him for in the first place. Surely that was how Stockholm syndrome began. But I *was* grateful. And it wouldn't hurt to have the goodwill of the man who was the biggest obstacle to my escape.

"Don't thank me, Delilah." He reached past me to slide the side of the cage open. "I'm not doing you a favor, I'm doing my job, and that won't always be pleasant for you." Gallagher lifted me into the wagon and handed me the costume Alyrose had made, without its hanger. "Get dressed. You go live in half an hour."

Live. I couldn't think about that without trembling, so I pushed the inevitable to the back of my mind and tackled the costume, though my concentration was hindered by the fact that I hadn't slept in almost thirty-two hours and had eaten nothing but a soggy slice of bread all day.

If not for the bathroom break in Alyrose's trailer, I would have had even more to worry about.

While I carefully puzzled my way into a configuration of satin and sequins that looked more like a harness than a costume, even over the tank top and bikini bottom, Gallagher moved around the tent, mounting and adjusting lights so that they didn't shine directly on my cage. He didn't offer to help me, in spite of my trouble with the claws. In fact, he hardly even glanced at me.

"Okay, this is as good as it's going to get," I said at last, and Gallagher looked up from the sign he was hammering into the ground in front of my cage.

Something raw and uncensored flashed behind his eyes, but it was gone before I could make sense of it. "Good. I'm almost done here, and I think they're ready for you out back." He gave the sign post one last blow, then set the hammer on the table next to the cattle prod.

"Out back? Is that secret code for something horrible?"

Gallagher crossed to the rear of the tent and knelt to unhook one of the canvas panels from its anchor. "In the menagerie, we don't hide 'horrible' behind code words. We put sequins on 'horrible,' drape ribbons around it, shine lights on it, and charge admission."

He pulled the tent flap back and the growl of heavy machinery crescendoed. Gallagher nodded to someone outside, then familiar, slow footsteps thudded toward us from behind the tent, a dull counterpoint to the incessant calliope music, the rumble of truck engines, and the ceaseless shouting of instructions from carnival employees.

"So, I'm that something horrible?" I sank onto my knees in my cage, already regretting the question. It didn't matter what he thought of me, since he could not be manipulated to benefit my escape.

Gallagher looked like he would answer, but then a shadow fell over the opening in the back of the tent. The minotaur ducked slowly beneath the canvas and his brown-eyed gaze met mine. For just a second, the drug-haze seemed to lift from his eyes as recognition filled them. But then his gaze fogged over again and his focus dropped to the ground in front of my cage.

"Over here, Eryx," Gallagher called. He harnessed the minotaur to the cage, then my cart began to roll toward the opening in the back of the tent.

Outside, daylight made me squint and the heat was like a quilt draped over me, suffocating me. Tree limbs rocked and bowed in the distance, well behind the fairgrounds, but tents and food trucks blocked the breeze from most of the carnival.

Behind the tent, I found a small truck pulling an open trailer stacked with the disassembled casing of a menagerie wagon—a frame designed to fit over my naked cage. Even I had to admit that the casing was beautiful. The side panels looked like huge hand-carved picture frames. They were red, trimmed with ornate gold edges and corners, and embellishments that curled over the arched facades. The end panels were solid red, with "Metzger's Menagerie" painted in scrolling gold lettering.

Gallagher waved to several men waiting for orders, and

two of the thick sweaty roustabouts lifted an ornate frame into place over one side of my cart, their arms bulging with effort. Two more rushed in with electric drills plugged into a generator on the back of the truck and began bolting the frame into place.

When all the facades were attached and my wagon sat low on its wheelbase from the additional weight, a man brought out a set of four matching wooden hubcaps, which were bolted to the front of the functional rubber tires to disguise them.

Just minutes after they'd started, the crew was done, and though I couldn't see any of it from the inside, I knew my cage had been transformed into a vintage-looking circus wagon, like the ones I'd seen the night before, as a carnival patron.

I exhaled, stunned and devastated by that thought. How could that possibly have been less than a day ago?

"Okay, Eryx, take her back in." Gallagher made a gesture toward the darker and slightly cooler interior of my tent, and as the minotaur pulled me into it, I noticed that though the roustabouts had all left, one red-clad handler had stayed behind to retrieve the bull.

When my embellished cage was in position and Eryx was gone, Gallagher closed and refastened the tent flap.

"So, these are my sequins?" I asked. He stood to look at me and I propped my hands on the glittery hips of my costume. "This new cage is my ribbons and lights, right? Because I'm that something horrible, that Metzger's charges admission to see?"

Gallagher crossed the tent and gripped the steel mesh separating us. "You are only *one* of the horrible things at Metzger's."

I started to argue, even though I could no longer reasonably claim to be normal, but he shook his head. "Most people have something horrible hidden inside. A beast. A secret. A sin. What makes you and the other exhibits different is that your inner monster can't be explained by the laws of physics and biology as we know them. What people don't understand, they fear. What they fear, they lock up, so they can come see whatever scares them behind steel bars or glass walls and call themselves brave. But that only tells you who *they* are, not who you are."

"You're one of them." The accusation in my voice surprised me. I wasn't telling either of us anything new.

"Yeah. I am."

"But you're not afraid of me." I looked right into his eyes, and his gaze stayed glued to mine. "Why don't I scare you, Gallagher?"

His voice was so low it could almost rumble in my bones. "If what scared other people scared me, I wouldn't be very good at my job." He turned and walked out of the tent, leaving me to puzzle through his meaning alone.

GALLAGHER

Gallagher stood just inside the tent, watching the crowd file by behind the red velvet rope. The space was dimly lit and the shadows near the tent wall hid him almost completely. Gallagher had many unusual skills, but his talent for going unnoticed was among those he valued most when the press of the crowd began to drain his patience and sharpen his temper.

Delilah's tent was square, with a red-and-white-striped canvas. It was eight and a half meters across and could easily have held two or three wagon cages plus the crowd, but for her debut, she had the tent all to herself. If they expected her to play ball just one day after being sold to the menagerie, with no training and no time to adjust to her new place in the world, they would have to give her some space. And carefully controlled lighting.

When Ruyle and the boss canvas man had tried to overrule him on the tent issue, Gallagher had stared them down with stony silence. Then he'd backed them down with blatant physical intimidation, and when push came to brutish shove, neither had been willing to openly deny the boss of livestock what he wanted.

Few ever were.

Rudolph Metzger and Delilah Marlow were two of the exceptions. Metzger was old as dirt, and he signed the paychecks, but Delilah...

Gallagher's gaze found the dimly lit cage, where she sat staring at the hay-strewn ground, the very picture of civil disobedience.

Delilah could not be controlled.

Ruyle and the rest of the staff believed she'd been damaged beyond any usefulness as an exhibit by the circumstance of her youth.

What they couldn't understand—what Gallagher himself was only just starting to realize—was that her tireless defiance stemmed as much from nature as from nurture. She could be caged, but she could not be restrained. She could be bought, but she could not be owned.

Despite Metzger's ironclad demand, she could not be broken.

Gallagher studied her from the shadows. She sat with her legs folded beneath her, theatrically made-up hands resting on her knees, where the only direct light shining into her cage glinted off the points of her fake claws. She would not transmute. She would not perform. She would not even look at the viewers who'd paid for the chance to gawk at her.

Delilah negotiated when she was cornered. She cursed at Clyde when he bullied her. She wore wit like armor. Even having known her for only twenty-four hours, he suspected she was one of the strongest people he'd ever met.

Which told Gallagher that he'd made a mistake.

The old man could have her beaten, stripped, starved, isolated, drugged, or whipped, or he could simply turn a blind eye while the least noble among his men came at her in the night, and eventually they might actually crack her mental armor, along with her bones. But that wouldn't be breaking Delilah. That would be psychologically obliterating her and, as Rommily had proved, a mentally shattered menagerie exhibit was no good to anyone.

If Chris Ruyle weren't as dim as a box of busted lightbulbs, he'd see that they were already close to losing little Geneviève, thanks to Jack and his damn cattle prod.

Gallagher's only regret over what had happened to Jack was that he hadn't played a role in the bastard's downfall. That was all Delilah, and he'd loved watching her work.

He craved another glimpse of her potential, not because exposing her beast would save his job, but because he needed to understand her.

Delilah wasn't mindless violence like the adlet, or uncontrollable temper like the ogres. She was destruction given form and purpose. Hers was an elegant savagery—he'd seen that the night before. She hadn't ripped open Jack's flesh or pulled apart his bones, as any of the other beasts would have. Somehow, she'd inspired him to inflict damage upon *himself*.

Her violence was art.

Delilah's incarceration hadn't gone as he'd hoped. He'd thought she would be safe in the menagerie—surely anyone foolish enough to anger a woman who could scramble the human brain like an egg deserved whatever he got. And secretly, he'd hoped to see that very thing.

No one was more surprised than Gallagher to realize that she'd thought she was human. That she had no idea how to call on her beast. And that no matter how strong she was mentally, without access to her cryptid abilities, she was as physically vulnerable in the menagerie as any of the cubs, foals, and hatchlings in the petting zoo.

Despite her strength, she needed him.

Something primal twisted in his chest with that thought. Something alarming and intoxicating. Something fierce and suffocating, and Gallagher wasn't sure whether he should fight its clutch or submit to this strange, powerful grip on his soul.

I am needed.

Gallagher had never been needed. After a lifetime of searching for a purpose—a drive as ingrained in him as the need to breathe—he'd given up hope of ever finding one. His grim cravings had never served anyone other than himself, but they could, with Delilah. They could *for* Delilah.

Yet many obstacles stood in the way of that possibility.

"What is she, Mommy?" a child's voice said near Gallagher's knee, and he looked down to find a small boy in khaki overalls holding his mother's hand while they both stared across the tent at Delilah in her display wagon.

"Some kind of monster." The mother pointed at the placard Gallagher had hammered into the ground in front of the cage. "That sign says they haven't figured out what kind yet, but that she's very dangerous."

"Is she gonna do something?"

"We've been standing here for ten minutes, and she hasn't moved a muscle," a man said from farther up the line. "I'm mermaid-bound. Who's with me?" His daughters squealed in delight, and Gallagher scowled as half of the crowd followed the young father out of the tent.

As intriguing as it was, Delilah's strength would be her ruin. If he couldn't bring out her beast and convince her to show it off, Metzger would sell her and she would be forever beyond his protection. Beyond his reach.

A young man stepped into the tent and slid into a dark alcove on the other side of the entrance instead of joining the line. His obvious desire to hide caught Gallagher's attention, and the familiarity of the man's features spiked the handler's temper. It took him several seconds to place the face half-hidden by the brim of a black cattleman-style cowboy hat, but then the circumstances fell into place.

The sheriff's station.

Tonight, Deputy Atherton wore civilian clothes.

Gallagher stepped out of the shadows, and three long steps later, he stood in front of the man in the cattleman hat, blocking his view and shielding him from Delilah's line of sight, should she actually open her eyes. "Out," Gallagher growled, and the deputy frowned up at him.

"Excuse me?"

Gallagher hauled him from the tent by one arm, heedless of the smaller man's spiritless protests, then pulled him behind a bank of blue portable toilets. "Leave now, or I will pop your skull like a balloon."

Atherton took off his hat and stared up at Gallagher. Sudden recognition lit his gaze. "I remember you. You bought her."

"My boss bought her. Yours sold her. We failed her in equal parts."

Atherton looked surprised by the admission. He scuffed one boot in the dirt. "Could I talk to her? Just for a minute? I want to tell her I'm sorry."

An inarticulate threat rumbled from the handler's throat. "If you're still here in two minutes, you'll never speak again."

Atherton put his hat back on, and with it, he seemed to find mettle. "She's not a monster. She doesn't belong here."

Gallagher seized handfuls of the deputy's shirt and pulled him close. Atherton grunted. Stitches popped beneath his armpits.

"You think she doesn't belong here because she looks

human?" the handler growled. "Or because you like her? You think deciding that she's the exception to everything you know about cryptids makes you noble, but it only exposes your ignorance. *No one* belongs here. But at least here she's accepted by her own kind."

"Maybe not." Still in the handler's grip, Atherton clumsily pulled a folded piece of paper from his back pocket and held it out.

Gallagher let him go, then snatched the paper and opened it. It only took him a few seconds to read the printout, but then he read it again. "This can't be right." He read it a third time.

Atherton shrugged. "Sheriff thinks there was a mix-up, so they're gonna run the sample again, but I thought you guys would wanna see this. I don't know what it would mean for her, if this is accurate, considerin' money's already changed hands…"

"This can't be right," Gallagher repeated, as doubt battered against what had seemed certain moments before. "I *saw* her."

Atherton nodded. "You and more'n a dozen other people."

"Leave," the handler growled.

The deputy blinked, obviously surprised to realize he was still being expelled from the menagerie. "Can I just talk to her for a minute?"

Gallagher advanced on him, wearing the threat of violence as casually as other men wore clothes. "You can walk out on your own, or I can tell the ambulance where to pick you up."

"I'm going." Atherton backed toward the portable toilets, headed for the midway. "Just…take care of her, okay?"

"She will come to no harm on my watch." The handler gave the deputy an unguarded moment of eye contact. "My word is my honor."

When Atherton had gone, Gallagher read the printed report one more time, and his focus lingered on the information in an official-looking box at the bottom, after several paragraphs of explanation.

Subject: Delilah Elizabeth Marlow
Classification: *Homo sapiens sapiens*.

Blood tests on the initial group of one thousand surviving children from last month's massacre have confirmed that, in fact, *not one* of them is human. Authorities aren't prepared to say exactly what species these things are, but it is becoming increasingly clear that women who gave birth in March of 1980 in the U.S. went home from the hospital cradling something *other* than their own natural children.

—From the front-page article of the September 20 edition of the *Detroit Daily Journal*

DELILAH

"Claudio, are you awake?" I practically had to shout to be heard over the road noise, lying curled up on my right side with my nose inches from the side of my cage. My blanket was too thin to provide any real padding and I'd woken up the day before with bruises on my hips from the floor of my wagon.

"*Oui. Que tu vas bien?*"

"Yeah, I'm fine." But I hadn't really been fine in eight days, twelve hours, and a handful of minutes, if the weak light oozing into the travel trailer through the vent at the top could be trusted. Hunger and exhaustion were chief among my complaints, but the lack of bathroom facilities was a growing concern. "How much longer do you think we'll be stuck in here? I really have to pee."

Claudio scooted closer to the side of his cage. "According to roustabout chatter, this is a nine-hour drive. We must be getting close."

Nine hours in the travel trailer, plus at least three before that, spent sipping from my bowl of murky water while I'd waited to be loaded with the other exhibits. So, twelve hours and counting, with no bathroom break. I could only imagine that the bestiary trailer reeked to high hell, since I was set to bust my personal record.

And possibly rupture my bladder.

But my biggest fear was that drinking dirty water and eating questionable meat would lead to some kind of bacterial infection. Unlike most of the other captives, I hadn't built up immunities in childhood.

"Papa," a soft voice called from Claudio's right, and I looked up to find Geneviève's golden eyes shining in the shadows. *"Dites-moi une histoire."*

"You need to go to sleep, *chère*," he replied, so softly I could hardly hear him over the road noise. But she would have heard him just fine. Shifters have great hearing.

"She wants a story?" Listening to the werewolves over the past week had brought back a lot of the French I'd learned in school.

"Oui," he said. "But she needs to sleep."

"Maybe a story would help her sleep. I know lots of stories."

Genni sat up, and I heard a high-pitched whine, which I interpreted as the lupine version of *"Pleeeeease,* Papa!"

Finally, Claudio nodded, and the pup settled in. "Have you heard about Hansel and Gretel?" I asked, practically shouting over the highway noise.

She shook her head, and Claudio chuckled. "She can hear you better than you hear her. You don't have to shout."

I nodded, then launched into the story about a girl who saved her brother from being eaten alive by a cannibalistic witch, and only halfway through did I realize Genni might miss the "girl power" message entirely, disguised as it was in action and gore. But when I finished, she curled up in the far corner of her cage and made a contented sound, deep in her throat.

Minutes later, she was asleep.

"Did you hear where we're going?" I asked, as Claudio's golden eyes shone at me in the gloom. Most of the handlers had stopped talking around me, since Ruyle had told them to quit arming me with information.

"Tomorrow's our first night in Texas." Claudio's blanket rustled. "Where is Texas?"

His question surprised me. "Have you ever seen a map of the U.S.?"

"I once saw one painted on the side of a ticket booth."

"At the bottom of the map, in the center." Claudio was smart, but he'd never been to school. He'd been born in a carnival near Avignon and sold to Metzger's as a teenager, and though he spoke fluent French and English, he could read neither language. "Texas is about the same size as France, but it's a lot dryer, and there's lots of open space. There are places in the western half where you can drive for hours without passing a single town." Which might explain our nine-hour ordeal.

Claudio nodded, taking it all in. "And where did we acquire you?"

"Oklahoma. That's just north of Texas. A century ago, it was full of buffalo, and horses, and cattle, and until the repeal of the Sanctuary Act, back in the eighties, we had skin walkers. A couple of the more prominent flocks of thunderbirds used to migrate through every fall."

I closed my eyes, trying to picture wide-open skies and magnificent giant birds, rather than the inside of a wide-load trailer, but the scents of hay and livestock were pervasive.

"Metzger's has a thunderbird," Claudio said. "Nashashuk. His mate died a few months ago, and *le vieil homme* is angry because Nashashuk is refusing food. Rommily says he'll die of an overdose of tranquilizer, though, so I suppose starving himself isn't going to work out."

"Rommily. What's her story?" I could see her across the

narrow aisle between rows of cages, curled up between her oracle sisters in their long faded skirts. Mirela and Lala were friendly enough. Lala had even offered to trade her mostly unmoldy slice of bread for my nearly cooked hunk of cow liver, an exchange I'd jumped on, even though my exhausted body cried out for protein.

But Rommily...

In the week I'd been incarcerated, I hadn't heard her complete a single coherent sentence.

Claudio sat up on his blanket and blinked at me from across the aisle. "Did she say something to you?"

"Just names."

"What names? People you know?"

I shook my head. "I don't think so." *Secret Mary. Princess Sara.* "She just said several names and called them fate's bastards. It doesn't make any sense."

"*Elle est folle.* Everyone has a limit. An end to what can be endured." Claudio glanced at the end of his cage, beyond which his daughter lay sleeping in a pen of her own, beyond his help when the handlers mistreated her.

"Rommily hit her limit a few months ago," he continued. "Clyde took her to the restroom near the end of the night, and she wasn't back by the time they closed the front gate. They had the whole staff looking for her, then she just came wandering down the midway in the rain, her clothes torn and bloodstained. Most of what she sees now is death, and everything she says comes out broken. The best she can do is...hint. Drop clues."

"Clyde." His name tasted rotten on my tongue, and I couldn't spit it out fast enough. "That bastard!"

Fire flared deep in my stomach and my scalp began to prickle, as if my hair wanted to stand upright, and with a shock, I recognized the symptoms. *Finally*, my inner monster wanted to come out and play.

"Clyde swears he turned around for a second, and she was gone. He says he has no idea what happened to her."

"*He* happened to her," I insisted. Clyde had shattered Rommily, physically and mentally, and maybe that's what he'd had in mind when he'd chained me to the front of my cage. Maybe that's what would have happened, if Gallagher hadn't come in.

Could I be broken that easily?

The tingling in my scalp faded and the flames in my stomach began to sputter, leaving me hollow and cold inside, and more than a little disappointed. I had no intention of performing in front of an audience, but if I had on-demand access to my beast, I could make sure Clyde got what he deserved. Just like Jack had.

"Clyde did it, and he'll pay for it," I whispered, lying down to stare at the ceiling of my cage. By the time sleep finally came, I was no longer sure whether I was promising Rommily or myself.

"Take off your clothes and slide them through the tray slot."

I didn't recognize the handler shouting orders at me, but I did recognize the hose he held, and I knew exactly what it was for. He'd already blasted it at the adlet, at Zyanya—the most feral of the cat shifters—and at poor little Geneviève, right there in their cages, lined up across from mine on a patch of grass behind the Denton County fairgrounds.

"I'm on hygiene plan A," I insisted, pulling myself to my bare feet with my fingers curled through the wire mesh. "I'm supposed to shower with the sirens, succubi, and oracles." I'd had enough trouble adjusting to group showers with sexual predators. Being hosed down in front of the entire carnival—that was too much to endure. "Ask Alyrose. She'll tell you."

"Today, you're on *my* list." Yet the handler made no effort to actually show me the list clipped to his clipboard. "So either you take your clothes off, or I accomplish your laundry and your shower in one convenient step."

Across the patch of grass, Genni sat shivering in one corner of her cage, even though the late-morning temperature had to be pushing ninety-five. She wasn't cold. She was nearly naked, soaked, and traumatized.

In the cage next to her, the drenched cheetah shifter prowled back and forth in feline form, hissing and spitting at anyone who came near. I understood why both the cat and the pup had been denied a proper shower, and the adlet was a no-brainer. He hadn't left his cage once in the week I'd been with the menagerie. But I was no obvious threat.

"Just go ask her. Or Gallagher. I'm supposed to shower with group A, then head to Alyrose's trailer for makeup."

"You're not going on tonight, which means no shower and no makeup for you. Now take off the dress. You smell."

What? Gallagher hadn't said anything about a change in my schedule, and he would never have okayed a public hosedown.

My temper overtook both fear and logic. My fingers clenched around the mesh. "No."

The handler set his clipboard on the ground and twisted the nozzle on his hose. Water slammed into my chest and punched the air from my lungs, driving me to the far side of my cage.

The blast trailed lower, stealing my breath and pounding the entire width of my body with a thousand needles. I clung to the side of the cage, determined not to curl up and hide. Not to show further weakness. I sucked air in and spit it back out in staccato bursts as the bruising jet pelted my stomach and my legs, then worked its way back up, over my breasts and shoulders. But when the water hit my neck—a thousand tiny fists pummeling my throat—I lost control. I threw my hands up to protect my face and let loose the scream clawing at the inside of my skull.

When the spray stopped, I wiped my face as I lowered my hands, thankful the hose water would disguise my tears.

"Turn around," the handler ordered.

My teeth chattered as I crossed my arms over my thin, soaked dress and refused as civilly as I could manage. "Go fuck yourself."

He shrugged and leaned to the left to nod at someone behind me. Before I could turn to look, a second blast hit the back of my head, throwing me face-first into the wire mesh on the opposite side. Metal bruised my face and I tried to push myself back, but the pressure was too strong. I could only cling to the side of my cage, soaked and gasping, trying not to drown.

Then the first handler turned his hose back on and reality splintered into sharp missiles pelting every inch of me, from every direction. My eyes burned from the chlorine, my throat was raw from screaming, and my skin felt like I'd been rolling in shattered glass.

When the spray finally stopped, I collapsed to the floor of my cage, soaked and gasping, bruised all over from the pressure of the blasts, and just as vulnerable to wandering gazes as if I'd taken off my linen dress, as ordered.

I crawled into one corner of my cage and tucked my knees up to my chest, struggling to control the hitching, but I couldn't stop shaking. I couldn't stop crying. And when I finally calmed down enough to push soaked hair from my face, my right hand came away bloody. My collision with the side of my cage had gashed open my head, just above my hairline.

With a groan, I swiped at my dripping nose and looked up.

Peeking through swollen eyelids, I found Clyde watching me, still holding the hose that had blasted me from behind.

By the time the sun hit the apex of its arch, my dress had dried, except where my back was pressed against the end panel of my cage. Hose water had been replaced by a thin sheen of sweat all over my body and my hair was a frizzy mass tangled around my face. My jaw ached from being clenched, and every time I looked up from the floor of my cage, I found someone staring at me as the staff worked to get everything ready for our first stop in Texas.

I'd been watching the parade of tent poles, massive sheets of canvas, and centaurs hauling cages for about an hour when the clanks and rattles of the food cart made my mouth water. I didn't *want* to want the scraps and entrails I'd come to expect from the food cart, but if every meal I'd been served in my week with Metzger's were to be scraped onto a plate, that pile would hardly equal two or three of my pre-captivity meals.

Hunger had become a perpetual state of being. Every time I passed a mirror, my cheekbones appeared sharper and my eyes a little bigger. My face seemed to be shrinking to the shape of my bones, and my knees looked knobbier than ever before.

My heart hurt when I saw Clyde in a stained apron, pushing the food cart between the two rows of cage wagons. Gallagher had never served a meal—the boss of livestock had more important things to do—so I hadn't really expected to see him, but I would have taken anyone other than Clyde.

Anyone.

"Hey, Drea, you all dried out yet?" Clyde stopped the cart in front of my cage, leering at me with one brow arched.

"That's not my name."

"It is now." He pulled a tray from the stack and filled one compartment with a ladle full of what appeared to be dark-meat chicken, swimming in broth so fragrant that saliva gathered in the corners of my mouth. I think I even saw a couple of noodles. "You can thank Gallagher for letting you keep your initial. Who knew he was such a softie?"

"You're all bastards." I tucked my feet beneath me and made myself let go of the wire mesh. "Someday someone's going to balance the scales, and I sure hope I'll be there to see it."

"Is that a prediction? You think you're an oracle now, *Drea*?" He pulled the heel from an otherwise empty bag of bread and dropped it right on top of my chicken soup.

"That's not my name." I couldn't drag my focus from the tray. My stomach cramped and my fingers clenched around handfuls of my dress. I couldn't think about anything but food.

"It's written on your placard. It's on the duty roster in the silver wagon. It's on the top line of the registration packet, all ready to send in and get you officially registered as a live exhibit, belonging to one Mr. Rudolph Metzger. We're still waiting for the blood test to tell us *what* you are, but the question of *who* you are has been answered."

Clyde flipped the latch on the tray slot, and the steel panel fell open. He slid my tray about a third of the way into the cage and I lunged for it, but he jerked it out of reach. "Say your name for me, and this is all yours. Chicken thighs in broth. The very last slice of whole wheat bread. And this fancy spring water. I brought it just for you, still cold from the fridge in my trailer." He pulled a bottle of water from the cargo pocket over his left thigh, and a drop of condensation rolled down the plastic to splat on the grass. "All you have to do is say your name."

My stomach growled. My throat ached and my tongue felt thick and unbearably dry. My fingers curled, as if they already held the tray. But to get fresh food and clean water, I'd have to give up my name—the only connection I still had to my mother.

I said a mental farewell to my lunch, then looked up to meet his expectant gaze. "I am Delilah Marlow."

"Oh, that's too bad, because there's no Delilah on the lunch list." Clyde's eyes narrowed and he shook his head in exaggerated disappointment. "This is for *Drea*." He dumped my lunch onto the ground, then set the empty tray back on the stack.

I blinked away tears and clenched my teeth against the sob building in my throat.

Clyde cracked the water bottle open and took a long swig from it, then screwed the lid back on and dropped the bottle into his pocket.

As he pushed the food cart past my cage, he planted one big black boot in my ruined lunch.

GENEVIÈVE

The pup huddled in one corner of her cage, knees tucked up to her chest, head buried in thin arms folded around her legs. Dirty toes peeked from beneath a curtain of long tangled hair that shone like gold when it was clean, but more often matched the grime the shower hose had managed to cake instead of rinse out.

"What'd the old man say?"

Genni peeked through her hair at the man with the mustache, but squeezed her eyes shut again the second his gaze met hers. Her arms tightened around her legs and her toes curled on the floor of her cage. She made herself as small as she could.

"He told me to make the deal," the tall man said. Genni knew he was the boss and that his name was Ruyle, though she couldn't read the letters sewn on his shirt. But her father secretly called him *l'imbécile grand*, and she thought that suited the tall man much better than his name. "He wants her gone before he gets back next week."

"But their offer's an insult. A werewolf bitch in perfect health is worth twice what they're quoting, and this one's never even been bred."

Geneviève cowered even tighter into her corner.

"Decision's not yours, Clyde," the tall man said.

"We're hardly getting paid as it is, and he just bought that arrogant free-range bitch when everyone knows the menagerie's in trouble," the shorter man grumbled.

Genni peeked above her arm to see his lip twitch, which made his mustache appear to crawl like a caterpillar.

"The equipment is outdated, the harnesses and muzzles are frayed, and if the government passes that new mandate, we'll have to upgrade to medical restraint cages. None of that will get any better if he accepts half what the pup's worth. I'm not taking another pay cut, Ruyle."

"With any luck, neither of us will have to," *l'imbécile grand* snapped. "The old man's looking at whatever we get for Genni as a down payment on a new bitch we can put in with Claudio. This time next year we'll have a cute little werewolf pup to sell, and hopefully another to keep in inventory. You know puppies bring in crowds."

"This one used to," the mustached man agreed.

Genni peeked through her hair again and saw *l'imbécile* shrug. "Yeah, but she's more trouble than she's worth now. We sell her to All American, and she becomes their problem. Let *them* try to breed the feral bitch."

Geneviève whimpered, and the sound of her own fear startled her so badly that she sank her teeth into her forearm until blood filled her mouth. The torn skin hurt, but that was nothing new. Ever since they'd put her in a cage of her own, pain had become a way of life. It was punishment, incentive, and bribe. It was the introduction to and the conclusion of every day. Pain told her to speak. Pain told her to shut up. Pain told her to move, and to be still. Pain was administered more reliably than either food or water, and there was no sure way to avoid it.

"Shit, she's bleeding." *L'imbécile* reached for the keys clipped to his belt, and Geneviève scooted as far from the door as she could, leaving a trail of blood across the floor of her cage.

"Shouldn't be." The man with the mustache frowned. "Werewolf bitches don't go into estrus 'til late November in the northern hemisphere. She's not even fertile right now."

"Someone's been doing his homework." Ruyle sounded impressed. "But that's not it. She bit herself again."

"Damn it!" the mustached man swore. "The electrical burns are bad enough. How are we supposed to tell All American she's in perfect health if she's covered in bite marks?"

"She's been like this since we sold her dam." *L'imbécile* slid the side panel open with a heavy metallic crash, and Geneviève flinched, but had nowhere left to flee.

"The problem isn't that we sold her dam," the mustached man insisted. "The problem is that we let dam and pup spend so long in the same cage. They should have been separated as soon as the pup was weaned. They *would* have been, if I were in charge of the livestock. I was next in line, after Venable."

Geneviève remembered Walter Venable. He'd been an old man with a shaky voice, firm hands, and even firmer opinions. When he'd retired the year before, she'd been sure that Clyde—the man with the mustache—would take his place, but then old man Metzger had hired Gallagher from outside the menagerie.

"You'll be in charge of livestock when the old man *puts* you in charge of livestock." *L'imbécile* reached into the cage for Genni's ankle, but she hissed and swiped at him with short, sharp claws growing from human hands. "Until then, you answer to Gallagher. But he answers to me." When Geneviève tried to tear his hand open again, *l'imbécile* turned back to the man with the mustache. "Give me the hypo."

Genni began to tremble when the man with the mustache slapped a syringe into his boss's palm. She clawed at him and tried to crawl away to avoid the needle, but only managed to tear open the boss's forearm, which made him curse at her in graceless, guttural English syllables.

On his third try, slippery from spilled blood, he grabbed the pup's left ankle and pulled as hard as he could. She slid across the cage toward him, thrashing and clawing at the blood-slick metal floor for purchase, but that was a struggle she had never won.

L'imbécile stabbed Genni in the thigh with the needle, then pressed the plunger, shooting fire into her leg. Geneviève screeched and the cage around her began to ripple and wave like a mirage. Her arms fell into the growing pool of blood. Her head rolled to one side and her eyelids grew insurmountably heavy as *l'imbécile* pulled her closer, widening the thick trail of blood on the floor.

"Muzzle." His voice seemed to distort the word like a funhouse mirror, stretching it thin in places and thickening it in others, but Geneviève knew that was the drugs at work.

The man with the mustache handed him a thick leather chin harness with straps on the sides and small holes in the part that would cover Genni's mouth. *L'imbécile* climbed into the cage to straddle her, staining both the knees of his pants and her grimy bikini bottom with his blood. He fitted the leather piece over her chin and mouth, then the man with the mustache lifted her head so the muzzle could be buckled at the back of her skull.

Genni moaned in protest, fighting the leaden darkness trying to suffocate her.

"Do everything you can while she's out." *L'imbécile* climbed down from the cage and pulled a white cloth from his pocket to press against his torn forearm. "Hose her down again, change her clothes, file her teeth and claws. Spray out this cage, and find out if Alyrose has anything to help heal those burn marks. Maybe a little of the phoenix tears. Then call All American back and renegotiate. You have less than a week to convince them she's domesticated and breedable, and worth more than they're offering."

"*I* have less than a week?" The man with the mustache turned from Geneviève to frown at his boss.

"If you can pull that off and Gallagher can't control that mutinous new monster of his, I'll see that you get his job."

"What about the old man? He likes Gallagher."

"He'll see the light if his boss of livestock costs him fifteen grand the same month you make a few thousand by selling Genni."

The mustached man's grin smeared across reality as the pup's vision began to lose focus. "Thanks, Ruyle. You won't regret this."

The last thing Geneviève saw before encroaching darkness washed away all sight and sound was the nozzle of a fat, heavy hose aimed right at her.

DELILAH

Hours later, I lay with my newly mildewing blanket draped over me, listening to the centaurs snort and shuffle in their sleep in their custom-height horse trailers. Several cages down from Zyanya, the adlet growled, accompanied by a metallic screeching I could only assume was the raking of his claws against the aluminum floor of his pen. He was an active dreamer.

From even farther down, the berserker snored, a troll grunted in his sleep, and one of the pretty little *djinn* teenagers sang softly to the other in a language I couldn't even identify.

She finished her lullaby around the time Zyanya's brother, Payat, stopped mewling in his sleep, and suddenly the most prominent sounds were crickets chirruping from the empty field behind the fairground and muffled country music coming from one of the trailers in the gravel lot, where all the staff campers were parked.

I closed my eyes, hoping for sleep, even though my dress had never truly dried in the damp heat, but minutes later, footsteps crunched on gravel and my eyes flew open, every muscle in my body suddenly tense and on alert.

My heart pounded against my sternum as those steps drew

closer, then stopped several feet away. I rolled over silently and stared into the moonlit aisle between the rows of wagons.

A handler stood in front of Zyanya's cage with his back to me. He was tall, and typically thick, but I knew from the lack of a cap at the top of his shadow silhouette that it wasn't Gallagher.

"Zy," the handler whispered, softly rattling the side of her cage, and I recognized his voice. It was Wallace, who'd driven the van that had brought me to Metzger's.

"What do you have?" she asked, and he lifted a paper-wrapped bundle. Her head appeared near the mesh wall of her cage, cat eyes flashing from a dark human face, and she sniffed the air. "Pork sausage?"

"Quarter pound, from one of the grease joints," he whispered. "I noticed dinner was a little sparse tonight."

"Dinner's sparse every night." But then she only stared at him through the wire mesh separating them. He shrugged and started to turn toward the other female cat shifter—Mahsa, a melanistic Persian leopard—and Zyanya finally nodded.

When Wallace fumbled for his cage key, I rolled over to face the other direction, newly nauseated by the price Zyanya was paying, yet unavoidably jealous of what she'd bought. Similar scenes had played out several times during my week with the menagerie, and though I wanted to believe myself unsusceptible to such a bribe, the cramping from my empty stomach made me wonder what I might be willing to do after a few more days without food.

Zyanya's cage door squealed as it slid open, and the last thing I heard before I stuck my fingers in my ears and hummed a soft tune to myself was the low-pitched feline growl coming from her brother Payat's cage.

After Wallace had gone and Zyanya had quietly devoured her snack and licked her fingers clean, I realized I'd been hearing a familiar rhythmic thudding for at least a minute before the sound actually sank in. By the time I rolled over, Eryx was only feet from my cage, and though the handler guiding him was drenched in shadows, I recognized the baseball cap in his silhouette.

I sat up, my blanket clutched to my chest.

Gallagher didn't say a word to me. He just moved Eryx into position at the end of my wagon and strapped him up to haul.

The minotaur snorted softly while he was being buckled into the harness, and I got the distinct impression that he was greeting me.

"Shh, Eryx," Gallagher said, blocked from my sight by the end panel of my cage, and I heard him pat the minotaur, probably on the shoulder as I'd seen him do many times in the past few days. "Let's go. Quietly."

"Gallagher?"

When he leaned around the corner of my cage, his focus found my bloody forehead, then skimmed the smelly blanket I still clutched to my chest, and his brows furrowed. He put one finger over his lips, silently ordering me to be quiet, then disappeared around the end of the wagon again.

I leaned against the rear wall of my cart as it rolled across the grass and through a back gate into the fairgrounds. Gallagher led Eryx into the first tent we came to, where, during operating hours, the berserker awed audiences by transforming first into a bear, then into a massive wolf by donning and shedding the necessary pelts.

Gallagher unhooked Eryx from the cart, then led him out onto the midway. Metal clanked as he secured the minotaur's chains to…something, then my handler appeared in the tent again and lowered the open sidewall, leaving us alone in the dark.

"What is this?" I whispered, my heart thumping in my ears.

What if I'd misread Gallagher completely? Was he about to show me a quarter pound of pork sausage and offer me a deal?

Something thudded in the dark, and he swore.

"Your phone probably has a flashlight app," I said, when another thud told me he was wandering around lost and blind.

"I don't have a phone." A second later, light flared from the pole at the center of the small tent, illuminating the blue-and-white-striped dome and sidewalls. Against one wall was a long table draped in a white cloth, on which were arranged samples of the berserker's bear and wolf hides to be felt by spectators waiting in line, along with a collection of photographs of past performances and several framed "fast-fact" cards about the Nordic shifter species.

Gallagher twisted a nob on the center pole, and the light dimmed. He turned to me with his arms crossed over his chest, dark brows bunched low over gray eyes, which seemed to be…assessing.

"Why don't you have a cell phone?" I said, still shielding myself with the stinky blanket.

"I don't need one."

"Because you have no friends and family? Or because they don't want to talk to you? Did you abandon them, too?"

His assessment landed on my face and stayed there. "You look pale."

"I'll have to take your word for that, unless you want to haul my cage past the mirror maze." Hearing the hostility in my voice felt like discovering a beam of steel at the center of my spinal column, and I clung to that hidden strength, the only thing holding me upright at that moment.

"What have you eaten today?"

"Humble pie, my own words, and a little crow." I tugged the blanket higher, afraid that my dress might still be wet enough to see through. "All three taste like shit."

"You're angry," he observed, his focus glued to my eyes, as if he'd just pulled that arcane secret from the mystic depths of my soul.

"And tired, and hungry, and bruised. Does any of that matter?"

"It doesn't affect my job, no." Gallagher shrugged and tilted his head, and in the harsh light from above, his cap looked oddly faded, as if it'd spent too much time in the sun. "But I don't enjoy seeing you suffer, Delilah."

"Well, then, I know how to make us both happy."

"I can't let you go."

"No, you *won't* let me go." I wanted to stand and pace, but the ceiling of my cage was too low, and because I'd hardly been out of it in two days, my legs were cramped from the lack of exercise. "You can keep lying to yourself about who and what you are, but don't expect me to believe it. You and your fellow handlers, the managers and acrobats and roustabouts and everyone else subsisting on the suffering of others—you're the real monsters."

Gallagher held my gaze.

"You're not going to argue?"

He shrugged broad red-clad shoulders. "Only a fool disputes the truth."

I blinked in surprise. "If you don't like seeing people suffer, then why—"

"I said I don't enjoy seeing *you* suffer."

I exhaled slowly, trying to interpret not just what he'd said, but what he hadn't said. My focus followed him as he crossed the sawdust-strewn ground and knelt to pull a backpack from beneath the table. "Why didn't I go on tonight?"

Gallagher pushed pictures and plaques out of the way and set his bag on the table. "Because Alyrose is running out of expensive supplies, and the time spent making you up to look like what you already are could be better spent on something else." He dug into the bag, then headed toward me with a bottle of water and a handful of protein bars. "The old man gets back in a few days, and if he doesn't see the real you, we're both screwed, Delilah."

"I'm screwed either way." I waved one hand at the cage surrounding me.

He shoved everything he held through the tray slot. The bottle of water only bounced off the floor of my cage once before I snatched it.

I needed both hands to crack the lid, and when Gallagher's focus found the blanket, slipping beneath pressure from my upper arms, I hesitated with the water halfway to my mouth. "Take it back." I closed the bottle and pressed it against the mesh side of the cage, even though my dry tongue and throbbing head begged me to reconsider. "I don't trade favors for food."

"Favors?" He scowled as understanding surfaced. "I told you not to insult me with such insinuations. I'm not going to molest you. I just realized I don't have anything clean and dry for you to wear. I didn't know you'd be…mildewed."

I stared at him, trying to determine the truth, and finally his expression cracked, and exhaustion leaked out.

"Delilah, drink the water. Eat the food. There's no price. There will never be a price. My word is my honor."

I gave him one more second to reconsider. Then I ripped into the first protein bar with my teeth and ate half of it in one bite. "Why are you doing this?" I asked around a mouthful of peanuts and oats.

"The food is free. Answers aren't." He headed for the loose canvas panel, and I probably would have pressed for more information if I weren't busy stuffing protein bars into my mouth. "I'll be back with some clean clothes and a fresh blanket."

"Thanks," I said, but Gallagher ducked beneath the untethered sidewall without acknowledging me.

I ate all four protein bars in a span of minutes, stopping only to chug from the bottle of water, and when I finished, my jaw ached from chewing so hard and fast. I drained the last drops from the bottle, then turned to gather my trash into a neat pile—and froze when I found the minotaur staring at me.

He stood in front of the sidewall Gallagher had left loose, an enormous chain trailing from his thick bovine ankle beneath the tent wall to whatever our handler had left him tethered to. Either my crunching had covered the sound of his entry or his chain was too heavy to rattle.

"Eryx?" My heartbeat thumped in my throat and echoed in both ears. The minotaur was nearly a foot taller than the top of my cage, and at least half as wide. For the first time since being conscripted into the menagerie, I was glad to be locked in a pen, even if the bull was drugged out of his mind.

There's never a good time to find out a minotaur has a bone to pick with you.

Eryx blinked, and his gaze held mine. He showed no inclination to ram my cart, or paw the ground, or even snort aggressively.

Fascinated, I scooted closer to the side of my cage, covering myself as best I could with the mildewy blanket. Ruyle had said the minotaur had the intellect of a cow, but his eyes looked human to me, and in my experience, rather than being the windows to the soul, they were the windows to one's thoughts. Which originated in the brain.

"Eryx, do you understand me?"

The minotaur's broad, thick forehead furrowed over his human eyes, and at first he only studied me. Then he nodded slowly, his enormous, curved horns dipping low with the movement, and I wondered if he'd ever nodded before. The gesture looked awkward and unpracticed.

"What are you doing in here?"

He tilted his head to the right, and though that gesture also looked awkward, his meaning was clear.

"Okay. Yes or no questions only. Um, did Gallagher send you in?"

Eryx shook his head.

"Does he know you're here?" I asked, and when he shook his head again, slowly, I wondered how much those massive horns weighed. If the thickness of his neck was any indication, they were quite a burden. "Do you need something?"

He seemed to think about that for a second, then shook his head again.

"Is there something you want to tell me?" I asked, and when he nodded, my pulse raced so fast I got light-headed. It took me a moment to realize that I wasn't about to pass out from exhaustion, hunger, or head trauma. I was exhilarated, like I hadn't been since long before Gallagher threw me into a cage like an animal. I had a mystery. A project. Maybe…a secret.

After a week trapped as much in my own head as in my cage, I finally had something to think about, other than my vague but persistent plans to escape.

"Eryx, does Gallagher know you understand…everything?"

He shook his head, and another little thrill of excitement shot through me. I felt like I suddenly had a secret ally.

"Does anyone know?" I asked, and when he didn't seem to know how to answer, I realized that my question was too broad. "Anyone on the staff?"

Another head shake, and I couldn't stop grinning. "Any of the exhibits?"

Eryx shook his head again, and frowned.

"Okay, what could that mean? Um…someone outside of Metzger's?" I said, and that time when the minotaur nodded, his eyes seemed to be shining. "Family?" He shook his head, so I tried again. "Friend?" But he only shook his head again. "Um…someone you knew before you came here?" He nodded, so I kept going. "A former…um…owner?"

That time when he nodded, I felt like my blood was on *fire*, and it wasn't just that I'd figured out something that Gallagher and Metzger didn't know. It wasn't just that I was now party to what was starting to feel like a triumphant conspiracy. It was the fact that Eryx's secret existed in the first place.

He had something private. Something all his own. Something they hadn't been able to take from him, in spite of the chains, and the drugs, and the forced labor and exploitation. Eryx had won, even if his victory was small, and his success was due not to his size or strength, but to his wit and his patience. The "dim-witted" beast had outsmarted his human captors, and if he could do it, I could, too. I would just have to be smart about it. Like Eryx.

"So, what did you want to tell me? Am I going to have to guess?"

Eryx shook his head, and that time I could swear he was trying to smile. Carefully, he lowered himself to one knee in the sawdust. I could tell the position wasn't comfortable for him, either because his lower legs were bovine, or because his head, arms, and torso were so massive that it was difficult for him to find balance off his feet. The minotaur slowly turned away from me and reached for the ground with one hand, resting his opposite elbow on his knee for stability. When he began to draw in the sawdust with one thick index finger, I realized I was holding my breath.

I scooted to one end of my cage and craned my neck, trying to see what he was drawing, and after several seconds, I realized he wasn't drawing at all.

"Holy shit, you can write! Which probably means you can read, too." Surely there were other exhibits who could read and write—though the siren Lenore was the only one I'd met so far who wasn't raised in a carnival—but it had never occurred to me that the minotaur might be one of them.

Suddenly I felt like a bigoted asshole.

Eryx nodded without pausing, and when he shuffled to the right to start on the second word, he revealed the first. He'd written *RED* in uneven capital letters.

"Red. Okay." I had to bite my tongue to keep from yelling at him to write faster, damn it! He clearly hadn't had much practice, but I was about to crawl out of my own skin in anticipation and Gallagher could be back at any moment.

Finally Eryx twisted on his knee to look at me, and the second word was revealed. *CAP* stood next to *RED*, written in those same shaky capital letters.

"Red cap." I frowned while he watched me expectantly. "Red cap. Whose cap, Eryx? Are you talking about Gallagher's hat?"

He shook his head, but then nodded, and I translated his frustrated contradiction into "no, but yes," a sentiment I'd often expressed with no more clarity, in spite of my fully functional human mouth.

"So, Gallagher's hat, but not his hat." And suddenly I got it. "You're talking about Gallagher himself, aren't you?"

Red cap was a descriptor. Maybe he didn't know how to spell *Gallagher.* Or maybe that would have taken too long.

Eryx nodded, and warmth spread throughout my chest. I was proud of us both, and not miserable for the first time since I'd woken up at the sheriff's station eight days before.

"Okay, so what about Gallagher? You want me to tell him

something for you? Why can't you just spell for him?" But the minotaur was already shaking his head. "You don't want me to tell him anything?" Eryx nodded, and I assumed that meant I was correct. "So…you want to tell me something about him?"

That time I was rewarded with a grand, exaggerated head nod, and I realized the minotaur was just as frustrated with my slow comprehension of his words as I was with his pace in writing them.

But before I could guess again, the untethered sidewall rustled and Gallagher called from outside the tent. "Eryx? Where did you—"

The minotaur swiped one huge hand over the words he'd written half a second before Gallagher pushed back the blue striped canvas flap and stepped into the tent with an armload of material.

"Eryx, what the hell are you doing in here?" Gallagher dropped the linen-and-wool bundle on the table, knocking over several of the berserker's pictures, then scowled at the minotaur, whose horns reached the handler's shoulders, even kneeling.

Eryx blinked up at him, and I realized that for whatever reason, the minotaur was playing dumb. And he was *good* at it.

"Well, get up!" Gallagher snapped. "Don't tell me you're stuck like that. It'd take a crane to lift you."

Eryx pushed himself to his feet slowly and with exaggerated effort, then let Gallagher lead him back outside. When the handler returned, he looked thoroughly perplexed. "What happened?" He plucked a clean dress from the pile on the table and shook it out on his way across the tent.

"I don't know," I lied. But my mental gears were grinding and smoking, trying to figure out what Eryx wanted to tell me about Gallagher, the man who held my safety and well-being in his big, rough hands.

"What was he doing in here?"

I shrugged, still clutching the dirty blanket. "He doesn't talk, remember?"

"A quality I'm starting to appreciate." Gallagher slid a fresh pair of underwear and a cotton bra through the tray slot in my cage. "Why was he on the ground?"

"He fell." I looked right into his eyes, but they narrowed with obvious suspicion.

"You're lying."

"Does that mean I don't get clothes?"

Gallagher huffed and let the dress hang from one finger. "This partnership is starting to feel a little one-sided. I give, and you take. Does that seem fair to you?"

My temper flared and my cheeks burned. "You said there would never be a price."

"I'm not asking you to pay. I'm telling you to learn how to transmute, so I can put you back in the show." He opened the tray slot again and pushed the clean dress inside. "That's not negotiable for either of us, Delilah."

"Don't you mean *Drea*?" I grabbed the dress, clutching the blanket to my chest with my free hand. "You can't change my name."

"I let you keep your initial."

"How magnanimous of you. Turn around," I snapped, and his growl was deep enough to impress a werewolf, but he turned.

I changed into the fresh underwear as quickly as I could. "I'm keeping my name." I pulled the clean dress over my head before he could get mad and decide to take the clothing back. "Is this really the best you could do?" I held out the hem of the new dress to show him that it was too small—more suited to one of the *djinn* girls than to a grown woman.

"You have a strange way of expressing gratitude."

"I'm better with logic, so let me put this 'gratitude' in perspective for you. I appreciate the fact that you've kept me alive, Gallagher, but I am entitled to life. I shouldn't need you to keep me from starving to death, and that's really all you're doing. You're flatlining on the morality EKG, expecting me to praise you as if you'd spiked an actual ethical pulse."

I threaded my fingers through the wire mesh and stood on my knees again, putting myself as close to eye level with him as I could. "I will get out of here. I can either go with you or through you."

His focus volleyed between my eyes, as if he were searching for something. "You're fearless." The pronouncement had the feel of an official ruling.

"Well, one of us should be."

He blinked, betraying a flash of anger. "You think I'm a coward?"

No. He'd taken plenty of risks for me. But at the end of the day, I was still locked in a cage. "I don't know what else to call a man who knows what's right, but refuses to act on it."

Gallagher was like a puzzle put together all wrong. The pieces shouldn't have fit, yet there he stood, made of equal parts compromise and rigidity. Compassion and mercenary determination to protect his paycheck.

"Don't mistake patience for cowardice, Delilah," he mumbled, and something grim and foreboding passed behind his eyes.

Anticipation raced through my veins like fire blazing along a trail of accelerant. Patience? I gripped the metal mesh tighter. "What does that mean? You're waiting for something? For what?" And what would he do when he got it?

I stared into his eyes, but the truth—if it was there—was buried too deep for me to see. "What are you doing, Gallagher? Are you planning something?" Or was he stringing me along with hope, to make me cooperate?

"You help me keep my job, and I'll tell you what you want to know."

"Promise? Because I hear your word is your—"

He scowled. "I swear on my life. And my word *is* my honor."

When I found no hint of doubt or hesitation in him, I exhaled. "Fine." I pushed the tray slot open and shoved both the mildewy blanket and my damp clothes onto the ground. "What do you want me to do?"

"Learn to transmute." He began to pace in front of my cage while he spoke. "I've been thinking about the one time it happened, and anger seems to have been the catalyst. But you're angry all the time, and that hasn't helped, so today I did what I could to re-create that kind of intense anger. However..." He shrugged, and the gesture looked all wrong on him. He had too powerful a build for such a casual motion.

"What does that mean? What did you do?"

Gallagher picked up the blanket, shaking sawdust from it. "I got out of the way." He crossed the tent and traded the dirty blanket for the clean one lying on the table.

"Out of the...? You...?" I sat back on my heels as the depth of his betrayal became clear. "You took the day off just to put me at Clyde's mercy. So he would piss me off." My throat felt tight.

"No." Gallagher spoke with such force that his denial could have driven a tent stake into the ground. "I had business in town today, and since I had to be gone, I took the opportunity to let him do what I couldn't." He slid the clean blanket through the tray slot, but I didn't even glance at it.

What he couldn't do. Starve me. Strip me. Humiliate me.

"Why couldn't you—" I hadn't realized how betrayed I felt

until my voice cracked in the middle of the question. Even if he was only doing his job—keeping me healthy enough to perform—I'd come to expect decency, if not actual kindness, from Gallagher. "Why couldn't you do it yourself?"

"My reasoning doesn't matter." His stone-gray eyes betrayed nothing.

"He threw out my food and drenched me with a hose in front of God and half of the menagerie. He gashed open my head, then left me to pass out in my cage!"

The iron clench of his jaw was the only hint that my suffering bothered him. "I know."

"You know?" Rage exploded inside me. I shook the wire mesh as hard as I could, but it barely rattled. Of course he knew. He'd expected most of that, which was the reason he'd left me with Clyde in the first place.

His expression was carefully blank as he studied mine. "How do you feel? Any change in vision? Does your hair feel…weightless?"

I jerked back from the side of the cage. He was still trying to turn me into a monster by making me mad. "Stop! It's not going to work!"

His forehead furrowed and he grabbed the metal mesh, his grip just outside of my own, and for the first time since he'd pinned Clyde to my cage, I saw something real—something raw and wild—flash in his eyes. "We're running out of time, Delilah." The urgency in his voice stole my breath. "If you can't perform by next week, they will take you aw—"

Gallagher's mouth snapped shut so quickly I wasn't sure what I'd almost heard. "They'll sell you," he finished. "And I won't be able to protect you."

"Protect me? Is that what you think you're doing?"

His gray eyes widened almost imperceptibly. "That's *all* I've done since you got here. I'm making enemies. I'm disobeying orders. I'm breaking laws, Delilah. All to keep the old man from selling you to a collector who'll wring every dime he can out of you, then let some sick bastard pay for the privilege of finally ending your miserable life."

"Why do you care?"

Gallagher blinked, and whatever I'd seen in his eyes was gone, suddenly concealed by the stone facade he wore as easily as other men wore sunglasses. He let go of the cage and stepped back. "That isn't relevant."

"It is." If I knew I could trust him—that he wasn't just manipulating me into performing to save his job—I might be willing to compromise. "Tell me the truth."

"I've never lied to you."

"Then don't start now. Talk, Gallagher."

He exhaled slowly, then met my gaze from across the tent. "I was wrong when I said you were just like all the other beasts in cages. You're not. You came to the carnival passing for human, and you could have left the same way. The only reason you're not at home in your own bed, wearing your own clothes right now, is that you exposed yourself to help Geneviève."

"I didn't know what I was doing." I shook my head. "I didn't know what it would cost me. I can't take credit—"

"You'd have done it even if you'd known," he insisted, though I kept shaking my head. "That's who you are. I've seen that in a dozen other, smaller ways since you got here. That draws people to you, Delilah. It makes assholes like Clyde want to conquer you, and it makes people like Claudio want to be your friend. It makes me want to keep you safe, even if that costs me things you can't possibly understand." And he clearly wasn't going to explain those things. "But the only way for either of us to protect you is to make sure you are valuable to the menagerie. You have to do what Metzger wants."

I was starting to concur, but not for reasons he'd like. I'd probably have significantly fewer chances to escape from a private collection than I would from the menagerie, where I was routinely removed from my cage and my handlers were often distracted by other duties.

"Gallagher, I don't know how. It's only happened that once, when Jack was hurting Genni."

"I'm still trying to figure that out." Gallagher stared down at me, frustration written in every line on his face. "Why is your transformation linked to the torture of a werewolf pup you'd never even met a few days ago?"

I had no answer. What did Genni have to do with—

"Maybe it isn't." I sat straighter as a fresh memory fell into place. "I felt it coming on in the travel trailer yesterday, but no one was being hurt." Though we were all suffering.

Gallagher came closer, and his shadow stretched across the ground. "What were you thinking about?"

"Rommily. Claudio was telling me about what happened to her, and I got so furious I couldn't think about anything else, and…" My words trailed off when I realized Gallagher was staring at me in astonishment. "What?"

"I can't believe I didn't see it." He stepped back and pressed both hands to the sides of his faded red ball cap. "The first time I saw you, I felt all this rage in you, but I misunderstood…"

I shook my head. He wasn't making any sense. "I wasn't angry until I saw Jack take a cattle prod to Geneviève." And I wasn't sure how he could have "felt" my anger, either way.

"The fury was always there," he insisted, and eyes that had previously looked as gray and unyielding as stone suddenly shone like polished steel. "You have an endless font of it, Delilah. You are made of rage and power, all tied up in this deceptively delicate form." His focus never wandered south of my face, but I felt his attention like a tangible force. "Your beast was just waiting for the right moment, for something to call it out of you."

"You're saying my inner monster is rage?" That didn't make any sense, but I could hardly think it through because he was still looking at me as if I were the only candle burning in a dark room—the first glimpse of light strong enough to lead the way.

As if I were something he *needed*.

"Yes, rage, but rage with a purpose. It's been there all along." Gallagher clutched the decorative frame of my cage and stared down into my eyes with an intensity I'd never seen from him. Or from anyone else. "This whole time I've been looking for your species, but it's not that simple. Nothing with you is ever simple. But my point is that you could be any species. You could be a siren, or an oracle, or—"

His sentence ended so abruptly I thought he might have bitten his tongue off with it.

Gallagher turned, and in three huge steps he'd crossed the tent and snatched his bag from the table. He rummaged through the front pocket, then came back clutching a folded sheet of paper in one huge fist, his gray eyes bright with fervor. He unfolded the page and held it up a foot from my face on the other side of the steel mesh.

The first thing I noticed was how deep and worn the creases were, as if he'd folded and unfolded the paper many times. Then I saw the date at the top. "This is a week old." My voice sounded strange. Hollow.

"Nine days," he corrected, and I realized I'd lost track of time. But by then I'd found the box at the bottom, where the result of my blood test was printed.

I blinked. Then I blinked again, but the words didn't change.

"This says I'm...human." But that couldn't be right. No human could do what I'd done to Jack.

"That's why they're running your blood work again." Gallagher stared down at me. "They don't believe it either."

Confusion warred with shock inside me. I couldn't think straight. "How long have you had this?"

"Since your second night in the menagerie."

"Why didn't you tell me?" I demanded.

"Because I thought it was a mistake, and believing you were human would not have helped you bring out your beast. But the test is right. You're not a cryptid, Delilah, not that it matters anymore—"

"You think that doesn't *matter*?"

"—because what you are transcends species. You're an ideal. An abstraction." He gripped the steel wire with his free hand. "You are the incarnation of justice."

"Wait. *What?* I'm human, but I'm also rage…and justice?" He clearly had no idea how little sense he was making.

Gallagher nodded, his gray eyes shining with feverish excitement. "You're a *furiae*, Delilah."

"Furiae?" I frowned, thinking back to a class I'd had in college. Not a crypto-veterinary class—a literature elective. "As in, the Erinyes?"

"Yes." He grabbed a folding chair from beneath the table and set it in front of my wagon. "Those who avenge unrighted wrongs. That's you." He looked so satisfied. Almost euphoric. As if what he'd figured out somehow meant as much to him as it should to me.

"But the Erinyes aren't real. They're just the personification of a concept." Many, many cryptids were once assumed to be folklore and myths, but the Erinyes… "They're just symbols, Gallagher. Stories intended to reassure people that justice would be meted out in the afterlife if it was overlooked in this one."

"Oh, the Erinyes are real." He sat in the low chair, and

for the first time since we'd met, he had to look up at me. "They're very rare, though, because they're not born. They're made."

"Made?" I wasn't sure how much to believe. I wasn't sure how much I *wanted* to believe. How could I be human, yet still have no rights? How likely were the authorities to believe a blood test, when at least fifteen people had seen me turn into a monster? "How are the Erinyes made?"

"Through sacrifice." Gallagher cleared his throat and leaned forward in his chair, capturing my gaze as if nothing in the world could mean more than whatever he was about to say. "People think they are masters of the universe because they've conquered the skies, and the seas, and the heavens. Because they can kill with the press of a button and speak to anyone else on the planet, anytime they like. But there are things older and wiser than humanity. Things more powerful and significant. Love, and loss, and birth. Pain, and bliss. Vengeance. They're more than just words, Delilah." The shine in his eyes was captivating. Practically hypnotic. "They're inalienable truths, in the most powerful sense of the word, and they're the only things that mankind can never truly touch, much less own.

"Every now and then, the universe decides to prove that by endowing a living being with the essence of one of those truths. You have been chosen to represent vengeance. To remind the world that mankind is not its own final authority. That burden is equal parts honor and curse, and it is nothing that humanity at large will ever accept. Or willingly allow to exist."

I could only stare at him, stunned by an outpouring of information I couldn't properly process. Most of it was churning in my head, slowly being ground into digestible chunks.

"What sacrifice put me here?" My voice echoed with shock.

"I don't know. Sometimes martyrs are brought back as *furiae*."

"But I'm not dead." Not that I knew of anyway. But then, the list of things I didn't know had never felt quite so comprehensive before.

"It's not always self-sacrifice. Each case is unique. We may never figure out how you became a *furiae*, but I have no doubt it's true. That's why you couldn't transmute when Clyde abused you." He finally refolded the paper and slid it into his pocket. "You can't avenge yourself—your calling is purely selfless."

My thoughts were racing. I didn't want to believe it, but I couldn't come up with anything to contradict his theory. "But I've seen plenty of unjust things, and none of them ever turned me into a monster. Why now? Why Genni?"

Gallagher was quiet, and I could tell he was searching through his knowledge of the mythology for an answer that made sense. "According to the lore, each of the Erinyes was responsible for avenging a certain kind of offense. Maybe your specialty is avenging abused cryptids."

Clarity rushed over me. I'd always been fascinated by cryptids and bothered by the way they were treated. That was why I'd majored in crypto-biology in the first place. I'd thought my degree would help me make a difference. If I'd gone on to crypto-veterinary school, surely I would have seen the abuse firsthand a lot sooner. My inner beast might have shown herself years ago.

"So, you're telling me that I can avenge any captive in the menagerie, but not myself?"

Gallagher nodded. "You may also be able to avenge humans, even if they're not your specific calling, but you can't take vengeance on your own behalf."

"So, I'm totally helpless."

"No." He stood and looked straight into my eyes. "You have intelligence and courage. And you have me."

Yet he didn't seem to see the conflict of interest. "You're a jailer."

"That sums me up no more thoroughly than the word *prisoner* describes you." He came closer to the side of my cage, piercing me with the intensity of his steel focus. "I'm working on something, Delilah. I can get you out of here, so that you can better serve the demands of your calling. But I'm going to need trust, patience, and cooperation from you, or it won't work. Can you do that?"

"Can you tell me what you're up to?" I said, and he shook his head, while mine spun with the possibilities. "Of course you can't. Do I have any other choice?"

"Not a good one. But my word is my honor, Delilah. Will you work with me?"

I exhaled and sat on my ankles in my cage. "Okay."

Gallagher nodded, and though he looked pleased, he did not smile. I wasn't sure he even knew how.

"The latest reports indicate that these 'surrogate' children brought home unbeknownst to their unwitting families somehow 'glamoured' parents into slaughtering all human siblings in a single bloody night. What kind of creatures are we talking about here, Ginger? Are they *fae*? What kind of *fae*, exactly?"

—Transcript from a September 24, 1986, interview with Ginger Cumberland, Head of Research at Yale's Crypto-biology Department, on *Wake Up America*

ERYX

The minotaur watched the carnival awaken from within his custom-made heavy-duty steel crate, but the carnival did not watch him back. The handlers and roustabouts never seemed to notice him until they needed him for heavy labor, and that was okay with Eryx.

The only advantage of having no speech was that most people assumed he also had no language and little comprehension beyond basic repetitive instructions.

Eryx was just fine with that assumption.

Before breakfast, Gallagher injected the usual dose of the usual drugs into his arm through the steel mesh and between the strong, thick steel bars. The bars on the minotaur's cage were twice as thick as those on the other cages because Eryx could have kicked out one of the regular bars in his sleep. In fact, he'd done that very thing during a bad dream the year he was fourteen and still in the possession of another carnival. The staff had risen to find him sleeping with one massive hoofed leg dangling from the side of his busted-open cage. The dislodged bar lay on the ground, and the wire mesh panel was twisted and torn around the bovine leg protruding through it.

Still, he'd never tried to run or to hurt anyone, and those

who worked with him on a daily basis were so accustomed to his benign presence and tractable disposition that even though he was four times heavier and nine times stronger than the average circus roustabout, few ever worried for their safety around the giant beast.

They worried even less about information spilled near him, and Eryx soaked it up like a sponge, patiently waiting for the opportunity and ability to use what he knew. And the information didn't just come from the staff. Many of his fellow captives—even those who recognized intelligence in his eyes—assumed him incapable of betraying the secrets they let slip in his presence.

Eryx knew about the siren's stealthy lover, and the ringmaster's closet fetish. He knew about the old man's hypocrisy and he knew where Gallagher went when he slipped away from the menagerie some nights and came back…rejuvenated.

The bull knew where Rommily had disappeared to on that rainy night months before. He knew who'd been with her, and what had happened to her, and he knew that she would never be the same again.

And as Gallagher marched him down the row of wagons, past cage after cage and captive after captive, Eryx saw Rommily, sitting between her sisters, and he understood—not for the first time—that they were the same in many ways, the fragile oracle and the mighty minotaur.

Both knew important things, yet could not speak them.

Rommily looked up as he passed, and when her wide-eyed, fevered gaze found his, the minotaur stopped walking, heedless of the ring tugging at his septum and the impatient sounds of the handler in the red cap.

"Steel trap," she murmured, but his ears were so attuned to her voice that he would have heard even the softest sound to fall from her tongue. "One track. Speak mine. Boggle yours. Think alike."

The bull snorted softly, and her wheat-colored eyes narrowed, studying him as the handler turned to assess the problem. "Eryx. Let's go."

"Labyrinth, deconstructed!" Rommily shouted, as Gallagher urged the minotaur forward. "Eccentric rings! Fools will tumble. Blood will flow. And the bull shall stand tallest of them all..."

DELILAH

Geneviève's cage, which had been ominously missing from the lineup last night, was in place next to her father's when I woke up. I couldn't have slept for more than a couple of hours, with my thoughts flying around like debris in a storm, but she looked like she'd been awake all night.

"Genni!" I called, when I noticed her curled up in one corner of her pen, and to my relief, she looked up at the sound of my voice. "We missed you last night. Are you okay?"

She blinked, but made no response, and I noticed the fresh bandage on her forearm.

"What happened to your arm, honey?"

"What's wrong with her arm?" Claudio sat up and looked to me for a reply because he couldn't see into his daughter's cage. "I don't smell fresh blood."

"Genni, hold your arm out please," I said, and after a moment's hesitation, she complied. "The bandage is clean," I told Claudio, but I didn't mention how thin her arm was or how prominent her elbow looked because of that. "If there was blood, it's dry and covered. Genni, what happened? Did someone hurt you?"

Just asking made my chest ache. In my former life, if she'd

said yes, I would have called child protective services. But because Genni was raised in the menagerie, her answer was largely irrelevant. If someone had hurt her, it wouldn't be the first time, and there was nothing I could do about it.

Or maybe there was.

If Gallagher was right, I might be the only one who *could* do something about it. But I wasn't quite ready to dive into the deep end of the vengeance pool.

I wasn't actually sure how to kick-start my inner *furiae*, and Gallagher and I had agreed that the rest of the staff should not know what we'd figured out. If they discovered that my life's purpose was at odds with their tendency to abuse the captives, I might very well be hurt—or at least isolated—beyond the ability to help anyone else. Yet what was the point of having a "calling," as Gallagher referred to it, if I couldn't perform the inherent duties?

Still, when Genni shook her head, relief rolled over me, taking some of the pressure off my response.

"Did you do that to yourself?" I asked, and she nodded, then mimed biting her own arm. "She bit herself," I told her father, and Claudio nodded in acknowledgment, his face a mask of worry. "Did they sew you up? Did they put cream on your arm before the bandage?"

Genni shrugged.

"She doesn't know," I said. "My guess is that she was unconscious."

"But she's okay now?"

"Seems to be," I said, well aware that "okay" was a relative term among menagerie captives.

Geneviève curled up on the metal floor of her pen and pulled her blanket up to her shoulders, then tucked both hands beneath her cheek like a pillow. *"Dites-moi une histoire, s'il vous plaît."*

"She wants to hear another story," her father translated, but I'd already figured that out. "She used her manners." He seemed pleased by that, and the rare glimpse at a normal parenting moment under such barbaric circumstances made my eyes water.

"Okay, let me think." She'd liked Hansel and Gretel, and I wanted to give her a story about a girl who triumphed over extraordinary adversity. Something relevant to her life. "Genni, do you know about the Black Bull-man of Norroway?" I asked, and when she shook her head, I sat cross-legged facing her and pulled my blanket into my lap, settling in for the story about a noble minotaur and his troubled young bride.

Halfway through, I looked up from where Genni lay watching me and discovered that Claudio, Zyanya, Payat, and Mahsa were all listening as well, and based on the silence from farther down the line, my audience had grown even bigger than I could see.

Breakfast was a small scoop of watery oatmeal—without utensils—and a boiled pig's foot, served by Abraxas. He didn't smile or chat with the captives, but he was a definite improvement over Clyde because everything he scooped onto the trays actually made it into someone's stomach.

I ate every bite of my meal, silently cursing myself for every scrap of food I'd ever wasted in my life before captivity.

I was leaning against the end panel of my cage, marveling at how much better I felt having eaten twice in a span of twelve hours, when Zyanya called my name from her ornate black-and-silver-framed crate across the aisle. "Hey," she said when I looked up. "Where did you go last night?"

"Excuse me?"

"I woke up in the middle of the night, and your cage was

gone, but this morning you have clean clothes and a fresh blanket. Where'd you go?"

"Gallagher took her," a female voice called from farther down my own line of cages, and I recognized Lenore's melodic siren voice. I knew most of my fellow captives by voice better than by sight.

"He didn't *take* me," I insisted, afraid someone would think I'd made a late-night concession for food. Which was when I realized my secret—*any* secret, actually—would be really hard to keep in the menagerie. "He just..."

"He made you work?" Claudio guessed, and I could have kissed him.

"Yes, actually. He says I can't go back on display until we figure out what I am." What he'd really said was that I couldn't go back on display until I figured out how to transmute without having to see someone else hurt. I'd come close on the travel trailer, but close wasn't good enough to charge admission for.

"Any clue yet?" Lenore asked from the wagon she shared with Finola.

Immediately the buzz of caged conversation swelled.

"I think she's a gorgon," the berserker called from three cages down. He was well out of my line of sight, but I'd grown to recognize the odd rattle in his voice. "Her hair looked like Medusa. I saw it that first night."

"I saw it, too, and there were no snakes," Zyanya insisted, seated with her knees sticking up near her shoulders, every bit the cat, even in human form. "No snakes, no gorgon. Plus, no one turned into stone."

"That stone part's bullshit," Finola, the other siren, called. I recognized her by the telltale melodic quality of her voice, even when she wasn't singing. "Gorgons don't actually petrify people—they exude some kind of hormone that paralyzes them. Besides, she can't be a gorgon. They're extinct."

After that, the discussion devolved into an argument over whether gorgons were actually extinct or just very, very endangered, and I let it proceed without me, grateful that everyone seemed to have forgotten about my illicit nighttime activities.

When the daily parade of captives toward the fairgrounds began, I watched with renewed interest, waiting for a glimpse of Eryx. Hoping he would look at me on his way past, or somehow acknowledge the new secret we shared, so I could stop worrying that I'd imagined him writing in the sawdust.

I wanted to know what he'd been trying to tell me. Did he know what Gallagher was up to?

Halfway through the cavalcade of weary exhibits in gilded cages, the white centaur and the buck pulled the oracle sisters by my crate and the moment my gaze met Rommily's, her eyes widened and glazed over with a white film.

"David! Dorothy! Heidi!" she shouted at me. "Siblings in serendipity, they welcome you!"

"Are those the names she said to you last time?" Claudio asked, and I could only shake my head, watching the oracles pass.

"Who are they?" Mahsa called from behind me.

"I have no idea."

"What were the other names?" the berserker asked, and in the aisle between rows, I could see his shadow silhouette turn toward mine.

"Um… Jane, and Pip, and Oliver. And a princess named Sara. And Secret Mary."

"*Sara, la princesse.*" Geneviève sat up and pushed her blanket off. "*Mon histoire préférée!*"

"What?" I turned to Genni, goose bumps rising on my arms. "Geneviève, what did you say?"

"She's talking about the girl in her favorite story," Claudio explained, pushing shaggy silver hair back from his face. "Mirela used to tell it to her, after Genni's mother... After they sold Melisande."

"A Little Princess." I'd read it over and over as a kid.

"Oui!" Genni looked so hopeful I hated to disappoint her by not telling the story, but my brain was racing too quickly to stop.

"Holy shit! They're all characters."

"What?" Zyanya blinked big orangish eyes at me.

"Rommily's names. They're all characters from books. Sara, from *A Little Princess*. Mary, from *The Secret Garden*. Pip, from *Great Expectations*. Oliver, from *Oliver Twist*. David, from *David Copperfield*. Dorothy, from *The Wonderful Wizard of Oz*. Heidi, from—well, from *Heidi*. I don't know who Jane is, but there must be a thousand characters named Jane."

Genni watched me, still waiting for her story, but her father looked puzzled. "Are they dead?"

"They're fictional. They were never alive in the first place." I shrugged. "You said Mirela told Genni about *A Little Princess*? Can she read? Weren't the oracles born here?" I had yet to meet anyone who'd learned to read after being born into captivity. Except maybe Eryx.

"No, they were bought as small children, after their parents were exposed and sold elsewhere," the werewolf papa said. "That was a couple of years after the old man brought me in from France."

"Were they old enough to read?"

"Mirela knows her letters," Mahsa said, smoothing long black hair over one dark shoulder, and I realized that everyone within hearing distance had gone quiet, listening. Most sat pressed against the aisle sides of their cages, trying to see as many fellow prisoners as possible. "She went to school for a couple of years before they were exposed. Sometimes she reads signs for us, so we know where we are. And I saw her teach letters to her sisters, in the dirt. When we were in the petting zoo."

The petting zoo.

An old memory flashed through my mind, and I connected the dots. I'd seen Mirela, Rommily, and Lala in the petting zoo when I was a kid. Mirela had been about my age, and I couldn't understand what three normal-looking girls were doing in the pen next to two small werewolves. They must have been new to the menagerie when I'd seen them.

The ache in my chest rivaled the rage in my soul. Small children ripped from their parents and sold into exhibition. That ache bruised even deeper when I realized I probably wasn't hearing about an isolated incident.

"She didn't read about Princess Sara, though," Claudio said. "She saw it on television. On a movie disk."

"A DVD." That made more sense. And if the oracle sisters had seen *A Little Princess* as a movie, they might have seen all the others the same way, long before they could have read the books.

"So why is she shouting the names of storybook characters at you?" Payat asked.

I could only shrug, my mind still racing. "Maybe she wants to tell me a story. Or maybe she wants me to tell one," I said, thinking of Eryx and our guessing game the night before.

Claudio shook his head once, firmly. "She doesn't ask for things anymore, and if her sisters didn't feed her, she would hardly eat. She has visions all the time, but she only shouts like that when she's seen something she really wants to tell someone."

What could Rommily possibly have seen involving a bunch of characters from books more than a century old, and what did any of that have to do with me?

Were any of them captives or prisoners?

Oliver Twist was stuck in a prison-like orphanage. Sara was forced to work for the owner of a girls' school, after her father died and left her penni—

"Orphans." The connection between the characters hit me like a punch to the gut. "They're all orphans. Sara, Mary, Pip, David, Oliver, Heidi, and Dorothy. And presumably Jane. Their parents are all…"

…*dead*.

Fate's bastards. "And I least among them…" My goose bumps receded beneath growing horror. "She's telling me I'm an orphan. Or that I'm going to be."

Movement to my right caught my eye and when the world zoomed back into focus, I saw Gallagher leading Eryx as he pulled a cage holding one of the squat, gnarl-limbed trolls.

"Gallagher!" I shouted, with no real forethought. He gave me a dark scowl, then kept walking without acknowledging me.

Normally, I would have let it go at that. Instead, I gripped the wire mesh and pulled myself onto my knees.

"Delilah, *don't*!" Zyanya whispered fiercely. "You're asking for trouble."

And I knew that. But my mother was the only person left in the world who'd cared about me both before and after captivity, and I didn't even know if she was alive. Getting ahold of her was worth whatever I'd have to endure for my insolence later.

So I steeled my nerve and raised my voice. "Gallagher! I need to talk to you."

His scowl became an angry glower and he handed Eryx's

lead rope to Abraxas, who was passing in the opposite direction, with a barked order to wait for him. Gallagher stormed toward me, every step a bolt of thunder, anger firing in his gaze like lightning.

"Delilah, don't make it worse," Claudio whispered. But I was already committed.

"What the *hell* are you doing?" Gallagher growled, and the look in his gray eyes froze the blood in my veins. He looked like he might have ripped my head from my neck, if not for the steel barrier.

My mother was worth the risk.

"I need a favor, and I'm willing to pay." Though I wasn't sure how. "I'll… You can put me in the show tonight. I'll figure out how to transmute. I *swear* I'll make it happen." And if I couldn't, he would already have granted my favor.

"Gallagher?" Chris Ruyle headed toward us from the silver wagon, wearing his authority like a badge, and my heartbeat echoed in my ears. "Is there a problem?"

"Nothing I can't handle." Gallagher held my gaze with fury dancing in his own. "Don't forget where you're sitting." His voice rolled over me with a chilling hostility that made me wonder if I'd imagined everything that happened the night before. "You do as you're told, or you pay the price, just like all the other monsters in metal boxes."

He turned to stomp off, and desperation warred with my common sense. "Gallagher, *please!*" I called after him, gripping the wire so tightly it cut into my fingers. "I wouldn't ask if it wasn't important!"

He stiffened. Two steps later, he grabbed Abraxas by the front of his red tee. "No lunch for Drea today. No dinner either. Got it?"

Abraxas nodded, clearly terrified, and Gallagher let him

go. "If you hear one more word out of her before I get back, hose her down."

His words were a shock almost as violent as the hose itself.

Gallagher snatched Eryx's lead rope and pulled the bull toward the rear entrance to the fairgrounds. As he was marched off, the minotaur turned to look at me, and I could swear I saw sympathy in his sad, human eyes.

Lunch came and went, and I was not served. Crews came to haul off the second troll, the lamia, the puca, the pair of *djinn*, and the berserker, but Gallagher did not return.

I didn't speak, even when Claudio and Zyanya both tried to draw me out of silence. Even when Geneviève asked politely in French for another story, I complied with Gallagher's gag order not for my own safety, but for my mother's. My last remaining parent, who was in serious trouble, if I'd interpreted Rommily's riddle correctly.

Or maybe she was already dead.

I would never know for sure without Gallagher's help.

After lunch, crew members leading pairs of drugged centaurs came to haul off the adlet and the cat shifters, leaving me alone with Geneviève and Claudio, who was trying to talk his daughter into performing her first live shift to keep her from being abused for refusal.

Early in the afternoon, two more hauling crews came for the werewolves, and my unadorned crate stood alone for the second day in a row. My growing hunger couldn't hold a candle to my need for a restroom, though I'd had nothing to drink since the small bowl of water that had come with my breakfast.

And through it all, I could think of nothing but my mother, hoping with every breath in my body that I'd misinterpreted the oracle's fractured prophecy.

Finally, as carnival performers headed toward the midway in black satin and red sequins glittering in the hot afternoon sun, Eryx and Gallagher appeared at the fairgrounds' back gate, headed my way. I could tell from my handler's gait that he wasn't as mad as he'd been earlier, but he didn't look happy either.

"Gallagher," I said as he fastened the minotaur's harness to my cage.

He leaned around the end panel. "Just shut up and sit still, and you might not end this day any worse off than you began it."

Out of options, I bit my tongue as Eryx pulled my cage through the gate, then into the alley behind a series of tents, avoiding the midway because the carnival was already open for business. Hours of operation were longer on the weekend, but I couldn't be sure whether it was Saturday or Sunday, and when I realized the day of the week no longer held any significance to me, I wanted to cry.

Eryx hauled me into my own small tent, and without a word, our handler unharnessed him and led him back outside, presumably to the hybrid tent, where the mighty minotaur should already have been on display.

Gallagher returned alone, still scowling from beneath the brim of his faded red cap. He hooked the bottom of the red-and-white tent sidewall into place, then stood to face me, thick arms crossed over an even thicker chest. "What the *hell* were you thinking?"

"That I need your help."

Gallagher's anger felt almost as ominous as Rommily's prophecy, but as tenuous as our partnership seemed, he was my only ally in the carnival. "That is *not* the way to get it," he growled as he unlocked my cage.

My legs ached in anticipation of truly stretching. Of walking. Of being out of that damn cage.

"If you ever pull something like that again, I'll have no choice but to let Ruyle punish you hard, fast, and in full view, just to keep my job." He pulled a pair of cuffs from a hook on the side of my cage, and I held my hands out so he could restrain me.

I didn't realize until the metal closed over my wrists that the restraint routine was so ingrained that I hadn't even given it conscious thought.

"There's *always* a choice," I insisted as he helped me to the ground. "Especially for those who aren't locked in metal boxes."

He led me out of the tent and through the back alley toward a row of blue portable toilets. "I *can't* lose this job, Delilah." The tension in his voice was an alarm, warning me that there was more to what he was saying than the sum of the words themselves. "Not yet."

"Why not? If you're going to break me out of here anyway, why can't we just go now?" Gallagher opened the toilet stall, but instead of stepping inside, I studied his gaze for some hint of what he was hiding. "We could leave tonight," I whispered. We could pile into his truck, or trailer, or whatever he drove, and I could call my mom from the road to check on her. Of course, I'd have to find a phone, since he didn't have a cell, and mine had been confiscated along with everything I'd owned.

"It's not that simple. Your escape is not my only concern, and this undertaking can't be rushed," he whispered. "I *cannot* lose this job before the time is right."

Tension twisted in my stomach. I suddenly felt as if I were standing in a pitch-black room, inches from some heinous danger I could sense, yet couldn't see. What would happen if I stepped forward? "What are you up to?" Why was he keeping me in the dark?

"You don't get to ask that question." Gallagher nudged me

toward the toilet, and I stepped inside. "What you get to do is turn yourself inside out, so we can all see the real you." His voice was muffled through the door. "You said you'd learn to transmute for tonight."

I stepped out of the stall, rubbing sanitizer from the dispenser onto my hands. "I said I was ready to make a deal. You help me, I'll help you."

"I'm *already* helping you. You have to do your part." Gallagher led me back to my tent and lifted me into my cage.

"Fine," I said as he locked me in. "But my condition stands. First I need you to call my mom and make sure she's still alive."

"Why would you think she's dead?"

"Because Rommily's spent the past two days trying to tell me that I'm an orphan. Or that I will be."

"No one knows what Rommily means most of the time, Delilah. That's why she doesn't work in the tent anymore."

But according to Claudio, banning Rommily from the oracle tent had more to do with the fact that since the day Clyde hurt her, her prophecies related almost exclusively to death, which wasn't marketable on the midway, because it scared the customers.

Her prophecy scared me, too.

"She called me an orphan, which either means that my mom is dead—or will be—or that she was talking about my biological parents. Whoever and wherever they may be. I'm not going to do another thing to help either of us until you find me a phone and let me talk to her."

A fierce, low growl rolled up from Gallagher's throat. "One phone call with your mother? One very *short* phone call, then you'll cooperate with me until the day you regain your freedom?"

"You have my word."

"Fine." He clipped the key ring back onto his belt. "I'll

be right back, and you better be ready to work." Then Gallagher unhooked one of the sidewalls and disappeared into the carnival.

Time dragged while he was gone, and I had no way to accurately count the minutes. The clomp of hooves had replaced the ticking of the clock since I'd been imprisoned by the menagerie, and the sun's position in the sky had become a cosmic hour hand, tracing time as it circled the world around me. But neither of those was accurate enough to tell me how long I lay awake at night, how soon breakfast would come, or how long Gallagher had left me alone, locked in a cage.

Finally, he ducked into the tent again and pulled a cell phone from his pocket. He slid it through the tray slot in the side of my cage.

I took the phone, and an ache swelled deep inside me, equal parts bitter loss and rose-tinted nostalgia. The juxtaposition of the *before* and *after* halves of my life could not have felt more bizarre if I'd worn shackles and chains to work at the bank.

"Whose is this?" I dragged my finger across the screen to wake the phone up and exhaled in relief when I wasn't asked for a password, a concept so removed from my new existence that for a second, I couldn't remember its purpose.

Authorization. Permission to use.

"Alyrose's. She's taking tickets for the hybrid tent tonight."

I dialed my mother's cell number, and the phone rang over and over in my ear. Finally, her voice mail picked up.

"Hello, this is Charity Marlow. I can't come to the phone right now, so leave me a message. Unless you're a reporter, in which case you can go fuck yourself. Have a great day!"

The beep speared my brain, and I couldn't help smiling, in spite of the circumstance.

Gallagher frowned. "What's funny?"

"I just realized how much of my personality can be credited

to nurture, rather than nature." How had I never noticed before how much like my mother I was? "Hey, Mom, it's me," I said, when I realized that my voice message was already recording. "I'm fine, but I need you to call me back if you get this within the next few minutes. After that, don't call, because I won't have access to this phone." I squeezed my eyes shut, and two tears rolled down my face as every moment of homesickness, memory, and isolation I'd suffered in captivity suddenly coalesced into a single devastating pang of loss. "I love you."

I hung up, and a minute later I was still staring at the phone when it buzzed in my hand.

Fresh tears gathered in my eyes when I saw my mother's number on the screen, and in my haste, I said hello before I'd actually accepted the call. "Mom?" I said again, with the phone pressed to my head.

She sobbed into my ear. "Lilah!"

She was alive.

Hearing her say my name felt amazing, yet it also hurt, deep inside.

"Yeah, it's me. I'm okay, but I don't have long. Are you okay?"

"No, honey, I'm not," she said over the rumble of road noise. "Last week a heartless, corrupt backwoods sheriff sold my daughter to a traveling menagerie. But the Cryptid Conservation Society gave me the name of a civil rights attorney from—"

"Mom." My throat felt thick, and the word almost got stuck in it. "Are you *physically* all right? Are you sick? Or hurt? Has anyone threatened you?"

She hesitated a second, as if the question surprised her. "The reporters are persistent, and there've been a few threats. But nothing serious. And I feel fine. Why?"

"No reason." I tried to make my pulse slow, but I couldn't

overlook the obvious—just because she wasn't sick or in danger now didn't mean she wouldn't be tomorrow. Or the next day. "I miss you."

"I miss you too, honey. You're in Texas now, right?"

I frowned, and a glance at Gallagher told me he'd heard her. "How did you know that, Mom?"

"Metzger's has a website, hon, and I'm not *completely* technologically incompetent."

"Okay." Gallagher held out his hand for the phone, as if I could just reach through the wire mesh and drop it onto his palm. "We don't have much time, Delilah."

"Who's that?" my mother asked.

"No one. I have to go." Tears blurred my vision, and I scrubbed my eyes with my free hand. Saying goodbye over the phone was just as hard as saying it in person had been.

"Can I call you back at this number?"

"No. I won't have access to a phone again." I sniffled and swiped at my nose with the back of my hand. "I just really needed to hear your voice."

"Me, too, hon, and I think I can do even better than that. The drive's not that long, and—"

"Don't," I said, and the word sounded like a sob. "Do *not* come here, Mom. I don't want you to see me like this."

"Delilah, there is no way I'm just going to leave you there to rot. I don't care if they declare you cryptid, or an alien, or the Antichrist, you're still my daughter, and they can't keep me away." Her engine noise softened and I heard a soft, familiar thump as she shifted into Park. "Anyway, I need pictures documenting your living conditions for the attorney—"

My chest ached fiercely. "Mom, do *not* hire an attorney." If she fought, Pennington and Metzger would throw her in jail.

She hesitated, and I could hear her breathing over the line. "Honey, it's starting to look like I'm going to have to hire her just to make them show me your blood test results. Unless you've already seen them?"

Gallagher tapped on the corner of my cage and I looked up to see warning in his stern expression.

"No." I felt bad about lying to my mother, but not bad enough to tell her the truth. After what I'd done to Jack, they wouldn't set me free no matter what my test results said, and she'd only be putting herself in danger if she kept digging. "Mom, I have to go, but I'm fine. Really. Don't come here, and don't hire the lawyer. That'll only make things worse."

My mother huffed. "I don't see how they could possibly be any—"

"Mom. Promise me!" My grip on the phone was so tight the plastic creaked.

After another moment's hesitation, she exhaled slowly. "Fine." I didn't believe her, but she would only have to keep her reluctant promise long enough for Gallagher to break me out. Which he'd said would be soon. "I love you, honey."

"I love you, too." I made myself hang up without thinking about it, so I couldn't lose my nerve. Then I pressed another series of buttons on Alyrose's phone.

"What are you doing?" Gallagher demanded, reaching for his keys.

"I'm just erasing my call from the log." I slid the phone back through the slot, and he took it. "Now, dial the weather line, or something generic like that. If you give the phone back and it doesn't show a call, Alyrose will get curious and ask you what you wanted."

"There's a weather line?" He stared at the phone as if he'd never held one.

"Yeah. It's archaic, thanks to the internet, but I think a lot of old people still use it." Like my mother. I gave him the number, and he dialed, then hung up a few seconds later.

"It's going to rain tomorrow." Gallagher slid the phone back into his pocket and when he left to return it, I huddled in the corner of my cage and let myself truly cry for the first time since waking up in the sheriff's station, in my own hometown.

Federal government rounds up more than 300,000 six-year-old "surrogate" children to be studied in secret labs

—Headline from the *Federal Inquirer*, September 30, 1986, edition

NALAH

The *ifrit* tucked a strand of wavy red hair behind her ear. She turned toward the sun, and the strand fell in front of her face again, subtle streaks of orange and yellow lit like a living flame. Nalah let the warmth soak into her skin, and when she closed her eyes, she could almost pretend she was back at home, a child of five lying on the grass behind the barn, waiting for her brother to finish feeding the cows.

The scent of manure fit. The warmth fit. The clanks and groans of wagons being hauled…that fit, too. The only thing left to ruin the illusion, as long as she kept her eyes closed, was—

"I can't stand this anymore."

Nalah opened her eyes and found Adira staring through the side of their cage, her pale fingers threaded through the wire mesh.

"It's too hot. Too dry. I'm going to shrivel up and blow away. Tell me we're almost home."

"We're almost home, Princess." The *ifrit*'s fingers found their way into Adira's long silver hair with no conscious thought, combing and gently untangling to provide comfort. "But the final mile is always the longest."

Adria twisted to frown at her companion, tugging her own hair in the process. "How can one mile be longer than any other?"

"I only meant that the most difficult part of the journey is yet to come."

The princess huffed. "What could be harder than sweltering for a year, locked in a cage, surrounded by beasts?"

"Overcoming distractions." Nalah gazed out at the alley behind their open tent, where she saw Gallagher leading an exhibit on foot. It was the new one—the girl with no notable features, aside from a crass tongue. Adira called her a "mongrel of nonspecific origin," but as was often the case, the merid could not see beyond the surface to the heart of the problem.

Nalah understood that no matter what the new girl's species turned out to be and no matter how diluted her bloodline, Gallagher did not think of her as a mongrel. She could see that in the gentle way he held her arm, as if he did not want to add to her bruises. In the subtle way his lips moved when he spoke to her, as if he did not want to be overheard.

But the most telling evidence that Gallagher did not think of the new girl as just another beast was the fact that he spoke to her at all.

In the year he'd been at Metzger's, Nalah had never seen Gallagher converse with an exhibit other than Adira and herself. He gave instructions, of course. Sometimes he gave soft words of encouragement to the mute minotaur, along with a companionable pat on the shoulder. But he didn't speak with the other exhibits, beyond the necessary exchange of information. Nalah couldn't think of a reason the new girl might need so much private instruction, unless she were feebleminded.

But Delilah was not feeble in any sense of the word.

The only reasonable cause for Gallagher's interest in her was, well, interest.

Pain flared deep in the *ifrit*'s chest, and she gasped with the sensation.

Nalah had felt quite a lot of pain in her fifteen years. She had been sick from want of home, when she was first given to Adira at the age of five. She'd been sick from drink not three months before they were imprisoned, the night Adira had told Nalah to sneak a bottle from the liquor stores, to wash away the fears accompanying the announcement of her betrothal to the *ifrit* crown prince. Nalah had been whipped by the menagerie's lot supervisor when she accepted blame for Adira's theft of a bottle of water, and she'd been consumed with the cramps of a consistently empty belly. She'd had hair pulled from her head, food taken from her hands, and flesh torn by the rough loss of innocence, but never in her life had anything hurt like the pain now stabbing at her chest like a spear of ice lodged deep in her heart.

She didn't realize she'd gasped again until Adira sat up with a frown. "Are you aware that the noises you're making are quite audible? Are you so very distressed that you must disturb my rest?"

"Apologies, Princess." Nalah took Adira's left hand and massaged it with both of hers.

Adira closed her eyes and squared her shoulders, as if to settle in for meditation. "And what was the cause for such a lapse?"

"Fear that Gallagher's attention has strayed from the task." Nalah's fingers never faltered, but her heart was not on the task. When Adira noticed, she opened her eyes and looked to where Gallagher and the new girl were passing by in the opposite direction. "She has already delayed your return and now seems poised to derail it entirely," the *ifrit* said softly.

"That is unacceptable." Adira pulled her hand free and turned to face the problem directly. Her pale blue eyes darkened like the ocean depths, and Nalah recognized the cruel edge in her voice. "How can we refocus his efforts?"

"By relieving him of the distraction."

"Fine. Kill her."

Nalah swallowed her initial, visceral excitement over the thought in favor of temperate council, but the words she could not say burned in her gut like lit coals. "I will roast her at the earliest opportunity, if that is your will, Princess. But Gallagher may gravely object to the loss, and he is precious to your cause."

Yet Adira seemed unconvinced that losing the mongrel to an agonizing, fiery death could sour the handler's loyalty to her.

"Also, in the aftermath of the roast, I will be executed, and you will have no companion," Nalah added. "No one to serve at your side." The *ifrit* had no doubt that if they'd been in the merid's homeland, among flowing rivers, glistening lakes, and an entire population eager to serve, the princess would not have hesitated to sacrifice her lifelong companion—her best friend in the world—for even the slightest comfort. But such a loss could not be endured under the current cruel circumstances.

"What recourse have we, then?" Adira asked with a resigned sigh.

"A wildfire consumes both the crops and the weeds together, Princess. What we need is a controlled burn..."

DELILAH

"Dreeeaa…"

My eyes flew open and I struggled to bring the ceiling of my cage into focus in the gloom. I'd fallen asleep after Gallagher left to return Alyrose's phone, but the light in my tent had been on. He must have turned it out to let me sleep, when he'd returned.

"Someone wants to see you," Clyde's voice taunted, and something clanged against the side of my cage.

I sat up, my heart pounding in alarm.

Bright lights came on in the empty tent with a low-pitched buzz and I sat up, rubbing my eyes to shield them from the sudden painful gleam. While I blinked, wiping defensive tears from my face, I heard a new sound—a soft, wordless mewling I recognized instantly.

"Genni?" I spun around on my knees, blinking against the glare, still sluggish from sleep and half-blind.

The mewling grew louder. I rubbed my eyes again, then fell backward, startled, when Geneviève's face was smashed into the side of my cage. Wire mesh dug into her cheek, her brow bone, and half of her nose. Her eyes were damp and wide with fear, her mouth covered with duct tape.

"Let her go!"

Clyde pulled her back, brandishing a cattle prod in his free hand. "Gallagher may let you order him around, but that's not how I run things."

"Where is Gallagher?" I demanded, when my brain finally caught up with the rest of me.

"There was a sudden crisis in the mermaid tank. Some asshole clogged the filter with a handful of hay—can't imagine who would do such a thing. Since Gallagher's fixing things in the hybrid tent, I thought I'd fix things in here."

"What is this? What are you doing?" I scooted to the end of my wagon, trying to follow as he hauled the poor werewolf cub out of sight.

Genni whined.

"Sit still, or I'll kick your teeth in." Clyde reappeared on the left side of my tent and hooked the corner of one canvas panel to another, so that it was held open like living room drapes.

He ducked out of sight for a second, then rose, hauling Genni up by her hair while her squeals crescendoed behind the makeshift gag. "We'll be right out there." He gestured with the cattle prod toward the space behind a large game booth, and I frowned, trying to figure out what he was up to.

Genni's cage stood open behind the game booth, visible to me, but not to the crowd I could hear talking and laughing on the midway.

"What are you doing? What do you *want*?" I demanded. "Take her back to her dad. She has nothing to do with… whatever this is."

"Oh, but she does, thanks to you." Clyde stretched toward a portable stereo on the table and pressed a button with one knuckle of the hand holding the prod. Music blared, dark and melodically haunting, and loud enough to make my ears ring.

Clyde set his prod on the edge of the table and held his free hand out toward me, fingers spread.

One, he mouthed, lowering his index finger. *Two*. When he got to five, he folded his thumb around his fist, then twisted to grab the cattle prod. Less than a second after he'd hauled Genni out of the tent and into the shadow of the game booth, two sidewall panels began to fold up at the front of my tent.

My pulse racing, I turned to find Abraxas standing at the entrance, wearing a red sequined vest. Sneakers peeked from beneath the hem of his baggy black pants. He held a battery-powered megaphone. Before I could ask what he was doing or demand that he go get Gallagher, he lifted the megaphone and began shouting into it.

"Step right up, ladies and gentlemen! Step right up! Metzger's Menagerie is proud to announce a brand-new exhibit, opening right here, right now, for the first time ever. How special is this creature? So special that we don't know what she is yet!"

People began to wander into my tent, attracted by the music and the fledgling "talker" and I noticed that a red-velvet rope had been set up several feet in front of my cage. When I looked through the side exit of the tent, I realized the rope wasn't meant to protect the audience from me, but to keep spectators too far back to see what was behind door number two: Clyde, holding the little-girl-werewolf by a handful of her hair while he brandished the cattle prod in his other hand.

"We know her name is Drea, and that she's not the innocent, harmless creature she appears," Abraxas continued, while I struggled to slow my breathing and keep the world in focus. "But her species has yet to be identified, so step right up and take a look! Maybe one of *you* has the knowledge to unlock the mystery! If you can correctly identify the species of our mystery monster, you will win a set of four deluxe tickets to tomorrow night's show, which includes a private behind-the-scenes tour for you and three friends."

"She doesn't look like anything special," one man shouted over the music, twisting to glance at Abraxas. "She looks human."

"Is she a surrogate?" a woman called out from the back. "Is this safe? I read that they can influence your thoughts just from looking at you."

The nervous buzz of the crowd swelled and they moved as one toward the midway.

"Wait!" Abraxas held both arms out as if to block their path, his eyes wide with panic. He was losing his audience.

I resisted the urge to deny that I was a surrogate, because their fear was working in my favor.

"She's not a surrogate!" Abraxas called out. "We don't know what she is, but we know that for sure, and if you'll hang out for a minute—" He stopped when he realized he'd broken character, and the kid looked so flustered I almost felt sorry for him.

But then Abraxas stood straighter and relaunched what was obviously a prepared spiel. "Don't let her appearance fool you, ladies and gentlemen! Behind that innocent face lies a monster capable of scrambling a man's gray matter with her bare hands. And you lucky folks will be the *first* to witness her live transformation."

I gaped at Abraxas, but he only grinned and extended a broad-armed gesture my way, as if we were coconspirators in Clyde's outrageous ambush.

I gripped the wire mesh, and my gaze flitted from face to rapt face within the growing audience. They stared. They pointed. They whispered in their friends' ears while they waited, and all I could think about was that I was wearing a short, grimy linen dress, with unwashed hair and dirty feet.

Yet that was just the latest in the string of mortifications that my existence had become.

If I couldn't figure out how to transform in order to save my own life, what made Clyde think I could do it for their entertainment? Or that I *would*, even if I could?

Rage built in my belly. He was conspiring against Gallagher and trying to humiliate me, and I didn't need creepy eyes or sharp claws to give him what he deserved.

"You're all being scammed!" I shouted, riding high on the sudden vengeful impulse.

The chatter stopped, though the music kept playing. Abraxas stared at me, the megaphone hanging limp in his hand.

"No, seriously." I stared straight at the man who'd said I looked like nothing special. "I'm human. Less than two weeks ago, I was a bank teller. I had a boyfriend, and an apartment, and a mother. They took me right off the street and threw me into this cage, and if they can do that to me, they can do it to any of your daughters. They don't even need proof that she's not human. They just need an accusation, and once they have that, they'll haul your daughter off and sell her to a carnival, or a lab, or a private collection, where they'll torture her to try to get her to show you what kind of monster she is, and when that doesn't work—because she's *not* a monster— they'll let her starve to death and inventory her corpse as a dead cryptid of unspecified origin."

Wives looked at their husbands. Parents clutched their children close. No one seemed to know what to say or do.

"Don't believe me? Look in that backpack over there." I pointed to the table near the entrance, where Gallagher's bag still sat. "Folded in the front pocket, you'll find the results of the test they ran on me. You!" I pinned a woman near the back of the crowd with my gaze. "Go look."

She hesitated for a second, while Abraxas stared, obviously

at a loss. Then she picked up the bag and unzipped the front pocket. She pulled the paper out and unfolded it. "It says she's human," the woman said, and the audience gasped.

Abraxas's eyes widened.

Several of the teenagers had their phone cameras aimed at me, in spite of the menagerie's rules, so I picked one and looked right at it. "Any minute now, they'll come out with a whip or a cattle prod, to try to shut me up, and when I collapse on the floor of this cage, still *completely human*, you'll know that what I'm telling you is true. And that if it can happen to me, it can happen to anyone."

I turned, ready to dare Clyde to come after me with his electrical prod, but he only glared at me through eyes narrowed into furious slits, his jaw bulging from being clenched.

Then he shoved the forked tip of the cattle prod at the inside of Geneviève's right thigh.

Genni convulsed and made a horrible sound from behind her duct tape, but no one in the tent could hear her over the music. Her legs folded, and she fell to the ground, but a thick clump of her hair remained in Clyde's hand.

I clutched the wire mesh so tightly it cut into my hands, but I couldn't make my fingers unfold. *Let her go!* I shouted, and only afterward realized the shout was trapped in my head, reverberating against the inside of my skull because my jaw would not unclench and release the words.

Clyde leaned over Genni and looked right at me. He brandished the cattle prod, then shoved it at her stomach.

Genni convulsed again. Her hands twitched and her head slammed into the grass over and over, and this time she seemed to be choking behind her gag.

No!

My skin began to itch, and my scalp started to tingle. My

fingertips burned, and I let go of the wire mesh, under the impression for just a moment that it was actually shocking me.

The audience stared at me, stunned, and whatever they were seeing—whatever my body was doing—had completely undermined everything I'd just said and everything printed on the report that woman at the back still held. It's much easier to believe what we see than what we are told.

The tingling in my scalp became a full-fledged burning, and on the edges of my vision, I saw strands of dark hair twisting around my face. Lights flashed as people took more forbidden pictures and video footage. Then the room slid into crisp, hyper-clear focus. Colors looked brighter. Edges looked sharper. I could see a tiny mole on the earlobe of the woman at the back of the tent, who still clutched my blood test results while she stared.

My fingers ached like knuckles in need of a crack, and when I held my hands up, I saw that my nails had tapered into curved, thin black points, more like needles than claws. I felt a steady pull to my left, as if the gravitational force had been reoriented to draw me toward Evan Clyde. I could practically *feel* his skin break beneath my hands, even with a steel cage and twenty feet of space standing between us.

The drive to make that act a reality was all-consuming.

Broiling with fury, I turned to find Clyde standing over Genni while she sobbed, fighting to breathe through her running nose. The cattle prod hung at his side. He was laughing. The bastard was *laughing*, because I'd given him exactly what he wanted.

He'd staged the entire thing to trigger my transmutation. In front of a live audience. Without Gallagher's knowledge or permission.

He'd hurt Genni for no reason at all.

"What did I—" Abraxas's voice cracked when his gaze met

mine. Then he blinked and cleared his throat. "What did I tell you, ladies and gentlemen? She's something else, isn't she?" He turned toward the midway and stumbled through his pitch, drawing more and more people into my tent, where cameras flashed and phones recorded my misery, in clear violation of the menagerie's policy. A couple of small children started to cry, but their parents only picked them up and continued to stare at me with kids clutched to their chests.

Clyde set his electrical prod on the ground behind the game booth, then picked Genni up and tossed her into her open cage. He slammed the door shut and locked it while she shook and sobbed behind her gag, blinking at me from twenty-five feet away. Then he stored his weapon on the step rail of her crate and sauntered into the tent as if he owned it.

As if he owned *me*.

"Ladies and gentlemen, I'm going to have to ask you to put away your cameras." He waited while the audience complied reluctantly. "What you just heard Drea say before she graced us with her true face is a prime example of why monsters that look human are the most dangerous of their kind. Cryptids like this are capable of masterful feats of deception. They are silver-tongued beasts who will lie right to your face to protect the illusion of their humanity, which is exactly how this particular cryptid spent *twenty-five years* passing for human.

"Now, folks, I don't want you to worry about your safety— Drea is securely locked in a steel cage—but again let me say that we *do not know* what she is. The experts are flummoxed, but it's possible one of *you* can identify her species. On the table next to the entrance, you'll notice an empty jar and a stack of notecards, which my assistant will be happy to pass out."

While Abraxas helped audience members fill out entry forms, I glared at Clyde, riding the current of fury coursing through my body, silently cursing the cage standing between me and a mind-scrambling end for the handler.

Justice for Geneviève.

The closer he came to my cage, the harder every cell in my body cried out for his suffering. I was drawn to him like metal to a human bastard of a magnet, but every time I reached for him, my claws slid through the wire mesh then stopped when my palms met metal.

I knew I couldn't get to him, but my body refused to accept that. The *furiae* within me suddenly felt like its own separate entity—inside of me, a part of me, but acting of its own accord.

People came and went with their kids and their astonished oohs and aahs. Abraxas continued to call spectators in from the midway. Clyde answered questions about where Metzger's had acquired me, and what I ate, and what havoc I might wreak if I ever escaped bondage. But as time passed after Genni's suffering, my inner beast slowly retreated beneath my skin, biding her time. She still wanted to crack Clyde's skull like an eggshell, but she seemed to finally understand that her chance had not yet come.

My twisty, stand-up hair had already begun to fall limp when Gallagher stormed into the tent and grabbed Abraxas by the front of his shirt. A beat of hope and relief pulsed through me when he hauled the boy off his feet and ripped the megaphone away. I couldn't hear what he said over the crowd and the music, but the shapes drawn by his lips were familiar enough.

"What the hell is going on?"

Abraxas pointed to Clyde, stuttering some explanation I couldn't make out.

Clyde watched the interchange in smug satisfaction, his arms crossed over his Metzger's polo, and the *furiae* inside me stretched beneath my skin, resurrecting my urge to reach for him.

Gallagher dropped the boy and barked an order I couldn't hear. Then he marched through the crowd, jostling people out of his way, and slammed one huge fist down on the small portable stereo. I jerked, startled. Slivers of plastic and electronics rained onto the table and the sawdust-covered ground.

The music died, and the crowd turned to stare at him. The sudden silence echoed in my ears and for a second I was sure I'd gone deaf. Then Gallagher faced the audience, his bearing stiff and his fists clenched. "This exhibit is now closed," he growled. "Don't forget to purchase a Metzger's T-shirt or commemorative minotaur mug on your way out."

For a moment, everyone stared in confusion. Then Abraxas lifted his megaphone and began directing the audience back onto the midway.

By the time Gallagher hauled the boy-crier into the empty tent and dropped the open sidewall, my hair hung lank and tangled over my shoulders and my vision had returned to normal. My fingernails were still pointed, but those points were receding right in front of my eyes. Yet I could still feel the *furiae* just beneath my skin, like the seething undercurrent beneath the calm surface of a lake.

I'd never felt anything so persistent. So bloodthirsty. She was a part of me—she *was* me—but this new appetite for violence was so foreign that I couldn't help thinking of her as a distinct division of me. A hungry splinter faction of Delilah that could only be controlled if it were fed regularly. Suddenly, the result of my blood test made more sense. Becoming a *furiae* hadn't cost me my humanity; it had made me capable of holding others of my species accountable for their cruelty.

"You're *fired*!" Gallagher roared at Clyde from across the tent, and I shivered as the words rolled over and through me, soothing my inner beast like a cat being stroked. The *furiae* liked seeing Clyde reproached. "Get the *hell* out of my menagerie!"

"You can't fire me." Clyde pulled a trash can from beneath the folding table and brushed the remains of his stereo into it with a jarring clatter.

"I'm your boss!" Gallagher shouted.

The sidewall rose behind him, and Ruyle stepped into the tent. "And I'm yours. Clyde stays."

Gallagher turned on the lot superintendent, and my pulse rushed in anticipation of the confrontation. "He sabotaged the mermaid tank, then usurped my act and launched an unauthorized showcase of an ungroomed exhibit! He's damn lucky I'm *only* firing him." But the tight clench of his fists told me he was actually hoping for a more extreme solution.

As was I.

"Clyde transformed a useless cryptid from a drain on carnival resources into a profitable exhibit and engaged the audience in the search for her species. They're talking about it up and down the midway. Videos are already surfacing online." Ruyle unlocked his cell phone with a swipe of the screen. "Two thousand hits in twenty-four minutes. Most asking where we'll stop next. That's the first time YouTube has ever worked in our favor." He held his cell up for Gallagher, and I couldn't clearly see the image paused on it, but I knew it was me.

Yet for the first time since discovering that I had an inner beast, I wasn't horrified or humiliated at the knowledge that she'd been gawked at. She'd *wanted* to be seen. But she'd wanted to be seen punishing Clyde for what he'd done, not as a monster sitting helpless in a cage.

"She's *my* project," Gallagher growled, and for once, I felt no need to object to the possessive nature of his claim. What he really meant but couldn't say was that I was his ally.

"Which is why you owe Clyde a debt—looks like you're going to get to keep your little pet." Ruyle turned to Abraxas, who still clutched the megaphone to his thin chest. "Take the jar to my office. There's a twenty waiting for you, as promised."

Ruyle glanced at me with a smug half smile, then he nodded at Clyde and ducked beneath the untethered side panel and out of the tent.

When Gallagher noticed Abraxas lingering, he turned to the boy with ice in his gray-eyed glare.

"I'm sorry." Abraxas started to hand him the megaphone, then set it on the ground between them instead. "I thought you knew. Clyde said this would be my chance to show Ruyle I could talk on the midway."

"Go," Gallagher growled. Abraxas blinked at him, then grabbed the jar full of paper slips and took off through the loose sidewall panel at a run.

"You, too," Gallagher said to Clyde, but the smaller handler only leaned with one hip against the folding table, smug and gloating.

"Don't you want to know how I got your pet freak to perform?"

"He tortured Geneviève." I turned to Clyde, and a resurgence of rage made my fingers tingle, but I swallowed the instinct, loathe to give him a second show. "He cuffed her, gagged her, and shocked her with the cattle prod for *no reason at all*." My voice had taken on a husky quality, just as it had that night in the hybrid tent.

"Oh, I had a reason." Clyde tapped on the end panel of my cage, and fire surged through me. He turned back to Gallagher. "At first I thought Drea was a lost cause, on account of her raising, but then I realized that could be used against her. This one thinks like a human bitch." He hooked one thumb in my direction. "Which means you can make her do any-thing you want, if you push the right button."

"Take Geneviève back to the row," Gallagher ordered through clenched teeth.

"She's scheduled for a live shift in the center ring tonight."

"Take her back," Gallagher growled. "Give her some water and let her rest. Claudio can go on in her place."

"You're too soft on them." Clyde pushed back the sidewall panel, but hesitated before he ducked beneath it. "They're going to run all over you."

"If I didn't repair the damage mental runts like you and Jack do to the inventory, the old man wouldn't have a thing to put on display. Now go do your damn job."

Clyde ducked beneath the loose canvas flap and disappeared, still grinning.

Gallagher slid his fingers through the wire mesh between us, just outside of my own grip on the metal, and when he only breathed deeply for several long seconds, I realized he was trying to rein in his temper.

Finally, he turned and secured the loose sidewalls to stakes in the ground, effectively locking all the doors. Then he opened my cage and motioned me forward until I sat in the threshold, my legs dangling from the edge of the wagon. "Are you okay?" He pulled a bottle of water from one of the pockets of his cargo-style jeans and handed it to me.

"You should be worried about Genni, not me." I cracked open the bottle and drank a third of it in several large gulps.

"I'll check on her when I'm done here." Gallagher scruffed his faded red cap over his short hair. "So, Clyde figured out how to bring out your beast, but not what it is?"

I wedged the open bottle between my thighs to keep from knocking it over, and the cold condensation was a shock to my overheated skin. "I think he just re-created the circumstance that triggered my first transmutation and hoped for the best." Gallagher and I could have done the same thing—if we'd been willing to hurt someone innocent.

Clyde wouldn't hesitate to do it again.

My hand tightened around the water bottle. I closed my eyes, trying to absorb the conclusions and ramifications spinning in my head, but only one thing became clear. "We can't wait. We have to go now."

"I told you. That's not an option."

I opened my eyes again to find him watching me from inches away. "They're going to have to hurt someone every time I go on display, and the only way they're going to make any money under that business model is if they use acts that aren't profitable on their own. Which is only Genni and Rommily, right?"

Gallagher nodded, his teeth clenched tightly.

"That is *not* okay with me!" The words grated against my throat on their way out, as the *furiae* asserted her influence on my vocal cords.

"Agreed, but we can't leave yet. I made a promise, and I can't go back on my word, Delilah. Not even to set you free."

"You made a promise to someone else?"

Gallagher nodded.

"To one of the other captives?" An odd beat of jealousy flashed through me at the thought.

"I can't... Look, I'd rather get you out of here tonight. Right now. But my word is my honor."

I knew I'd lost before he even finished the familiar phrase. Anger ground my teeth together, and I tried to scoot back into my cage, to put distance between us.

He caught me with one hand around my ankle. "Delilah. I'm *going* to set you free." Gallagher tugged me forward until my legs dangled from the cage again, and we were inches apart. "You have my word. But now I need yours. I want you to promise me you're going to be patient and wait. No more stunts like you pulled yesterday."

"I'm not promising you anything. You said it yourself—I'm supposed to be avenging unrighted wrongs. Instead, I'm the reason Genni was tortured tonight, and that's going to happen over and over unless we do something about it. Clyde was right. As long as I'm in this cage, I'm worth less than the food it takes to keep me alive."

Anger flashed across Gallagher's face. "That is *not* true," he growled. "You are judge, jury, and executioner—the physical embodiment of retribution." Fervor burned in his eyes, kindling a blistering response deep inside me, where the *furiae* was stirred by his words. "You serve no one and nothing except the concept of justice itself, and no ignorant brute of a handler could possibly understand your worth."

For a second, I couldn't breathe. The conviction in his voice was stunning. It was absolute. No one had ever in my life believed in me as much as Gallagher did in that moment. I could see that in his eyes as clearly as I could hear it in his voice.

"What you do is important to the world. Who you are is important to me. You are worth fighting for, and *I will fight for you*. But you have to be willing to compromise until the time is right."

I stared at him, trying to understand. Where had his conviction come from? Every other human I'd met since being sold to the menagerie had treated me like an animal, but Gallagher seemed to be polishing a pedestal for me.

I didn't deserve his conviction. Regardless of whatever calling I served, all I'd done so far was get people hurt. I couldn't let that happen again.

"I can't compromise someone else's safety just so Metzger's can get a show out of me," I insisted.

"Then figure out how to give them what they want some other way. On your own terms."

As if I hadn't thought of that. "How?"

Gallagher closed his eyes and scruffed his hat over his hair again as he thought out loud. "Injustice triggers your transmutation, but do you have to actually *see* that injustice, live?" His eyes opened, and his gaze met mine. "Could you possibly just think about an instance in the past? Meditate about it?"

"I think that's what was happening that time in the travel trailer, and I've tried that a couple of times since, but I was never able to make it work. But tonight when I saw Clyde hurting Genni, my inner beast was just *there*. She was drawn to him, in a way she couldn't be when I was locked up in the travel trailer, because he wasn't there."

"Because *he* wasn't there…" Gallagher's eyes brightened, and after a second, I caught on.

"Clyde wasn't close enough to be punished in the travel trailer, so my beast never fully manifested. I don't need to see the abuse—I just need to see the abuser!"

Gallagher nodded. "That's what it sounds like anyway."

I frowned as a new realization dawned. "But I see Clyde all the time without sprouting claws."

"So maybe part of it is that meditation," he suggested. "Maybe if you visualize giving him what he deserves?"

"We need a trial run." Warmth blossomed in my gut and my fingers began to itch. My beast was still there, just beneath the surface of my skin. She was still eager. And she was pissed off that she hadn't gotten the man she'd shown up for.

Gallagher shrugged. "I could send Clyde in here on an errand."

I shook my head. "I want a *real* trial run." My voice took on that fuller quality, as if the words were somehow heavier than they should have been. "Give him a reason to unlock my cage, and I'll take care of the rest." I was suddenly viscerally certain that I could do it. That now that she'd been unlocked, the *furiae* wouldn't let me truly rest until she'd drawn blood.

"Delilah, I can't let you kill Clyde."

I could feel my beast crawling around inside me, restless, stretching to fill the shape of my limbs. "I don't know that he'll die. What I do know is that I'm supposed to hurt him. He deserves it."

Gallagher frowned and took a step back, and I realized he'd heard the beast in my voice. He stared into my eyes, then stepped closer again. "Delilah?"

"I can feel her." I reached out for him, and he took my hands. "She wants him, Gallagher, and I *have* to give him to her."

"But—"

"She won't rest until she draws blood." I hardly recognized the sound of my own voice, or the odd echo it carried.

Gallagher's eyes widened, but instead of backing away, he leaned closer to me, as if he were drawn to my beast. His pupils dilated until his irises almost disappeared, and his hands tightened around mine. "Okay."

"Okay?"

He nodded. "But I can't give you Clyde." His voice was deep and even gruffer than usual, similar to how Brandon had sounded when he was aroused. Only Gallagher's interest didn't look or feel like anything as simple as physical titillation. The fire in his eyes was part empathy and part fascination— a vicarious anticipation of what he'd just agreed to let me do. "Will your beast take anyone else, for now?"

"Wallace." I didn't even have to think about it. His name was just there, along with the memory of him standing in front of Zyanya's cage, extorting sexual favors from a half-starved captive in exchange for food.

Gallagher let go of my hands and reached for the door to my cage. Each movement was fast and sharp, as if he couldn't wait to fulfill my request. "I'll send him to take you to the bathroom."

"No, it can't happen here," I said. "The staff has to see me transmute while no one's being hurt." To protect Genni and Rommily from future pointless abuse.

Gallagher nodded again, breathing faster now. He swallowed, and I realized he was trying to rein in his excitement. "Give me five minutes," he said as he slid my cage door closed and locked it. He wanted to see what I could do. He could hardly wait.

That made two of us.

Leaders of the cryptid community deny any knowledge
of or involvement in the mass slaughter of innocent
children now known nationally as "the reaping," but
most government officials remain skeptical.

—Opening line from a front-page article in the
Chicago Post, October 4, 1986

GALLAGHER

The boss of livestock hardly saw the crowd that split before him, instinctively making way for the large man marching down the center of the paved midway, clearly on an urgent mission. He hardly heard the organ music or smelled the fried food either, because he was lost in his own thoughts. In the memory of Delilah's eyes, before color had returned to them and the veins had faded. Of her voice when the *furiae* had seized it, adding a dark and thrilling depth to the normally mellow notes.

That voice had called out to him, not with the actual words spoken, but with the power of the tone itself. Listening to Delilah speak had triggered wordless flashes behind his eyes—images he kept buried not because they bothered him, but because they *excited* him.

Blood. Unseeing eyes. Torn flesh. Broken bone.

Not thinking those thoughts was an exercise in willpower—a way to control his craving for violence—but the more time he spent with Delilah, the harder it became to maintain that willpower. She made him want to give in to a basic nature neither of them could ever truly escape.

But that would not be wise.

Not yet.

Gallagher never lied, not even to himself, so denying that he had an interest in Delilah wasn't possible. In truth, he thought about her all the time, but he couldn't say precisely when this captivating new fascination had developed. It was a strange feeling: part burning curiosity about what she could do, part utter fixation on why she'd been charged with that task. But it was her purpose—the clear-cut objective of her existence—that occupied most of his idle thoughts.

The universe had a plan for Delilah. She'd been given an exquisite and devastating ability and had been burdened with its use because she was everything Gallagher was not.

He marched past the sirens' tent, then the oracles' tent, and he was halfway to the red-trimmed succubi tent before he realized he'd taken off in the wrong direction. Wallace was at work in the hybrid tent. Gallagher's head was not in the game. Because Delilah was in his head.

Growling to himself, the boss of livestock executed an abrupt about-face, without noticing the strange look that Rommily's handler gave him from outside the oracles' tent. Gallagher was thinking about Mike Wallace, a man he'd been working alongside for a year. A man he'd eaten with, traveled with, and shared the occasional drink with.

A man he was about to deliver into the claw-fingered hands of Lady Justice herself.

Gallagher wondered if Wallace would die. That thought did not bother him.

He wondered if Wallace would bleed and scream. That thought excited him, dumping adrenaline into his veins with every beat of his heart. He itched to see Delilah standing over a limp body. Blood dripping from her fingers. Hair floating around her face. Power emanating from her every pore.

He ached to be the one who put her in that position, yet he could not quite swallow his envy of her.

The world would never embrace his cravings as it would embrace Delilah's, once those in need of justice understood what she was. She would be their champion; he would be their nightmare, as fate had decreed on the day of his birth.

Unless she gave him purpose.

Gallagher stopped in midstride and several passersby had to dart around him to avoid a collision. He could ask her. The words were there—written long before he was born, memorized before he'd even learned to spell them—but the precedent was not. Tradition did not support the most radical impulse Gallagher had ever had. Delilah was not a proper candidate for the position, and even if she were, he had not yet earned the right to request her consideration.

There were preliminary advances. Prescribed offerings. A conventional exchange of sentiment. But there was no time for most of that, and she would understand little of it anyway.

Gallagher's plan would not work.

Yet he could think of nothing else. She needed him, and he needed purpose.

Resolved, the boss of livestock marched on with his head high and his spine straight, headed for the hybrid tent with fresh intent. The sacrifice of Mike Wallace would serve three different but vital functions. The handler's suffering would feed the *furiae*'s appetite for justice and it would free both Genni and Rommily from the pain of triggering Delilah's transmutation.

But most important, Mike Wallace would serve as Gallagher's official tribute of blood to Delilah—the first sacrament of formal devotion.

PART 3

ÉMANCIPE

DELILAH

While I waited in my cage in the quiet, empty tent, I could feel the *furiae* moving inside me. It was a strange sensation, and every time I decided it was psychosomatic—after all, she and I were one and the same—she would stretch again, as if she were trying to break free of my body, and I would reconsider.

I'd never felt her like that before. Not even the day she'd attacked Jack in the hybrid tent. In the nearly two weeks I'd been at Metzger's, I'd tried countless times to call her forth with no luck, but now that she'd been awakened, she would *not* go back to sleep. At least, not until she got what she wanted.

It reminded me of how my mother had described her pregnancy to me once. She'd said that when I'd finally kicked hard enough to make my presence known, she realized I'd been kicking for days, but she'd had no understanding of the sensation.

Of course, as it turns out, she wasn't feeling me at all. She was feeling Elizabeth.

I'd been jittery and uneasy for the past few days, except when I'd been too weak from hunger to move. I'd attributed that psychological unease to being cooped up in a cage, but in looking back, I could see that much of my discomfort was the *furiae* pacing inside me, eager to avenge injustice hidden beneath the striped canvas and behind the bright lights.

In a sudden surreal moment of epiphany, I realized I was incubating not a child, but a cause. I had become the mother of retribution, and my vengeful offspring would kick until she got her way.

She wouldn't have to wait long.

Gallagher never came back. Wallace ducked into my tent holding the minotaur's guide rope, grumbling that the assignment was beneath him as he led Eryx into my tent. The minotaur met my gaze, and I wondered how much he knew about our trial run. I wondered how much he knew about *everything*. The handlers' tongues wagged freely around him because they thought he was mindless.

No one ever seemed to truly notice him, except for me. And Gallagher.

Eryx blinked at me deliberately as Wallace harnessed him to the end of my cage, and I wondered what he was trying to tell me.

"They ever figure out what you are?" Wallace slapped Eryx on the shoulder, and the massive minotaur hauled my cage slowly toward the rear of the tent.

"They figured out I'm dangerous," I said, and Eryx snorted.

Wallace lifted a flap at the back of the tent. "You've been misinformed. What you are is caged."

"Only a fool believes his eyes above all other senses." I could tell from his dismissive glance that he had no idea I was quoting Gallagher.

Wagon row was still nearly empty when Eryx hauled my cage into place. Most of the hybrids were still performing in the big top, but Genni was there in her cage, as were several of the humanoid captives, who had no role in the final show. Several roustabouts were carrying supplies toward the rear entrance to the fairgrounds, and the man who ran the pie car was headed toward the silver wagon.

My audience was small, but it would have to do.

Wallace left Eryx harnessed to my wagon while he ordered me to put my hands through the tray slot, so they could be cuffed. Then he unlocked my cage door. He wasn't supposed to leave the minotaur unattended while he took me to the portable toilet, but like most of the other handlers, Wallace assumed he had nothing to fear from the docile, drugged beast, as long as he was tied to something.

The *furiae* twisted frantically inside me as Wallace slid the door open. Anticipation tingled in my fingers.

"Make it quick," the handler snapped, waving me forward, and he seemed to have no idea that by cuffing my hands in front instead of at my back, he'd underestimated me just like he'd underestimated the minotaur.

My vision sharpened dramatically as I shuffled on my knees toward the open side panel. My fingertips burned, and I heard several soft cracking sounds as the nails lengthened and hardened into needle-points.

"What the hell?" Wallace's eyes widened as my hair began to rise off my shoulders under its own power. He tried to slam the door shut as I reached for him, and he might have crushed my hands if Eryx hadn't lurched forward at that very moment, pulling the cage side panel right out of Wallace's grip.

I swayed with the sudden motion, then the *furiae* threw herself over the threshold. My knees crashed into Wallace's stomach. He hit the ground on his back, screaming.

The *furiae* grabbed his head. My sharp, narrow nails slid through the flesh at his temples.

The handler's screaming soon stopped, but by then, several others had risen to fill the shocked silence. Wallace's eyes rolled up until only the bottoms of his irises were visible. He began to shake as if I were electrifying him.

Footsteps pounded toward us as he writhed in pain beneath me.

When I stared down at Wallace, I saw him not convulsing on the ground, but standing in front of Zyanya in the middle of the night. I heard him unlock her cage and unzip his pants.

How do you *like it?*

"Help him!" someone shouted. Shadowed silhouettes fell over me, but I didn't look up.

Frenzied cheering echoed from the cages behind me.

"Someone get a mallet! And a muzzle!" Ruyle shouted. He'd emerged from the silver wagon, but was scared to get too close to me.

"I got it," Gallagher called, and I finally looked up. He held a tranquilizer gun, aimed right at me. He fired, and pain bit into my thigh.

Stunned, I fell back on my heels and my fingers were ripped from Wallace's temples. I collapsed against a wagon wheel as the world swam around me.

Blood dripped from the sides of Wallace's head as he struggled to sit up, but his eyes regained no focus.

Gallagher marched toward me, rifle aimed at the ground, and though his gray-eyed glare betrayed no involvement in my little trial run, I could tell from his easy gait that he was as pleased with the result as I was.

The last thing I saw before the world went dark was Mike Wallace's bloody right hand, clawing at his own gory groin through the unzipped crotch of his jeans.

He'd torn his briefs—and what lay beneath the material—to shreds.

It was late when I woke up in my cage on wagon row, which I only knew because the carnival was dark and quiet.

The silver wagon's windows were unlit, as were most of the personal trailers in the dirt parking lot.

As far as I could tell from my limited perspective, all the other cages had been hauled back into the usual configuration of two parallel lines, and I thought everyone was asleep until Claudio sat up across the aisle from me.

"Delilah." His long thin fingers gripped the side of his cage. Dim light from the edge of the parking lot shone on nails that were thick, curved, and yellow, even in human form. "*Mon Dieu*, what have you done?"

I frowned at Claudio, well aware that he could see me much better than I could see him in the dark. "I don't..." I knew who I was and where I was but everything else was kind of foggy.

"Gallagher said you tried to escape. He had to tranquilize you."

And all at once, the whole thing came back with a rush of adrenaline, remembered pain, and primal satisfaction. I could practically feel the *furiae* purring inside me like a smug cat.

"Wait, Gallagher said I tried to escape?" But Gallagher never lied. His word was his honor.

Claudio shrugged. "He said you got out of your cage." And that much was true. Claudio—and everyone else—had probably assumed the rest. "You're lucky they didn't put a bullet in your head."

"No, *they're* lucky she didn't rip them all wide-open," Zyanya said from her the cage. All I could see of her was the light reflecting from her feline eyes in the dark. "Whatever she did to Wallace left a bucket of blood soaking into the dirt." Her silhouette moved among the darker shadows, and her next words were half whisper, half throaty growl. "Smells like dinner."

"I didn't do that." I'd hardly even seen it, before Gallagher's tranquilizer knocked me out. "All I did was touch him." I'd touched skin, then pushed through that into skull, then into the fragile, malleable tissue of his brain.

"Then what the hell happened to the bastard?"

"He tried to rip off his own man parts," Lenore whispered from farther down the row. Even at a volume almost too low to hear, her melodic voice made me want things I couldn't possibly articulate. Dark things. Primal, violent things. "He might have actually succeeded."

"Why would he...?" Mahsa began, but the leopard shifter didn't seem to know how to finish her sentence.

"Because Delilah touched him," Lenore whispered, and her cage wagon creaked as she moved around in it. "Whatever she did made him want to hurt himself."

The groan of metal and whispered murmurs from farther up wagon row told me that others were waking up. Listening.

"But why like that?" Payat asked, from Zyanya's other side. "Why not make him dig his own eyes out, or bite off his tongue?"

"I didn't know." I couldn't explain what I'd been thinking when the *furiae* took over. I wasn't even sure I understood it. "I just wanted justice. I wanted him to understand what he'd done wrong and to punish himself in some manner that fit the offense."

"That was *his* choice?" the berserker called. "Why wouldn't he just climb into a cage?"

"She's talking about a different offense," Payat said, and I could tell from the angle of his glowing eyes that he was staring at the end panel of his cage in his sister's direction.

"You..." Zyanya crawled forward until I could see her in the light thrown from the lamp in the parking lot. She sat in a deep squat, with her knees up near her ears. "You did that for me?"

"And for everyone else he's coerced with threats or promises to give something he had no right to deprive you of in the first place."

"That's a crime?" Zyanya sounded stunned.

Lenore huffed, and even that rough exhalation of air seemed to carry oddly expressive notes. "No," she said. "Not here. Not against us."

"I deal in morality, not in law," I whispered, oddly pleased by the opportunity to twist Sheriff Pennington's words into a more satisfying truth. "Wallace can't misuse a body part he doesn't have."

"Yeah, well, I can't digest meat I don't eat," Zyanya snapped, but I could hear the truth in the raw, vulnerable quality of her voice, as if she were on the edge of relieved tears. She was pleased not just by the fact that someone had acted on her behalf, but by the knowledge that she'd been found worthy of the action.

The fact that she'd had reason to doubt that broke my heart.

"They won't underestimate you again," Claudio warned.

I was fine with that, because they would also never again torture someone innocent to make me perform.

My gaze landed on Genni, who lay in her wagon, unmoving, and I couldn't distinguish most of her from the shadows.

"Is she okay?" I whispered.

"I don't know." Claudio was pressed against the side of his cage, trying to get as physically close to his daughter as possible. "I've been calling her name, but there's been no response."

"I can't see her very well either," Finola said from the crate on my right, which she shared with Lenore. "But her wagon was already here when we got back, and I don't think she's moved since then."

"What happened to her?" Claudio's voice was thick and

growly with worry, as if his vocal cords were more canine than usual. "Did anyone see?"

"Clyde electrocuted her." I tried to strip all emotion from my voice, half-afraid that now that I'd unleashed the *furiae*, she would be on a hair trigger.

The father pressed his face into the side of his cage until the mesh made a grid on his face, pale in the moonlight. "Why?"

"To trigger my transmutation." The last word got lost in a sob I couldn't choke back. "I'm so sorry, Claudio. I couldn't make him stop."

"You can't blame yourself for what they do," Lenore insisted.

"Well, you *can*," Zyanya purred from the cage on the papa wolf's other side. "But that won't fix anything."

Claudio spoke into the corner of his cage closest to his daughter. "Geneviève? Genni, *chère, dis quelque chose.*"

The werewolf pup rolled toward the side of her cage, but her eyes did not open.

"She's okay. I think." I'd almost said *she's alive*, but I didn't want her father to know I'd had any doubts. "Genni, wake up, honey." The duct tape was gone, and I couldn't see or smell any vomit.

"Geneviève!" Claudio snapped, his voice sharp and commanding, with more than a hint of fabled werewolf aggression. *"Réveille-toi!"*

"Papa?" she whispered, and Claudio exhaled deeply.

"Are you okay, *chère?*"

"J'ai mal à la tête."

Her head. "She hit her head on the ground." A lot. "Are you nauseated?" I asked.

"Comment?"

"Do you feel like you're going to vomit?" I clarified. "Throw up?"

"Non."

"Does anything look...strange? Are you seeing okay?"

"Oui." She pushed herself upright, and her knee brushed something that crinkled like cellophane. When I squinted into the dark, I made out one of Gallagher's ubiquitous protein bars. He must have slipped them to her at some point after I'd been recaged.

"There's a snack bar next to your left knee. I think you'll feel better a lot faster if you have something in your stomach."

Genni reached down for the bar, then tore into the wrapper with her teeth. For a couple of minutes, we all listened to her chew. Farther down my row, one of the *djinn* was singing to the other, and both trolls had started to snore again.

"So..." Zyanya said, when Genni didn't vomit or pass out, and everyone had relaxed a little. "What are you?" Her golden eyes shone at me in the dark. "Why would they have to torture Genni to bring out your beast?"

"It doesn't have to be Genni." I crossed my feet beneath me on the aluminum floor, which was already warm from my skin. "Clyde electrocuted her because that's what was happening when I transmuted the first time. He still doesn't know what I am."

"But you do." Zyanya's cat eyes practically glowed at me from the shadowy depth of her cage, and I realized she was shrewder than I'd given her credit for. "How long have you known?"

"Known what?" the berserker asked from a couple of wagons down.

"What is she?" one of the succubi called, though I couldn't tell if I was hearing Trista or Zarah—the sisters sounded just alike.

"Born of blood and wrath!" The shout came from a cart several down and across the aisle from mine, and I recognized Rommily's voice. "The crone is set upon her path!"

Zyanya pressed against the steel mesh to see as far down the aisle as she could. "What the hell does that mean?"

"She's a *furiae*," Mirela said, and I could tell from how surprised she sounded that even Rommily's sisters were rarely able to interpret her riddles.

"As in…an Erinyes?" Lenore's voice was high-pitched with excitement. Or maybe with disbelief. "My grandmother's people called them the Eumenides—the kindly ones—to avoid insulting them."

I scooted closer to the Lenore end of my cage, so I could hear her better. "Did she say what they look like?"

"The old stories describe them with snakes for hair, bodies as black as coal, wings like a bat, and bloodshot eyes."

I was two for four, assuming twisting, gravity-defiant locks could be seen as the logical interpretation of "snakes for hair."

"But the truth is that no two Erinyes look alike, because 'Erinyes' isn't a species," Lenore added. "It's a… It's like a calling. A pull from some higher purpose. An Erinyes can be a werewolf, or a dryad, or an elf, or any other species capable of feeling the sting of injustice."

"Yeah, that fits with what Gallagher told me," I said, and when the *djinni*'s lullaby ended abruptly, I realized my audience had grown. "As it turns out, I actually am human. How's that for irony?"

"Delilah, this is wonderful!" Lenore's voice sounded like sunshine. Like hope, joy, faith, and anticipation, and when she spoke, I started to feel all those things, too. Which was why her handlers wore earplugs during her performances— the modern-day Odysseus really could've sailed his ship into the rocks under a siren's influence.

"They will have to let you go!" Claudio said, his accent thicker than usual with emotion.

"Oh, no, they won't." I'd been thinking about that a lot.

"I'm not sure my test results will matter, considering that there's footage out there showing my transmutation. I'm still a monster in their eyes. And even if by some miracle I actually got a court to verify my test results and get me out of here, they'd just charge me for what I did to Jack and to Wallace, which would either get me locked up and isolated for the rest of my life or executed."

"But Gallagher knows?" Claudio said.

I started to answer, then thought better of it. Gallagher couldn't afford to be seen as less than loyal to the menagerie, and he'd already given Genni a protein bar, probably in full view.

"He thinks there was a mistake at the lab. They're rerunning the test. But that won't help me."

"Mysterious ways…" Rommily murmured, so softly I could hardly hear her.

"What does that mean?" I asked the world at large, and to my surprise, Lenore had an answer.

"The Lord works in mysterious ways." The siren's crate squealed. "My grandmother said it all the time. Rommily means that you're meant to be here. Don't you see? You were sent to us, Delilah. My grandmother said the Eumenides would only be called forth when and where they are needed."

And that was exactly what had happened. Gallagher was right. My purpose was to avenge the wrongs committed against cryptids, and I'd been called forth when and where I was first needed.

"You're where you're supposed to be." Lenore's voice felt like a call to action, and my heart pounded harder. My inner *furiae* was eager to accept that call. "No place on earth needs you more than we do. You can *avenge* us." Her pitch dropped into a range most women weren't capable of, and a shiver rolled through me, accompanied by the phantom taste of blood on my tongue. "You can kill them all, and…set us free."

Lenore could have launched ships and formed armies with nothing more than her voice—her pull was much stronger than I'd realized. Claudio had told me once that the only reason she and Finola didn't try to talk their way out of their cages in broad daylight was because Finola's older sister had been shot on sight for doing that very thing.

Fear is often more effective than chains at keeping people in captivity.

"You chameleons are all alike," Zyanya growled, breaking the siren's spell. "You pass for human for most of your lives, then when you get captured, you think you can just overthrow the system and take your life back, but that's not how it works. Even if Delilah could kill them all and set us free, how long do you think we'd stay free? Where would we go? There's no place for cryptids in this country, except as entertainment and playthings. And even if we make it to the Mexican border alive, it's not like they're welcoming everyone across the river with open arms." Moonlight reflected from her cat eyes and shone on the tips of her elongated canines. "You dream all you want, songbird, but leave the rest of us out of it. Hope is much more dangerous than any damn cattle prod."

With that, the cheetah shifter slunk to the other side of her cage and curled up in the shadows.

"Don't listen to her," Lenore insisted. "You're here for a reason, Delilah. You can do what the rest of us can't."

And for the first time since I'd been locked up, I realized that my escape from Metzger's would feel more like abandonment to those I left behind.

I wasn't sure either part of me could live with that.

CHARITY

"You in town for the circus?" The convenience store clerk rang up Charity Marlow's coffee, breath mints, and two energy drink cans with a handheld scanner, then swiveled the display to show her the total.

"No." Charity dug a twenty from her wallet and laid it on the counter. "Just passing through." And anyway, the menagerie would be pulling up stakes first thing in the morning, according to the schedule posted online.

"Too bad." The clerk counted out her change. "I saw it last night. Hell of a show. The Courtyard Inn on the highway is booked solid for the first time I can remember."

"Is that the only hotel in town?"

"It's really more of a motel, but yeah, that's all we got since the Bluebell shut down a few years ago. You need a place to stay?"

"No," Charity lied, as the cashier packed all of her purchases except the coffee in a small brown paper bag. "Thanks." She slid her change into her pocket and took the bag, then headed out into the brightly lit parking lot with her new cell phone in her hand.

Alone in her car, she locked the doors and set her coffee in the cup holder, then touched a series of icons on her phone screen. Shelley Wells had shown her what to buy and helped her set up her email account on a device that had only one button, yet about a million functions. She still only understood three of them—telephone, email, and internet.

The texting program seemed promising, but Charity had no one to text. Most of her friends had quietly backed away from her after Delilah was arrested. Shelley had made it clear that her involvement ended with setting up the cell phone and, as hurt as she was, Charity couldn't blame her. Any good mother would be willing to take risks for her daughter, but she couldn't justify dragging someone else into danger.

The progress icon cycled for a minute or so, while Charity stared at the tiny email inbox, mentally crossing her fingers. She'd been waiting for a reply from Paige Wilmington, the civil rights attorney, for three days, and as far as she was concerned, any attorney whose services required old women to mortgage their homes should be on call twenty-four hours a day.

Wilmington's work was usually pro bono, at least on the front end; if she won her clients' cases, she took a percentage of the settlement. She'd successfully sued police departments, school systems, and even the Veteran's Administration, multiple times. But because she'd never won a case brought on behalf of a cryptid, she couldn't afford to work for free.

In the end, Charity had decided she'd rather have her daughter back than keep her home. No one who knew her was surprised. But at some point along the way, Ms. Wilmington had decided that she stood a much better chance of keeping Charity out of jail than of freeing Delilah.

Finally, the email program loaded, and a single new message appeared. Charity's hand tightened around her phone as she read, squinting at the small print.

Mrs. Marlow,

I'm sorry to say that we've been denied access to Delilah's blood test results based on your own admission that you are not her biological mother. This is a setback, for sure, but it's not a road-block. I'm appealing the decision, and while we're likely to get the same ruling from the circuit court, the appeal will put us on the judicial radar on a national scale, and that kind of attention can really only help our cause.

Either way, we're still going to need those pictures. Let me know when you have them.

Sincerely,

Paige Wilmington

Charity pressed the only actual button on her phone and dropped it onto the passenger-side floorboard in disgust.

That was the problem with civil rights lawyers. They were always more concerned with the big picture—with throwing light onto the problem—than with fighting for any single oppressed individual.

Delilah couldn't spare that kind of time, and Charity's budget could not support a two-year fight toward a—likely unfavorable—Supreme Court ruling.

Still, nearly two weeks of research and planning had revealed only two other alternatives. She could try to buy Delilah from Metzger's, but that would be financially unfeasible, even before she applied for the necessary permits and bought the required equipment and facilities.

Or she could help Delilah escape. The obstacles in that case were both financial and logistical. How would she break Delilah out of the menagerie? Even if they managed to escape, where could they go? The last cryptid to escape from official custody was shot to death in the street like a dog, and the relative who'd helped him escape was sentenced to life in prison.

Charity started her engine and backed out of the parking lot, then drove east for a mile and a half to an empty lot she'd scouted on the way into town. She'd slept in her car before, and she could do it again, especially fueled by the knowledge that Delilah now slumbered under much harsher conditions.

Charity dreamed about the woman in the mirror and the baby in her arms, then woke up with tears on her cheeks. Failure as a mother had already torn Elizabeth from her.

She was *not* going to lose Delilah, as well.

DELILAH

The squeal of metal woke me, and I had to blink several times to bring the man-shaped shadow standing in front of Genni's wagon into focus. The lock clicked, then he slid the side of her cage open slowly, to dampen the noise. The *furiae* stirred inside me. Geneviève was only thirteen!

I sat up, ready to wake the whole world with my outrage, but then I recognized Gallagher's distinctive, broad outline as he helped the werewolf cub from her wagon.

She stood mute and docile while he closed and locked her cage, then opened Claudio's. Genni curled up next to her father, and Gallagher slid two bottles of water and a few more of his ubiquitous snack bars into the cage before he closed it.

"You lied to me," I whispered, as he quietly unlocked my wagon.

His brows rose in silent question.

"You told me you weren't a nice guy."

He shook his head as he slid open the side pancl of my cage. "I have never lied to you, Delilah."

He cuffed my hands and helped me out of my cage, and a few steps later, I spoke too softly for anyone else to hear. "Where are we going? Is tonight the night?" I still had no idea what his plan for breaking me out entailed, and I felt almost as imprisoned by that ignorance as by my chains.

"Gallagher!"

The strained whisper came from my left as Gallagher led me toward a fairgrounds service entrance, and we both turned to see the teenage *djinn* seated side by side on their knees, in their shared cage.

Gallagher groaned, but veered toward their wagon, positioned first in the double row. "What?" he growled, pulling me to a stop at his side.

The one on the left—the paler one with the silver hair—turned to her cage mate expectantly.

"I need feminine supplies." The redhead's voice was soft, and she stared at the floor of her cage while she spoke, her face flushed even beyond what was normal for an *ifrit*.

Gallagher groaned again, and I scowled at him. The poor thing was already humiliated by the circumstance, and he wasn't making that any easier.

"Just go get her something!"

His eyes flashed at me in silent censure, but he knelt to chain one of my ankles to the axle beneath their cage, then took off toward the supply trailer at a jog.

"You are called Delilah, are you not?" The silver-haired *djinni* was young and coldly beautiful. Her wide blue eyes literally twinkled in the light from the parking lot, and her hair shimmered like water flowing through a starlit river.

"Yes. And you're... Nalah?"

She flinched, as if I'd insulted her. "I am Adira, a merid, highborn among glittering fountains and glistening seas. Nalah is my *ifrit* companion." She tossed a careless gesture at the girl next to her.

Nalah was one of the most stunningly beautiful girls I'd ever seen. Her smooth skin was golden bronze and nearly glowing, her long hair so many shades of crimson it seemed actually to be on fire, even in the dim light from the parking lot. Next to her, the merid looked pale and cold.

"Nalah hails from a land of roaring flames and broiling deserts, but I would never hold her unfortunate origin against her. She serves me very well." Adira gave her companion a lofty smile, and I had to bite my tongue to hold back the criticism ready to leap from it.

"Okay…" It was hard for me not to frown. "Good for her."

Adira nodded, accepting my congratulations with haughty ease. "Delilah, why are you out of your cage in the middle of the night?"

I scrambled for a logical explanation, since I couldn't tell her that my handler and I needed to discuss his plan to set me free. "Gallagher wants me learn how to call my inner *furiae* on demand. Without having a…target to aim for."

That was close enough to the truth that I didn't feel bad about lying to my fellow captives.

"You seem strangely eager to cooperate," Adira said, and the criticism in her voice made me bristle.

"If I'm not useful, Metzger will sell me to a collector." I shrugged. "We do whatever it takes to survive, right?"

Nalah nodded solemnly, the oranges and yellows of her irises leaping like flames, practically glowing from the shadowed interior of their wagon.

"Of course," Adira agreed. "But we'd heard that *you* were above such concessions." Her tone was full of reprimand and I wondered whether she was using the royal "we" or was including Nalah in her backhanded compliment. "We're especially surprised to see that you've submitted to Gallagher, out of all the handlers, considering his role in your captivity."

I bit back the urge to defend him. "He had no role. Metzger put him in charge of me."

Adira and Nalah exchanged a private, ominous look, then the merid turned back to me. "Did he mention why?"

Unease crawled beneath my skin at the suggestive arch of her brow. "No."

Adira turned to her young companion, wringing her hands in sudden, overblown uncertainty, and I couldn't tell whether she was a drama queen by nature or intentionally putting on a show. "Maybe we shouldn't tell her. I can't see how it would help."

"Would you want to know, if your positions were reversed?" Nalah's voice was soft and steady. Comforting, but somber, just like both her bearing and her expression. My attention was repeatedly drawn to her, in spite of her cage mate's histrionics.

"I would." Adira nodded. "Manipulation is their strongest weapon, and I'd want to know if it were being wielded against me." She seemed completely ignorant of her own hypocrisy.

"Then you must afford her the same rights you would claim for yourself," Nalah advised. "She deserves no less."

"Your counsel is wise without fail." Adira turned back to me with exaggerated solemnity. "Gallagher was put in charge of you because he is the reason you're here."

"What?" I backed away from their wagon as far as the ankle chain would allow. That couldn't be true. They were playing some kind of cruel prank. "No." I shook my head firmly. "Metzger bought me. I was there."

"The old man wrote the check, but Gallagher advised the purchase," Adira insisted. "Gallagher told him what you'd done and where they'd taken you after…your display in the hybrids tent." She paused for dramatic effect, and my heart thudded painfully. "You're here, locked up, a possession of those who were once your equals, because of Gallagher."

"No. You're wrong." I reveled in the numbness of denial,

a psychological narcotic, because they couldn't be right. They *couldn't*. "I don't know what kind of stupid adolescent game you two are playing, but I've sat through enough community theater to know an amateur performance when I see one."

"She doesn't believe us." Adira shook her head in exaggerated pity.

"I'm sure she means no slight against your honor, Princess," the companion murmured. "Delilah has obviously grown fond of Gallagher, and hearing the truth about him must be difficult." Nalah laid her free hand over her heart. "Truly, she has my sympathy."

"Mine as well." Adira studied my expression, but I could find only ice in her blue-eyed gaze. "If you don't believe us, ask Gallagher. I'm sure he will tell you the truth." The merid watched me closely as she struck the final blow. "His word is his honor."

I flinched, and she noticed. She'd been waiting for it.

Gallagher had told them the same thing he'd told me—that his word was his honor. Were they the other captives he'd made a promise to? If so, what had he promised them?

I sank to the ground on my knees and ran both hands through my tangled hair. I wanted to believe the *djinn* were lying—their delivery hadn't exactly reeked of sincerity—because from the very beginning, Gallagher had treated me better than any of the other handlers had, and it wasn't just the extra food and water. He spoke to me like a person. He spared my dignity. He argued with me.

People do not bicker with cats and dogs. They give pets orders and expect to be obeyed.

I didn't want to believe that the only Metzger's employee who thought of me as a person was actually the reason for my imprisonment.

Cryptids have been warned by the federal government to stay in their homes as the investigation continues into the origins and instigation of "the reaping," amid growing pressure from the public.

—Public service announcement, issued October 10, 1986

DELILAH

"**G**et up."

Startled, I looked up to see Gallagher walking toward me carrying a plastic grocery store bag. He opened the *djinn*'s cage and handed the bag to Nalah, then locked the cage again and freed my ankle. The whole time, I watched him, trying to see if I'd missed something. Maybe it was naive of me to believe him just because he'd told me I could, but I'd never caught him in a lie to anyone. Not to my fellow captives or to his own coworkers.

He'd said I was meant to be free, yet the *djinn* girls claimed he was the reason I'd been bought by Metzger's in the first place.

I had no reason to trust Adira and Nalah over Gallagher, yet in spite of their manipulative delivery, everything they'd said made sense. Gallagher was in the hybrid tent when I was exposed. He came with Metzger to buy me from the sheriff. The old man had put him in charge of me, as if he'd had some reason to hold Gallagher accountable if I failed to perform.

I probably never should have trusted him in the first place, but because I had, the sting of his betrayal was sharp and deep.

"Let's get moving." Gallagher reached for my arm, but instead of hauling me to my feet, he simply helped me up, and again my resolve faltered. I couldn't decide from one heartbeat to the next whether I was being unfair to him by suspecting him or unfair to myself by wanting him to be innocent.

He frowned with one look at whatever conflict showed on my face. "What's wrong?"

"I'm a captive in a traveling zoo," I snapped, caught between a pressing need to demand the truth and a fear that doing so would end any chance I had of escaping with him. "A better question would be 'What's right?'"

Gallagher's frown deepened, but instead of replying, he led me through the service entrance to the deserted fairgrounds, which sported a blacktop midway and kiosks built like little storybook cottages. I felt like a hostage in a warped fairy tale as we passed a cobbler's shop, a small castle tower, and what appeared to be the cabin from Goldilocks's infamous home invasion.

With every step, my leg shackles scraped the blacktop, reminding me that my status as a prisoner might be Gallagher's fault.

I assumed we were going to my usual tent until he guided me through another service entrance. Just outside the carnival proper, a camper sat about fifty feet from a flatbed pickup truck with the Metzger's logo painted on one door and an empty livestock cage lashed to the bed.

"We took the long way, so no one would see us, but everyone else is parked just around that corner—" he pointed at a curve in the exterior fairgrounds fence "—so we still have to be quiet."

"Why are we here? Is that yours?" I gestured toward the camper.

Gallagher nodded. "I thought you might like a break from tents and cages and folding furniture. Not that I have much better to offer." He led me to the camper and unlocked the door. "There's a light switch on your left, but don't flip it until I get the door closed."

He helped me up the steps in my chains, then followed me inside, and for a moment, he seemed to take up the entire tight space.

Fear skittered up my spine until it hit the lump in my throat. I couldn't even breathe without brushing his arm or chest, and I was suddenly, terrifyingly certain that I'd just made the biggest mistake of my life. Not that I'd had any choice.

I stumbled forward to put much-needed space between us and collided with what felt like a hollow wall.

The door latched behind me with a solid click. A second later, the light came on, and I found myself staring at a small wood-paneled refrigerator.

"Have a seat." Gallagher scooted past me and pulled two bottles of water from the fridge. "Anywhere's fine," he said, when my focus skipped from the booth-style table against one wall to a small sofa, then to an unmade bed at the back of the trailer.

I sat on the closest of the padded booth benches.

Gallagher set both bottles of water on the table, then he knelt in front of me and removed my handcuffs. They hit the chipped top of the table with a clank.

He sank onto the sagging built-in couch, his elbow resting on the tiny kitchen counter. "Water?" He gestured at the bottles, but I shook my head. "What's wrong, Delilah?"

"Are you the reason I'm here?" The words fell out before I could rethink my approach. "Did you tell Metzger to buy me?"

For one single, unprecedented instant, Gallagher's thoughts were unguarded, and I saw the truth. He leaned forward on the couch, his bearing instantly tense. "Okay, first of all, Rudolph Metzger doesn't do anything he doesn't want to do—"

I stood, and he rose to slide between me and the door, and suddenly oxygen seemed to be in short supply.

"Delilah, wait. Please listen." He reached for me, and when I backed away, I hit my hip on the edge of his tiny kitchen cabinet.

"Is it true?" I snatched the handcuffs from the table top, which was only an arm's length away in the tight space. "Is this because of you?"

He exhaled heavily, but held my gaze. "Yes."

"You soul-rotting *bastard*!" I threw the cuffs at his face and tried to push past him for the door, all promises to bide my time—to wait for his mysterious plan to unfold—forgotten. "You lied to me!"

Why did that knowledge hurt, when I should have expected it? Why did I feel so betrayed, when I should have known better than to trust anyone who dressed me in linen scraps accessorized with steel cuffs?

Gallagher refused to budge, and I realized he was actually broader than the door—he probably had to turn sideways to get into his own home. "I have *never* lied to you." His gray eyes flashed in anger, as if he were mortally wounded by the insult. "You never asked if buying you was my idea. If you had, I would have told you the truth."

"You lied through omission," I insisted, glaring up at him, and bewildered lines creased his forehead. "You intentionally withheld information I had a right to."

His confusion cleared like clouds blown away to expose the sky. "That's not a lie, that's a *deception*," he said as if the distinction somehow relieved him of guilt. "Deceit is a much more complicated, nuanced concept. I've never lied to you, or to anyone else. Ever." He looked like he wanted to say more, but no more came.

A river of lava pumped through my veins. "Are you seriously trying to absolve yourself using semantics?"

"Please sit and let me explain."

"I don't have any choice, do I?" Yet he'd already said "please" twice since closing the door behind us. "You give the orders and I follow them. That's how the relationship between captor and captive works, right?"

"I'm not your captor," he growled. "And you sure as *hell* aren't my captive."

"I'm wearing several pounds of metal that would suggest otherwise." I lifted one foot, and the chain connecting it to my opposite ankle clanked against the floor. "You were never going to set me free, were you? So what was your plan? Get Metzger to buy me like a piece of meat, then swoop in and string me along with snacks and water and promises you never make good on?" I frowned up at him, still trying to puzzle it through. "What was the point?"

He hadn't asked me for anything, other than patience and cooperation with my "act," and the only deception I could pinpoint was his admission about buying me.

"You don't understand." Gallagher reached for me, but I backed up until my spine hit the narrow bathroom door. "I don't want to hurt you—I want to protect you."

"Is that what you said to those pretty little *djinn* girls? Did you buy them, then promise to let them go, too?" Despite the lack of evidence, in the absence of a more logical theory, the obvious—and vile—conclusion seemed most likely. "They're *children*, Gallagher!"

"Adira told you...?" Gallagher lifted the faded cap from his head and raked his fingers through his hair. "Damn it!" His fist slammed into the table with an iron thud and it broke into two pieces, then fell apart.

I jumped, startled, and bumped the bathroom door again.

The table *fell apart*, like a stack of children's blocks. I stared at it, stunned, and my vague need to escape his trailer became a command to flee, from every muscle in my body.

Gallagher stepped in front of the broken furniture, as if out of sight really might mean out of mind. "It was old and poorly constructed. Delilah, Adira's…" He rubbed his forehead and started again, but I hardly heard him. I was still staring at the table he'd destroyed as easily as I might rip a sheet of paper. "In her homeland she was royalty—given everything she ever wanted, no matter what it cost anyone else—and she refuses to acknowledge that her circumstances have changed." Gallagher tilted my face so that my gaze met his.

I flinched away from his touch, but had no more room to retreat.

"She manipulates people into doing what she wants," he said. "She's a troublemaker."

"But is she a liar?" I didn't care about her motives. "Or was she telling the truth?"

"She doesn't even know the truth. She told you something she heard out of context, because she got scared. I've never touched either of those girls beyond my duties as a handler, and I had nothing to do with Metzger buying them," he growled, huge fists clenched in response to accusations that clearly offended him. "They were here before I took this job." He stood straighter, and the top of his cap brushed the ceiling. "I swear on the solemn honor of my name."

I frowned, caught off guard by archaic phrasing he didn't seem to have noticed, and suddenly I remembered how my mother's Southern accent had always thickened when she was angry or upset.

"Moreover, I will tolerate no further unwarranted denigration of my character, from you or from anyone else."

"Denigration of your…?" Fire flushed my cheeks and

scalded my ears. *"You're* the bastard who put me here, and you never had *any* intention of setting me free."

He reached for me again, and when I sidestepped his touch, I almost fell onto his bed. "I talked Metzger into buying you to save your life."

I rolled my eyes. "Because I'm so safe here, half-starved, surrounded by child-abusing rapist handlers." I half expected him to deny the circumstances I'd described, but I should have known better. I had yet to catch him in a lie.

"You're safer here than you'd be anywhere else." When he took a step back, I realized he was trying to set me at ease. As if it had just then occurred to him that closing in on me would have the opposite effect.

"Why on earth would I be safer here?"

"Because *I'm* here!" His spine straightened with the claim, and his next words carried the first hint of vulnerability he'd shown. "Because if you'll let me, I'll make sure no one can hurt you."

With a sudden bolt of surprise, I realized I was finally seeing a crack in the steely facade he'd worn from the moment I'd first met him. The longing that showed through that crack was somewhere between the lust for a beautiful woman and the craving of a juicy steak.

Gallagher was looking at me like Shelley might look at a pair of designer shoes she could never afford. Like my mother had looked at the only new car she'd ever had, convinced she didn't deserve it, but resolved to take care of it.

He was looking at me the way I looked at freedom, with ironclad determination to take it for myself and make the most of it.

"Clyde hurt me," I whispered, stunned and disoriented by the strange, restrained desire I could hear in his voice and see in his eyes, yet couldn't make sense of. It felt cleaner than lust and more formal than physical attraction. Almost like… chivalry.

Real chivalry—not simple manners, but archaic courtly valor.

Suddenly I remembered Gallagher helping me dress with his gaze averted, after Clyde had cut my clothes off. The clean clothes and blanket he'd brought me, after my confrontation with the hose. The food and water he gave me. How *fundamentally* insulted he'd looked when I'd asked what his favors would cost me.

Whatever he was showing me felt…urgent. Significant, in some way I couldn't truly understand.

"You said if Clyde touched me, you'd rip him apart. Then you let him hose me down." I'd considered that a failed threat, rather than a broken promise, but Gallagher flinched, and I was fascinated by his reaction.

"I apologize. I didn't know how else to bring out your beast and keep you from being sold into a situation I couldn't protect you from. I chose to let him hurt you a little now to keep someone else from hurting you worse later. But I swear on the solemn honor of my name that I will keep my word. Evan Clyde will pay for what he did to you. He will pay in pain, and in terror, and in pints and pints of glistening blood."

Chills rolled through me not just at his words, but at the hushed, reverent quality of his voice when he said them. At the eager look in his eyes. He felt and sounded nothing like the steely-eyed boss of livestock I'd come to know. This Gallagher felt larger and more powerful in some captivating way that had nothing to do with his physical size. It was as if he'd just put on a costume.

Or had finally taken one off.

"If you'll let me, I will rip apart anyone who lays a hostile hand on you. I swear on my life, and my word is my honor,

Delilah." This time when he reached for my hands, I let him take them, because I believed him. His voice sounded like truth. His every utterance felt like fact.

My head swam and my pulse roared in my ears.

He squeezed my hands, the pads of his fingers rough against my palms. "I can protect you. I *want* to protect you. I want to fight for you."

Warmth gathered low in my stomach. "What does that mean?" Why did the intensity of his voice hint at more than his words seemed to say?

Gallagher knelt and unlocked the cuff around my right ankle. He looked up at me from his knees, still holding my dirty foot. "My people believe that from birth, each of us owes the world a service, in exchange for the seeds we sow and the air we breathe."

His people? What people? How could I have spent so much time with him, yet know so little about him, beyond his role in the menagerie?

Why would a man who kept sentient beings in cages be so concerned with truth and honor?

"That service must be selfless and it must cost us something, because that which costs nothing is worth nothing." He gently lowered my right foot and lifted my left. "I have nothing to offer the world except physical strength, the simplest, most humble of all gifts. But *you* have something truly extraordinary to give, and it has cost you everything."

My chest felt so tight that breathing had become a blissful agony.

He unlocked the other cuff, and the shackles fell away, but his hands did not. His fingers felt warm and strong, yet made no demands and took no liberties. "You are bold, and fearless, and even the darkest parts of you serve at the discretion of your compassion and empathy. You *exist* to seek justice, and it has become increasingly clear to me since I met you that the most worthy service I will ever be able to offer the world is the facilitation of your work."

"Facilitation? You want to help me be a *furiae*? How? By getting me out of here?" Was that why he wanted to help me escape—so he could feel like he deserved every breath he took?

That sounded pretty odd, but who was I to criticize someone else's culture, especially if it led him to set me free?

"By freeing you, and by protecting you, so you can live out your purpose with no fear for your personal safety."

"Wait, like a bodyguard?" That was hands-down the strangest proposition I'd ever received, and on the surface, it seemed to make little sense. Yet somehow it *felt* reasonable. Gallagher looked and sounded sincere, and I had no trouble picturing him in that role. "You're serious?"

"Of course." He looked up at me from his knees. "I've spent my entire life searching for an opportunity to serve. You are that opportunity, Delilah." He cleared his throat. "Will you consider me as your champion?"

"My champion?" That sounded like a hell of a lot more than a bodyguard. And I was suddenly very aware that he was still holding my bare, filthy foot.

"Yes. Your defender and guardian."

My heart thumped so loudly I was sure he could hear it. Those words obviously meant something very specific to him. Something primal, which the *furiae* stirring contentedly inside me seemed to understand, but I couldn't quite wrap my mind around.

"What does that entail, exactly?" Hadn't he already sworn to rip hands off for me?

Gallagher released my foot, then stood straight and tall—all six and a half feet of him. His speech took on the cadence of a formal vow, and I could only stare up at him, riveted. "As your champion, I will serve at your side. I will protect you with every bone in my body and every beat of my heart. I will rip apart anyone who comes between us, and I will litter the ground with the corpses of our enemies. I will be your sword and your shield, in all matters. If you will have me."

"My sword and shield." My throat felt inexplicably tight, and his camper suddenly looked unsteady, as if it might start spinning at any second. "Do you understand how strange that sounds?"

"To you? Yes. But for my people, it's an honored tradition. It's a way of life."

"And just who are these people?" I knew of several religions and a couple of cults which required less formal vows.

Gallagher's expression softened, and he looked pleased by my interest. "You have my word that when I have the chance, I will tell you everything you want to know about my people and our traditions. But right now, we're pressed for time, and I need your decision."

He looked nervous for the first time since I'd met him, as if I had the power to break him with a single word, when he'd spent the past year working with beasts strong enough to pull his head from his shoulders. Literally.

"I'm not sure I understand what I'm getting into," I admitted, my thoughts racing. "Would I be obligated to *do* anything?"

His brows rose. He looked almost impressed that I'd thought to ask. "Only to seal our alliance when the probationary period concludes, if you choose to continue the partnership."

"Seal...how?" I was assuming he had something more *mature* in mind than cutting our palms and shaking hands. Was that why he'd brought me to his home?

I glanced at his bed, but I should have known better.

Gallagher looked painfully offended.

"Delilah, this is the most honorable relationship my people recognize. More so even than marriage, because conjugal pairings are typically built upon a foundation of lust, which is notoriously capricious. I know you don't understand, but assuming that I'm asking for anything improper from you is a grave insult to my honor."

"Oh. I'm—I'm sorry." I looked down at my bare feet, my face flaming. But I wasn't sure what other conclusion I was supposed to draw. I'd never met a man who valued honor over sex. That wasn't human nature—honor didn't propagate species.

"No need to apologize. Our relationship would be sealed with your acceptance of four offerings and the recitation of a sacred vow."

"Presents and a promise?"

"No. Offerings and a vow," he insisted, and finally I understood that for him, words were as important as actions. His words were specific. They seemed to carry power.

"Gallagher, your people... They aren't human, are they?"

For a moment, he only stared at me, his features so perfectly blank they had to be hiding something big. Something important. Then I understood the problem. His word was his honor, so he couldn't lie. But telling the truth would be dangerous.

"It's okay," I said. "I won't tell anyone. You have my word."

Gallagher exhaled slowly. "No. They aren't human."

Exhilaration surged through me with each beat of my heart. He was hiding in plain sight, in a position of authority, and had been for at least a year. No wonder he didn't abuse the captives. No wonder he'd talked Metzger into buying me. He really did think he could protect me. Maybe he could.

"What are—"

Gallagher shook his head. "I can't tell you anything else right now, but I will hold you to your word. And you still haven't answered my question. Will you consider me as your champion, Delilah? I swear on my honor—on my life—that *no one* will get to you without going through me."

An alliance with a strong and by all appearances honorable ally, who had the keys to my cage and a personal interest in keeping my secrets. An alliance with a trial period. That was exactly what a woman with a big mouth, no self-defense skills, and no civil rights needed.

"Okay," I said, and adrenaline rushed through me, amplifying my heartbeat until I could hear it in my ears, the rhythm of my very existence. I'd been certain the universe owed me a break, and what it had given me was Gallagher. I'd have been a fool to turn his offer down.

"Are you sure?" His gaze searched mine, looking for doubt.

I shrugged. "If we're allies, you'll *definitely* get me out of captivity? Soon?"

"I swear on my honor."

"Then, yes, I'm sure."

"You have to say the words," he insisted, taking my hands as he looked down into my eyes, and he was almost smiling. Almost.

"There are words?" Of course there were words. Words, evidently, meant everything to his people. Whoever they were. "What are these words?"

He grew solemn again, as if someone had flipped a switch. His eyes even looked darker, and a beat of doubt pulsed along with my heart. "You have to say you'll take me as your sword and shield."

I sucked in a deep breath and swallowed my doubt. I would get no better opportunity to escape, and he'd already taken many risks for me. "Gallagher, I will take you as my sword and shield." *Probationally.*

Without releasing my hands, he gave me a formal nod—almost a bow. "And so you shall have me."

"Great." I gently pulled my hands from his grip and took a step back, just then realizing that I was both unbound and uncaged for the first time since being sold as livestock. "So, now what? How are we going to get me out of here? Where are we going to go? Can we leave tonight?"

"We're going to Mexico, and no, we can't leave tonight." Gallagher leaned back against the kitchen countertop, and I realized he towered over his own refrigerator. "And we're taking Adira and Nalah."

I started to ask why, when Genni and Rommily were clearly faring much worse in captivity, but then I understood. "You made them a promise, too." I frowned. "Wait, are you championing them, too?"

That hint of a smile was back, as if he wanted to laugh, but wasn't allowed. "No. A champion can only have one benefactor. And I didn't promise the girls. I promised Adira's father. He hired me to return his daughter."

"What?" I sank onto the couch, trying to puzzle through that unexpected revelation.

"I applied for the job at Metzger's so I could stay close enough to break her out when the menagerie swings near the southern border. That's the only way to avoid going on the run during a nationwide manhunt. Adira and Nalah can't pass for human." He shrugged. "We'll never make it if border patrol—not to mention the rest of the country—knows to look for us."

"How did you get this job without lying?"

Gallagher's gray eyes shone. "Fortunately, in the entire year I've been here, waiting for the southern loop of the menagerie circuit, no one's ever actually asked me if I'm here to free the *djinn* from captivity."

"A year." I had **trouble wrapp**ing my mind around that. "Her dad must be offering one hell of a payout."

"He can afford it." Gallagher sat on the edge of one of the padded benches and propped one elbow on the broken table. "Her father is Bruhier, sultan of the merids."

"Wait, she really is royalty?" He'd told me, and *she'd* told me, but I hadn't really believed it. "How did she wind up in the menagerie?"

"She ran away a week before her wedding, and because she's not the brightest merid in the pond, she fled north, into the U.S. She'd been here less than a week before she and Nalah were captured, and old man Metzger swooped in with his checkbook."

"She was a runaway bride more than a year ago?" Adira looked very young, even having lived in such rough conditions. "How old is she?"

"She's sixteen now." Gallagher shrugged. "Each culture has its own customs. That's no different for cryptids than for humans. Adira's marriage to the crown prince of the *ifrits* is supposed to unite the two *djinn* kingdoms, or something like that. My job is just to take her home. What happens after that has nothing to do with me."

"But she doesn't want to get married." Anger stirred in the pit of my stomach at the thought of a teenager forced into marriage.

"And I'm not going to make her. I told her what her father was offering, and she decided she'd rather take her chances at home than sit in a cage here."

I couldn't blame her for that. "Do the other handlers know who she is? Does Metzger?"

"Everyone's heard her talk, but I don't think many believe her. Which is probably for the best. She's worth quite a lot to her father."

"Which is why you took the job?" That didn't sound much like the man who'd volunteered to be my champion. "For the money?"

"There is no money. I wanted to go south of the border, and the sultan has provided passage."

"You have passage into Mexico?" Even having grown up human, I knew what that was worth. Few cryptids even made it to the border thanks to the U.S. Border Patrol, and of those who did, fewer than half were accepted into Mexico. Worried about a flood of refugees, the sultans south of the border only took in those who could pay, or who could otherwise benefit the kingdom.

"Sultan Bruhier sent a pass for each of the girls, and one for me."

Passage for three. "No wonder the girls are scared. They're afraid I'll take one of the spots."

"Yes, but it won't come to that. My trip into town the other day was so I could contact Adira's father, to ask for a fourth pass."

"What did he say?"

"He's considering it. I'm supposed to call again from the next town."

"Can't you just borrow another cell phone?"

Gallagher shook his head and shifted on the couch. "I can't risk anyone finding a call to Mexico on their bill, or someone walking in while I'm on the phone. But I'll get another pass, Delilah. I'm not going to leave you here. My word is my honor, remember?"

How could I forget?

Gallagher stood and scruffed his sun-bleached baseball cap back and forth over his short hair, a habit I'd noticed my first day in the menagerie.

"You need a new hat." I stood and reached up to thump the bill, and he tensed. "This one's all faded."

"I'll wash it soon, and it'll look as good as new," he insisted, but I had my doubts.

Gallagher picked up the cuffs and leg shackles, and a familiar, devastating dread glued my bare feet to the cheap linoleum.

"I can't put those back on." I couldn't climb back into that horrible cage. Not with liberty so close. Not with Gallagher's promise to free me still echoing in my head.

"It's not for long. We drop stakes near Laredo in a couple of days, then this'll all be over."

"Swear?" I said, as he reached for the doorknob.

Gallagher hesitated, his brows tugged low by the weight of what I was asking for. "I can't foresee all the possible complications, but I swear I'll do my best to set all four of us free there."

"Thank you," I said, when I realized that was the best I was going to get.

Gallagher gave me an almost formal nod, then gestured for me to precede him outside. He turned off the light, then followed me onto the steps, clanking like a captive thanks to the metal he carried. He was about to recuff me when a growl cut through the night, too loud to have come from wagon row.

"What the hell?" I whispered.

"Pipe down, Papa, or I'll light you up until your insides boil," Clyde said, and I gasped at how close his voice was. He had to be right behind the camper.

"Stay here," Gallagher whispered, carefully lowering the cuffs and shackles to the ground, so they wouldn't clank again. He rounded the end of the RV, and after a moment's hesitation, I followed, barefoot.

I'd recognized that growl, and I'd sure as *hell* recognized the soft canine whine accompanying it.

Geneviève was in trouble.

Congress officially repeals the Sanctuary Act, stripping cryptids of protection under the U.S. Constitution. Millions lose their jobs and homes in the immediate aftermath.

—From a December 12, 1986, article in the *Tulsa Herald*

DELILAH

From the shadow of Gallagher's camper, I could see the figures gathered near the flatbed truck, but they hadn't noticed me yet.

Eryx was harnessed to Claudio's wagon, which he'd obviously hauled from wagon row toward the truck with an animal crate strapped onto the bed. The truck's headlights threw two cones of bright light over the grass, which made the ambient darkness look even darker.

"Come here, you little bitch, or we'll have to do this the hard way." Clyde had opened the side panel of the werewolf's cage and was brandishing a cattle prod at the father and daughter inside, both in canine form.

Gallagher stepped into the beam of the headlights, and Eryx's brown eyes widened. "What the hell are you doing?"

"My job." Clyde didn't turn, nor did he seem surprised by Gallagher's presence; he'd obviously recognized the camper. "Ruyle signed the papers on the little bitch this afternoon, and I'm supposed to have her in Wichita by noon."

That's when I realized Clyde had parked the menagerie's flatbed truck next to the camper *hoping* to attract Gallagher's attention. Because he wanted to gloat.

My hands curled into fists. He couldn't sell Genni. She was just a kid—the only child her father had left!

Clyde brandished the prod at Claudio, who scuttled back, growling while he shielded his daughter with his own body. "Unfortunately, separating the whelp from her sire is a real pain in the ass. Any idea why this cage is at double capacity?"

Gallagher ignored the question. "Ruyle didn't say anything to me about selling Geneviève."

"That's because you are no longer in the loop. Once the old man gets back and signs off on it, you'll be answering to me. If you wanna get a head start on that, come help me get her onto the truck."

"She's not going anywhere until Ruyle verifies that you're not just poaching menagerie assets. Close the door and back away from the cage," Gallagher ordered.

"I don't answer to you anymore." Clyde turned back to the werewolves. "Papa, send the pup out here before you both get hurt."

Claudio growled louder, baring sharp teeth, still firmly installed between his daughter and the handler.

"Have it your way." Clyde thrust the electrical prod at Claudio. The wolf lunged. He began to convulse from the voltage just as his muzzle clamped down on Clyde's bare right forearm, and for one long, stunning moment, mutual foes shared a splendid dance of agony.

A high-pitched squeal leaked from Clyde's lips, but it contained none of the volume or power I'd expected in response to a brutal werewolf bite. All at once I realized the electrical voltage was flowing into him through the werewolf, completing a circuit that prevented Claudio from letting go of Clyde's arm and Clyde from letting go of the cattle prod.

Genni's whine crescendoed into a yowl of terror. Eryx twisted in his harness, trying to get a look at the problem.

Gallagher lurched forward to interrupt the cycle, but I darted out of the shadows to pull him back. "Use something that doesn't conduct. Like...wood. Or plastic." We glanced around and found nothing on the ground, so I raced to the flatbed truck and pulled a shovel from the large tool bin behind the cab. Gripping it by the wooden handle, I swung the shovel at the cattle prod, knocking it out of Clyde's grip.

The prod thumped onto the grass four feet away.

Claudio let go of the handler and backed shakily into the corner of his cage, where Genni began to lick his face and nuzzle him. Clyde collapsed onto the grass in a bright beam from the truck's headlights, clutching his mauled forearm, jaw clenched to deny the pain an outlet. For one long, tense moment, no one moved. No one spoke.

Then Eryx stamped one hoof, his human eyes wordlessly demanding an update—he hadn't seen much from his position at the front of the cart.

"It's okay." I crossed my fingers, hoping I was right. I had no idea how much voltage had gone through Claudio, but I couldn't reasonably hope it had fried the handler without mentally damning the werewolf to the same fate.

Clyde looked up at the sound of my voice, still clutching his arm, and at first his stare was blank. Then he frowned, and I froze like a deer in oncoming headlights when I realized he was coming out of his stupor. And that he recognized me.

"What's..." Clyde cleared his throat and pushed himself to his feet, still holding his ruined arm, while blood ran between his fingers. He slammed the cage door shut without ever taking his focus from me, but he was speaking to Gallagher. "What the *fuck* is she doing out here, and where the *hell* are her restraints?"

"You're hurt," Gallagher observed, with an almost clinical

detachment. Clyde was also shiny with sweat and pale, even in the glare from the headlights. He'd lost a lot of blood.

"You need to go to the hospital." I glanced at the Metzger's truck, then at Gallagher, and the rage I found etched into his face sent chills deep into my bones. His fists were clenched. His teeth were grinding. His eyes had darkened until I couldn't be sure they held any color at all.

Clyde glanced from Gallagher to me, then back, and the obvious misunderstanding surfaced in his eyes, already glassy with blood loss. "You have five seconds to deal with your little whore, before I wake up the whole damn menagerie."

The snarl that rumbled from Gallagher was like no sound I'd ever heard. It wasn't human. It wasn't feline, or canine, or ursine, or anything like the grunts and grumbles of a troll, or giant, or even the berserker. It was a sound of raw power and pure rage.

Gallagher seemed to be standing on the edge of some crucial precipice. The monster within me understood the storm of violence roiling off him like clouds in advance of a downpour, but the rest of me couldn't make sense of what I was seeing. What I was feeling. What the very charge in the air told me was about to happen.

"Gallagher?" I kept my voice low and steady out of instinct, the way one might address a gunman with his finger on the trigger, or a dog with its teeth already buried in flesh.

He turned to me, and Clyde dived for the cattle prod. Gallagher lunged at him so fast I could hardly track the movement. His massive right shoulder slammed into Clyde's solar plexus, driving the air from his body an instant before they both hit the ground.

Gallagher clamped one broad hand over Clyde's mouth, then reached for the cattle prod. I thought he'd rip it from Clyde's grasp. Instead he ripped Clyde's arm from his body, with no more effort than it might take to tear a breadstick in two.

I blinked, shocked beyond all words. All thoughts. Then blood began to soak through Clyde's empty left sleeve, and my legs folded beneath me. Horrified, I held back screams with both hands over my mouth while Clyde howled into Gallagher's palm.

Eryx snorted and pawed at the ground with one hoof. Claudio and Genni stood on all fours in their cage, panting while they watched, evidently unbothered by the savage spill of blood.

My sight lost focus and I started to shake while Gallagher pulled Clyde apart. Piece by piece. One-handed. An arm landed several feet in front of me, followed by a blood-filled left boot. A bare leg hit the side of Claudio's cage and he and Genni both scuttled back, then edged forward again to watch the show.

When it was over, Clyde lay in blurry, red-streaked pieces on the grass between the werewolf cage and Gallagher's camper. Empty, blood-soaked scraps of clothing littered the ground. More blood gathered in out-of-focus pools on the grass and dripped from the wire mesh side of the crate.

I couldn't breathe. I couldn't think.

I couldn't believe what I'd seen, even with evidence of it lying all around me in gruesome bits and pieces.

"What…what…what…?" My chin quivered, and I couldn't get beyond that one word. I swallowed and started over, staring up at him from my knees in the blood-splattered grass. "What the *fuck*, Gallagher?"

He turned to me slowly, moonlight shining on an arc of blood splattered across his face. "I said I would rip him limb from limb for touching you. My word is my honor."

My teeth began to chatter, in spite of the heat. I had no idea what to say.

Gallagher knelt among the dismembered remains of his foe and took his faded baseball cap off. I watched, stunned, while he set his cap upside down in a pool of blood and stared at it. At first, I thought he was praying.

Then a drop of blood rolled up and over the edge of Clyde's empty black boot, and I gasped. Once I'd noticed that one small motion, I could see all the others.

I could see the pattern.

Blood flowed all around me—from everywhere it had landed during the massacre, as well as from the severed body parts—but it flowed *toward* Gallagher's hat. It rolled, and streamed, and gathered in defiance of gravity, over blades of grass and twigs and trash blown from the carnival midway. Blood trickled through the wire mesh side of Claudio's cage and fell in fine beads from Gallagher's face and clothing. It all collected in the pool beneath his hat, but that pool didn't widen. It didn't deepen. In fact, it seemed to be shrinking.

As I watched, the blood from the puddle soaked into Gallagher's hat, pulled up through the fibers like a spill into a paper towel, and I couldn't look away.

"What's happening?" I whispered, and when he didn't answer—didn't even look away from his bloody hat—I tried again. "Gallagher, what the hell is happening?"

He didn't answer, but Eryx snorted, so I tore my gaze from the deliberate flow of blood and looked at the minotaur. And that's when I finally realized that whatever was happening, he'd known about it all along.

Red cap. He'd written it in the sawdust, but I hadn't understood what he'd been trying to tell me.

I still didn't.

"Is this what you were saying?"

Eryx nodded. Geneviève whined and I looked up to find her father sitting next to her in human form, casually nude as shifters often seemed to be by necessity, one arm wrapped protectively around her canine shoulders. "Did you know about this?" I whispered, and he shook his head. "Do you know what's happening?"

Claudio shook his head again, and Eryx snorted in obvious frustration. Claudio could speak, but had no answers, and Eryx clearly understood, yet couldn't speak.

Finally, when the last drop of blood had soaked into Gallagher's gruesome baseball cap, leaving the gory crime scene eerily absent of mess, he picked up his hat, which now glistened with thick, dark blood.

"No!" I cried, when I realized what he was about to do, but he set the hat on his head anyway.

I braced myself for the sight of blood running down his face, into his eyes, and over his chin. But that didn't happen.

The blood stayed in his hat, and after a few seconds, the hat stopped glistening. It looked...dry. It looked normal—as clean and bright red as it must have been the day he'd bought it.

Assuming such a hat *could* be bought.

"Delilah." Gallagher stepped over Clyde's torso and veered around his right leg, then sank to his knees in the grass next to me. "Delilah," he said again, and when I didn't look at him— when I could only stare at my hands, clenched around handfuls of my dirty linen skirt, he lifted my chin until I met his gaze.

His eyes looked normal. Gray and...worried. "Delilah, are you okay?"

"What is this? What happened?" I brushed his hand away and tried not to be swayed by the fact that the rare glimpse of true concern in his expression was for me. "What are you?"

"I am a redcap." He answered without hesitation, and seemed almost relieved by the opportunity.

"A redcap." I thought back through everything I'd learned about cryptids in college, but couldn't place the species.

"We're also known as *fear dearg*." He took my hands, and they finally stopped shaking. "It means 'red man' in—"

"In Celtic," I finished for him. And suddenly I understood. "You're *fae*."

"*Fae*, yes, but of the solitary variety. I serve no king or queen." There was something oddly fragile in the admission, and for once, his eyes hid nothing. His pain was mine to observe. "I have no home."

"How are you here? There are no *fae* here, Gallagher."

"None that you know of." He squeezed my hand, then brushed hair back from my forehead. "The *fae* are better equipped than any other cryptid species to blend in with humanity."

Which was why I'd learned as much about them in mythology class as in any of my biology courses.

"Glamour," I said, and he nodded. "What do you really look like?"

He seemed surprised by the question. "This is my actual appearance."

"But *fear dearg* is small—like, three feet tall—and his teeth are sharp and pointy, and his fingers—"

Gallagher scowled. "Yes, and *furiae* are hideous old hags who fly on bat wings and have snakes for hair. How often have you known folklore to be completely accurate, Delilah?"

"Okay. Fair point." But shock still dulled my thoughts and slowed my tongue. "I guess the blood part's real, though? You have to kill to survive?"

"Yes." His gaze was open. Brutally honest. "If the blood ever completely dries from my cap I will die," he explained, one side of his face brightly lit by the headlights. "We are warriors by nature—*fear dearg* crave slaughter. In the past, we've been mercenaries, assassins, and hunters. Some worked for pay, but most would work for the thrill of the kill. However, a few centuries ago, a group of *fear dearg* who did not relish the death of innocents broke away to form their own tribe. The *honora militem*. Members of the *militem* swore to take as victims only those who deserve a painful end. They took an oath promising to repay the earth for the resources they used by dedicating their lives to selfless service. Most became champions."

The strange tradition. The formal words. The strong drive to facilitate my calling. "You're *militem*."

"I am what's left of *militem*." He shifted on his knees in the grass, as if the admission made him uncomfortable. "When I was a boy, there was a civil war, such as has never been fought among humans. I and a few others are all that remain, scattered across the globe."

"Your word is your honor..." I mumbled, and another piece of the puzzle slid into place. "*Fae* cannot tell an outright lie." But according to conventional wisdom, they were masters of deception.

No wonder he'd stressed the distinction.

"Which is why we take the oath—it prevents us from killing the innocent, even in desperate times, when our caps begin to dry. Without the oath, most *fear dearg* would give in to the irresistible lure of violence. Even now, having just bathed my cap, my hands itch to rip flesh and break bone."

I could see the stress that resisting the biological urge put him through. No wonder he was always tense. Living in such close proximity to fragile flesh and pumping blood must have been torture similar to that of a celibate man walking through a nudist colony.

"Your cap looks dry now." I stared at his hat, remembering how faded it had been minutes earlier, yet how bright on the day we'd met.

"I use glamour to disguise my traditional red cap as a human baseball cap and the drying of blood as the fading of color, but I have no choice about the truth behind the illusion. Clyde had to die. I had to dip my hat in blood. And you had to know the truth. Though this is not how I would have chosen to show you."

The truth. "You're a monster. Like me." I wanted to condemn what he'd done. I wouldn't sentence my worst enemy to the mutilation Clyde had suffered. But what right did I have to denounce Gallagher's nature, when mine wasn't so very different?

"No." He took me by both arms and stared right into my eyes. "Your calling is sacred. You are the physical incarnation of justice. The force that balances the scales. You are everything antithetical to my nature. *I* am a monster. And now I must clean up a monster's mess."

Gallagher stood and pulled me up with him, and I realized the wolves and the minotaur were still watching us. And that the sun would soon be up. And that the ground was still littered with body parts.

"Stay here. Don't touch anything," Gallagher said, and before I could nod, he disappeared around the corner of his camper. A second later, the front door squealed open, and I heard his footsteps as he walked through the small space.

"Are you okay?" I asked Claudio. I wanted to get closer, to see for myself, but I couldn't make myself step over Clyde. Any part of him.

The werewolf nodded. "A redcap. How could we not have known?"

"Eryx knew," I said, and the minotaur snorted in acknowledgment.

"This won't stop them," Claudio said, and I realized he'd

moved past the recent slaughter to his own tragedy. "They'll still sell Geneviève. The deal's already been struck."

"No." I wrapped my arms around myself, shivering in spite of the warm night. "Gallagher won't let it happen." He might be at Metzger's for Adira, but that hadn't stopped him from treating Eryx with respect and helping me. He would help Genni, too. She was an innocent.

Claudio shook his head. "There's nothing he can do without exposing himself."

Genni whined, her muzzle resting on his leg.

"He's right," Gallagher said, and I whirled to find him headed our way, carrying a large black trash bag.

"You can't just let them give Genni to another carnival," I insisted, crossing my arms over my thin linen dress. "What's the point of being strong enough to rip a man limb from limb if you can't stop bad people from selling children?"

"I can't stop them, and if I try, I'll either lose my job or expose my species." He bent to pick up Clyde's arm, then dropped it into the open bag. "There'll be nothing I can do to help *anyone* if that happens."

"Fine. I'll get her out of here." I held my hand out, palm up. "Give me your keys."

"No." He bent for another body part, and his trash bag began to bulge with morbid shapes.

"I'm not just going to let them take her, Gallagher. She's only a kid!" I said, and Genni whined in what I assumed was agreement. "You're supposed to be facilitating my life's work!"

"Which I'm doing, by keeping you from getting yourself killed." Gallagher stood and met my gaze. "Beyond that, I have another promise to keep, which I can't do if I have to expose myself by killing anyone who touches you when they hunt you and Genni down."

"What?"

He exhaled slowly, obviously grasping for patience. "As you might recall, I swore to rip apart anyone who lays a hostile hand on you."

Alarm coursed through me with the stunning realization. "You meant that literally." As evidenced by the body parts still scattered all over the grass.

"Of course." Gallagher shoved a severed hand into his bag. "My word is my—"

"Honor." I gripped handfuls of my own hair, too frustrated to think straight, then combed through the tangled strands with my fingers. "I know."

"Then you understand that if you let them sell Genni, she will live, as will all the police and idiot civilian hunters who won't have to go through me to get to you."

"He's right," Claudio said. "Sell her, but sell me with her. We'll go without a fuss, and I promise that if you keep us together, neither of us will ever tell a soul that you're not human. Ever."

Gallagher dropped the last arm into his bag and stepped closer to Claudio's cage. "I swear that I will try, but I can't promise it'll work." Claudio nodded, and Gallagher held his gruesome goody bag out to me. "Will you hold this open?"

"No way in hell." I stepped back, arms folded firmly over my chest.

Gallagher rolled his eyes, then handed the bag to Eryx, who held the opening wide while the handler picked up Clyde's torso and dropped it inside with a leaden thunk. Gallagher took the bag back and pulled the red drawstrings tight, then glanced around the scene of the crime in satisfaction.

My gaze was drawn to his gruesome bundle. "An hour ago, I would have sworn that a man's body wouldn't fit in a standard trash bag, and that even if it did, it'd be too heavy to lift."

"Pieces always fit better than the whole," he said. "And a corpse weighs less after you drain the blood."

"Spoken like a true psychopath." And I was starting to suspect that Gallagher could have lifted several corpses at once, even still full of their lifeblood.

"This is what I am." He threw the bag over his shoulder like Santa with a really morbid surprise, then stepped closer. "I am a monster, born and bred to kill. This is what that looks like. I cannot change my nature. I can only use my oath to reshape it, like tight clothes will reshape the physical form." He reached for my hand, and I let him have it. "Or I can unleash it, and let the bodies fall where they may. Delilah, I've sworn to unleash the violence that swims in my veins for *you*."

"You killed Clyde because you had to."

"I had to kill someone, but it didn't have to be him. I killed him because he saw you unrestrained. Because he hurt you. I killed him because he humiliated you and made you bleed. I killed him because you were not safe here while he still breathed."

"I know." And killing a coworker couldn't have been the ideal scenario—there would be questions, and possibly an investigation. "Thank you."

"There is no need to thank me. My honor is sullied when you suffer, and it shines when you are well." He stepped closer and lowered his voice, but I was pretty sure the werewolves could still hear him. "Unfortunately, we have to endure your captivity for a little while longer."

My gaze followed his to where my chains still lay on the grass. Reluctantly, I let him recuff my wrists, and when he knelt to do my ankles, the black bag recaptured my attention. "What about the body? I mean, the pieces."

Gallagher gave me a small, morbid smile. "Fortunately, we

travel in the company of several different species of flesh eaters, each of whom will be glad for the treat."

"The adlet?"

"And the trolls. And the ogres. And the wendigo, the as-
wang, and the cyclops. And the lamia, if we had the corpse
of a child, though I try never to have the corpse of a child.
But the lion head of the chimera will be good for a hand or
foot, as will the griffin."

"Sounds like you've done this before."

"Many times. But never with the body of a coworker."

The sky was beginning to lighten when Gallagher led us
all back to wagon row, my arm in his left hand, Eryx's lead
rope in his right, Claudio and Geneviève trailing behind in
their wheeled cage. "How can you stand this?" I whispered
as we walked. "You're one of us. How can you stand to keep
the rest of us in chains and cages?"

"If I could free them all, I would. But that's well beyond
one man's ability. Even mine," he added, before I could cite
his supernatural strength as an asset. "I can't stop a bullet with
bare flesh, and I can't stop the slaughter that would result when
everyone I set free is hunted down. The best I can do is get
you, Adira, and Nalah over the border, and hope that the others eventually find their way south." He spoke softly because
neither the wolves nor Eryx knew Gallagher's true reason for
being at Metzger's, and I'd promised not to tell.

Most of the others were asleep when he locked me into my
cage, then did the same for Genni and Eryx, and by the time
he came back through with his black bag full of horrors, Geneviève was already deep asleep in her cage.

Though he hadn't gotten much sleep either, and I'd had
none at all, neither Claudio nor I were able to close our eyes

for more than a long blink, and I couldn't help wondering if I'd ever sleep again without dreaming of flying body parts and blood-soaked hats.

DELILAH

While Abraxas was serving breakfast to Payat two cages down from mine, one of the handlers came running toward wagon row and skidded to a breathless stop a few feet from the food cart. My heart thudded in my ears while I waited to hear that body parts had been found in one of the cages or that Gallagher had been arrested. But the handler only asked Abraxas if he'd seen Clyde.

I glanced at Claudio. He said nothing, so I followed his lead.

"Not since last night." Abraxas dropped a ladleful of oatmeal on Payat's tray, then cursed when he remembered that cat shifters were supposed to receive 70 percent protein.

"He was supposed to be halfway to Wichita by now with the werewolf bitch," the handler said. "But no one's seen him since he got up at four this morning to load her onto the flatbed truck."

Abraxas slid Payat's tray into Lenore's cage, then leaned back and glanced down the row in my direction. "Genni's right there."

"I *know* she's there. Gallagher found her cage sitting by the side entrance to the fairgrounds, not fifteen feet from the flatbed, with Eryx still harnessed to the cart. He put her back in line and locked up the minotaur, and says he didn't know anything about the sale until he reported the incident to Ruyle this morning."

"I didn't know about the sale either." Abraxas scooped several chunks of organ meat onto another tray for Payat. "Are we sure it's legit? Did anyone call Clyde?"

"Been calling him all morning, but he's not answering. Ruyle's so pissed off his face is purple."

Abraxas shrugged and slid Zyanya's tray through the slot in her cage. "Clyde'll probably show up with a hangover in a couple of hours."

The other handler looked doubtful, but he only nodded, then tapped the side of the food cart. "Hurry up with this. We're shorthanded with Clyde missing, and that'll get worse when Gallagher heads to town for supplies."

When Abraxas had served everyone and pushed the food cart back to wherever it belonged, Zyanya looked up from her empty tray and arched one brow at me. "So, what really happened last night?"

"How should I know?" I avoided looking at her, hoping there wasn't some weird cheetah shifter trait that let her hear my racing pulse.

"You left with Gallagher in the middle of the night, and you were with him when he brought the wolves back this morning." She made a show of sniffing the air in my direction. "Though you're not carrying enough of his scent to have done much rolling around."

"It wasn't like that." Yet I could feel my cheeks flush.

"What about the predawn snacks Gallagher handed out to all the fastest, most thorough eaters?" Payat asked, holding his tray aloft, ready to be licked clean. "They smelled an awful lot like a certain missing asswipe handler."

I shrugged. He didn't need me to confirm what his nose and eyes had already told him. "Are you going to report him?"

Zyanya laughed out loud, exposing the sharp cat canines jutting from an otherwise human mouthful of teeth, and several softer chuckles echoed from farther down the row. "For feeding one monster to several others? No, and neither will anyone else. Though I don't understand why he did it." She turned toward Claudio, though he was blocked from her sight by the end panels of both of their cages. "Why would he cover for you, Papa wolf?"

I blinked, surprised by the conclusion she'd drawn, until I realized she could probably smell some trace of Clyde on Claudio, from the big pre-mortem bite the werewolf had taken out of the handler.

"To cover his own rule breach," Claudio said, looking right at me. "For letting Genni into my cage and for taking Delilah out for the night. We agreed to call it even."

Zyana snorted. "I'd say you came out ahead on that one, Papa."

No one argued.

"What did Ruyle say about Claudio?" The question tumbled from my tongue the minute Gallagher finished anchoring the canvas flap.

He crossed the tent toward me, digging his keys from his pocket, and his steps looked a little lighter, his eyes a little brighter, probably thanks to the newly bright hue of his blood-hat.

"Ruyle won't let him go with Genni. The old man plans to breed him with a new purchase." He unlocked the side panel of my cage and slid it back, and I sat on the edge, with my legs dangling over. "I'm sorry. I tried."

"I know."

Gallagher lifted me out of the cage and set my bare feet in dry sawdust.

My gaze found the handcuffs hanging from a hook on the end of my cage. "Should I put those on? What if someone comes in looking for Clyde?"

"Ruyle had the entire menagerie searched before 10:00 a.m. All they know for sure is that Clyde's not here. The gate opens in a couple of hours, and everyone else is too busy covering for him to bother us before then. So, no restraints for the moment." He leaned to his left and smacked the handcuffs, which made them swing like a pendulum. "Two days from now, if you like, we will throw these on the fire and watch as flames consume them."

"Does steel burn?"

"Only at very high temperatures. Fortunately, an *ifrit*'s fire can burn anything."

I stepped back for a better look at his expression. "Wait, you mean Nalah can just melt through her cage anytime she wants?"

Gallagher shrugged. "She's young, so if she can't yet, she'll be able to soon. But not without frying Adira in the process, which is why they're in the same cage. Nalah is the only captive *ifrit* in the country kept unsedated—none of the others have a reason not to burn through both cage and handlers." He set up two folding chairs in front of my cage. "We should all be thankful that she's even-tempered and fanatically loyal to that spoiled little merid."

"Wow." I sank onto one of the chairs. "Speaking of double occupancy, most of my fellow inmates think Claudio killed Clyde. He's not correcting them."

Gallagher's eyebrows rose. "Why do they think that?"

"Zyanya smelled Clyde on him. And she saw me come

back with you, so now everyone seems to think we're doing something…illicit."

Gallagher frowned. "This isn't some unseemly fling to fuel gossip. We're upholding an esteemed traditional imperative."

"Yes, but we're doing that *illicitly*," I pointed out. "People are going to talk."

"Well, they're wrong. And to demonstrate the honorable nature of this merger, I have something for you." Gallagher sank onto both knees in front of my chair and pulled what appeared to be a narrow leather envelope from his backpack on the ground. His steady eye contact told me that whatever was inside was important to him, and I wondered if I was being given some kind of test.

He reached into the leather wrapping and pulled out a short, thin blade with a simple leather-wrapped handle. "I took this from the corpse of my first kill—a soldier fighting against the *militem* during our civil war."

"I thought you were just a kid during the war." I stared at the knife. It was humbly appointed, but the edge of the blade looked as thin as a sheet of paper. I knew nothing about weapons, yet even I recognized the extraordinary skill that went into its production.

"I was eleven. This is my oldest possession, and it represents the day I accepted my calling as a warrior. I would be honored if you would accept it, as a symbol of my devotion to our partnership."

"Gallagher, I can't take your knife." It was clearly his most precious possession, and beyond that, I had nowhere to hide it.

His brows dipped low in dismay, bordering on bafflement. "There is no more appropriate offering from a champion to the one he serves. This knife holds great value to me, and giving it to you means that I hold you in equal worth. If you refuse the blade, you'll be refusing my services. My honor will never recover from the blow."

"Wait, if I don't take your knife, you can't be my champion?" Meaning he couldn't free me from captivity?

"Yes. This is the last of the four offerings. You readily accepted the others, and you seemed satisfied with the probationary period of our arrangement. This is the last step required to seal our union."

"Wait, are you saying the trial period is over? It's only been twelve hours!" By my best guess, in the absence of a watch.

Gallagher nodded. "The probationary period is defined by action, not by the passage of time."

"What?" I felt like a child floating in the ocean, fighting an undertow she could neither see nor understand. "What action?"

Gallagher spoke as if the answer should have been obvious, and maybe it would have been to a redcap. "My first kill on your behalf."

Clyde. But… "Are you saying the probationary period lasted less than an hour?"

"Twenty-three minutes, by my count." His gray eyes shone. "A feat that would have been celebrated, if I still had friends or relatives with which to share the news."

"I don't have any either, anymore." None except my mother, who would only be put in danger by contact with me.

"If you accept the knife, you'll have *me*," he said, and I could see the truth of that burning in his hungry gaze. "For the rest of your life, or until mine is taken as the price for failure."

I stared at him, stunned. "For the rest of my life? That's a hell of a commitment." And not what I'd signed up for.

"A redcap may only take the role of champion once—it's a lifelong devotion. It's your choice, whether or not to accept me, but you need to decide. You've already accepted the first three offerings and we have concluded the probationary period."

What had I accepted from him, other than kindness and a modicum of respect? He seemed to sense my confusion.

"The champion must offer and have accepted gifts of food, shelter, blood, and weapon—the pillars of life for a warrior."

Food. Well, yes, I'd taken his food.

Shelter. I hadn't... But, yes, I had. Clyde had said my private tent was Gallagher's doing.

"Okay, I took food and shelter from you, but I didn't know what I was doing. You said there'd never be a price."

"There is no price." Gallagher shrugged. "I would have given them to you regardless. But the point is that you accepted them from me, which indicates that you found me worthy of the offering."

"Okay, but what about blood? I haven't taken your blood."

"It's the blood of an enemy, delivered into your hand." Gallagher's eyes flashed with what could only have been bloodlust with the memory. "Michael Wallace." Whom he had, in fact, sent right to my cage.

Shit. "So... I accept your knife and get a champion for life, or I reject it and lose—" Any hope of getting out of Metzger's. "—you?"

He gave me a single, solemn nod. Despite the multitude of doubts rolling around in my head, I saw no other choice. Without him, even if I escaped, I would never get to the border. And even if I did make it, I would have no way to cross.

"There is no more sacred union among my people, Delilah. I will serve at your side with every beat of my heart and every breath in my body. If you will have me."

His words—and the righteous hunger fueling them—gave me chills.

I nodded. "Fine. I'll accept your knife, and with it, your

service." I lifted the knife from his palm, and the next word caught in my throat. "Forever."

"I swear you will never regret those words." Gallagher stood with the ease of a much smaller man. "Redcaps are the greatest warriors in the world." His gray-eyed gaze shone with the first glimpse of true pride I'd ever seen in him. "Once, there were entire armies of us, each pledged to defend the crown we swore loyalty to. We stormed kingdoms and left battlegrounds littered with the bloodless corpses of our enemies. We don't exist in such large numbers anymore, and I have no crown to serve. Instead, I lay all that I have and all that I am at your feet. Use me well, and ours will be a union spoken of for centuries to come."

His words were obviously part of some ancient ceremony, but as I listened, I realized they were also true. If I gave the *furiae* full reign and he ripped people apart to protect me, we would be spoken about, and not just in oral traditions passed down by a fearsome but unknown species of *fae*. We would make history on television and online, and in any newspapers still being printed. We would gain twenty-first century notoriety the likes of which he probably couldn't even imagine.

Humanity would *have* to see us. They would have to see what they'd done.

"May I hold that for you, until you are free to wear it?" Gallagher asked, and I realized he was staring at his knife.

My knife.

"Oh. Yes, please." I gave it back to him, and he slid it reverently into its humble sheath.

"How much time do we have left?" I gripped the seat of the metal chair on either side of my thighs, and he glanced at his watch. "A couple of hours until the gates open. Another hour after that before your show. Genni will be gone by then."

He met my gaze with regret. "Tonight Ruyle's going to use Claudio to force you to perform."

"But they don't need to torture anyone! That was the whole point of the Mike Wallace incident."

"They know you can transmute on your own," Gallagher explained. "But they don't know that you *will*. They're holding Claudio in reserve, just in case."

My fist curled around a handful of gray linen. "We can't let him torture Claudio."

Gallagher slid the knife back into his backpack. "Even if we could stop him, Ruyle would just replace Claudio with one of the kids from the petting zoo. That was actually discussed this morning, Delilah."

Anger flared like a bonfire in the pit of my stomach, and bitter irony was fuel for the flames. Lenore had been so sure I could save them, but Geneviève had been hurt because of me, and her father could soon suffer the same fate. They'd both be better off once I was gone, I told myself. But that was a lie, and I damn well knew it.

My escape wouldn't stop handlers from abusing their authority or management from stripping new acquisitions of their very identities. My absence wouldn't give the captives better food or more substantial clothing, nor would it free them from chains or cages.

After I left, the menagerie would still load captives in sweltering cargo trucks, where they would be forced to soil themselves. Handlers would still starve, strip, whip, and hose down the captives. They would still put children on display in their underwear. They would still extort sexual favors in exchange for food. And one night, another missing captive might be found wandering down the midway, dripping blood.

My escape would only benefit me.

And without Gallagher there to prevent the worst of the abuse...

I stood, and the metal chair squeaked with the motion. "Gallagher, we can't go."

"What?" He looked up from his bag, his forehead furrowed.

"You can send Adira and Nalah over the border but we can't just leave the rest of them here to suffer. I'm supposed to *avenge* them, not abandon them."

"Delilah, there's nothing else we can do for them. Ruyle already wants me fired, and when Metzger finds out I didn't break you—that I wasn't even the one who got you to transmute—he'll be ready to send me packing. We can't stay."

He turned to pick up his bag, but I seized his hand and with it, his attention. "Gallagher, I can't walk away from this place while they're all still locked up! They're just like us. You said you'd be my sword and shield in all things. I thought your word was your honor."

"And both are beyond reproach." He set his bag on the ground and glared down at me. "If we stay here, they'll eventually kill you, even if they have to go through me, and I will have failed. I'm leaving, and I'm taking you with me."

"No! I'm staying, and so are you. You're a warrior, right?" I stared up at him, reckless exhilaration firing through me with each beat of my heart.

"You know I am." He was still scowling, but something stirred behind his eyes in response to my excitement. What moved me would move him, evidently. For the rest of our lives.

"Then why wouldn't you want to fight? War is all or nothing, right? You take everything, or you lose everything?"

He nodded, and curiosity showed through his stern facade like the bulge of muscles through his sleeves. "When it's done right, war is a *glorious* commitment to a cause. The fallen die as heroes. The survivors change the world. There is no more noble commitment."

"That's excellent, because I have an idea." A crazy, dangerous, impractical, and quite possibly ill-conceived idea that would either bring freedom to every sentient, sane captive at Metzger's or get every last one of us killed. "We're not going to leave the menagerie. We're going to *take* it."

"Take the menagerie? As in mutiny?" His narrowed eyes said he couldn't tell whether or not I was joking.

"Yes. A hostile takeover. A mini-emancipation. Blood will be shed, and wrongs will be righted. This is *our fight*, Gallagher. This is what we were meant to do."

"Delilah…" Each syllable of my name was weighted with his skepticism. "Even if we could take control of Metzger's— and what glorious bloodshed that would be—what are we going to do with a caravan full of cryptids?"

"Any chance the sultan would let us drive the whole menagerie over the border?" I was mostly kidding—I hadn't thought that far ahead—but Gallagher frowned as he leaned back against my wagon, clearly considering the possibility.

"Not literally. But if the captives were all willing to swear fealty, and there was good press to be gained…" He shrugged. "Maybe, if I pitch the idea with just the right spin."

Anticipation tingled in my every nerve ending. "Can you go back into town and give that your best shot?"

He nodded. "But I need to know exactly what you're planning here, Delilah."

"We're a couple of days from the border, right?" I said, and he nodded again. "You can pass for human, obviously, and I *am* human." Not that my species had mattered, in the end. "Lenore passed for, like, twenty years, and there are others who could pass for employees with sunglasses, or hats, or work gloves, just long enough to get us to the border." I stood, grateful for the freedom to pace as I thought. "And if we could get Alyrose on board, with her skills and supplies…"

Gallagher took my arm before I could pace very far. "Speaking of Alyrose, what are you planning to do with all the human employees? I can only kill the ones who directly threaten you."

"And those will be yours to tear apart. But with any luck, the rest will simply walk away," I said, and when his frown deepened, I patted his massive left biceps. "How much do you know about *encantados*?"

Gallagher's frown lingered for a second, then his eyes widened, and I knew he'd caught on. "We have two. Renata and Raul. As a species, they're very smart, very curious, and very mischievous. In captivity, they're kept heavily sedated, which only works because they transmute into dolphins instinctively every time they hit the water."

"How long would it take for the sedation to wear off?"

He shrugged. "I administer a specially formulated dose every twelve hours."

"There's no vet?" No wonder I'd never been examined by one.

He shrugged. "Cryptid vets bill as much per hour as a lawyer, and even if we could afford one full-time, they don't typically favor the camper-and-pie-car lifestyle. The old man brings one in every three months to perform the required quarterly exams and reassess all the dosages."

For the first time since graduation, I could actually see a potential use for my crypto-biology degree. "So, if you were to skip a dose, both *encantados* would be fully functional in less than twenty-four hours?"

"Functional, and a hazard to every human in the room. There's a good reason the name of their species means *enchant* or *bewitch*." Gallagher's eyes widened as understanding dawned in them. He studied me with what looked suspiciously like respect, not for the beast that could make men spill their own blood, but for the idea that might let us take the menagerie without shedding a single innocent drop. "You may be the most brilliant woman I've ever met."

"I *may* be? Come back when you're sure." I climbed into my cage, for once eager to be locked up so he could put in motion the first stage of my plan.

"I'm sure," Gallagher said as he slid the door closed between us. He placed one hand against the mesh, and I laid mine against it, fascinated by the combination of warm flesh and cold steel. "It is my profound honor to serve at your side."

GALLAGHER

The name of the town closest to this latest county fair-grounds escaped Gallagher. He'd seen too many in the past year to count, but what he did remember about this particular town was that it lacked pay telephones entirely. The day before, he'd been forced to purchase a six-pack of some beer he'd never heard of for the privilege of using the convenience store's line for a call to Mexico.

If he hadn't mastered the art of the phone card nine months before, he might have had to wait and pray that the next town had a telephone booth.

The bell over the convenience store door chimed, and an unnaturally cold blast hit Gallagher as he stepped inside. The air smelled stale—like artificial coolant and dust—and as he headed for a row of cold glass cases at the back, he was struck with the sudden certainty that the owner was preserving himself through refrigeration just as surely as he was preserving his beer and soft drinks.

At the register, Gallagher set a small carton of cheap beer on the counter, along with a twenty-dollar bill, and the man behind the register handed him the wireless phone handset without being asked. He remembered Gallagher from the day before.

Few people ever forgot the man in the red cap.

Gallagher dialed from memory as he walked to the other side of the store, and someone answered on the second ring. "Gallagher for Sultan Bruhier," the menagerie handler said, without waiting for a greeting from the other end.

An unfamiliar voice replied, "One moment," and a second later Bruhier was on the line.

"You've called for a decision about your friend's passage?" The sultan rarely wasted time with pleasantries, and Gallagher respected that about him.

"Actually, I have a revised proposal for you. I will deliver your daughter and her companion as promised, and if you grant Delilah passage under the same terms you've granted me—admission with no obligation of fealty—we promise to bring with us up to three dozen others prepared to swear allegiance in exchange for citizenship."

For a long moment, the sultan was silent. "You're asking for additional passage for thirty-six?" His lyrical accent stressed odd sounds and syllables.

"I'm offering up to thirty-six new citizens to add strength to your kingdom and honor to your name. The whole world will know that the generous merid sultan has taken mercy upon a host of abused refugees. Your people will further adore you. There is nothing but benefit for you in this arrangement."

"Yet not enough," the sultan insisted. "I will accept your terms with one condition. You must also bring me a human named Christopher Ruyle. My eyes and ears in the U.S. tell me he is responsible for the purchase of Adira and her companion."

Gallagher could not verify the truth of that statement, but

Ruyle was far from innocent. "Agreed. Look for us in two days, at the crossing near Laredo."

"If I may ask," Bruhier said, before Gallagher could hang up, "who is this woman, that you would go through so much trouble for her?"

"She is…" Gallagher considered his reply carefully. "Worthy. I have offered myself as her sword and shield, and she has accepted."

"You're her champion?" the sultan said, surprise thick in each word, and Gallagher gave an affirmative grunt. "Does she mean that much to you?"

"She means that much to the *world*." Gallagher pressed the button that would end the call, then he returned the telephone to the clerk. As he walked out into the heat of the day without the beer he'd paid for, Gallagher reveled in a private moment of triumph.

He'd been waiting for this day his entire life.

Millions flee the country as the federal government begins assigning cryptids to walled-in reservations, to protect the human community from the threat of further attack.

—January 2, 1987, headline in the *Toledo Tribune*

DELILAH

They came for Geneviève in the middle of the afternoon. Two of them—handlers I recognized but couldn't name—with Ruyle driving the transport flatbed. Genni began to whine the minute she saw him. She'd been in wolf form all day.

Claudio growled when Ruyle got out of the truck and took a tranquilizer rifle from the gun rack mounted behind the seats. "Settle down, Papa," the lot supervisor said. "You know how this works."

Claudio's growl only deepened, and when a feline yowl joined in, I looked up to see that Zyanya and Payat were both in cheetah form, pacing back and forth in their cages, while on the other side of Payat, Mahsa sat on her haunches, growling, her black tail swishing angrily behind her.

"Fuss all you want," Ruyle said. "This is happening."

When the handlers approached Genni's cage, she huddled in one corner, her silver tail curled protectively around the rest of her body. One of the handlers unlocked the side panel and slid it open just far enough for Ruyle to stick the barrel of his rifle inside.

Genni whined and trembled. Claudio paced and growled.

Zyanya, Payat, and Mahsa made deep, angry bleating sounds. The trolls and ogres grunted. From farther down wagon row, metal clanked and clanged as the other captives rattled cage doors in protest.

The communal outrage made my heart ache.

Ruyle fired his rifle. Genni yelped, and her whole body twitched. She blinked twice. Then her head sank onto her front paws and her eyelids fell.

The supervisor lowered his gun and the other handler slid the cage door all the way open. He reached inside, hesitantly, and when Genni didn't move, he grabbed her left rear paw and pulled her to the opening. The handlers carried her to the cage strapped onto the flatbed of the transport truck, and Ruyle followed, still aiming the rifle, just in case.

When the cage slammed shut behind his daughter, Claudio howled. The sound was an outpouring of anger and grief, and it pierced me like a spear straight through my soul.

One of the handlers slid into the driver's seat and started the engine, and the cacophony from wagon row rose into an earsplitting din of growls, howls, grunts, screams, and clanking steel. When the truck drove off and Genni was gone, I sat with my knees pulled up to my chest, and I only realized I was crying when tears fell onto my arm.

Claudio howled for his lost daughter until he lost his voice, as well.

"Claudio," I whispered, as the thud of Eryx's hooves faded into the distance, along with the squeal of the loose wheel beneath Payat's cage. There was no one left on wagon row now except Lenore and Finola, in the crate to my right, and Zyanya and Claudio across from us. "Can you hear me?" I asked softly, but the werewolf didn't even look up from the corner of his cage.

"He can hear you," Zyanya said, and I realized I would have to take her word for it.

"You're going to get Genni back," I said, and the cheetah shifter clucked her tongue to scold me.

"Don't give him false hope. How can he get her back when he can't even get out of that cage?"

"I'm going to get him out," I whispered, and Zyanya snorted. "I have a plan, and it's going to work," I insisted. "This time tomorrow, we will all be free."

Zyanya made another rude sound from deep in her throat and Claudio didn't even open his eyes, but from my right, Lenore cleared her throat. "Do you mean it?"

"Yes. Be ready," I told her. "We'll need your help."

Hours later, I realized none of them had asked me who else "we" included.

"We've only got an hour before you're due in Alyrose's trailer for costuming," Gallagher said, lifting the sidewall as he stepped into my tent.

"Did you talk to the merid…king? Or whatever?" I asked, the instant the canvas fell closed behind him.

"He's a sultan. His name is Bruhier." Gallagher pulled a bottle of water and a cylindrical silver package from his backpack, then dropped the bag on the table beside the tent entrance. "And, yes, I called him from town. He's agreed to everything we asked for—"

Relief washed tension from my limbs, and I had to fight the urge to squeal with excitement.

"—on the condition that we deliver Chris Ruyle to him." Gallagher opened the tray slot and slid the bottle of water through, along with what turned out to be a hot dog fresh from the midway.

"Thanks," I said, my mouth already watering from the scents of beef and mustard. "Why does the sultan want Ruyle?"

"So he can take the pound of flesh he feels he's owed. Though no doubt it'll be much more than an actual pound. Ruyle is the one who bought Adira and Nalah for the menagerie," Gallagher explained.

I swallowed my first blissful bite, then gulped from the bottle of water. "So you're just going to hand him over to be tortured?"

"Yes." Gallagher didn't even blink. "That's the price for your freedom and for that of every other sentient cryptid at Metzger's."

Ruyle was an asshole and a generally reprehensible human being, but death by torture at the hands of a *djinn* sultan? At least Clyde's death had been quick. If brutal and messy. "There has to be another way."

"He's not innocent, Delilah."

"I know, but torture? Are you sure he deserves it?" I was supposed to be avenging injustice, not perpetuating it.

Gallagher frowned. "He sanctioned what Clyde did to Genni to bring out your beast. He's the one who'll be torturing Claudio tonight. And he's the one who suggested bringing in one of Zyanya's cubs from the petting zoo, if hurting Claudio doesn't work."

"Zyanya has kids?" How had I not known? In the two weeks I'd been with the menagerie, she hadn't been taken to see them once, and they certainly hadn't been brought to her.

"Three-year-old twins. A boy and a girl. And Ruyle would see them electrocuted just to make you perform."

My dinner went tasteless on my tongue and in spite of my empty stomach, I had to force myself to swallow. Fire burned in my gut at the thought of Ruyle anywhere near Zyanya's babies. He was a monster. The *furiae* stirring inside me agreed.

"Give him to the sultan."

Gallagher laid one hand on the beautifully carved frame of my wagon. "I was thinking we could hand him over in your cage."

"Poetic justice. I like it." I took another bite of my hot dog, then spoke around it. "Why didn't you just use Clyde's cell to call the sultan? It's not like he'll be around to check the call list."

"The *fae* can't use cell phones. Or computers. Or most other electronic devices. They crash about a minute after I start pushing buttons, which is one of the reasons my camper is thirty years old. That, and it was cheap." He curled his fingers through the mesh side of my cage.

"Wow. No electronics?"

He nodded. "After millennia of hiding from humanity— often in plain sight—the avoidance of electronic technology will no doubt be what someday exposes us. On an individual basis, at least."

I chewed my last bite of hot dog while I thought about that, and I decided that most of the *fae* were safe for the moment— no state in the union had enough manpower to go door to door checking for cell phones and digital cable.

"Where do we stand with the *encantados*?" I asked as I slid the hot dog wrapper to Gallagher through the tray slot.

"Both received an injection of pure saline at noon today. By midnight, any human who gets within earshot of them will completely lose touch with reality."

"Does that include me?"

Gallagher frowned. "I guess we'll find out. I'll bring earplugs, just in case."

"Thanks. What time do the gates close tonight?"

"Eleven," he said.

My pulse spiked at just the thought of what we were about

to attempt. "So we should start introducing the staff to Raul and Renata around…what, 2:00 a.m.?"

He nodded. "That should work. With any luck, by the time the sun rises, you'll be a free woman."

That night, they gave me a real talker and a bigger tent, which was open across the front so the crowd could spill out onto the midway. Alyrose had dressed me all in black and applied sparkly, scrolling black makeup, which, she'd assured me, would only enhance my "natural look," once I'd "become the monster."

I caught a glimpse of myself in the mirror, when Freddie—chest hair still poking from the unbuttoned top of his Metzger's polo—pulled me out of the dental chair to haul me out of Alyrose's trailer. The makeup artist had left my hair down in a wild tumble of dark waves so they would be free to twist on their own later. She'd emphasized my newly hollow cheekbones and enlarged my eyes with several shades of powder and lots of blending. The sequined costume hid my visible ribs, yet emphasized my narrow waist. Alyrose had given me the kind of dangerous, ethereal beauty both sirens and succubi were born with, and I hardly recognized myself.

Yet the beast within me stirred, content with what she saw and eager to add to the effect.

A sheet of canvas was draped over my cage when they opened my tent, so I could be revealed with a splash at the appropriate time. I could hear chatter from the audience. I could smell their popcorn and corn dogs, their beer and their sweat. I could feel their excitement.

It was hard not to hate every single one of them.

"We don't know what she is yet," the talker called from outside my tent. "But we know what she can do, and you do not want to miss one of the most dramatic transformations in the cryptid kingdom!"

That was a flat-out lie. The phoenix bursting into flames, then rising from his own ashes—that was dramatic. The shifters taking on two completely different forms—three, in the berserker's case—that was dramatic. My bloodshot eyes, long nails, and crazy hair didn't really compare.

However, I took a certain amount of petty satisfaction from the fact that Gallagher and most of my fellow captives knew what I was, while the rest of the staff did not.

When the sheet of canvas slid off my cage, the audience and I stared at each other, but they seemed...disappointed. Even with the dramatic black makeup and sparkly costume, I looked human.

"She may seem normal now, but you've seen the posters," the talker said, draping the canvas he'd removed from my cage over a folding chair. "Our mystery monster is a sight to behold."

They'd made posters?

I turned to my left and saw Chris Ruyle standing next to Claudio's cage, just outside my tent, concealed from both the audience and the midway by a large framed canvas panel, probably printed with an ad for one of the acts. Claudio lay on the ground in wolf form, muzzled so that he could not howl. He wore a nylon harness—a sturdier version of the kind guide dogs wear—which was chained to a tent stake.

Ruyle stood just out of Claudio's reach, holding an electrical prod, but Claudio didn't even seem to know he was there. At first I thought the wolf had been sedated, but when he blinked, I saw that his eyes looked clear.

He wasn't medicated. He was in mourning.

My heart broke for him, but my blood...my blood *boiled* for him.

I let that anger flow through me unchecked, and the *furiae* took over from there. My fingers and scalp began to tingle. My vision sharpened until I could see individual hairs on Claudio's pelt, and when the audience *oooohed*, I knew that my eyes had changed. Static electricity propelled my hair away from my head, and my throat throbbed with a dull ache even as my fingertips began to burn.

I stared out at the spectators through my cage and found all gazes on me. Mothers held their infants. Fathers clutched older kids' hands. Teens and single adults were filming with their cell phones, and no one told them to stop.

"Drea, why don't you turn a circle and give us a good look?" the talker said, his chest all puffed out, as if he'd had something to do with making me perform.

"Fuck you," I said, nice and clear, in spite of my fuller voice, so everyone could hear.

A couple of teens near the back of the crowd laughed, but the mothers scowled and covered their children's ears.

"Sorry about that, ladies and gentlemen," the talker called with an amiable chuckle. "Most of our exhibits were born and raised in the carnival, and they hear a lot of rough language."

"Most of our handlers are full of shit," I added, drawing more laughter from the back of the crowd. "I learned to cuss the same place all of your kids did. In middle school."

I'm pretty sure my online debut went viral.

Because I drew a pretty big crowd, Ruyle kept me on display until shortly before the main gate closed, and for the first time since I'd been sold into the menagerie, I was one of the last to make it back to wagon row.

My pulse raced for the entire two hours it took the staff to get everything sealed up and put away for the night, and I couldn't have fallen asleep if my life had depended on it.

By 1:00 a.m., by my best guess, the independent contractors had packed up their rides and booths and moved on toward their next stop, and most of the circus performers, handlers, and roustabouts had retired to their trailers and campers.

Over the next half hour or so, I watched the Metzger's employees' lights go out one by one. After that, there was nothing left to do but measure the passing seconds in the snores and grunts of trolls and ogres.

When Gallagher finally stepped silently out of the shadows, I was so startled I nearly screamed.

"You ready?" he whispered, pulling his key ring from the loop on his belt.

"I've never been more ready for anything in my entire life."

He unlocked the cage and helped me down, and when I stepped onto the grass unfettered, my heart pounded so hard I was afraid it would wake every shifter on wagon row.

"Let's go," he whispered, and I followed him through the unlocked rear gate and across the darkened menagerie into the empty hybrid tent, where a single pole-mounted light remained lit. Gallagher knelt to pick up a bag stowed just inside the entrance. "I had to guess at your size. Alyrose's clothes looked like they'd be the best fit."

I reached into the bag and pulled out a red Metzger's polo and a pair of jeans. At the bottom of the bag was a pair of black hightop sneakers.

"In the dark, if we put your hair up, I don't think anyone will recognize you."

He was right, but that had less to do with the dark than with the fact that no one on staff would ever expect to find me uncaged, unchained, and dressed like a normal human being.

Alyrose's shirt and jeans were loose, but by some miracle, her shoes fit me perfectly. When I was dressed, Gallagher led me across the hybrid tent toward the special canvas room adjoining it, where several of the rarer cryptid hybrids—including the minotaur—were displayed during operating hours.

My friends and I hadn't made it that far during our tour the day I'd been exposed.

"Let me know immediately if you start to feel strange at all," Gallagher said, and when I nodded, he pushed open the tent flap and gestured for me to precede him inside.

Eryx had already been returned to wagon row, but the other two acts spent all of their time, except during transit, in that canvas room, and once I saw them, I understood why.

The largest of the two mermaids couldn't have been longer than four and a half feet, and maybe weighed eighty pounds, at most. Yet despite their small stature, if I'd come across them in the wild, they would've been more than enough to keep me out of the water.

Isla and Havana had webbed hands, scales climbing the sides of their necks, and bulbous eyes on either side of pointy, fishlike faces. The mermaids had human mouths and noses, along with a set of gills just below their ears. Though they were clearly able to breathe both in and out of water, only a few inches of air stood between the surface of the water and the tank's covering, and there was too little space inside the tank for them to do more than slowly circle each other, their long seaweed-like hair floating around their faces.

"Delilah," Gallagher called, and when I reluctantly tore my gaze from the poor mermaids, I found him waiting for me next to the other, even larger tank. A young man and woman, each about the size of a human twelve-year-old, sat on Plexiglas benches built into the aquarium, near the open top, their bare human feet dangling in the water. "This is Raul." Gallagher gestured to the man. "And this is his sister, Renata."

"Nice to meet you," I said, trying not to notice the fact that they were completely nude, and fully mature, despite their size.

Raul grinned. *"Encantado,"* he replied, and when Renata laughed, I realized he'd made a pun out of the greeting.

Their age was difficult to determine because their pale skin was flawlessly smooth and completely hairless. And like the dolphins they would become the minute they were submerged in water, each had a small blowhole—vestigial, in human form, if I remembered correctly—at the top of his/her smooth, bald head.

"Gallagher says you're to thank for clearing our minds," Renata said, and after hearing her voice, I decided she was a little older than my original guess. "To what do we owe the pleasure, of both lucidity and your company?"

I shrugged. "We're staging a coup, and we need your help."

Raul's bright blue eyes widened and he turned to Gallagher. "Is she serious?"

Gallagher nodded. "But first, we need to know whether or not you can enchant her."

"We can't," Renata said, and when I shot a suspicious glance her way, she shrugged. "I've been trying to make you cluck like a chicken since you walked into the room."

"What are you?" Raul asked.

"Human."

He frowned and pulled himself up on the edge of their tank, his arms dangling on the outside while his feet kicked gently in the water. "What else?"

"She's a *furiae*," Gallagher said. "We don't—"

"And what are you?" Renata demanded, leaning forward on her Plexiglass bench for a better look at him. She'd just discovered that Gallagher—whom she'd been too sedated to try to enchant before—wasn't human either.

"He's a redcap." I propped both hands on my hips and stared up at them. "Look, if you're on board, we need to get—"

"On board?" Raul repeated, and I wondered if they were ever going to let me complete a sentence. "You're asking us?"

"If we were ordering you, this wouldn't be much of an emancipation," I pointed out. "No chains. No cuffs. No sedatives. We want you to voluntar—"

Renata's hairless brows rose. "If this is truly our choice, what's to stop us from just walking out of here right now?"

"The fact that on your own, you'll almost certainly be caught, and probably shot on sight." Because few humans would be willing to get very close to them. "However, if you help us, we can guarantee you full citizenship in a sultanate south of the border. The deal's already in place. But we need you to help us take the menagerie."

Renata turned to her brother, and for a moment, the *encantados* only stared at each other. Then she shrugged, and he returned the gesture, and as one, they turned back to us. "How can we help?" Raul asked.

It took serious effort to conceal my excitement. "By doing what you do best…"

We got Raul situated in the small canvas room with two folding metal chairs, which—he insisted—were all he needed. He didn't even want any clothes. I set up two more chairs for Renata in the main hybrid tent, just outside the red circus ring, where the wagons would have been on display during business hours.

When everything was ready, Gallagher headed into the employee lot to get the first staff member, while I went back to wagon row to recruit some help.

"Eryx," I whispered, standing next to the first cage in line—a reinforced steel crate mounted on a custom heavy-duty wagon base. The minotaur's cage didn't have a fancy frame because during exhibition hours, he stood for hours on end chained to a tent stake in the ground.

"Eryx," I whispered again, and the bull snorted, startled out of whatever dreams made his thick human fingers twitch. His eyes opened and slowly focused, and when I was sure he recognized me, I smiled and put one hand on the corner of his cage. "How would you like a permanent change of address?"

I held up Gallagher's key ring, and the minotaur's eyes widened. "Shhh…" I said while I unlocked his crate, and he peered out into the dark, on the lookout for trouble. "We're letting the staff know that they're no longer needed, and we could use your help."

I led him—unchained, possibly for the first time in his life—to the back of wagon row. Several of the other captives twitched or rolled over in their sleep, but they were accustomed to sleeping when and where they could, and if any of them woke up, I couldn't tell.

At the end of the row, I asked Eryx if he would be willing to help, and in response, he harnessed himself to my empty wagon, eagerness shining in his brown human eyes.

On the way to the hybrid tent, I caught movement in the shadows to one side of the deserted midway and froze, one hand on Eryx's arm to bring him to a silent halt. A second later, Gallagher stepped out of the shadows, flanked by two large handlers in jogging shorts and tees they'd obviously slept in. I couldn't hear what he was telling them, but as per the plan, it sounded urgent.

When they disappeared into the hybrid tent, I waited several seconds, then tapped Eryx's shoulder. "I think we're good."

We followed them inside just in time to see Gallagher lead the second handler into the small canvas room. The first sleep-groggy handler stood in the middle of the main tent, hands clasped at his back, as if he were waiting for an important meeting to start.

"Come on in, David," Renata said, and the man in shorts jumped, startled, as if he hadn't seen her sitting right in front of him. "Have a seat." She waved one hand at the folding metal chair facing hers, and I watched, amused, while David sat, his spine straight, picking nervously at his fingernails.

"Is something wrong, Mr. Metzger?" he asked, staring right at the *encantado*.

"Unfortunately, I have to let you go today," Renata said, and the handler frowned, his mouth already open to object. "It's nothing you did. This is a budgetary issue. We're making cutbacks in every department."

"But I've been with the menagerie for three years!" David cried, and I wondered what he was seeing. Did he think he was in the silver wagon, staring across one of the metal desks at old man Metzger?

"And I'm sure you'll find work with another outfit in no time. I think you'll find that if you head out immediately, you'll miss the morning rush hour. Please leave your uniforms and any menagerie property with Gallagher. Best of luck to you, son." Renata gave him a dismissive nod, then pretended to shuffle papers on a desk that didn't exist.

Stunned but compliant, David stood and walked out of the tent without even a glance at me or at Eryx, who still stood harnessed to the wagon. When the tent flap fell closed, Renata stood and stretched with her thin pale arms over her bald head, beaming a smile that seemed to take up the width of her entire face. "Damn, that felt good! How was I?"

"You were incredible." Far better than I'd had any reason to expect from a cryptid who'd spent most of the past few years in a medicated stupor. "He thinks he was let go?"

"He *was* let go. By the old man himself, in his office. The images were already in his memory. I just had to dig them out and project them for him," she explained, and suddenly I understood why Renata and her brother spoke more like my former, human friends than like most of the other captives—even sedated, they were inundated by thoughts and images from the minds of every human they saw. "Right now, David wants nothing more than to drive his camper back to Alabama and park it in his ex-wife's driveway until she agrees to take him back."

"That's brilliant, Renata!" I couldn't believe how well the plan had worked.

"I hear this whole thing was your idea," she said, as I helped Eryx out of his harness.

I shrugged. "We couldn't do it without you. Or you," I added, turning to Eryx, who blinked at me in acknowledgment. "Okay, two employees down, many still to go. It's going to be a long night." Yet it was already the best night of my entire life.

"Hey, what's going on?" a voice called from behind me, and I spun to see Abraxas standing in the entrance, holding the loose canvas flap back. His eyes widened when he recognized me, in spite of my Metzger's uniform, and before I could stop him, he turned and took off down the midway, headed straight for the employee lot.

"Damn it! Gallagher!" I yelled over my shoulder. Then I raced into the dark after a terrified kid armed with knowledge that could derail our plans before we'd even gotten them off the ground.

ABRAXAS

His heart pounding like thunder in his chest, Abraxas Lasko raced up the aluminum camper steps and hammered on the door with his fist. When he got no response after two seconds, he glanced into the dark around him, on alert for any movement from the shadows, then banged on the door again.

"What?" Chris Ruyle yelled from inside. "It's two-thirty in the morning!"

"Mr. Ruyle?" Abraxas called in as loud a whisper as he could manage. "You gotta come now. Something's wrong!"

Footsteps echoed from within the camper, and the boy heard a scraping sound as Ruyle flipped the latch. He swung the door open, and Abraxas barged inside, then slammed the thin door at his back. "What's—"

"Some of the beasts got loose." His chest heaving with each breath, the boy peeked through the dusty curtains over the grimy sink. "They were in the hybrid tent, no chains or nothin', just walking around and talking to each other!"

"Fuck!" Ruyle pulled on a pair of boots without socks, then clipped his key ring to his belt. "Let's go get Gallagher. Stupid brute doesn't have a phone."

"I tried him first." Abraxas turned and peeked through a window on the other side of the small room, completely missing Ruyle's irritated glance at the admission. "He's not in his camper. I can't find Freddie either, and Clyde's still gone. We gotta do something! Do you have a tranq rifle?"

Ruyle shook his head and unlocked the door. "They're in a crate—at the back of the hybrid tent."

"We might be able to get to them," Abraxas whispered, following the lot supervisor quietly down the steps and onto the gravel lot. "The beasts chased me when I ran out, so they may not be in the tent anymore."

"How many were there?" Ruyle stepped carefully, to keep his boots from crunching on loose rocks, and the boy tried to follow his example. "What kinds?"

"Three, that I saw. That new female we picked up a couple of weeks ago—"

"I *hate* that bitch," the supervisor mumbled.

"—and one of the dolphin shifters. And the minotaur."

Ruyle cursed beneath his breath. "It'll take several darts to bring the bull down. Come on."

"Should we wake someone else up?"

"They'd only be in the way," the supervisor said as they stepped out of the lot and onto grass, and he seemed to breathe easier now that every footstep didn't call attention to them. "The only men as qualified as me to bring down the minotaur are Clyde and Gallagher. It'll probably take half a dozen of us to move him once he's out."

"This ever happened before?" Abraxas asked, adrenaline firing through his veins, and Ruyle snorted.

"A centaur broke his lead rope once and made it a couple hundred yards before I dropped him with a hunting rifle. But we never had one break out of his cage, much less three at once. They had to've had some help. Someone's head's gonna roll."

"Any guess who?" Abraxas asked, and Ruyle eyed the boy in the moonlight as they passed through the menagerie's rear entrance.

"How old are you, kid? Eighteen?"

The boy followed his supervisor between two tents and past a bank of portable toilets. "Nineteen in a couple'a weeks, sir."

"And how long you been with us now?" Ruyle whispered, rolling his feet on the paved midway to mute his footsteps.

"Three months." Something moved in the gloom to his left, and Abraxas jumped, but when he stared into the darkness, he found only shadows.

"Welcome to the trenches, kid. You ever shot a tranq rifle?"

"I shot my dad's Winchester .38," the boy whispered, as they approached the hybrid tent.

"I guess that's close enough." Ruyle put one finger to his lips and aimed an exaggerated wide-eyed look at Abraxas, who nodded. Then the handler pushed open the loose canvas panel and stepped into the tent.

Abraxas followed him in, then immediately stepped to the right of the entrance, his pulse swooshing in his ears.

"What the— Mr. Metzger?" Ruyle frowned and glanced around the tent, but Abraxas could tell he wasn't seeing the red ring in the middle, or the striped canvas sidewalls, or Delilah Marlow's circus wagon. Nor was he seeing Renata, the smooth-skinned dolphin shifter, who calmly told him to have a seat and remove his key ring from his belt.

"Did you have any trouble?" Delilah whispered from the shadows to his right, and Abraxas shook his head, grinning, and crossed his arms over his thin chest.

"Worked like a charm," he said, as the lot supervisor sat in a folding chair near the middle of the tent, as if he could neither see nor hear them. "This was really your idea?" That's what Gallagher had told him, when he'd chased the boy down and offered him a choice.

Delilah nodded.

"How many is this?"

"Ruyle's the fifth, but he's a special case," she said. "We still have a long way to go, and it'll get trickier once the first few start leaving."

The minotaur snorted, towering over them both from her other side, and Abraxas laughed softly. "Eryx thinks you've got it in the bag. I agree." He reached in front of Delilah to extend his fist toward the minotaur, who only stared at it, brows drawn low. "You have to make a fist and bump mine," Abraxas whispered. "For solidarity."

"Like this." Delilah returned the fist bump in demonstration.

When Eryx gave it a try, he knocked the boy back by several steps.

Abraxas chuckled softly and rubbed his knuckles. "I just fist-bumped a minotaur."

Eryx snorted, and Delilah grinned. "Well, I hope you're both right, and the rest of them go this smoothly."

"So, everyone will think they were fired?" the boy asked, watching as Ruyle approached the empty circus wagon under the mistaken impression that the opening was an air conditioner vent in need of repair.

"The ones I don't hate will think they quit, and Ruyle here is headed somewhere special, but yeah, that's the general idea," Delilah said. "No bodies. No questions from the authorities or from worried relatives."

"Hey!" Abraxas called as Ruyle gripped the side of the cage, preparing to climb into it. The supervisor's eyes widened in surprise; he'd obviously forgotten all about the boy. "If I say something to him, will he remember later?"

"Not if you don't want him to," Renata said.

"I want him to." Abraxas crossed the sawdust-strewn ground toward the handler, and Ruyle's expression grew more confused with every step the boy took. "Remember that Winchester .38 I told you about?"

The supervisor nodded hesitantly, his eyes half-focused.

"I fired it at the hunter chasing my cousin Thea into the woods, to keep him from selling her at auction. She was half-dryad on her dad's side. Thea got away, and I've been trying to find her and bring her home ever since." Abraxas pulled himself up to his full—if slight—height and punched the handler in the face. Ruyle stumbled backward and hit his spine on the cage.

Renata calmly told the former supervisor to climb into the vent and begin his repairs and when Ruyle had obeyed, Abraxas slammed the door shut and locked it. "The bastard who tried to take my cousin died facedown in the dirt. Ask me, you're getting off easy."

DELILAH

It took us three hours to convince all the handlers and performers that they had been fired or had quit jobs they were no longer satisfied with, and it would have taken a lot longer than that without Abraxas's help. Once Raul and Renata really got into the swing of it, they were able to convince about half of their victims to leave their campers in the possession of the menagerie and hitch a ride home with a friend, which left us with more vehicles than we had people qualified to drive them.

By the time we started firing the miscellaneous staff, at about four-thirty in the morning, Raul, Renata, Eryx, Abraxas, Gallagher, and I were running on nothing but adrenaline and the thrill of tentative success. About a third of the trucks and campers had left the campgrounds, carrying two-thirds of the employees we'd already dealt with, and all of wagon row was awake and wide-eyed, buzzing with rumors of the staff exodus.

When Gallagher had escorted the petting zoo "nannies" to the hybrid tent to convince them both that they'd quit, Eryx hauled the children one cage at a time toward wagon row, where I used Gallagher's keys to reunite parents with children.

Zyanya cried when she saw her twins. "You did it!" she whispered, clutching the side of her cage while I unlocked it. "I can't believe you did it." Yet fear echoed in her voice and was evident in her grip on the metal wire. As excited as she was, she expected our coup to fail and dreaded the price we would pay.

"It's not over yet," I admitted. "But as soon as we're rid of the staff, we'll let you all out. In the meantime, I thought you'd like some company while you wait."

I lifted both squirmy toddlers into their mother's cage, and when she scooped up her excited, mewling, human-form kittens, my vision blurred beneath tears of my own. Even Eryx sniffled. I gave them two packs of hot dogs and three bottles of water from Clyde's refrigerator, then left them to their reunion.

While Zyanya coddled and examined her kittens, checking every inch of their tiny bodies for marks or injuries, speaking to them in hushed, tender tones, I opened the next wagon. Claudio looked up when I set some scavenged clothes and a pair of shoes on the pressed aluminum cage floor, along with a backpack full of food and water, and a pair of dark sunglasses. "Go get your daughter," I said.

Claudio ran his hand over the blue tee, and his eyes watered.

"You can throw them in the backpack, if you want to go after her in wolf form. It has a strap here that'll fasten around your stomach." I demonstrated clicking the fasteners together. "You should be able to run with it on—"

"It's not that," he said. "I've never worn such a shirt. Or such a color. I've never carried…possessions."

I smiled. "Welcome to emancipation. New clothes for everyone."

"Enjoy it, for however long it lasts," Zyanya said, and when I leaned back to scowl at her, she shrugged, a quiet child cradled in each arm, their pudgy little hands clutching possessively at their mother's dress, as if they were afraid to let her go. "You know it's true. They'll catch him. Or they'll kill him. They'll probably kill all of us when we're caught, to make an example." She nudged one of the packets of hot dogs, which she couldn't open with her hands full of toddler. "Your heart's in the right place, but you've just served our last meal."

"That's not true," I insisted as Claudio began to pull on the new clothes with a shifter's typical immodesty. "You all have passage over the border and guaranteed citizenship in the merid sultanate. We'll reach the border tomorrow. No more cages. No chains. No late-night visits in exchange for food. You and your kids are going to be free, Zyanya. For good."

Her laugh was harsh and bitter, and I instinctively recoiled from the sound. "You don't get it, do you? These aren't my only children, Delilah," she said, and it took a moment before a brutal understanding crashed over me. "Two more were sold off years ago, separately. I can't leave them here to suffer any more than Claudio can leave Genni. Half of wagon row will refuse to cross the border for the same reason."

"But what about *these* children?" I demanded, gesturing to the curly-headed toddlers. Surely she wouldn't condemn them to captivity just because the older ones were locked up.

"If they truly have passage, I'll send them over the border with Payat."

Her brother grunted in consent from the cage on her other side.

I could only stare at her, frustrated almost beyond words by how much I'd failed to consider. How little I'd seen of the larger picture. Still, there was only so much even a *furiae* could do, and she might not get another chance at freedom. "Zyanya, if you stay here, they'll catch you eventually."

"I know. Claudio knows it, too." She carefully laid her

mewling twins side by side on her blanket, then crawled closer to the side of her cage and lowered her voice. "But how could either of us live in peace while our children are suffering?" Her orangish gaze pinned me from a foot away, as light from the parking lot shone on her dark skin, and despite the differences in their ages and appearances, something in Zyanya's expression reminded me of my mom.

My mother would move heaven and earth if she thought it would help me, and Zyanya would do the same for her children.

"Okay. Maybe we can wait another day or two," I said as a new idea began to form. "Do you know where your other kids are? Maybe we could buy them back in Metzger's name before we cross." I turned back to Claudio, who was trying to figure out how to tie his new boots. "We could do the same for Genni. Gallagher knows who bought her."

"What about my daughter?" one of the succubi demanded from farther down the row.

"And my son," the berserker added.

"Our parents," Lala called from the oracles' cage.

"And my mother and my little sister," Lenore said. "We were separated when we were exposed. I can't leave the country without them."

Calls rang out from the full length of wagon row, and the demands were overwhelming. My heart thumped too hard and my throat felt tight. I hadn't understood the breadth of the problem. The scale of their suffering.

I'd never felt like such a fool in my life.

"Did you really think it would be that easy?" Zyanya demanded softly, with one look at my stricken face. "Did you honestly think you could spend two weeks in our shoes, then swoop in and solve all our problems?"

"I…" Is that what I'd thought? Had I truly been that naive?

"I get that you want to fix this, Delilah," Zyanya said, as she pulled open one of the hot dog packets. "It's in your nature. But this isn't the kind of thing that can be fixed by making a couple of men claw their own privates off." She took a bite from the first stick of beef. "You're in way over your head, *furiae*."

"We can't go," I said, before the bathroom door could even swing shut behind Gallagher. I'd dragged him into the nearest building I could find, and only realized it was a men's room when I noticed the urinals.

"We can't go where?" But his deeply furrowed forehead told me he knew exactly what I was talking about.

"Gallagher, they won't cross the border with us. They all have family members who were sold off, and I can't leave knowing they're all going to be recaptured or killed just for trying to save their kids. Or their parents. Or their siblings."

"So, what, we get captured along with them?" he demanded. "How will that help?"

"We won't get captured. We've taken the menagerie, and no one knows! Don't you get it? Metzger's can travel all over the country, and as long as it looks like we're keeping cryptids in cages, no one will know any different. We could buy back their relatives as we go, then just drive the whole caravan back to Mexico. We might even be able to pick up a few strays, like you guys picked me up. We'd be *saving lives*, Gallagher. That's making a difference."

"Delilah, that's a beautiful thought, but—"

"Don't patronize me!" I snapped, anger sizzling beneath my skin.

His gaze hardened. "I'm not patronizing you. I'm telling you it won't work. Metzger's is broke. Maybe we could get Genni back. We haven't been paid for her yet. But then we'd only be able to buy one or two more—assuming we can find them—before the funds are exhausted. And that's if we don't spend anything on food or fuel, which is well beyond the bounds of practicality."

I crossed my arms over my chest and stared up at him in the fluorescent glow from overhead. "Isn't the menagerie a business? Won't people pay to come see us?"

"Yes, but—"

"Wouldn't that be the most satisfying irony ever?" I demanded. "Using the money we take from human audiences to buy freedom for cryptids?"

He nodded. "There is a certain poetic ring to it, but are you sure they'd want to perform?"

"I think that's a question worth asking." I shrugged. "We'd only have to use the cages for performances, and we could change the show. Cut out anything demeaning or cruel. We could be showing off, instead of being exploited. We could show people how much beauty there really is in the cryptid world!"

Gallagher's resistance was starting to weaken. "Okay, I'm not saying it's not possible, for a little while anyway," he said. "But, Delilah, you said it yourself—the menagerie is a business. There are fees, and inspections, and bookkeeping, and advertisement. The administrative aspects never end, and we've just fired everyone who knows about that stuff."

"We haven't fired everyone yet. We know Abraxas will stay—he's looking for his cousin. And there's Alyrose."

"She won't—"

"She might," I insisted, leaning against one of the grimy gray toilet stalls.

"She'd be risking jail time if we're caught."

"We're risking a hell of a lot more than that. I'm going to ask her."

"Delilah." Gallagher put a hand on each of my shoulders. "If this is what you want to do, I'm with you. I always will be. But I want you to think about this for a minute. You're less than a day away from absolute freedom. No running. No hiding. No chains. Are you willing to give that up for a chance—a very *slim* chance—that we can find a handful of cryptids spread out all over the country?"

"Am I willing to risk my own freedom for the chance to give that same thing to several dozen others?" I stared up at him. "Gallagher, that's the *only* thing I'm willing to risk my freedom for."

I sneaked Renata through the thickest shadows to Alyrose's trailer, where Abraxas had promised to meet me with Kevin—the last of the handlers—in tow. The costume mistress answered her door in a blue satin robe, her normally spiky purple hair hanging limp around her ears. Her sleep-puffy eyes widened when she recognized me. "What the—"

Then she noticed the *encantado* standing behind me, still nude, because every piece of clothing we'd offered her had irritated her smooth, sensitive skin.

Alyrose made an inarticulate sound and tried to slam the door in my face. I stuck my foot in the jam, and when she backed farther into her trailer, I led Renata inside.

"We're not here to hurt you," I said, but Aly couldn't tear her gaze from the *encantado*. Renata looked around the trailer with wide eyes, taking in the furniture, and costumes, and makeup, and I wondered if that was the first time she'd ever physically existed in the kind of setting she'd been re-creating for her victims for the past couple of hours.

Alyrose shifted nervously, reclaiming my attention. "We're taking the menagerie, and I'm offering you a choice few of the other staff members are getting. Because I think you're a decent person."

"You're *taking* the menagerie?" Her eyes swam in fear; she still thought we'd come to kill her.

"Yes. Total mutiny. In fact, we're almost done. Do you know what Renata is?" I asked, and when her gaze strayed to the *encantado* again, as Renata ran her fingers over a feather boa hanging from a full clothing rack, I stepped between them to regain her focus. "Aly. Do you understand what she and her brother can do?"

The costume mistress nodded, and her focus shifted back and forth between us. "They can alter memory and perception."

"Exactly. Renata and Raul are helping us send the staff away peacefully. There hasn't been a single injury so far. If you want, we can do that for you. You wouldn't remember any of this. You'd just believe you decided to move on from the carnival lifestyle. Or...you can stay. We'd love to have you, and we could really use your help."

"With what?" Finally, she looked more curious than scared.

"We're going to run the menagerie ourselves. *For* ourselves. The only way we can stay free in the U.S. is to maintain the illusion of the traveling menagerie, as if nothing's changed. And we could use a good costume mistress. But you need to understand up front that it won't be like it was before. Sentient, nonviolent cryptids will only be in cages for performances."

"The adlet?" Fear lined Aly's forehead.

"We can't set him free. He's a predator through and through. But he'll have decent facilities and food. We'll do what we can for him, and for anyone who's truly a threat to others, within those limitations. You'll be safe here with us if you stay, but if we get caught, you'll get caught with us." I wanted to be up-front about that, too. "So...what do you say?"

Her eyes were painfully wide, and her fingers were curling and uncurling at her sides, as if she didn't know what to do with them. "Do I have to decide now?"

"Five minutes ago would have been good. If you choose to stay and later decide you don't like it, you can leave then, under the same terms."

Alyrose looked from me to Renata, as if to confirm what I'd promised. Or maybe to make sure this whole conversation wasn't really just an enchantment.

"If I were enchanting you, you wouldn't see me," Renata said, as she thumbed through a book of fabric samples, but her reassurance sounded more like a threat.

Alyrose took a deep breath, and finally she nodded. "Okay. I'm in."

On our way out of Alyrose's trailer, I stopped and turned back to her. "Hey, do you have anything Renata could wear while she's out of the water? Everything we've given her irritates her skin."

When Aly pulled off her own satin robe and gave it to the *encantato*, I knew that I'd been right to trust my gut. Regardless of her species, Alyrose was one of us.

We passed wagon row on the way back to the hybrid tent, and halfway down, I put one hand on Renata's satin-clad shoulder to stop her. Something was wrong. Turning, I studied the wagons. Everyone was awake, and many of them were still slowly nibbling the snacks I'd brought, obviously worried that my plan would fail and it might be a long time before they were fed again.

I could understand that fear.

But one of the cages looked...

I let go of Renata and marched toward the siren cage—

where Finola sat alone. "Where's Lenore?" I demanded, panic painting my voice in shrill tones.

"Kevin came for her, but—"

I took off running with Renata on my heels, and behind me Finola was still shouting, "Delilah, wait…!"

KEVIN

Kevin was already awake when Gallagher knocked on the door of the camper next door. He was already dressed, and had brushed his teeth and combed his hair nearly an hour before. Holding one boot, he peeked between the dusty metal blinds, as paranoid men were apt to do, and saw Gallagher lead Hallie and Farah—the human contortionists—toward the fairground. At two in the morning.

And they weren't the first to go.

Kevin's hands shook as he pulled his last boot on, listening carefully for more footsteps. More knocks on hollow metal doors.

Over the past half hour, he'd seen the boss of livestock come for two other staff members. Then Abraxas, that kid they'd picked up near Saint Louis a few months before, had pounded on Ruyle's door across the way, spouting some story about a breakout. Kevin might have fallen for it, too, if anyone had sounded the alarm. And if he hadn't already seen several other handlers lured quietly from their beds in the middle of the night.

Two of them had come back, climbed into their campers, and driven right off the lot. The others had yet to return.

Something very strange was going on. Maybe it was nothing. Maybe there was a perfectly good explanation. But a man with secrets like Kevin's couldn't afford to take that chance.

Kevin sneaked out of his camper the moment Gallagher and the acrobats disappeared around the corner, his keys jingling in his pocket, his left boot untied. He stuck to the shadows on his way toward wagon row, and ducked behind a portable toilet when he saw a dark-headed female employee jogging toward the fairgrounds as if her feet were on fire.

One glance at wagon row had confirmed that something was wrong. The cheetah shifter was cradling her cubs—in her cage! Several others were eating what looked like raw hot dogs, probably stolen from one of the vendor's carts. And they all had bottles of water.

If this was a breakout, why were none of the exhibits loose? Who was feeding them? Why were the employees abandoning the menagerie one by one in the middle of the night?

Lenore sat up straight when she saw him, her eyes wide with obvious relief. "Kevin!" she whispered around a bit of… Was that a candy bar clutched in her right hand? No, a power bar. Who had given her a power bar?

"Come on. Something's wrong, and this is our chance." He unlocked her cage with practiced ease, then hauled her onto the ground with one arm around her waist.

"Wait, I have to tell—"

"Shh…" Kevin slid the cage door shut and locked it with a regretful glance at Finola, who stared at him in bewilderment. He felt bad about leaving her there, but he really had no other choice.

Kevin's grip on Lenore's hand tightened as he pulled her across the gravel lot toward his trailer. She stumbled and cried out for him to wait, but he kept running, hauling her along as fast as he could, his heart pounding against his sternum. Whatever was going on would soon attract the cops, and they'd have to be long gone by the time that happened.

"Kevin, wait!" Lenore's voice flowed over him like water over a riverbed, eroding his willpower. Washing away his immediate haste, but leaving his deeper-rooted anxiety intact. It was a soft insertion of her will over his, and it was his irritation that stopped him, as much as it was the pull from her voice.

"You swore you'd never do that," he snapped, skidding to a halt on the gravel beneath his boots.

"It's an emergency," she said, by way of an apology. "It's a coup, Kevin. A mutiny. The cryptids are taking over the menagerie."

"So I see. We need to be at least sixty miles away before anyone else figures that out," he insisted, tightening his grip on her hand when she tried to pull free. "This is our chance to get away." He'd been waiting for an opportunity for years, biding his time in a red polo that bound him to the carnival as surely as her chains bound her. But he'd been expecting a simple distraction, like a tent fire, or an escaped centaur. He'd never dreamed of an opportunity like this.

"No," Lenore said. "This is our chance to *stay*."

"But when the cops get here—"

"The cops won't get here. No one's going to report this, Kevin. The employees don't even know this is happening. They all think they've been fired, or that they quit. It's really kind of funny. And pretty smart."

"They think...?" Well, that would explain why they were all leaving, instead of sounding an alarm. "How?"

Lenore smiled, and her entire face lit up. "The *encantados*. Delilah woke them up."

"Delilah?"

"Yes. I told you, she was sent to us. She did this for us, and we *owe* her."

"We don't owe anyone anything. Not after what you've been through."

Kevin had ached to touch her since the moment he'd first seen her, so long ago, and no matter how many times his greedy hands fulfilled that wish, he couldn't get enough of her.

He would *never* have enough of her. But this was his chance to try. "Come on. We're leaving, and we're going to put this all behind us."

"No." Lenore's voice held no pull, but neither did it hold any doubt. She tugged her hand from his grip and stood firm. "You leave if you want. Maybe you should. If I come with you, we'll always be on the run."

"Lenore..." he said, but she shook her head.

"This wasn't fair to you." She spread her arms to indicate the entire menagerie. "But running won't be either. Maybe you should go find someone whose most frequent accessory isn't steel bracelets. Someone you can share a real life with."

Anger flared deep in his chest. He pulled her close, and when she flinched, a pang of guilt rang through him, but he didn't release her. He couldn't. "Don't ever say that again," Kevin growled through clenched teeth. "I will never let you go, Lenore. You're mine, and I don't care what some scrap of paper in an old man's filing cabinet says. I have a document that predates his."

"Let her go."

Kevin heard the words a split second before he was pulled off his feet. Lenore gasped, jerked forward by his desperate grip on her arm until his fingers loosened and she slid free.

Gallagher lifted the smaller handler until his boots barely dragged on the ground. Light from the parking lot shone on his bright red cap. His thick left hand curled into a fist, already drawn back for a blow that would surely shatter Kevin's cheek.

"Wait!" Kevin's focus slid from Gallagher's face—half-shadowed from the light by the bill of his hat—to where the new exhibit stood behind him, unshackled and dressed in a Metzger's polo. "This isn't what you think."

"I think you're a predatory asshole who's about to get a free makeover," Gallagher growled.

"No!" Lenore stepped forward, pulling at Gallagher's arm. "Leave him alone. Please." Her wide violet eyes and furrowed forehead pled just as hard as her words, threaded through with a calming undertone. "You don't understand." She sucked in a deep breath, then let it out slowly. "He's my husband."

DELILAH

"If I could have everyone's attention, I think we're ready to get started." I cleared my throat and stepped up onto the center platform of the white three-tiered podium in the middle of the red ring. The circus wagons—holding all of the sentient cryptids, except for the adlet—were arranged around the outside of the ring in two rows, staggered so everyone could see. "And while we talk, Abraxas and Gallagher are coming around with more water."

I nodded, and the kid began distributing bottles from the cooler full of ice Gallagher hauled behind him, as if it weighed nothing.

"When do we get out of these cages?" the berserker shouted, and both trolls echoed the sentiment in their slightly less articulate...style. "If this is a coup, why are we still locked up?"

"Why are *they* here?" Mirela, the oldest of the oracles, asked, glaring at Alyrose and Kevin.

"Why are they already unlocked?" Adira demanded, eyeing Eryx, Claudio, and Lenore.

"You're all going to be let out in a few minutes," I assured them. "I just want a chance to explain what's happening before any of you decide to wander off."

"You're going to let us go?" one of the succubi—Zarah? Or maybe Trista?—said, disbelief thick in her husky voice.

"Of course, if that's what you want. But I'd like to invite you to stay and—"

"Why the hell should we stay?" one of the giants demanded in his booming voice, and that triggered another outbreak of questions. Which was when I remembered that crowd control was more of a problem in a democracy than in any other version of society.

"Be quiet and let her speak." The voice was soft, yet it cut through the cacophony like an oar through water, and when I glanced to my right, I saw Lenore smiling at me, clutching her husband's hand.

"Thank you," I said, then I turned back to the wagons. "In case any of you haven't figured it out yet, we've taken over the menagerie. Renata and Raul have helped us get rid of all the staff members except for Alyrose, Kevin, and Abraxas without spilling a single drop of blood." Which I was proud of on a personal level—even though Gallagher was disappointed—because if we were caught, at least the headlines couldn't read Savage Cryptids Slaughter Staff and Seize Circus. Not truthfully anyway.

Our actions would speak louder than our words ever could. People would know that we'd spared our human captors, though they had rarely spared us.

"Alyrose, Kevin, and Abraxas have agreed to stay and help us because they're sympathetic to our cause. For those who don't know, Kevin is Lenore's husband. He took a job at Metzger's years ago, to stay near her."

"What about Gallagher?" someone shouted, but I couldn't identify the speaker.

"He's a redcap," Adira said with a petulant pout, obviously irritated that she hadn't been let in on our coup before the fact.

Nalah was curled up in the opposite corner of their cage, her yellow-orange eyes burning brighter than ever.

"Yes," I said. "Gallagher's been working here on behalf of Adira's father, in order to return her to her homeland. Which brings me to my next point. Adira's father, Sultan Bruhier, has offered each of you full citizenship in the merid sultanate. Those of you who wish to accept can cross the border with Adira and Nalah tomorrow.

"However, those of us standing before you plan to keep the menagerie open and run it as a masquerade of sorts. We plan to use whatever money we earn to reunite whoever stays with us with their lost relatives. Those who choose to stay will still look like prisoners to the outside world, but in reality, we'll all be living free behind the facade of captivity. We will continue to put on exhibitions and charge admission, but the money will go toward feeding us and freeing your children, parents, and siblings from whatever institutions they were sold into."

A cautiously optimistic buzz rose from the cages, as my fellow former captives discussed my plan and questioned its chances of success. The conversation encouraged me. I'd been worried most of them would be too scared of reprisal to seize freedom when it was offered, but that didn't seem to be the case.

"Will we still be in the ring?" Mahsa shouted, to be heard over the other voices.

"Yes, but the acts will be all ours. We'll redesign the show. You can wear whatever you want and perform whatever tricks you like, so long as they'll impress a human audience and bring in cash without hurting anyone. You can show them whatever you want them to see of your culture and your abilities."

"What about cages and chains?" Finola called, with her seductive siren voice.

"And sedatives?" That came from the back, maybe from one of the centaurs.

"No sedatives," I said. "And we'll only use chains and cages during exhibitions and inspections, to maintain the illusion that Metzger's is still a real menagerie. You'll all have a healthy diet and better facilities. And real clothes. And proper hygiene. You'll have everything Metzger's can possibly give you. Including autonomy. You'll decide what you want to eat, and when. You'll choose your clothes. You will raise your own children."

Stunned reactions buzzed from the wagons, and I recognized both eager acceptance and disbelief. Fear, skepticism, and astonishment. Some of them were instantly won over, and even those who seemed convinced we were doomed to fail sounded inclined to at least give it a chance.

"Of course, all this comes with a risk," I continued, from the top tier of the podium. "If we get caught, we'll all be back where we were before, if not worse. That means more captivity and abuse for the cryptids, and jail time for human accessories. I need you all to understand that before you decide. Nothing is gained without risk." I took Ruyle's key ring from Gallagher when he held it up for me. "Now we're going to come around and unlock everyone, and Alyrose has brought over a selection of clothing for you to look through—"

On the left edge of my vision, one of the tent panels rose, letting in the first rays of sunlight, and I turned toward the movement just as my mother stepped hesitantly into the hybrid tent.

I froze in midsentence, momentarily convinced that I was hallucinating. That Renata had been lying about her inability to enchant me, and now she was either trying to give me the gift of a reunion or throw me entirely off my game.

Then Gallagher made an aggressive move toward my

mother, and I lurched after him and grabbed his arm. "Wait! That's my mom."

Gallagher stopped and made a confused sound deep in his throat, but I couldn't tear my gaze away from my mother. "Delilah?" she said, and tears blurred my vision. My mother was alive, and she was fifty feet away, and I wasn't an orphan after all.

I hopped down from the podium and raced across the saw-dust-strewn ground toward her. The tent flap fell closed at her back, and her arms opened. I slammed into her so hard I almost knocked us both over, then she was crying, and I was laughing, and we were both talking at once.

"What's happening, Lilah?" she asked, as I buried my face in her hair and breathed in the scent of her shampoo. With that scent came random memories from my childhood, relevant to that moment only because she'd smelled the same in each of them, and because the scent of artificial strawberry would forever be linked to the safest, most stable moments of my life.

"We're taking over the menagerie," I said, still caught between laughing and crying, and when my mother pulled away to look at me, I realized that the rest of the tent had gone still and quiet, watching our reunion.

"You're taking the menagerie?" my mother said, and I almost laughed at her expression. "And here I thought you'd need to be rescued."

"She does," Ruyle said, and when I turned toward his cage, intending to tell him exactly where to shove his unwanted commentary, I found him standing in deep shadows three feet away, one hand at his ear.

He was aiming a rifle at my head.

DELILAH

"I want you to climb back in your cage," Ruyle said. "Right now."

A glance to the right revealed that my cage stood wide-open against the rear sidewall.

How the hell had he gotten out, when I still held his keys?

Gallagher growled from my right, and I realized he'd followed me across the tent. I could tell from his stiff bearing and from the anger emanating from him like heat from a fire that he was mentally ripping the former lot supervisor limb from limb.

"Put the gun down," Lenore said, and the compulsion in her voice rolled over me on its way to Ruyle. I knelt beneath the power in her words, intending to put down the key ring just in case it might be mistaken for a gun, until Gallagher caught my arm and pulled me back up, breaking the siren's spell. Which probably wouldn't have been possible, if it'd actually been aimed at me.

When Ruyle didn't respond, I squinted and noticed the orange tip of an earplug sticking out of his left ear. To his right, a crate of supplies—including guns, tranquilizer rifles, handcuffs, and earplugs—stood open. I still couldn't understand how he'd gotten free, but with his mind clear once the *encantados'* enchantment had faded, he'd obviously raided the stock in the shadows while I'd talked and everyone else was distracted by the prospect of freedom.

I scanned the tent, looking for Raul or Renata, but they'd returned to their tanks to rest and rehydrate after hours of work on our behalf. They could not help us.

"Gallagher, cuff your cryptid slut, then cuff yourself. Kevin, cuff your wife, then slap some duct tape over her mouth." When no one moved to comply, Ruyle cocked his rifle—still aimed at my head. "Do it! Or I'll blow Drea's face wide-open!"

Gallagher growled again, putting to rest any doubt that he wasn't human.

Heart slamming against my chest with every beat, I slowly slid my hands into the air, and Gallagher did the same, demonstrating that he didn't have any cuffs and would have to find some. Kevin acted out the same concept, charades-style, since the former supervisor couldn't hear us.

"Lift up the top of the podium." Ruyle gestured to the platform I'd stood on. "We keep extras in there."

Kevin knelt to do as instructed, his jaw tightly clenched.

"Where's the bull?" Ruyle demanded, as Kevin tossed a set of cuffs to Gallagher, and that's when I realized Eryx had disappeared at some point during my speech.

Kevin stood with another set of cuffs, while everyone else stared, most too terrified to move.

Gallagher was wound so tight I was afraid he'd explode and take half the tent with him. His glare was fixed on Ruyle with the savage hatred of a thousand *fear dearg*, and for a second, I could almost imagine him on the battlefield, surrounded by his red-capped brothers in arms, ready to paint the earth red with the blood of their enemies. "I'm going to tear you—"

"Don't say it!" I hissed, as he slowly pulled my arms behind my back, stalling for time. "We need him alive."

Suddenly another side panel was lifted from the outside, and bright morning light poured into the tent, momentarily blinding us all. "Hey, where the hell is every—" Carter, the handler who'd driven off with Genni in her cage, stepped into the tent and froze, as blinded by the darkness as we were by the light of day.

Startled, Ruyle turned toward the new arrival, and his aim tracked away from me. Gallagher tackled his former boss, and the rifle went off as they fell, gunfire echoing within the walls of the tent.

Someone screamed—a bloodcurdling, primal screech of agony—and as I turned to see who'd been shot, I spotted Eryx in a dark corner of the tent, suddenly exposed by the intrusion of light. The bull snorted and pawed the ground, and my pulse tripped too fast. I saw no sluggishness in his eyes. No drugged glaze.

What I *did* see was a very familiar destructive rage.

"No—!" I shouted.

Gallagher stood and pulled the lot supervisor to his feet, ripping the rifle from him at the same time.

The minotaur charged, and the ground trembled with every thundering step.

Gallagher turned to look just as Eryx drove his curved right horn through the supervisor's stomach, tearing him from the redcap's grip.

Ruyle made a gruesome, wet choking sound, which I could hardly hear over the screaming, and my stomach pitched.

Eryx stood up straight, snorting in triumph, with Ruyle still impaled on his gore-smeared horn. The lot supervisor howled. He struggled and kicked, eight feet in the air, but the huge bull-man didn't even sway beneath the weight. Blood poured down Eryx's head, between his eyes, then dripped off his bovine nose as Ruyle's struggles quickened his own gory demise.

"Eryx, put him down!" I shouted, horrified not just by the violence, but by the loss. We *needed* Ruyle alive.

The minotaur blinked at me, and what I saw in his eyes bruised me all the way to my soul. The source of his rage was pain. Deep, profound pain and loss.

He shook his head slowly, declining my request while Alyrose and Lenore and several of the cryptids still locked in cages wailed, horrified by what we were witnessing. Eryx seized the feet flailing weakly in front of his face and pulled with such force that his horn ripped Ruyle's torso in two, from belly button to left shoulder.

Blood poured over the mighty minotaur. Ruyle's arms stopped flailing.

I gasped, and my hands flew up to cover my mouth, along with my horror.

Eryx gave a mighty bovine bellow, then hurled Ruyle's dripping, half-bisected corpse far over my head, where it smacked the opposite side of the tent and slid down the sidewall, leaving a thick, gory smear in its wake.

All the air leaked from my lungs. No Ruyle, no passage. The sultan would not let our people in. All of our hope and effort and ideas had been for nothing.

Zyanya was right. I was hopelessly naive. I'd just sentenced us all to death.

Terrified into motion, Carter dropped the tent flap, temporarily blinding us all again, and dived toward the open crate of weapons. On my right, Kevin overcame his shock in time to reach into the open podium and pull out a pistol, just as Carter aimed a gun in my direction with one shaky hand.

"No!" My mother stepped in front of me as Carter pulled the trigger. Kevin fired four times, in rapid succession.

My mother fell into my arms as the handler stumbled backward into the tent wall, blood pouring from his chest. He slid to the ground as a dark pool quickly formed around him.

I sank onto the sawdust with my mother on my lap. Tears blurred the red mess her chest had become, and my screams joined the other voice still shrieking over another casualty I hadn't yet discovered.

My mother blinked up at me, pain tugging her features into a mask of suffering. "Mom…" I pressed both hands over the hole in her chest, but blood poured between my fingers. Her wound was too big. There was nothing I could do.

"I always loved you best," she whispered, and I leaned closer to listen, as my tears fell onto her hair. "Maybe that was wrong, but it's the truth. I always loved you most…" Her body stiffened beneath my hands, then her eyes fluttered closed. She took two more short, halting breaths. Then she went still.

I threw my head back and screamed.

"Delilah." Gallagher tried to pull me up, but I fought him, determined to stay with my mother. "Delilah!" He took me by both arms and hauled me to my feet, heedless of my blows, as if he didn't feel them. "Your mother died an honorable death, and the earth welcomes her nourishing blood. Don't take that from her by letting her death be in vain."

I choked back another sob and scrubbed tears from my eyes, finally pulling his face into focus.

"Warriors die, Delilah, and your mother was a soldier. I know that without ever having met her. Make her proud. Keep fighting. There are still people depending on you."

I nodded shakily, and he let me go. "I'm okay," I said. Later that might not be true, once my loss had a chance to sink in, but for the moment, he was right. I had to stand straight and keep going, or I might never get up again.

The sidewall behind Eryx swished. I couldn't see the source

of the movement, with the minotaur blocking it, but Gallagher let out a mighty roar, then lunged for the loose panel. I hardly processed his absence. All I could see was blood. All I could think about was how badly I'd failed everyone I'd tried to help.

A hand settled onto my arm, and I looked up to find Eryx staring down at me, blood still dripping from his horn and rolling down his face and chest.

"Did you let Ruyle out of the cage?" I demanded, tears standing in my eyes as another chunk of hope died a fiery death, deep within my soul. The minotaur nodded, and I found no remorse in his eyes. "Why?"

Eryx pointed at the ground, where I found letters written in the sawdust, in the minotaur's labored but legible print. One word.

Rommily.

When I looked up to ask for more, I found him pointing at Ruyle's ruined corpse, still propped against a far sidewall of the tent.

"It was Ruyle? Ruyle broke Rommily?" I said, and Eryx nodded slowly. Firmly. "Are you sure?" I asked, and again he nodded. "I understand. He had to pay." But now, unless Gallagher could renegotiate with the sultan, we would all pay for the sins of one horrible man.

I turned to look at Rommily and found her standing on her knees in her cage, between her sisters, all three gripping the metal mesh.

Rommily met my gaze boldly. "And the bull shall stand tallest of them all."

Chills rose all over my skin. I had no idea what she was talking about, but it seemed to mean something to Eryx. He walked toward the oracles' cage with slow, deliberate steps, then slid his thick fingers through the mesh. With bulging arms and a mighty bellow, he ripped the sliding panel right off the cage and dropped it on the ground at his feet. Then he reached out for Rommily.

She placed her small hand in his huge grip and let him help her out of her cage, unfettered. Then she wrapped her thin arms around him as far as they would go and laid her cheek on his massive human chest, heedless of the fresh blood.

When I finally looked away from their private, bittersweet moment, I saw that Alyrose, Kevin, Abraxas, and Lenore had started unlocking crates. People were climbing out of their cages, many for the first time, unfettered. But they were not celebrating. They weren't even talking. They stared, almost as one, at a cage near the center of the circle, where the screaming that had begun right before my mother was shot had become a high-pitched keening.

I pushed my way through the crowd, dread eating at me from the inside, but before I'd gotten close enough to see, the crowd began pushing against me, backing up as one unit. I slid between the berserker and one of the giants and gasped at what I saw.

Nalah sat on the floor of her cage, holding Adira's limp body. Blood covered the merid from the bullet hole in her neck all the way to her waist. But Nalah was clean. She was also completely nude, and I didn't understand why until I felt the heat radiating from the cage. Her internal temperature had risen so steeply it had burned both the blood and clothing from her flesh.

"You!" Her gaze met mine, and the yellows and oranges in her irises burned brighter. Her normally golden skin had taken on a darker hue, glowing from within like a lit coal. "*You* did this." Nalah stood and laid Adira on the floor, where the merid's skin sizzled against aluminum that glowed red with heat. "You took *everything*. You had no right. Now she is gone." Nalah extended one hand toward her companion's corpse. "And he is pledged." She threw her other arm out toward the wall of the tent, and I realized she was talking about Gallagher. "And you will pay for your theft with the fire of a *thousand* suns."

My pulse leaped into my throat as a wave of heat washed over me, and the *djinn* cage began to melt right in front of us. Adira's corpse burst into flames, but Nalah didn't seem to notice. She gripped the metal mesh, and it melted beneath her fingers, just as the floor began to bow beneath her feet.

Heart pounding, face flushed from the heat, I took a step back as she pushed her way through the melting metal screen and stepped onto the ground. "I will sear the flesh from your bones and make a stew from your organs." Sawdust burst into a thousand tiny sparks beneath her feet. "I will dance in your ashes. I will—"

A soft thwack echoed from behind me. A tranquilizer appeared in the *ifrit*'s bare thigh, and she crumpled to the ground. A drift of sawdust burst into flames beneath her hair, then died as the fuel was consumed.

Gallagher pulled me back from Nalah's still form and clutched me close. "She doesn't know what she's saying. She's lost everything." He aimed the tranquilizer rifle at the ground.

"She has us," I said, as—deep inside me—the *furiae* seemed frustrated by the injustice of the young *ifrit*'s loss, and by the fact that there was no vengeance to be had on her behalf. The princess's killer was already dead. "But we'll have to keep her sedated until she can accept Adira's death."

Gallagher nodded. "That may take a while. I hope your masquerade idea works, because we may need it long-term.

Bruhier will *never* let us in now. We'll be lucky if he doesn't take out a contract on us both."

"No Mexico?" Lenore said, and I looked up to find the siren and her husband standing over Carter's corpse. The pistol still dangled from Kevin's hand.

"I'm so sorry," I said, but Kevin didn't seem to hear. He was staring at his former coworker's body.

"You didn't have any choice," Lenore told him. "You saved Delilah's life."

Eryx and Rommily stepped closer, and the oracle's eyes were huge as she stared down at the corpse. "Multiple gunshot wounds to the torso," she said.

Kevin's eyes went wide, and he stared from the oracle to the body at their feet. His empty hand went to his own chest, as if to verify that he was still whole, and Rommily's smile looked satisfied, as if she'd finally broken through a barrier she'd been chipping away at for years.

"Hey, Gallagher, what do you want me to do with him?" Abraxas called. I turned to ask what he was talking about, and my jaw nearly fell open. Rudolph Metzger lay unconscious at his feet.

Gallagher had lunged at the moving tent flap to find the old man, about to make an entrance and discover the coup.

"The hood of his truck is still hot—he must have just gotten back. I want to see if the sultan will accept him as a peace offering." Gallagher bent to pick the old man up like a baby, then slid him into the cage Ruyle had vacated. "Would you like the honor?" He stepped back and leveled a grand gesture at my open wagon.

Nodding, I grabbed the cage door, ready to slam it shut.

"Wait!" Mirela ran toward us and skidded to a barefoot halt, with Lala not two steps behind her. "Don't forget this!"

She tossed the old man's top hat into the cage, and it landed square on his little potbelly.

"And this!" Lala slid his formal black walking stick in next to him.

I slammed the cage shut, severing Rudolph Metzger from his liberty, once and for all.

RUDOLPH

The old man woke up on his side, in the dark, and no matter how many times he blinked, his surroundings would not come into focus. There was not enough light to see by.

His head ached fiercely, and a gentle probe with his fingers revealed a tall, tender bump on the back of his head, but for his life, Rudolph could not recall how he'd gotten it.

The world jostled and bounced beneath him, jarring him terribly, and when he tried to stand, his knees and hips screamed with arthritic pain. The room jumped beneath him again, and he smacked his elbow on something hard.

Rudolph sucked in a deep, calming breath through his nose, trying to get a handle on impending panic, and that's when he noticed the smell. Stale hay, and...manure.

And urine.

Fear began to gather at the back of his mind. Rudolph felt around on the floor, and his fingers bumped over a raised pattern. His heart began to thump. His throat constricted. He reached a little farther, and the tips of his fingers brushed something hard and thin. He slid his hand up, and his fingers pushed through a grid of some kind. A hard, metal...grille. Like a chain-link fence. Or the side of an animal crate.

No!

The room jostled him again, and that time Rudolph recognized the motion and racket for what they were. Road noise. The harsh bounce of low-quality shocks. The squeals and groans of one of his custom-built wide-load cryptid transport trucks.

"No!" Rudolph shouted aloud that time, but there was no response. "Gallagher, let me out of here, you son of a bitch!"

His voice was reflected back to him from the steel sides of the cavernous cargo trailer. He was alone. But as the trailer sped toward the Mexican border, Rudolph Metzger understood that the blessing of solitude would not last much longer.

And if he was very, very lucky, neither would he.

DELILAH

"Here they come," Zyanya whispered as she approached the ticket booth, staring over my shoulder at the first few cars as they pulled into the gravel parking lot. She tugged at the elastic hem of her sequined leotard, where it met her thick black tights. "Why is there no music? They'll never believe this is a real menagerie if there's no calliope music, Delilah."

"We're having technical issues. Abraxas is on it," I assured her.

"Great." Zyanya rolled her eyes, which looked very dark, but human, thanks to Alyrose's contact lenses. "Put the kid in charge of all the technical equipment. How could that possibly go wrong?"

"He's the only one who's ever seen it run," I reminded her, powering up the ancient credit card machine in my booth. "And anyway, kids always know how to work new technology before adults do. It's like their birthright." I neglected to tell her that the broadcast system was at least a decade older than Abraxas and hopelessly outdated, just like everything else at Metzger's.

Zyanya nodded, but her left hand strayed into her apron

pocket to fidget with her emergency sunglasses. I'd given them to her in case she lost a contact lens, and she kept touching them to reassure herself that they were still there.

"Are you ready?"

She nodded again, her lips moving silently as she went over the prices in her mind. Zyanya had never gone to school, and after a week of lessons, she still couldn't spell her own name, but she'd picked up simple change-making very quickly, earning herself a place in the cash-only booth. She was the first disguised cryptid our customers would see—a test case of sorts—and I could practically hear the anxiety in her voice.

A door slammed shut in the parking lot, and she jumped. "Maybe you should have put Lenore here. Or Finola."

"You're gonna be fine," I said as she stepped into her booth. Besides, I needed them taking tickets at the bestiary and the hybrid tent, which were unsupervised positions. "Just don't open your mouth very wide." So the customers wouldn't see her sharp canines.

"Are humans so easy to fool?"

I shrugged. "People see what they expect to see, and you look the part." She was *stunning* in the glittery costume and makeup Alyrose had fixed up for her, and as long as she kept her gestures grand and her smile small, she'd be just fine. We'd already fooled the independent contractors who'd provided the game booths, pie carts, and rides. In comparison, customers should be easy.

"Delilah!" Lala skidded to a halt next to my booth, kicking up a cloud of dust around her sparkly black slippers. She would spend the evening as a talker for Mirela in the fortune teller's tent. "The berserker's cage clasp broke, and he won't let us chain it shut. He seems to truly think we won't let him back out again."

"Okay." That was understandable. Most of the former captives viewed their freedom as a tenuous state, and for some, the illusion of captivity was still too realistic to be endured. "Turn his cage around, so that the door's on the back side, and leave it closed, but unlatched. If that doesn't satisfy him, remove his cage from the lineup and let him work as a handler tonight. Alyrose left extra red shirts in the supply trunk. If the customers notice him missing, tell them the vet pulled him from the exhibit because he's sick."

Worry melted from Lala's expression when it became clear that I wasn't going to kill the messenger. Time was the only thing that could heal the flinch response they'd all acquired from years of abuse, and that fact broke my heart on an hourly basis. "Okay. I'm on it!" She smiled and turned to run back the way she'd come. Lala ran everywhere she went, now that there was no cage to restrict her.

"Lala!" I called, with a glance at the parking lot, where the first families were already heading toward us. "Hurry. The hybrid tent will have customers in less than five minutes."

She nodded and raced back the way she'd come. I laughed as I watched her go.

"Family of four," Zyanya mumbled, as the first group approached. "That's four tickets, at one hundred four dollars each. If they pay with four hundreds and a twenty, I'll give them back four one-dollar bills..."

"Relax." I smiled at her from across the space between our booths. "You've got this." And most people would pay with a credit card anyway.

"I hope you're right."

Before I could insist that I was, static buzzed from the speaker over our heads, followed by a loud burst of calliope music, adding the sound track necessary to complete our illusion. Zyanya visibly relaxed. She ran one hand over the top of her head, toward the bun pinned at the back of her skull, and gave me a small smile. "I'm ready."

"All right. Let's do it!" I whispered as the first family approached. The father wore a skeptical frown, but the mother looked excited. The kids—a boy and a girl—had wide eyes and timid smiles.

I reached into my pocket for a wad of flash cotton and a flint wheel, mentally crossing my fingers as I prepared the only magic trick I knew. When the kids were about five feet away, I lit the cotton and presented my handful of flames with a flourish. In my open palms sat four shiny red tickets.

The children's eyes brightened and their jaws dropped open.

I smiled and waved them through the gate. "Welcome to the menagerie, where beauty and grace shine from every cage and peek from every shadow. You've never seen anything like the exotic wonders within, so keep your eyes open, ladies and gentlemen, because in our world of spectacle and illusion, what you see isn't always what you get."

★ ★ ★ ★ ★

ACKNOWLEDGMENTS

Thanks first and foremost go to Mary-Theresa Hussey, whose initial confidence in this project got the ball rolling. Your influence and excitement continue to mean the world to me.

Thanks also to Michelle Meade, my new editor, whose enthusiasm and guidance have been nothing short of brilliant. Your vision for this project is stunning, and I only hope I've risen to meet the challenge. Thanks for ideas and rapid-fire brainstorming phone calls, and for bringing everything together.

Gratitude, as always, goes to my agent, Merrilee Heifetz, who's never dropped a ball in her life. She even picks up mine, when my juggling falters.

Thank you to my critique partner, Rinda Elliott, for being the world's best sounding board, and for all the crazy text messages she answers, at all hours.

Thank you to the amazing art and production teams at MIRA Books. I am honored to say I work with the best!

And finally, a big thank-you to Holly, Sarah, and Kelley, for talking me through the initial mental roadblock I erected in spite of my own efforts. You ladies are amazing, and I am in your debt!

Turn the page for a special sneak peek at
SPECTACLE,
book two in THE MENAGERIE SERIES,
by New York Times *bestselling author Rachel Vincent.*

DELILAH

Calliope music shrieked from the speaker mounted high on a pole just off the midway, its grating notes bouncing around my head like the ricochet of a whimsical bullet. Night after night, the iconic circus music managed to overwhelm all the other sounds of the menagerie, no matter how loud the cries of the barkers and buzz of the crowd grew.

Not that there was much of a crowd on the midway after ten o'clock. The main event drew most of the customers into the big top for the last two hours of every evening, leaving only stragglers to knock down mermaid-shaped cutouts with water guns and toss rings onto an inflated minotaur's plastic horns, or visit the other exhibits along the midway.

"Delilah!"

I turned toward the sound of my name to find Lala at her post in front of the fortune teller's tent—the first of our exhibits after a string of locally subcontracted food carts and game booths. I folded my arms over the clipboard I held and crossed the sawdust-strewn path toward her, sidestepping a little boy eating a melting ice cream cone while his father threw darts at the balloon breasts of a cartoon-style siren. My head throbbed from the music and my feet ached from another eighteen-hour workday, but I put on a smile for Lala.

She was living her dream.

"How'd we do?" the youngest of the three oracles asked, crossing her arms over a red Metzger's Menagerie polo. She'd filled out a bit with proper nutrition since our coup of the menagerie, but the true source of her newfound confidence was the hours she spent watching television and listening to the radio while she worked, immersing herself in human culture. Despite her youth—she was barely nineteen—Lala had become one of our most self-assured and dependable liaisons with human society, and it certainly didn't hurt that she looked completely human when she wasn't in the grip of a vision.

"Um…" I checked the figure at the bottom of the form listing the night's earnings. "Fifty-one thousand, two hundred seventy-two dollars." Gross. In one night.

"That's almost a thousand dollars more than last night." Lala's brown eyes shone in the light from a nearby pole. "That's good, right?"

"It's very good." It was nearly twice what I'd made in a year as a bank teller, before I'd been "exposed" and sold into the menagerie. I should have been thrilled, especially considering that at $104 per ticket, admission wasn't exactly affordable for the nine-to-fivers and minimum-wagers who made up most of our customer base. Yet people kept paying, night after night, in town after tiny, rural town.

"We'll be near Tucson in a couple of days right? I know we have bills and things, but do we have enough?" Her eyes were wide and hopeful. Her optimism made me feel guilty for being the bearer of bad news.

"Lala, we don't have *any*. The money's spent before we even make it."

"What? All of it?" Unshed tears seem to magnify her eyes. "But we're going to be within a few miles of Gael's son."

Like most of us, Lala got invested in every cryptid we tried to buy from the menageries, preserves and labs that owned them. But this one was personal for her. She was the one who'd found the berserker's son, in a vision.

"We have to buy him, Delilah. That's the whole point of this, right?" She spread her arms to take in the entire menagerie, and our perilous, secret possession of it. "So pay something late. We only need twelve thousand dollars."

And right after we'd taken over the menagerie, I would have paid it in a heartbeat to free one of our fellow cryptids from captivity. In fact, I'd done just that before I had a handle on the menagerie's finances. Before I'd realized how dire our financial situation really was.

I'd handled tens of thousands of dollars in cash nearly every night since we took over the menagerie, but the vast majority of it went to paying our operating costs. Taxes. Licenses and permits in every single town. Fairground rental fees. Inspections. Food. Fuel. Maintenance. And insurance. That was the big one. Insurance alone cost Metzger's Menagerie more than a million a year. And we were only getting off that easily because Rudolph Metzger hadn't reported most of our recent "incidents" to the insurance company—some because the old man was trying to cut corners, and some because he was no longer in a position of authority at the menagerie.

We'd shipped him south of the border in one of his own menagerie cages as a gift to the *merid* sultan, whose only daughter had died during our revolt.

If the insurance company knew about everything Metzger had covered up, our coup of the menagerie would have been exposed long ago—not because a customer saw through our masquerade, but because of simple, stupid bankruptcy.

Even so, we sat on the verge of that very catastrophe on a nightly basis.

"Lala, we're already paying bills late. If that gets any worse, they'll start foreclosing on things." Old man Metzger had bought much of his equipment on credit. Ironically, we no longer needed most of it, since we were running our own show now and only selling the illusion of captivity. But we couldn't return or sell any of it without explaining why our creatures and hybrids no longer needed to be restrained or sedated.

"There has to be a way," the young oracle insisted, heartbreak in her eyes.

"Maybe there is. I don't want everyone to get their hopes up, but I was thinking about asking Renata if she'd be willing to help."

"Oh!" Lala jumped and clenched her fists in excitement.

"Shh!" I stepped in front of her, trying to shield her delight from the man running the funnel-cake stand. The subcontractors had no idea that Metzger's Menagerie was being run by the very cryptids who made up its exhibits and performances, and if any of them ever found out, our ruse—and our freedom—would come to a violent end.

"Sorry," Lala whispered, as she recomposed herself into the role of tired carnival worker. "I just… I thought it was too dangerous to let the *encantados* play with people's minds."

"It is. But we don't have a lot of choice this time, do we?" I pulled my ink pen from the top of the clipboard while she tried to control her smile. "I have to go collect the stats. What was your head count?"

"Two hundred and seven. We had a thirty-minute line late this afternoon."

"Mirela must be exhausted." The oldest of the three oracles was alone inside the tent, since it was Lala's turn to play carnival employee.

Lala shrugged. "That just makes the bed feel that much softer at the end of the night."

I gave her a smile as I moved on to the next tent. Her upbeat outlook never failed to amaze me. At the end of the day, as grateful as I was for my freedom, I couldn't help missing the apartment and belongings I'd lost when I was arrested and sold. I resented the fact that, even in freedom, I had to hide. But Lala lived for every minor liberty and moment of comfort, as if indulging in them might someday make up for everything she was denied in her sixteen years as a captive.

I continued down the sawdust path, taking head counts from the few tents that were still open, until I got to the bestiary, where the nonhuman hybrids were on display in a series of vintage circus cage wagons. Ember, the phoenix, was easily my favorite. From her head down, her plumage graduated through shades of red, yellow, and orange, ending in long, wide tail feathers that looked like living flames in the bright light thrown from high, pole-mounted fixtures. But she could hardly even stretch those tail feathers in the confines of her cage.

Darkness shifted behind the next enclosure, a subtle blending of one shadow into another, and though I heard neither footsteps nor breathing, I knew I was no longer alone.

"This isn't fair to them." I tucked my clipboard under one arm and stared up at the phoenix.

"I know." Gallagher stepped out of the shadows, yet they seemed to cling to him, giving him a dangerous look that most humans would fear without truly understanding why. They would blame their instinctive fear on his towering height. On his massive musculature. But they wouldn't really grasp his destructive potential.

If they were lucky.

"I got a quote on bigger cages, but considering that our

budget is around zero, it's not going to happen anytime soon."
Three months after our coup, we had yet to come up with a
solution for the beasts' confinement. Their enclosures were
inhumanely small, but much like the lions in any zoo, the
chimera, the gryphon and the others were all far too dangerous to simply keep on leashes. "We're going to have to raise
ticket prices."

Gallagher shook his head, and light shone on the red baseball cap covering most of his short dark hair. "The menagerie's customer base is blue-collar. They're already paying more
than they can afford. We need to be touring larger venues.
Exhibition grounds. Amusement parks."

"No." I was already weary of the argument we'd been putting off for two months. "Bigger venues are too much of a
risk."

"Eryx brings in five hundred people in every tiny town
we visit. Imagine the thousands he'd attract in a larger venue.
In bigger cities."

I turned to look up at him. "The cryptids... We're all still
skittish, Gallagher. Most of them are terrified to deal with
vendors and carny subcontractors, and with good reason. That
would only be worse if we played larger venues, with more
inspections and more invasive oversight."

His brows furrowed low over dark eyes. "It's almost September, Delilah. Schools are already back in session, and the
county-fair circuit will dry up in the next few weeks. If we're
not prepared to step into the big interior venues—stadiums and
concert halls—we won't make it through the winter, because
we certainly can't raise funds the way old man Metzger did."

The very thought gave me chills.

During the off season, when the carnival circuit shrank to
virtually nothing, Rudolph Metzger had rented the most exotic of his cryptids to various private collections, where they

were exhibited in a more intimate setting for high-dollar clientele who wouldn't frequent a sweaty, dirty, outdoor carnival.

"We're not renting anyone out, and we're not risking larger venues."

In our menagerie, we ran the shows and set our own limits. Except for the required inspections, there was no third-party oversight. Under Gallagher's plan, all it would take was one suspicious stadium employee to blow our ruse wide-open, and we'd all be back in cages. We couldn't take that risk.

"We'll find another way," I assured him.

Our original plan had been to take the entire menagerie south of the border. But when Sultan Bruhier's daughter, Adira, died during the coup, he'd closed his borders, leaving us trapped in the US, where exposure would mean imprisonment and, in many cases, torture.

"We could send Bruhier another gift," Gallagher said. I shook my head, but he kept talking. "I could call one of the old handlers and offer him a job, then throw him in a cage and ship him down to the sultan."

"We gave him Metzger. If that didn't work, sending a lower-ranking menagerie employee won't, either. And even if I was okay with sending someone else to be tortured to death at the hands of the sultan, we can't make another person disappear. It took forever for the *encantados* to make the old man's family think he ran off with an acrobat. We can't do that again."

"We can't let everyone starve to death, either."

"I know." I cleared my throat and took the pen from my clipboard again. "What was the bestiary's head count?"

"Four hundred sixty."

"Are we all set for takedown?"

"As soon as the gates close."

"Good." I turned to head to the hybrids' tent, but Gallagher took my hand before I made it two steps.

"Delilah." He tugged me closer, and when I looked up at him, I found his eyes shrouded in the shadow cast by his hat bill in the light falling from overhead. "My oath to protect you includes protecting you from starvation. And from yourself. Buying the incubus nearly bankrupted us."

"I couldn't just leave him there, Gallagher—"

"But now we're rationing food. Something has to give."

I nodded. I knew that. "I have to get a head count from the big top. I'll think of something. I swear."

Gallagher frowned at my choice of words. Swearing meant something different to him than it did to the rest of the world because the *fae* couldn't go back on their word.

Nor could they lie.

Redcaps are *fae* soldiers from their birthing cries to their dying breath, but the few who survived their brutal civil war each swore to find and serve a noble cause. To fight a battle worthy of the blood they must spill to survive.

Gallagher chose to serve and protect me because as a *furiae*, a force driven to avenge injustice and corruption wherever I find it, I am helpless to defend myself against those very things.

I chose to believe that fate sent me Gallagher to make up for what it took from me. My friends. My family. My property. My freedom.

Gallagher's oath to protect me at any cost was the driving force in his life. His oath was unbreakable.

For the rest of my life, he would literally rip my enemies limb from limb to keep me safe.

At eleven fifty, I stepped inside the massive striped tent and watched the big-top finale from the west entrance. Though I saw the show nearly every night, I was still awed by the strength and ingenuity of the performers. By their grace and beauty. By the pride they took in their performances, now that the show was truly theirs.

In the ring—we only assembled one of them, now that our show was smaller—Zyanya and her brother, Payat, had already completed their live shift into cheetah form. As I watched, the draco named Ignis breathed fire over the first of two steel rings suspended from a sturdy steel frame, and the audience *oohed* as the ring burst into flames.

Ignis was a three-foot-long winged serpent whose fire-breathing range had been surgically reduced from over seven feet to a mere eighteen inches long before old man Metzger had bought me for his menagerie. Even with his surgical handicap, Ignis represented the biggest risk we were willing to take in the ring, because he was difficult to communicate with and impossible to retrain without using the abusive tactics his previous trainers had employed.

Once Ignis had swooped to light the second steel ring, heralded by a crescendo in the soaring big-top soundtrack, Zyanya and Payat leaped through the blazing hoops in sync, still in cheetah form, and landed gracefully on the backs of a matching set of thickly muscled centaurs—part Belgian horse, part man.

Several minutes later, the show culminated in a flaming, twisting, glittering, swooping spectacle that utilized Eryx, the minotaur, as the base of a diamond-shaped formation of hybrid acrobats stacked to within mere feet of the aviary net, while Ignis swooped and glided through the air around them. The music soared and the crowd stood on collapsible risers, stomping and clapping for a show they would credit to a huge staff of human handlers and trainers.

For nearly a minute, the performers remained frozen in their ending pose, breathing hard, basking in applause from spectators who would have run screaming if they'd known the truth about what they'd just seen.

Then the music faded, and smoke machines fired a gray mist into the ring. Under the cover of smoke, the performers dismounted and filed from the ring toward the back of the tent while the audience climbed down from the bleachers and headed for marked exits in pairs and small clusters. Children clutched their parents' hands, chattering about the massive minotaur and the graceful leopard shifter. Adults recounted their favorite parts, from the berserker in bear form throwing glittering rings for the harpies to catch in their beaks, to the wolf and the cheetahs transforming from man into animal right in front of them.

I stood at my post, thanking them all for coming, directing them toward the main exit, past the closed ticket booth. I shook hands with fathers and high-fived young boys wearing souvenir Metzger's hats with minotaur horns, and little girls who'd bought headbands with cat ears or fake teeth with wolf or cheetah incisors poking into their lower lips.

At exactly midnight, as I was ushering the crowd from the big top, Abraxas—one of our three human employees—turned off the calliope music and played a light instrumental intended to signal the night's end. The intercom crackled, then Lenore's smooth siren voice spoke over the music, urging the audience members to make their way straight to the exit, then proceed directly to their cars.

Only the fact that I knew who she was and what she was doing allowed me to resist the sudden compulsion to leave the carnival and drive straight home. Even though I no longer had a car. Or a home, outside the menagerie and the camper I shared with Gallagher.

Abraxas and Alyrose, our human costume mistress, still

had to wear earplugs during the nightly farewell, but Lenore's human husband, Kevin, was used to it.

Caught in the siren's pull, the spectators headed for the entrance as one. But as I watched, an odd movement caught my eye. One tall man in the crowd had his hand over his ear, not cupped like he was covering it, but as if…he'd just put in an earplug. The light was too dim for me to see for sure, but the possibility set me on edge.

Everyone else was with a friend or a date or a family, yet this man walked alone, amid the jostle and flow of the crowd. Watching. When his gaze met mine, he smiled, but the expression seemed localized to his lips, one of which was bisected by a thick line of scar tissue that hooked down and over the edge of his chin.

He looked familiar, but I couldn't quite place him, and the mental disconnect hovered on the edge of my thoughts like an itch that couldn't quite be reached.

When the crowd had gone and the smoke had cleared, Abraxas turned off the sound system. Gallagher locked the gates. All over the menagerie, creatures with scales and horns and tails shed their chains and emerged from their cages like monstrous butterflies from steel cocoons. They shook off the pretense of captivity and stretched muscles stiff from hours in confined spaces.

It was my favorite part of the evening.

Together, we closed things down for the day and set up for tomorrow, our last night in this small Southern town. While I swept the bleachers in the big top, I listened to Zyanya and Payat laughing as they broke down and stored the equipment in the ring. Zyanya's toddlers ran circles around their mother and uncle and made the occasional mad dash into the stands, playing as children should. As they'd never been allowed to do, before the coup.

Afterward, I met Gallagher as he fed the last of the beasts and nonhuman hybrids—the menagerie residents we couldn't simply let out of their cages, because of safety concerns.

"Did you see the man with the scar?" I asked as he opened the feeding hatch on one side of the wendigo's cage and tossed a live rabbit inside.

"No. Why?" Using the two-foot-long steel-clawed grabber, Gallagher plucked the last rabbit from the box we'd bought at the local pet store that morning.

"I think I saw him put plugs in his ears during Lenore's farewell message. And he was here alone. No one goes to the menagerie alone." I opened the feeding hatch on the adlet's cage and Gallagher shoved the rabbit inside. The adlet—a wolf-man stuck in a perpetual in-between state—ripped it nearly in half before it even hit the floor of the pen.

"You think he suspected something?"

"Maybe. But obviously we haven't heard any police sirens. I'm probably imagining it." I'd been living under a constant cloud of paranoia since the moment we'd locked Rudolph Metzger in one of his own cages.

"Maybe not." Gallagher shrugged. "The last time I had a feeling about one of our patrons was when you visited the menagerie, and that changed everything. For all of us. Tell me about this man," he said as he picked up the empty rabbit box. "What did his scar look like?"

"It ran through his lip and over the edge of his chin, and—"

Gallagher stopped walking so abruptly that I almost ran into him. His sudden tension made my pulse trip faster. "Which side of his chin?"

"The left."

He dropped the empty box, alarm darkening his eyes. "That's Willem Vandekamp."

"Vandekamp. Why do I know that name?" Why was his

face familiar? If I'd seen him before, how could I possibly have forgotten that scar?

"He owns the Savage Spectacle." At my blank look, Gallagher explained, his words rushed and urgent. "It's a private cryptid collection catering to wealthy, high-profile clients. But he also has a specialized tactical team. Vandekamp is who the police call when they need to bring in a cryptid they're not equipped to handle. They've called him in, Delilah. This is over."

Fear raced down my spine like lightning along a metal rod. "This? The *menagerie* is over?"

Gallagher dug a set of keys from his pocket and pressed them into my palm. "Go straight to the fairground's main office and play the alarm tone over the intercom, then run back to our camper. We have to go."

A chill raced through the length of my body. Everyone knew that if they heard an unbroken alarm tone over the intercom, they were to get in their designated vehicles and run. But our emergency procedure was so new we hadn't even practiced it yet.

Despite the risks, we hadn't really thought we'd need it.

"*Go*, Delilah. I'll get all the cash from the silver wagon, then meet you at the camper."

I nodded, but before I could take two steps, a man in a protective vest stepped out of the shadows, aiming a stun gun at Gallagher's chest. "Don't move." His right hand hovered over the butt of a pistol holstered at his waist. The name Brock was embroidered in shiny silver thread on the left side of his vest. Beneath that were the initials SS, stylized and intertwined, as if they belonged on an expensive hand towel or pillowcase.

I eyed the soldier, my pulse racing. *Willem Vandekamp had his own tactical team.*

"Put your hands up," Brock ordered. "Or I *will* tase you." He thought we were human.

Gallagher didn't move, but I could feel the tension emanating from him. Every muscle in his body was taut. Ready to explode into motion. "Vandekamp deals in exotic fetishes. He'll rent them out by the hour," Gallagher said, trying to convince me of what needed to be done. "They'll die in captivity, Delilah. And in great pain."

Chains. Cages. Fists. Whips. Blood.

My heart ached at the memories. The terror. My lungs refused to expand. If Vandekamp knew about the coup, others knew, too. Gallagher was right. The menagerie was over.

We had to sound the alarm and give people the chance to escape.

Kill him. My words carried no sound, but Gallagher read them on my lips. He turned, impossibly fast, and ripped the stun gun from the soldier's hand. It broke apart in his grip like a child's toy.

Brock grunted and reached for his real gun, his movements clumsy with shock. Gallagher grabbed his head in both hands and gave it a vicious twist.

I heard a distinct crack. The man's arms fell to his sides, but to my surprise, his head remained attached to his body. Gallagher hadn't spilled a single drop of blood, even though he needed it to survive.

"You're not going to…?" I gestured to his faded red cap as the body fell to the ground at his feet.

"No time. We have to—"

Something whistled softly through the air, and Gallagher stumbled. He slapped one hand to his thick thigh and pulled out a dart attached to a tiny vial that had already nearly emptied into his flesh. He growled as he stepped in front of me, shielding me, and turned toward the direction the dart had come from. "Get down."

As I knelt behind him, I heard another soft whistle. He flinched, then fell onto his knees. "Gallagher!" My pulse racing, I pulled a second dart from his leg and stared into the dark, trying to spot the threat.

"Get the gun," Gallagher said, but his voice was much too soft. His eyes were losing focus.

I spun toward Brock's corpse and was reaching for the pistol still strapped into his holster when Gallagher fell to the ground with a heavy thud.

"No!" The gun forgotten, I dropped onto my knees to put one hand on his chest. It rose, then fell. He was completely unconscious, his hat still firmly seated on his head.

"Delilah Marlow."

Fear electrified every nerve ending in my body as I twisted to see the man with the scar staring down at me, his tranquilizer rifle aimed at my chest. But I shoved my terror down to feed the rage burning out of control in my gut.

"You have three seconds to get the hell out of my menagerie before I scramble your brain."

His brows rose in an insulting blend of fascination and amusement. "Do your worst."

My worst was already on its way. Deep inside me, the *furiae* stretched as she woke up, intent on avenging Gallagher, and as her righteous anger rapidly filled me, my nails hardened and began to lengthen into needlelike points.

Vandekamp's gaze flicked to my hands, but his expression did not change.

I stood, and my vision zoomed into an extraordinary clarity and depth. My hair began to rise on its own, defying gravity as my rage mounted.

Vandekamp held his ground three feet away. He twisted a small knob on his rifle and aimed it at my thigh.

I lunged for him, my thin black claws grasping for his head. He pulled the trigger, and pain bit into my thigh. I gasped and stumbled sideways, then tripped over Gallagher's thick leg. The world rushed toward me as I fell. My shoulder slammed into the dirt path.

Gallagher lay a foot away, his eyes closed.

The dart burned fiercely in my thigh, and my vision blurred. My arms were too heavy to lift. I couldn't move my legs.

From somewhere in the fairgrounds, a scream rang out, then was suddenly silenced.

"Don't do this," I begged, as a second scream split the night. But my voice was too soft. The world was starting to lose focus.

Vandekamp put his boot on my shoulder and pushed me onto my back. He knelt next to me, his rifle hanging from one shoulder, and stared into my eyes, apparently fascinated by the black orbs they had become when the *furiae* awoke. "I've heard a lot about you, Delilah." He brushed hair back from my face and tucked it behind my ear. "My name is Willem Vandekamp."

I blinked, and his face blurred as darkness engulfed me.

"You belong to me now."